A HANDFUL OF DUST is Evelyn Waugh's scathing commentary on the well-mannered death struggles of the upper classes —an irrepressibly amusing picture of society politely blowing its own brains out, with a defiant smile.

It tells of Brenda, Tony and their friends— a wonderfully congenial group who live by a unique set of social standards. According to their rules, any sin is acceptable provided it is carried off in good taste.

In *DECLINE AND FALL*, Mr. Waugh has a delightful time taking the sacred cows of England (e.g., the English public school, the traditions of Oxford, British sportsmanship, the titled gentry, the remittance man) for a blithe and madcap ride.

Extravagantly exaggerated, brilliantly nonsensical, it yet manages to tread somehow upon the lunatic fringe of reality.

A
HANDFUL
OF DUST

EVELYN
WAUGH

DECLINE
AND FALL

A Laurel Edition

Published by
DELL PUBLISHING CO., INC.
750 Third Avenue
New York 17, N.Y.

Laurel ® TM 674623, Dell Publishing Co., Inc.

Dedication: To Harold Acton in homage and affection

First Dell printing—February, 1959
Second Dell printing—January, 1960
Third Dell printing—December, 1960
Fourth Dell printing—May, 1962
Fifth Dell printing—May, 1963
Sixth Dell printing—December, 1964
Seventh Dell printing—December, 1965
Eighth Dell printing—October, 1966
Ninth Dell printing—September, 1967
Tenth Dell printing—September, 1968

Printed in U.S.A.

CONTENTS

A Handful of Dust

Decline and Fall

A HANDFUL
OF DUST

. . . I will show you something different from either
Your shadow at morning striding behind you
Or your shadow at evening rising to meet you;
I will show you fear in a handful of dust.

THE WASTELAND

CHAPTER ONE

Du Côté de Chez Beaver

"Was anyone hurt?"

"No one I am thankful to say," said Mrs. Beaver, "except two housemaids who lost their heads and jumped through a glass roof into the paved court. They were in no danger. The fire never properly reached the bedrooms I am afraid. Still they are bound to need doing up, everything black with smoke and drenched in water and luckily they had that old-fashioned sort of extinguisher that ruins *everything*. One really cannot complain. The chief rooms were *completely* gutted and everything was insured. Sylvia Newport knows the people. I must get on to them this morning before that ghoul Mrs. Shutter snaps them up."

Mrs. Beaver stood with her back to the fire, eating her morning yoghort. She held the carton close under her chin and gobbled with a spoon.

"Heavens, how nasty this stuff is. I wish you'd take to it, John. You're looking so tired lately. I don't know how I should get through my day without it."

"But, mumsey, I haven't as much to do as you have."

"That's true, my son."

John Beaver lived with his mother at the house in Sussex Gardens where they had moved after his father's death. There was little in it to suggest the austerely elegant interiors which Mrs. Beaver planned for her customers. It was crowded with the unsaleable furniture of two larger houses, without pretension to any period, least of all to the present. The best pieces and those which had sentimental interest for Mrs. Beaver were in the L-shaped drawing room upstairs.

Beaver had a dark little sitting room on the ground floor behind the dining room, and his own telephone. The elderly parlourmaid looked after his clothes. She also dusted, polished and maintained in symmetrical order on his dressing table and on the top of his chest of drawers, the collection of sombre and bulky objects that had stood in his father's dressing room; indestructible presents for his wedding and twenty-first birthday, ivory, brass bound, covered in pigskin, crested and gold mounted, suggestive of expensive Edwardian masculinity—racing flasks and hunting flasks, cigar cases, tobacco jars, jockeys, elaborate meerschaum pipes, button hooks and hat brushes.

There were four servants, all female and all, save one, elderly.

When anyone asked Beaver why he stayed there instead of setting up on his own, he sometimes said that he thought his mother liked having him there (in spite of her business she was lonely); sometimes that it saved him at least five pounds a week.

His total income varied around six pounds a week, so this was an important saving.

He was twenty-five years old. From leaving Oxford until the beginning of the slump he had worked in an advertising agency. Since then no one had been able to find anything for him to do. So he got up late and sat near his telephone most of the day, hoping to be called up.

Whenever it was possible, Mrs. Beaver took an hour off in the middle of the morning. She was always at her shop punctually at nine, and by half past eleven she needed a break. Then, if no important customer was imminent, she would get into her two-seater and drive home to Sussex Gardens. Beaver was usually dressed by then and she had grown to value their morning interchange of gossip.

"What was your evening?"

"Audrey rang me up at eight and asked me to dinner. Ten of us at the Embassy, rather dreary. Afterwards we all went on to a party by a woman called de Trommet."

"I know who you mean. American. She hasn't paid for the toile-de-jouy chaircovers we made her last April. I had a dull time too; didn't hold a card all the evening and came away four pounds ten to the bad."

"Poor mumsey."

"I'm lunching at Viola Chasm's. What are you doing? I didn't order anything here I'm afraid."

"Nothing so far. But I can always go round to Brat's."

"But that's so expensive. I'm sure if we ask Chambers she'll be able to get you something in. I thought you were certain to be out."

"Well I still may be. It isn't twelve yet."

Most of Beaver's invitations came to him at the last moment; occasionally even later, when he had already begun to eat a solitary meal from a tray (. . . "John, darling, there's been a muddle and Sonia has arrived without Reggie. Could you be an angel and help me out. Only be quick, because we're going in now"). Then he would go precipitately for a taxi and arrive, with apologies, after the first course . . . One of his few recent quarrels with his mother had occurred when he left a luncheon party of hers in this way.

"Where are you going for the week-end?"

"Hetton."

"Who's that? I forget?"

"Tony Last."

"Yes, of course. She's lovely, he's rather a stick. I didn't know you knew them."

"Well I don't really. Tony asked me in Brat's the other night. He may have forgotten."

"Send a telegram and remind them. It is far better than ringing up. It gives them less chance to make excuses. Send it tomorrow just before you start. They owe me for a table."

"What's their dossier?"

"I used to see her quite a lot before she married. She was Brenda Rex, Lord St. Cloud's daughter, very fair, under-water look. People used to be mad about her when she was a girl. Everyone thought she would marry Jock Grant-Menzies at one time. Wasted on Tony Last, he's a prig. I should say it was time she began to be bored.

They've been married five or six years. Quite well off but everything goes in keeping up the house. I've never seen it but I've an idea it's huge and quite hideous. They've got one child at least, perhaps more."

"Mumsey, you are wonderful. I believe you know about everyone."

"It's a great help. All a matter of paying attention while people are talking."

Mrs. Beaver smoked a cigarette and then drove back to her shop. An American woman bought two patch-work quilts at thirty guineas each, Lady Metroland telephoned about a bathroom ceiling, an unknown young man paid cash for a cushion; in the intervals between these events, Mrs. Beaver was able to descend to the basement where two dispirited girls were packing lampshades. It was cold down there in spite of a little oil stove and the walls were always damp. The girls were becoming quite deft, she noticed with pleasure, particularly the shorter one who was handling the crates like a man.

"That's the way," she said, "you are doing very nicely, Joyce. I'll soon get you on to something more interesting."

"Thank you, Mrs. Beaver."

They had better stay in the packing department for a bit, Mrs. Beaver decided; as long as they would stand it. They had neither of them enough chic to work upstairs. Both had paid good premiums to learn Mrs. Beaver's art.

Beaver sat on beside his telephone. Once it rang and a voice said, "Mr. Beaver? Will you please hold the line, sir, Lady Tipping would like to speak to you."

The intervening silence was full of pleasant expectation. Lady Tipping had a luncheon party that day, he knew; they had spent some time together the evening before and he had been particularly successful with her. Someone had chucked . . .

"Oh, Mr. Beaver, I *am* so sorry to trouble you. I was wondering, could you *possibly* tell me the name of the young man you introduced to me last night at Madame de

Trommet's? The one with the reddish moustache. I think he was in Parliament."

"I expect you mean Jock Grant-Menzies."

"Yes, that's the name. You don't by any chance know where I can find him, do you?"

"He's in the book but I don't suppose he'll be at home now. You might be able to get him at Brat's at about one. He's almost always there."

"Jock Grant-Menzies, Brat's Club. Thank you so *very* much. It *is* kind of you. I hope you will come and see me some time. *Good*bye."

After that the telephone was silent. At one o'clock Beaver despaired. He put on his overcoat, his gloves, his bowler hat and with neatly rolled umbrella set off to his club, taking a penny bus as far as the corner of Bond Street.

The air of antiquity pervading Brat's, derived from its elegant Georgian façade and finely panelled rooms, was entirely spurious, for it was a club of recent origin, founded in the burst of bonhommie immediately after the war. It was intended for young men, to be a place where they could straddle across the fire and be jolly in the card room without incurring scowls from older members. But now these founders were themselves passing into middle age; they were heavier, balder and redder in the face than when they had been demobilized, but their joviality persisted and it was their turn now to embarrass their successors, deploring their lack of manly and gentlemanly qualities.

Six broad backs shut Beaver from the bar. He settled in one of the armchairs in the outer room and turned over the pages of the *New Yorker*, waiting until someone he knew should turn up.

Jock Grant-Menzies came upstairs. The men at the bar greeted him saying, "Hullo, Jock old boy, what are you drinking?" or simply "Well, old boy?" He was too young to have fought in the war but these men thought he was all right; they liked him far more than they did Beaver, who, they thought, ought never to have got into the club at all. But Jock stopped to talk to Beaver. "Well, old boy," he said. "What are you drinking?"

"Nothing so far." Beaver looked at his watch. "But I think it's time I had one. Brandy and ginger ale."

Jock called the barman and then said:

"Who was the old girl you wished on me at that party last night?"

"She's called Lady Tipping."

"I thought she might be. That explains it. They gave me a message downstairs that someone with a name like that wanted me to lunch with her."

"Are you going?"

"No, I'm no good at lunch parties. Besides I decided when I got up that I'd have oysters here."

The barman came with the drinks.

"Mr. Beaver, sir, there's ten shillings against you in my books for last month."

"Ah, thank you, Macdougal, remind me some time, will you?"

"Very good, sir."

Beaver said, "I'm going to Hetton tomorrow."

"Are you now? Give Tony and Brenda my love."

"What's the form?"

"Very quiet and enjoyable."

"No paper games?"

"Oh, no, nothing like that. A certain amount of bridge and backgammon and low poker with the neighbours."

"Comfortable?"

"Not bad. Plenty to drink. Rather a shortage of bathrooms. You can stay in bed all the morning."

"I've never met Brenda."

"You'll like her, she's a grand girl. I often think Tony Last's one of the happiest men I know. He's got just enough money, loves the place, one son he's crazy about, devoted wife, not a worry in the world."

"Most enviable. You don't know anyone else who's going, do you? I was wondering if I could get a lift down there."

"I don't I'm afraid. It's quite easy by train."

"Yes, but it's more pleasant by road."

"And cheaper."

"Yes, and cheaper I suppose . . . well, I'm going down to lunch. You won't have another?"

Beaver rose to go.

"Yes, I think I will."

"Oh, all right. Macdougal. Two more please."

Macdougal said, "Shall I book them to you, sir?"

"Yes, if you will."

Later, at the bar, Jock said, "I made Beaver pay for a drink."

"He can't have liked that."

"He nearly died of it. Know anything about pigs?"

"No. Why?"

"Only that they keep writing to me about them from my constituency."

Beaver went downstairs but before going into the dining room he told the porter to ring up his home and see if there was any message for him.

"Lady Tipping rang up a few minutes ago and asked whether you could come to luncheon with her today."

"Will you ring her up and say that I shall be delighted to but that I may be a few minutes late."

It was just after half past one when he left Brat's and walked at a good pace towards Hill Street.

CHAPTER TWO

English Gothic—I

BETWEEN *the villages of Hetton and Compton Last lies the extensive park of Hetton Abbey. This, formerly one of the notable houses of the county, was entirely rebuilt in 1864 in the Gothic style and is now devoid of interest. The*

grounds are open to the public daily until sunset and the
house may be viewed on application by writing. It con-
tains some good portraits and furniture. The terrace com-
mands a fine view.

This passage from the county Guide Book did not cause
Tony Last any serious annoyance. Unkinder things had
been said. His aunt Frances, embittered by an upbringing
of unremitting severity, remarked that the plans of the
house must have been adapted by Mr. Pecksniff from one
of his pupils' designs for an orphanage. But there was not
a glazed brick or encaustic tile that was not dear to Tony's
heart. In some ways, he knew, it was not convenient to
run; but what big house was? It was not altogether amenable to modern ideas of comfort; he had many small improvements in mind, which would be put into effect as
soon as the death duties were paid off. But the general
aspect and atmosphere of the place; the line of its battlements against the sky; the central clock tower where quarterly chimes disturbed all but the heaviest sleepers; the
ecclesiastical gloom of the great hall, its ceiling groined
and painted in diapers of red and gold, supported on shafts
of polished granite with carved capitals, half-lit by day
through lancet windows of armorial stained glass, at night
by a vast gasolier of brass and wrought iron, wired now
and fitted with twenty electric bulbs; the blasts of hot air
that rose suddenly at one's feet, through grills of cast-iron
trefoils from the antiquated heating apparatus below, the
cavernous chill of the more remote corridors where, econ-
omizing in coke, he had had the pipes shut off; the dining
hall with its hammer-beam roof and pitch-pine minstrels
gallery; the bedrooms with their brass bedsteads, each with
a frieze of Gothic text, each named from Malory, Yseult,
Elaine, Mordred and Merlin, Gawaine and Bedivere,
Lancelot, Perceval, Tristram, Galahad, his own dressing
room, Morgan le Fay, and Brenda's Guinevere, where the
bed stood on a dais, its walls hung with tapestry, its fireplace like a tomb of the thirteenth century, from whose
bay window one could count the spires of six churches—
all these things with which he had grown up were a source

of constant delight and exultation to Tony; things of
tender memory and proud possession.

They were not in the fashion, he fully realized. Twenty
years ago people had liked half timber and old pewter;
now it was urns and colonnades; but the time would come,
perhaps in John Andrew's day, when opinion would rein-
state Hetton in its proper place. Already it was referred to
as "amusing" and a very civil young man had asked per-
mission to photograph it for an architectural review.

The ceiling of Morgan le Fay was not in perfect repair.
In order to make an appearance of coffered wood, moulded
slats had been nailed in a chequer across the plaster. They
were painted in chevrons of blue and gold. The squares
between were decorated alternately with Tudor roses and
fleur-de-lis. But damp had penetrated into one corner,
leaving a large patch where the gilt had tarnished and the
colour flaked away; in another place the wooden laths had
become warped and separated from the plaster. Lying in
bed, in the grave ten minutes between waking and ringing,
Tony studied these defects and resolved anew to have them
put right. He wondered whether it would be easy, nowadays, to find craftsmen capable of such delicate work.

Morgan le Fay had always been his room since he left
the night nursery. He had been put there so that he would
be within calling distance of his parents, inseparable in
Guinevere; for until quite late in his life he was subject to
nightmare. He had taken nothing from the room since he
had slept there, but every year added to its contents, so
that it now formed a gallery representative of every phase
of his adolescence—the framed picture of a dreadnought
(a coloured supplement from *Chums*), all its guns spouting
flame and smoke; a photographic group of his private
school; a cabinet called 'the Museum,' filled with a dozen
desultory collections, eggs, butterflies, fossils, coins; his
parents, in the leather diptych which had stood by his bed
at school; Brenda, eight years ago when he had been trying to get engaged to her; Brenda with John, taken just
after the christening; an aquatint of Hetton, as it had
stood until his great-grandfather demolished it; some

shelves of books, *Bevis, Woodwork at Home, Conjuring for All, The Young Visitors, The Law of Landlord and Tenant, Farewell to Arms.*

All over England people were waking up, queasy and despondent. Tony lay for ten minutes very happily planning the renovation of his ceiling. Then he rang the bell.

"Has her ladyship been called yet?"

"About quarter of an hour ago, sir."

"Then I'll have breakfast in her room."

He put on his dressing gown and slippers and went through into Guinevere.

Brenda lay on the dais. She had insisted on a modern bed. Her tray was beside her and the quilt was littered with envelopes, letters and the daily papers. Her head was propped against a very small blue pillow; clean of make-up, her face was almost colourless, rose-pearl, scarcely deeper in tone than her arms and neck.

"Well?" said Tony.

"Kiss."

He sat by the tray at the head of the bed; she leant forward to him (a nereid emerging from fathomless depths of clear water). She turned her lips away and rubbed against his cheek like a cat. It was a way she had.

"Anything interesting?"

He picked up some of the letters.

"No. Mama wants nanny to send John's measurements. She's knitting him something for Christmas. And the mayor wants me to open something next month. Please, needn't I?"

"I think you'd better, we haven't done anything for him for a long time."

"Well you must write the speech. I'm getting too old for the girlish one I used to give them all. And Angela says will we stay for the New Year?"

"That's easy. Not on her life, we won't."

"I guessed not . . . though it sounds an amusing party."

"You go if you like. I can't possibly get away."

"That's all right. I knew it would be 'no' before I opened the letter."

"Well what sort of pleasure can there be in going all the way to Yorkshire in the middle of winter . . ."

"Darling, don't be cross. I know we aren't going. I'm not making a thing about it. I just thought it might be fun to eat someone else's food for a bit."

Then Brenda's maid brought in the other tray. He had it put by the window seat, and began opening his letters. He looked out of the window. Only four of the six church towers were visible that morning. Presently he said, "As a matter of fact I probably *can* manage to get away that week-end."

"Darling, are you sure you wouldn't hate it?"

"I daresay not."

While he ate his breakfast Brenda read to him from the papers. "Reggie's been making another speech . . . There's such an extraordinary picture of Babe and Jock . . . a woman in America has had twins by two different husbands. Would you have thought that possible? . . . Two more chaps in gas ovens . . . a little girl has been strangled in a cemetery with a bootlace . . . that play we went to about a farm is coming off." Then she read him the serial. He lit his pipe. "I don't believe you're listening. Why doesn't Sylvia want Rupert to get the letter?"

"Eh? Oh well, you see, she doesn't really trust Rupert."

"I *knew* it. There's no such character as Rupert in the story. I shall never read to you again."

"Well to tell you the truth I was just thinking."

"Oh."

"I was thinking how delightful it is, that it's Saturday morning and we haven't got anyone coming for the week-end."

"Oh you thought that?"

"Don't you?"

"Well it sometimes seems to me rather pointless keeping up a house this size if we don't now and then ask some other people to stay in it."

"*Pointless?* I can't think what you mean. I don't keep up this house to be a hostel for a lot of bores to come and gossip in. We've always lived here and I hope John will be able to keep it on after me. One has a duty towards one's employees, and towards the place too. It's a definite part of English life which would be a serious loss if . . ." Then Tony stopped short in his speech and looked at the bed. Brenda had turned on her face and only the top of her head appeared above the sheets.

"Oh God," she said into the pillow. "What have I done?"

"I say, am I being pompous again?"

She turned sideways so that her nose and one eye emerged. "Oh no, darling, not *pompous*. You wouldn't know how."

"Sorry."

Brenda sat up. "And, please, I didn't mean it. I'm jolly glad too, that no one's coming."

These scenes of domestic playfulness had been more or less continuous in Tony and Brenda's life for seven years.

Outside, it was soft English weather; mist in the hollows and pale sunshine on the hills; the coverts had ceased dripping, for there were no leaves to hold the recent rain, but the undergrowth was wet, dark in the shadows, iridescent where the sun caught it; the lanes were soggy and there was water running in the ditches.

John Andrew sat his pony, solemn and stiff as a Life-Guard, while Ben fixed the jump. Thunderclap had been a present on his sixth birthday from Uncle Reggie. It was John who had named her, after lengthy consultation. Originally she had been called Christabelle which, as Ben said, was more the name for a hound than a horse. Ben had known a strawberry roan called Thunderclap who killed two riders and won the local point-to-point four years running. He had been a lovely little horse, said Ben, till he staked himself in the guts, hunting, and had to be shot. Ben knew stories about a great many different horses. There was one called Zero on whom he had won five Jimmy-o-goblins at ten to three at Chester one year. And there was a mule he had known during the war, called Peppermint, who had died of drinking the company's rum rations. But John was not going to name his pony after a drunken mule. So in the end they had decided on Thunderclap, in spite of her imperturbable disposition.

She was a dark bay, with long tail and mane. Ben had left her legs shaggy. She cropped the grass, resisting John's attempts to keep her head up.

Before her arrival riding had been a very different thing. He had jogged around the paddock on a little Shetland pony called Bunny, with his nurse panting at the bridle. Now it was a man's business. Nanny sat at a distance, crocheting, on her camp stool; out of ear shot. There had been a corresponding promotion in Ben's position. From being the hand who looked after the farm horses, he was now, perceptibly, assuming the air of a stud groom. The handkerchief round his neck gave place to a stock with a fox-head pin. He was a man of varied experience in other parts of the country.

Neither Tony nor Brenda hunted but they were anxious that John should like it. Ben foresaw the time when the stables would be full and himself in authority; it would not be like Mr. Last to get anyone in from outside.

Ben had got two posts bored for iron pegs, and a whitewashed rail. With these he erected a two foot jump in the middle of the field.

"Now take it quite easy. Canter up slow and when she takes off lean forward in the saddle and you'll be over like a bird. Keep her head straight at it."

Thunderclap trotted forwards, cantered two paces, thought better of it and, just before the jump, fell into a trot again and swerved round the obstacle. John recovered his balance by dropping the reins and gripping the mane with both hands; he looked guiltily at Ben, who said, "What d'you suppose your bloody legs are for? Here take this and just give her a tap when you get up to it." He handed John a switch.

Nanny sat by the gate re-reading a letter from her sister.

John took Thunderclap back and tried the jump again. This time they made straight for the rail.

Ben shouted "Legs!" and John kicked sturdily, losing

his stirrups. Ben raised his arms as if scaring crows. Thunderclap jumped; John rose from the saddle and landed on his back in the grass.

Nanny rose in alarm. "Oh what's happened, Mr. Hacket, is he hurt?"

"He's all right," said Ben.

"I'm all right," said John, "I think she put in a short step."

"Short step my grandmother. You just opened your bloody legs and took an arser. Keep hold on to the reins next time. You can lose a hunt that way."

At the third attempt John got over and found himself, breathless and insecure, one stirrup swinging loose and one hand grabbing its old support in the mane, but still in the saddle.

"There, how did that feel? You just skimmed over like a swallow. Try it again?"

Twice more John and Thunderclap went over the little rail, then nanny called that it was time to go indoors for his milk. They walked the pony back to the stable. Nanny said, "Oh dear, look at all the mud on your coat."

Ben said, "We'll have you riding the winner at Aintree soon."

"Good morning, Mr. Hacket."

"Good morning, miss."

"Goodbye, Ben, may I come and see you doing the farm horses this evening?"

"That's not for me to say. You must ask nanny. Tell you what though, the grey carthorse has got worms. Would you like to see me give him a pill?"

"Oh yes, please, nanny, may I?"

"You must ask mother. Come along now, you've had quite enough of horses for one day."

"Can't have enough of horses," said John, "ever." On the way back to the house, he said, "Can I have my milk in mummy's room?"

"That depends."

Nanny's replies were always evasive, like that— 'We'll see' or 'That's asking' or 'Those that ask no questions, hear no lies'—so unlike Ben's decisive and pungent judgments.

"What does it depend on?"

"Lots of things."

"Tell me one of them."

"On your not asking a lot of silly questions."

"Silly old tart."

"*John.* How dare you? What do you mean?"

Delighted by the effect of this sally John broke away from her hand and danced in front of her saying, "Silly old tart, silly old tart" all the way to the side entrance. When they entered the porch his nurse silently took off his leggings; he was sobered a little by her grimness.

"Go straight up to the nursery," she said. "I am going to speak to your mother about you."

"Please, nanny. I don't know what it means, but I didn't mean it."

"Go straight to the nursery."

Brenda was doing her face.

"It's been the same ever since Ben Hacket started teaching him to ride, my lady, there's been no doing anything with him."

Brenda spat in the eye black. "But, nanny, what exactly did he say?"

"Oh I couldn't repeat it, my lady."

"Nonsense, you must tell me. Otherwise I shall be thinking it something far worse than it was."

"It couldn't have been worse . . . he called me a silly old tart, my lady."

Brenda choked slightly into her face towel. "He said *that?*"

"Repeatedly. He danced in front of me all the way up the drive, *singing it.*"

"I see . . . well you were quite right to tell me."

"Thank you, my lady, and since we are talking about it I think I ought to say that it seems to me that Ben Hacket is making the child go ahead far too quickly with his riding. It's very dangerous. He had what might have been a serious fall this morning."

"All right, nanny, I'll speak to Mr. Last about it."

She spoke to Tony. They both laughed about it a great deal. "Darling," she said. "*You* must speak to him. You're so much better at being serious than I am."

"I should have thought it was very nice to be called a tart," John argued, "and anyway it's a word Ben often uses about people."

"Well, he's got no business to."

"I like Ben more than anyone in the world. And I should think he's cleverer too."

"Now you know you don't like him more than your mother."

"Yes I do. *Far* more."

Tony felt that the time had come to cut out the cross talk and deliver the homily he had been preparing. "Now, listen, John. It was very wrong of you to call nanny a silly old tart. First, because it was unkind to her. Think of all the things she does for you every day."

"She's paid to."

"Be quiet. And secondly because you were using a word which people of your age and class do not use. Poor people use certain expressions which gentlemen do not. You are a gentleman. When you grow up all this house and lots of other things besides will belong to you. You must learn to speak like someone who is going to have these things and to be considerate to people less fortunate than you, particularly women. Do you understand?"

"Is Ben less fortunate than me?"

"That has nothing to do with it. Now you are to go upstairs and say you are sorry to nanny and promise never to use that word about anyone again."

"All right."

"And because you have been so naughty today you are not to ride tomorrow."

"Tomorrow's Sunday."

"Well next day, then."

"But you said 'tomorrow.' It isn't fair to change now."

"John, don't argue. If you are not careful I shall send

Thunderclap back to Uncle Reggie and say that I find you are not a good enough boy to keep him. You wouldn't like that would you?"

"What would Uncle Reggie do with her? She couldn't carry him. Besides he's usually abroad."

"He'd give him to some other little boy. Anyway that's got nothing to do with it. Now run off and say you're sorry to nanny."

At the door John said, "It's all right about riding on Monday, isn't it? You did *say* 'tomorrow.' "

"Yes, I suppose so."

"Hooray. Thunderclap went very well today. We jumped a big post and rails. She refused to first time but went like a bird after that."

"Didn't you come off?"

"Yes, once. It wasn't Thunderclap's fault. I just opened my bloody legs and cut an arser."

"How did the lecture go?" Brenda asked.

"Bad. Rotten bad."

"The trouble is that nanny's jealous of Ben."

"I'm not sure we shan't both be soon."

They lunched at a small, round table in the centre of the dining hall. There seemed no way of securing an even temperature in that room; even when one side was painfully roasting in the direct blaze of the open hearth, the other was numbed by a dozen converging drafts. Brenda had tried numerous experiments with screens and a portable, electric radiator, but with little success. Even today, mild elsewhere, it was bitterly cold in the dining hall.

Although they were both in good health and of unexceptional figure, Tony and Brenda were on a diet. It gave an interest to their meals and saved them from the two uncivilized extremes of which solitary diners are in danger—absorbing gluttony or an irregular regimen of scrambled eggs and raw beef sandwiches. Under their present system they denied themselves the combination of protein and starch at the same meal. They had a printed catalogue telling them which foods contained protein and which starch. Most normal dishes seemed to be compact of both so that it was fun for Tony and Brenda to choose the menu. Usually it ended by their declaring some food 'joker.'

"I'm sure it does me a great deal of good."

"Yes, darling, and when we get tired of it we might try an alphabetical diet, having things beginning with a different letter every day. I would be hungry, nothing but jam and jellied eels . . . What are your plans for the afternoon?"

"Nothing much. Carter's coming up at five to go over a few things. I may go over to Pigstanton after luncheon. I think we've got a tenant for Lowater Farm but it's been empty some time and I ought to see how much needs doing to it."

"I wouldn't say 'no' to going in to the 'movies.' "

"All right. I can easily leave Lowater till Monday."

"And we might go to Woolworth's afterwards, eh?"

What with Brenda's pretty ways and Tony's good sense, it was not surprising that their friends pointed to them as a pair who were pre-eminently successful in solving the problem of getting along well together.

The pudding, without protein, was unattractive.

Five minutes afterwards a telegram was brought in. Tony opened it and said "Hell."

"Badders?"

"Something too horrible has happened. Look at this."

Brenda read. *Arriving 3.18 so looking forward visit. Beaver.* And asked, "What's Beaver?"

"It's a young man."

"That sounds all right."

"Oh no it's not, wait till you see him."

"What's he coming here for? Did you ask him to stay?"

"I suppose I did in a vague kind of way. I went to Brat's one evening and he was the only chap there so we had some drinks and he said something about wanting to see the house . . ."

"I suppose you were tight."

"Not really, but I never thought he'd hold it against me."

"Well it jolly well serves you right. That's what comes of going up to London on business and leaving me alone here . . . Who is he anyway?"

"Just a young man. His mother keeps that shop."

"I used to know her. She's hell. Come to think of it we owe her some money."

"Look here we must put a call through and say we're ill."

"Too late, he's in the train now, recklessly mixing starch and protein in the Great Western three and six-penny lunch . . . Anyway he can go into Sir Galahad. No one who sleeps there ever comes again—the bed's agony I believe."

"What on earth are we going to do with him? It's too late to get anyone else."

"You go over to Pigstanton. I'll look after him. It's easier alone. We can take him to the movies tonight and tomorrow he can see over the house. If we're lucky he may go up by the evening train. Does he have to work on Monday morning?"

"I shouldn't know."

Three-eighteen was far from being the most convenient time for arrival. One reached the house at about a quarter to four and if, like Beaver, one was a stranger there was an awkward time until tea; but without Tony being there to make her self-conscious, Brenda could carry these things off quite gracefully and Beaver was so seldom wholly welcome anywhere that he was not sensitive to the slight constraint of his reception.

She met him in what was still called the smoking room; it was in some ways the least gloomy place in the house. She said, "It is nice that you were able to come. I must break it to you at once that we haven't got a party. I'm afraid you'll be terribly bored . . . Tony had to go out but he'll be in soon . . . was the train crowded? It often is on

Saturdays ... would you like to come outside? It'll be dark soon and we might get some of the sun while we can ..." and so on. If Tony had been there it would have been difficult for she would have caught his eye and her manner as châtelaine would have collapsed. And Beaver was well used to making conversation, so they went out together through the French windows on to the terrace, down the steps, into the Dutch garden, and back round the orangery without suffering a moment's real embarrassment. She even heard herself telling Beaver that his mother was one of her oldest friends.

Tony returned in time for tea. He apologized for not being at home to greet his guest and almost immediately went out again to interview the agent in his study.

Brenda asked about London and what parties there were. Beaver was particularly knowledgeable.

"Polly Cockpurse is having one soon."

"Yes, I know."

"Are you coming up for it?"

"I don't expect so. We never go anywhere nowadays."

The jokes that had been going round for six weeks were all new to Brenda; they had become polished and perfected with repetition and Beaver was able to bring them out with good effect. He told her of numerous changes of alliance among her friends.

"What's happening to Mary and Simon?"

"Oh, didn't you know? That's broken up."

"When?"

"It began in Austria this summer ..."

"And Billy Angmering?"

"He's having a terrific walk out with a girl called Sheila Shrub."

"And the Helm-Hubbards?"
there's a new night club called the Warren ..."

"That marriage isn't going too well either ... Daisy has started a new restaurant. It's going very well ... and there's a new night club called the Warren ..."

"Dear me," Brenda said at last. "What fun everyone seems to be having."

After tea John Andrew was brought in and quickly

usurped the conversation. "How do you do?" he said. "I didn't know you were coming. Daddy said he had a weekend to himself for once. Do you hunt?"

"Not for a long time."

"Ben says it stands to reason everyone ought to hunt who can afford to, for the good of the country."

"Perhaps I can't afford to."

"Are you poor?"

"Please, Mr. Beaver, you mustn't let him bore you."

"Yes, very poor."

"Poor enough to call people tarts?"

"Yes, quite poor enough."

"How did you get poor?"

"I always have been."

"Oh." John lost interest in this topic. "The grey horse at the farm has got worms."

"How do you know?"

"Ben says so. Besides you've only got to look at his dung."

"Oh dear," said Brenda, "what would nanny say if she heard you talking like that?"

"How old are you?"

"Twenty-five. How old are you?"

"What do you do?"

"Nothing much."

"Well if I was you I'd do something and earn some money. Then you'd be able to hunt."

"But I shouldn't be able to call people tarts."

"I don't see any point in that anyway."

Later in the nursery, while he was having supper, John said: "I think Mr. Beaver's a very silly man, don't you?"

"I'm sure I don't know," said nanny.

"I think he's the silliest man who's ever been here."

"Comparisons are odious."

"There just isn't anything nice about him. He's got a silly voice and a silly face, silly eyes and silly nose," John's voice fell into a liturgical sing-song, "silly feet and silly toes, silly head and silly clothes . . ."

"Now you eat up your supper," said nanny.

That evening before dinner Tony came up behind Brenda as she sat at her dressing table and made a face over her shoulder in the glass.

"I feel rather guilty about Beaver—going off and leaving you like that. You were heavenly to him."

She said, "Oh it wasn't bad really. He's rather pathetic."

Further down the passage Beaver examined his room with the care of an experienced guest. There was no reading lamp. The ink pot was dry. The fire had been lit but had gone out. The bathroom, he had already discovered, was a great distance away, up a flight of turret steps. He did not at all like the look or feel of the bed; the springs were broken in the centre and it creaked ominously when he lay down to try it. The return ticket, third class, had been eighteen shillings. Then there would be tips.

Owing to Tony's feeling of guilt they had champagne for dinner, which neither he nor Brenda particularly liked. Nor, as it happened, did Beaver, but he was glad that it was there. It was decanted into a tall jug and was carried round the little table, between the three of them as a pledge of hospitality. Afterwards they drove into Pigstanton to the Picturedrome where there was a film Beaver had seen some months before. When they got back there was a grog tray and some sandwiches in the smoking room. They talked about the film but Beaver did not let on that he had seen it. Tony took him to the door of Sir Galahad.

"I hope you sleep well."

"I'm sure I shall."

"D'you like to be called in the morning?"

"May I ring?"

"Certainly. Got everything you want?"

"Yes thanks. Goodnight."

"Goodnight."

But when he got back he said, "You know, I feel awful about Beaver."

"Oh Beaver's all right," said Brenda.

But he was far from being comfortable and as he rolled

patiently about the bed in quest of a position in which it was possible to go to sleep, he reflected that, since he had no intention of coming to the house again, he would give the butler nothing and only five shillings to the footman who was looking after him. Presently he adapted himself to the rugged topography of the mattress and dozed, fitfully, until morning. But the new day began dismally with the information that all the Sunday papers had already gone to her ladyship's room.

Tony invariably wore a dark suit on Sundays and a stiff white collar. He went to church, where he sat in a large pitch pine pew, put in by his great-grandfather at the time of rebuilding the house, furnished with very high crimson hassocks and a fireplace, complete with iron grate and a little poker which his father used to rattle when any point in the sermon attracted his disapproval. Since his father's day a fire had not been laid there; Tony had it in mind to revive the practice next winter. On Christmas Day and Harvest Thanksgiving Tony read the lessons from the back of the brass eagle.

When service was over he stood for a few minutes at the porch chatting affably with the vicar's sister and the people from the village. Then he returned home by a path across the fields which led to a side door in the walls garden; he visited the hot houses and picked himself a button-hole, stopped by the gardeners' cottages for a few words (the smell of Sunday dinners rising warm and overpowering from the little doorways) and then, rather solemnly, drank a glass of sherry in the library. That was the simple, mildly ceremonious order of his Sunday morning, which had evolved, more or less spontaneously, from the more severe practices of his parents; he adhered to it with great satisfaction. Brenda teased him whenever she caught him posing as an upright, God-fearing gentleman of the old school and Tony saw the joke, but this did not at all diminish the pleasure he derived from his weekly routine, or his annoyance when the presence of guests suspended it.

For this reason his heart sank when, emerging from his

study into the great hall at quarter to eleven, he met
Beaver already dressed and prepared to be entertained; it
was only a momentary vexation, however, for while he
wished him good morning he noticed that his guest had an
A.B.C. in his hands and was clearly looking out a train.

"I hope you slept all right?"

"Beautifully," said Beaver, though his wan expression
did not confirm the word.

"I'm so glad. I always sleep well here myself. I say I
don't like the look of that train guide. I hope you weren't
thinking of leaving us yet?"

"Alas, I've got to get up tonight I'm afraid."

"Too bad. I've hardly seen you. The trains aren't very
good on Sundays. The best leaves at five-forty-five and gets
up about nine. It stops a lot and there's no restaurant car."

"That'll do fine."

"Sure you can't stay until tomorrow?"

"Quite sure."

The church bells were ringing across the park.

"Well I'm just off to church. I don't suppose you'd care
to come."

Beaver always did what was expected of him when he
was staying away, even on a visit as unsatisfactory as the
present one. "Oh yes. I should like to very much."

"No, really I shouldn't, if I were you. You wouldn't enjoy it. I only go because I more or less have to. You stay
here. Brenda will be down directly. Ring for a drink when
you feel like it."

"Oh, all right."

"See you later then." Tony took his hat and stick from
the lobby and let himself out. 'Now I've behaved inhos-
pitably to that young man again,' he reflected.

The bells were clear and clamorous in the drive and
Tony walked briskly towards them. Presently they ceased
and gave place to a single note, warning the village that
there was only five minutes to go before the organist
started the first hymn.

He caught up nanny and John also on their way to
church. John was in one of his rare confidential moods;

he put his small gloved hand into Tony's and, without introduction, embarked upon a story which lasted them all the way to the church door; it dealt with the mule Peppermint who had drunk the company's rum ration, near Wipers in 1917; it was told breathlessly, as John trotted to keep pace with his father. At the end, Tony said, "How very sad."

"Well *I* thought it was sad too, but it isn't. Ben said it made him laugh fit to bust his pants."

The bell had stopped and the organist was watching from behind his curtain for Tony's arrival. He walked ahead up the aisle, nanny and John following. In the pew he occupied one of the armchairs; they sat on the bench at his back. He leant forward for half a minute with his forehead on his hand, and as he sat back, the organist played the first bars of the hymn.

"Enter not into judgment with thy servant, O Lord. . . ." The service followed its course. As Tony inhaled the agreeable, slightly musty atmosphere and performed the familiar motions of sitting, standing, and leaning forward, his thoughts drifted from subject to subject, among the events of the past week and his plans for the future. Occasionally some arresting phrase in the liturgy would recall him to his surroundings, but for the most part that morning he occupied himself with the question of bathrooms and lavatories, and of how more of them could best be introduced without disturbing the character of his house.

The village postmaster took round the collection bag. Tony put in his half-crown; John and nanny their pennies.

The vicar climbed, with some effort, into the pulpit. He was an elderly man who had served in India most of his life. Tony's father had given him the living at the instance of his dentist. He had a noble and sonorous voice and was reckoned the best preacher for many miles around.

His sermons had been composed in his more active days for delivery at the garrison chapel; he had done nothing to adapt them to the changed conditions of his ministry and they mostly concluded with some reference to homes and dear ones far away. The villagers did not find this in any way surprising. Few of the things said in church seemed to have any particular reference to themselves. They enjoyed their vicar's sermons very much and they knew that when he began about their distant homes, it was time to be dusting their knees and feeling for their umbrellas.

". . . And so as we stand here bareheaded at this solemn hour of the week," he read, his powerful old voice swelling up for the peroration, "let us remember our Gracious Queen Empress in whose services we are here and pray that she may long be spared to send us at her bidding to do our duty in the uttermost parts of the earth; and let us think of our dear ones far away and the homes we have left in her name, and remember that though miles of barren continent and leagues of ocean divide us, we are never so near to them as on these Sunday mornings, united with them across dune and mountain in our loyalty to our sovereign and thanksgiving for her welfare; one with them as proud subjects of her sceptre and crown."

("The Reverend Tendril 'e do speak uncommon high of the Queen," a gardener's wife had once remarked to Tony.)

After the choir had filed out, during the last hymn, the congregation crouched silently for a few seconds and then made for the door. There was no sign of recognition until they were outside among the graves; then there was an exchange of greetings, solicitous, cordial, garrulous.

Tony spoke to the vet's wife and Mr. Partridge from the shop; then he was joined by the vicar.

"Lady Brenda is not ill I hope?"

"No, nothing serious." This was the invariable formula when he appeared at church without her. "A most interesting sermon, vicar."

"My dear boy, I'm delighted to hear you say so. It is one of my favourites. But have you never heard it before?"

"No, I assure you."

"I haven't used it here lately. When I am asked to supply elsewhere it is the one I invariably choose. Let me see now, I always make a note of the times I use it." The old clergyman opened the manuscript book he was carrying. It had a limp black cover and the pages were yellow with age. "Ah yes, here we are. I preached it first in Jelalabad when the Coldstream Guards were there; then I used it in the Red Sea coming home from my fourth leave; then at Sidmouth . . . Mentone . . . Winchester . . . to the Girl Guides at their summer rally in 1921 . . . the Church Stage Guild at Leicester . . . twice at Bournemouth during the winter of 1926 when poor Ada was so ill . . . No, I don't seem to have used it here since 1911 when you would have been too young to enjoy it. . . ."

The vicar's sister had engaged John in conversation. He was telling her the story of Peppermint ". . . he'd have been all right, Ben says, if he had been able to cat the rum up, but mules can't cat, neither can horses . . ."

Nanny grasped him firmly and hurried him towards home. "How many times have I told you not to go repeating whatever Ben Hacket tells you? Miss Tendril didn't want to heart about Peppermint. And don't ever use that rude word 'cat' again."

"It only means to be sick."

"Well Miss Tendril isn't interested in being sick . . ."

As the gathering between porch and lych gate began to disperse, Tony set off towards the gardens. There was a good choice of button-hole in the hot houses; he picked lemon carnations with crinkled, crimson edges for himself and Beaver and a camellia for his wife.

Shafts of November sunshine streamed down from lancet and oriel, tinctured in green and gold, gules and azure by the emblazoned coats, broken by the leaded devices into countless points and patches of coloured light. Brenda descended the great staircase step by step through alternations of dusk and rainbow. Both hands were occupied, holding to her breast a bag, a small hat, a half finished panel of petit-point embroidery and a vast dis-

ordered sheaf of Sunday newspapers, above which only
her eyes and forehead appeared as though over a yashmak.
Beaver emerged from the shadows below and stood at the
foot of the stairs looking up at her.

"I say can't I carry something?"

"No, thanks, I've got everything safe. How did you
sleep?"

"Beautifully."

"I bet you didn't."

"Well I'm not a very good sleeper."

"Next time you come you shall have a different room.
But I daresay you won't ever come again. People so seldom
do. It is very sad because it's such fun for us having them
and we never make any new friends living down here."

"Tony's gone to church."

"Yes, he likes that. He'll be back soon. Let's go out for
a minute or two, it looks lovely."

When Tony came back they were sitting in the library.
Beaver was telling Brenda's fortune with cards. ". . . Now
cut to me again," he was saying, "and I'll see if it's any
clearer. . . . Oh yes . . . there is going to be a sudden death
which will cause you great pleasure and profit. In fact you
are going to kill someone. I can't tell if it's a man or a
woman . . . yes, a woman . . . then you are going to go on
a long journey across the sea, marry six dark men and
have eleven children, grow a beard and die."

"Beast. And all this time I've been thinking it was
serious. Hullo, Tony, jolly church?"

"Most enjoyable; how about some sherry?"

When they were alone together, just before luncheon,
he said. "Darling, you're being heroic with Beaver."

"Oh, I quite enjoy coping—in fact I'm bitching him
rather."

"So I saw. Well I'll look after him this afternoon and
he's going this evening."

"Is he, I'll be quite sorry. You know that's a difference
between us, that when someone's awful you just run away
and hide, while I actually enjoy it—making up to them

and showing off to myself how well I can do it. Besides
Beaver isn't so bad. He's quite like us in some ways."

"He's not like me," said Tony.

After luncheon Tony said, "Well if it would really
amuse you, we might go over the house. I know it isn't
fashionable to like this sort of architecture now—my Aunt
Frances says it is an authentic Pecksniff—but I think it's
good of its kind."

It took them two hours. Beaver was well practised in
the art of being shown over houses; he had been brought
up to it in fact, ever since he had begun to accompany
his mother, whose hobby it had always been, and later,
with changing circumstances, the profession. He made apt
and appreciative comments and greatly enhanced the
pleasure Tony always took in exposing his treasures.

It was a huge building conceived in the late generation
of the Gothic revival, when the movement had lost its fantasy and become structurally logical and stodgy. They
saw it all: the shuttered drawing room, like a school
speech-hall, the cloistral passages, the dark inner court-
yard, the chapel where, until Tony's succession, family
prayers had been daily read to the assembled household,
the plate room and estate office, the bedrooms and attics,
the watertank concealed among the battlements; they
climbed the spiral staircase into the works of the clock
and waited to see it strike half past three. Thence they descended with ringing ears to the collections—enamel,
ivories, seals, snuff boxes, china, ormolu, cloisonné; they
paused before each picture in the oak gallery and discussed
its associations; they took out the more remarkable folios
in the library and examined prints of the original buildings, manuscript account books of the old abbey, travel
journals of Tony's ancestors. At intervals Beaver would
say, "The So-and-sos have got one rather like that at Such-
and-such a place," and Tony would say, "Yes, I've seen it
but I think mine is the earlier." Eventually they came
back to the smoking room and Tony left Beaver to Brenda.

She was stitching away at the petit-point, hunched in

an armchair. "Well," she asked, without looking up from her needlework, "what did you think of it?"

"Magnificent."

"You don't have to say that to me, you know."

"Well, a lot of the things are very fine."

"Yes, the *things* are all right I suppose."

"But don't you like the house?"

"Me? I *detest* it . . . at least I don't mean that really, but I do wish sometimes that it wasn't *all*, every bit of it, so appallingly ugly. Only I'd die rather than say that to Tony. We could never live anywhere else, of course. He's crazy about the place . . . It's funny. None of us minded very much when my brother Reggie sold *our* house—and that was built by Vanburgh, you know . . . I suppose we're lucky to be able to afford to keep it up at all. Do you know how much it costs just to live here? We should be quite rich if it wasn't for that. As it is we support fifteen servants indoors, besides gardeners and carpenters and a night watchman and all the people at the farm and odd little men constantly popping in to wind the clocks and cook the accounts and clean the moat, while Tony and I have to fuss about whether it's cheaper to take a car up to London for the night or buy an excursion ticket . . . I shouldn't feel so badly about it if it were a really lively house—like my home for instance . . . but of course Tony's been brought up here and sees it all differently . . ."

Tony joined them for tea. "I don't want to seem inhospitable, but if you're going to catch that train, you ought really to be getting ready."

"That's all right. I've persuaded him to stay on till tomorrow."

"If you're sure you don't . . ."

"Splendid. I *am* glad. It's beastly going up at this time, particularly by that train."

When John came in he said, "I thought Mr. Beaver was going."

"Not till tomorrow."

"Oh."

After dinner Tony sat and read the papers. Brenda and Beaver were on the sofa playing games together. They did a cross word. Beaver said, "I've thought of something" and Brenda asked him questions to find what it was. He was thinking of the rum Peppermint drank. John had told him the story at tea. Brenda guessed it quite soon. Then they played 'Analogies' about their friends and finally about each other.

They said goodbye that night because Beaver was catching the 9.10.

"Do let me know when you come to London."

"I may be up this week."

Next morning Beaver tipped both butler and footman ten shillings each. Tony, still feeling rather guilty in spite of Brenda's heroic coping, came down to breakfast to see his guest off. Afterwards he went back to Guinevere.

"Well, that's the last of *him*. You were superb, darling. I'm sure he's gone back thinking that you're mad about him."

"Oh, he wasn't too awful."

"No. I must say he took a very intelligent interest when we went round the house."

Mrs. Beaver was eating her yoghort when Beaver reached home. "Who was there?"

"No one."

"No one? My poor boy."

"They weren't expecting me. It was awful at first but got better. They were just as you said. She's very charming. He scarcely spoke."

"I wish I saw her sometimes."

"She talked of taking a flat in London."

"*Did she?*" The conversation of stables and garages was an important part of Mrs. Beaver's business. "What does she want?"

"Something quite simple. Two rooms and a bath. But it's all quite vague. She hasn't said anything to Tony yet."

"I am sure I shall be able to find her something."

Two

If Brenda had to go to London for a day's shopping, hair-cutting, or bone-setting (a recreation she particularly enjoyed), she went on Wednesday, because the tickets on that day were half the usual price. She left at eight in the morning and got home soon after ten at night. She travelled third class and the carriages were often full, because other wives on the line took advantage of the cheap fare. She usually spent the day with her younger sister Marjorie who was married to the prospective conservative candidate for a South London constituency of strong Labour sympathies. She was more solid than Brenda. The newspapers used always to refer to them as 'the lovely Rex sisters.' Marjorie and Allan were hard up and smart; they could not afford a baby; they lived in a little house in the neighbourhood of Portman Square, very convenient for Paddington Station. They had a Pekingese dog named Djinn.

Brenda had come on impulse, leaving the butler to ring up and tell Marjorie of her arrival. She emerged from the train, after two hours and a quarter in a carriage crowded five a side, looking as fresh and fragile as if she had that moment left a circle of masseuses, chiropodists, manicurists and coiffeuses in an hotel suite. It was an aptitude she had, never to look half finished; when she was really exhausted, as she often was on her return to Hetton after these days in London, she went completely to pieces quite suddenly and became a waif; then she would sit over the fire with a cup of bread and milk, hardly alive, until Tony took her up to bed.

Marjorie had her hat on and was sitting at her writing table puzzling over her cheque book and a sheaf of bills.

"Darling, what *does* the country do to you? You look like a thousand pounds. Where *did* you get that suit?"

"I don't know. Some shop."

"What's the news at Hetton?"

"All the same. Tony madly feudal. John Andrew cursing like a stable boy."

"And you?"

"Me? Oh, I'm all right."

"Who's been to stay?"

"No one. We had a friend of Tony's called Mr. Beaver last week-end."

"John Beaver? . . . How very odd. I shouldn't have thought he was at all Tony's tea."

"He wasn't . . . What's he like?"

"I hardly know him. I see him at Margot's sometimes. He's a great one for going everywhere."

"I thought he was rather pathetic."

"Oh, he's *pathetic* all right. D'you fancy him?"

"Heavens, no."

They took Djinn for a walk in the Park. He was a very unrepaying dog who never looked about him and had to be dragged along by his harness; they took him to Watt's *Physical Energy;* when loosed he stood perfectly still, gazing moodily at the asphalt until they turned towards home; only once did he show any sign of emotion, when he snapped at a small child who attempted to stroke him; later he got lost and was found a few yards away, sitting under a chair and staring at a shred of waste paper. He was quite colourless with pink nose and lips and pink circles of bald flesh round his eyes. "I don't believe he has a spark of human feeling," said Marjorie.

They talked about Mr. Cruttwell, their bone setter, and Marjorie's new treatment. "He's never done that to me," said Brenda enviously; presently, "What do you suppose is Mr. Beaver's sex-life?"

"I shouldn't know. Pretty dim I imagine . . . You *do* fancy him?"

"Oh well," said Brenda, "I don't see such a lot of young men . . ."

They left the dog at home and did some shopping—towels for the nursery, pickled peaches, a clock for one of the lodge-keepers who was celebrating his sixtieth year of service at Hetton, a pot of Morecambe Bay shrimps as a surprise for Tony; they made an appointment with Mr. Cruttwell for that afternoon. They talked about Polly

Cockpurse's party. "Do come up for it. It's certain to be amusing."

"I might . . . if I can find someone to take me. Tony doesn't like her . . . I can't go to parties alone at my age."

They went out to luncheon, to a new restaurant in Albemarle Street which a friend of theirs named Daisy had recently opened. "You're in luck," said Marjorie, as soon as they got inside the door, "there's your Mr. Beaver's mother."

She was entertaining a party of eight at a large round table in the centre of the room; she was being paid to do so by Daisy, whose restaurant was not doing all she expected of it—that is to say the luncheon was free and Mrs. Beaver was getting the order, should the restaurant still be open, for its spring redecorations. It was, transparently, a made-up party, the guests being chosen for no mutual bond—least of all affection for Mrs. Beaver or for each other—except that their names were in current use—an accessible but not wholly renegade Duke, an unmarried girl of experience, a dancer and a novelist and a scene designer, a shamefaced junior minister who had not realized what he was in for until too late, and Lady Cockpurse; "God, what a party," said Marjorie, waving brightly to them all.

"You're both coming to my party, darlings?" Polly Cockpurse's strident tones rang across the restaurant. "Only don't tell anyone about it. It's just a very small, secret party. The house will only hold a few people— just old friends."

"It would be wonderful to see what Polly's *real* old friends were like," said Marjorie. "She hasn't known anyone more than five years."

"I wish Tony could see her point."

(Although Polly's fortune was derived from men, her popularity was chiefly among women, who admired her clothes and bought them from her second hand at bargain prices; her first steps to eminence had been in circles so obscure that they had made her no enemies in the world to which she aspired; some time ago she had married a good-natured Earl, whom nobody else happened to want at the time, since then she had scaled all but the highest peaks of every social mountain.)

After luncheon Mrs. Beaver came across to their table. "I *must* just come and speak to you though I'm in a great hurry. It's *so* long since we met and John has been telling me about a *delightful* week-end he had with you."

"It was very quiet."

"That's just what he *loves*. Poor boy he gets rushed off his feet in London. Tell me, Lady Brenda, is it true you are looking for a flat, because I think I've got just the place for you? It's being done up now and will be ready well before Christmas." She looked at her watch. "Oh dear, I must fly. You couldn't possibly come in for a cocktail, this evening? Then you could hear all about it."

"I *could* . . . " said Brenda doubtfully.

"Then *do*. I'll expect you about six. I daresay you don't know where I live." She told her and left the table.

"What's all this about a flat?" Marjorie asked.

"Oh just something I thought of . . ."

That afternoon, as she lay luxuriously on the osteopath's table, and her vertebrae, under his strong fingers, snapped like patent fasteners, Brenda wondered whether Beaver would be at home that evening. "Probably not, if he's so keen on going about," she thought, "and, anyhow, what's the sense? . . ."

But he was there, in spite of two other invitations.

She heard all about the maisonette. Mrs. Beaver knew her job. What people wanted, she said, was somewhere to dress and telephone. She was subdividing a small house in Belgravia into six flats at three pounds a week, of one room each and a bath; the bathrooms were going to be slap-up, with limitless hot water and every transatlantic refinement; the other room would have a large built-in wardrobe with electric light inside, and space for a bed. It would fill a long felt need, Mrs. Beaver said.

"I'll ask my husband and let you know."

"You *will* let me know soon, won't you, because *everyone* will be wanting one."

"I'll let you know very soon."

When she had to go, Beaver came with her to the station. She usually ate some chocolate and buns in her carriage; they bought them together at the buffet. There was plenty of time before the train left and the carriage was not yet full. Beaver came in and sat with her.

"I'm sure you want to go away."

"No, really."

"I've got lots to read."

"I *want* to stay."

"It's very sweet of you." Presently she said, rather timidly, for she was not used to asking for that sort of thing, "I suppose you wouldn't like to take me to Polly's party, would you?"

Beaver hesitated. There would be several dinner parties that evening and he was almost certain to be invited to one or other of them . . . if he took Brenda out it would mean the Embassy or some smart restaurant . . . three pounds at least . . . and he would be responsible for her and have to see her home . . . and if, as she said, she really did not know many people nowadays (why indeed should she have asked him if that were not true?) it might mean tying himself up for the whole evening . . . "I wish I could," he said, "but I've promised to dine out for it."

Brenda had observed his hesitation. "I was afraid you would have."

"But we'll meet there."

"Yes, if I go."

"I wish I could have taken you."

"It's quite all right . . . I just wondered."

The gaiety with which they had bought the buns was all gone now. They were silent for a minute. Then Beaver said, "Well, I think perhaps I'll leave you now."

"Yes, run along. Thank you for coming."

He went off down the platform. There were still eight minutes to go. The carriage suddenly filled up and Brenda felt tired out. "Why *should* he want to take me, poor boy?" she thought, "only he might have done it better."

"Barnardo case?"

Brenda nodded. "Down and out," she said, "sunk, right under." She sat nursing her bread and milk, stirring it listlessly. Every bit of her felt good for nothing.

"Good day?"

She nodded. "Saw Marjorie and her filthy dog. Bought some things. Lunched at Daisy's new joint. Bone setter. That's all."

"You know I wish you'd give up these day trips to London. They're far too much for you."

"Me? Oh, I'm all right. Wish I was dead, that's all . . . and please, please, darling Tony, don't say anything about bed, because I can't move."

Next day a telegram came from Beaver. *Have got out of dinner 16th. Are you still free.*

She replied: *Delighted. Second thoughts always best. Brenda.*

Up till then they had avoided Christian names.

"You seem in wonderful spirits today," Tony remarked.

"I feel big. I think it's Mr. Cruttwell. He puts all one's nerves right and one's circulation and everything."

Three

"Where's mummy gone?"

"London."

"Why?"

"Someone called Lady Cockpurse is giving a party."

"Is she nice?"

"Mummy thinks so. I don't."

"Why?"

"Because she looks like a monkey."

"I should love to see her. Does she live in a cage? Has she got a tail? Ben saw a woman who looked like a fish, with scales all over instead of skin. It was in a circus in Cairo. Smelt like a fish too, Ben says."

They were having tea together on the afternoon of Brenda's departure. "Daddy, what does Lady Cockpurse eat?"

"Oh, nuts and things."

"Nuts and what things?"

"Different kinds of nuts."

For days to come the image of this hairy, mischievous Countess occupied John Andrew's mind. She became one of the inhabitants of his world, like Peppermint, the mule who died of rum. When kindly people spoke to him in the village he would tell them about her and how she swung head down from a tree throwing nutshells at passers-by.

"You mustn't say things like that about real people," said nanny. "Whatever would Lady Cockpurse do if she heard about it."

"She'd gibber and chatter and lash round with her tail, and then I expect she'd catch some nice, big, juicy fleas and forget all about it."

Brenda was staying at Marjorie's for the night. She was dressed first and came into her sister's room. "Lovely, darling, new?"

"Fairly."

Marjorie was rung up by the woman at whose house she was dining. ("Look here are you absolutely sure you can't make Allan come tonight?" "Absolutely. He's got a meeting in Camberwell. He may not even come to Polly's." "Is there *any* man you can bring?" "Can't think of anybody." "Well we shall have to be one short, that's all. I can't think what's happened tonight. I rang up John Beaver but even *he* won't come.")

"You know," said Marjorie, putting down the telephone, "you're causing a great deal of trouble. You've taken London's only spare man."

"Oh dear, I didn't realize . . ."

Beaver arrived at quarter to nine in a state of high self-approval; he had refused two invitations to dinner while dressing that evening; he had cashed a cheque for ten pounds at his club; he had booked a divan table at

Espinosa's. It was almost the first time in his life that he had taken anyone out to dinner, but he knew perfectly how it was done.

"I must see your Mr. Beaver properly," said Marjorie. "Let's make him take off his coat and drink something."

The two sisters were a little shy as they came downstairs, but Beaver was perfectly at his ease. He looked very elegant and rather more than his age.

'Oh, he's not so bad, your Mr. Beaver,' Marjorie's look seemed to say, 'not by any means,' and he, seeing the two women together, who were both beautiful, though in a manner so different that, although it was apparent that they were sisters, they might have belonged each to a separate race, began to understand what had perplexed him all the week; why, contrary to all habit and principle, he had telegraphed to Brenda asking her to dine.

"Mrs. Jimmy Deane's very upset that she couldn't get you for tonight. I didn't give away what you were doing."

"Give her my love," said Beaver. "Anyway we'll all meet at Polly's."

"I must go, we're dining at nine."

"Stay a bit," said Brenda. "She's sure to be late."

Now that it was inevitable, she did not want to be left alone with Beaver.

"No, I must go. Enjoy yourselves, bless you both." She felt as though she were the elder sister, seeing Brenda timid and expectant at the beginning of an adventure.

They were awkward when Marjorie left, for in the week that they had been apart, each had, in thought, grown more intimate with the other than any actual occurrence warranted. Had Beaver been more experienced, he might have crossed to where Brenda was sitting on the arm of a chair, and made love to her at once; and probably he would have got away with it. Instead he remarked in an easy manner, "I suppose we ought to be going too."

"Yes, where?"

"I thought Espinosa's."

"Yes, lovely. Only listen: I want you to understand right away that it's *my* dinner."

"Of course not . . . nothing of the sort."

"Yes, it is. I'm a year older than you and an old married woman and quite rich, so, please, I'm going to pay."

Beaver continued protesting to the taxi door.

But there was still a constraint between them and Beaver began to wonder, 'Does she expect me to pounce?' So as they waited in a traffic block by the Marble Arch, he leaned forward to kiss her; when he was quite near, she drew back. He said, *"Please,* Brenda," but she turned away and looked out of the window shaking her head several times quickly. Then still fixed on the window she put out her hand to his and they sat in silence till they reached the restaurant. Beaver was thoroughly puzzled.

Once they were in public again, his confidence returned. Espinosa led them to their table; it was the one by itself on the right side of the door, the only table in the restaurant at which one's conversation was not overheard. Brenda handed him the card. "You choose. Very little for me, but it must only have starch, no protein."

The bill at Espinosa's was, as a rule, roughly the same whatever one ate, but Brenda would not know this so, since it was now understood that she was paying, Beaver felt constrained from ordering anything that looked obviously expensive. However she insisted on champagne, and later a ballon of liqueur brandy for him. "You can't think how exciting it is for me to take a young man out. I've never done it before."

They stayed at Espinosa's until it was time to go to the party, dancing once or twice, but most of the time sitting at the table talking. Their interest in each other had so far outdistanced their knowledge that there was a great deal to say.

Presently Beaver said, "I'm sorry I was an ass in the taxi just now."

"Eh?"

He changed it and said, "Did you mind when I tried to kiss you just now?"

"Me? No, not particularly."

"Then why wouldn't you let me?"

"Oh dear, you've got a lot to learn."

"How d'you mean?"

"You mustn't ever ask questions like that. Will you try and remember?"

Then he was sulky. "You talk to me as if I was an undergraduate having his first walk out."

"Oh, is this a walk out?"

"Not as far I am concerned."

There was a pause in which Brenda said, "I am not sure it hasn't been a mistake, taking you out to dinner. Let's ask for the bill and go to Polly's."

But they took ten minutes to bring the bill, and in that time Beaver and Brenda had to say something, so he said he was sorry.

"You've got to learn to be nicer," she said soberly. "I don't believe you'd find it impossible." When the bill eventually came, she said, "How much do I tip him?" and Beaver showed her. "Are you sure that's enough? I should have given twice as much."

"It's exactly right," said Beaver, feeling older again, exactly as Brenda had meant him to.

When they sat in the taxi Beaver knew at once that Brenda wished him to make love to her. But he decided it was time he took the lead. So he sat at a distance from her and commented on an old house that was being demolished to make way for a block of flats.

"Shut up," said Brenda. "Come here."

When he had kissed her, she rubbed against his cheek in the way she had.

Polly's party was exactly what she wished it to be, an accurate replica of all the best parties she had been to in the last year; the same band, the same supper, and, above all, the same guests. Hers was not the ambition to create a sensation, to have the party talked about in months to come for any unusual feature, to hunt out shy celebrities or introduce exotic strangers. She wanted a perfectly straight, smart party and she had got it. Practically everyone she asked had come. If there were other, more remote worlds upon which she did not impinge, Polly did not know about them. These were the people she was after, and here they were. And looking round on her guests, with Lord Cockpurse who was for the evening loyally putting in one of his rare appearances at her side, she was able to congratulate herself that there were very few people present whom she did not want. In other years people had taken her hospitality more casually and brought on with them anyone with whom they happened to have been dining. This year, without any conscious effort on her part, there had been more formality. Those who wanted to bring friends had rung up in the morning and asked whether they might do so, and on the whole they had been cautious of even so much presumption. People, who only eighteen months before would have pretended to be ignorant of her existence, were now crowding up her stairs. She had got herself in line with the other married women of her world.

As they started to go up, Brenda said, "You're not to leave me, please. I'm not going to know anybody," and Beaver again saw himself as the dominant male.

They went straight through to the band and began dancing, not talking much except to greet other couples whom they knew. They danced for half an hour and then she said, "All right, I'll give you a rest. Only don't let me get left."

She danced with Jock Grant-Menzies and two or three old friends and did not see Beaver again until she came on him alone in the bar. He had been there a long time, talking sometimes to the couples who came in and out, but always ending up alone. He was not enjoying the evening and he told himself rather resentfully that it was because of Brenda; if he had come there in a large party it would have been different.

Brenda saw he was out of temper and said, "Time for supper."

It was early, and the tables were mostly empty except for earnest couples sitting alone. There was a large round table between the windows, with no one at it; they sat there.

"I don't propose to move for a long time, d'you mind?" She wanted to make him feel important again so she asked him about the other people in the room.

Presently their table filled up. These were Brenda's old friends, among whom she used to live when she came out and in the first two years of her marriage, before Tony's father died; men in the early thirties, married women of her own age, none of whom knew Beaver or liked him. It was by far the gayest table in the room. Brenda thought 'How my poor young man must be hating this'; it did not occur to her that, from Beaver's point of view, these old friends of hers were quite the most desirable people at the party, and that he was delighted to be seen at their table. "Are you dying of it?" she whispered.

"No, indeed, never happier."

"Well I am. Let's go and dance."

But the band was taking a rest and there was no one in the ballroom except the earnest couples who had migrated there away from the crowd and were sitting huddled in solitude round the walls, lost in conversation. "Oh dear," said Brenda, "now we're done. We can't go back to the table . . . it almost looks as though we should have to go home."

"It's not two."

"That's late for me. Look here, don't you come. Stay and enjoy yourself."

"Of course I'll come," said Beaver.

It was a cold, clear night. Brenda shivered and he put his arm around her in the taxi. They did not say much.

"There already?"

They sat for a few seconds without moving. Then Brenda slipped free and Beaver got out.

"I'm afraid I can't ask you in for a drink. You see it isn't my house and I shouldn't know where to find anything."

"No, of course not."

"Well, goodnight, my dear. Thank you a thousand

times for looking after me. I'm afraid I rather bitched your evening."

"No, of course not," said Beaver.

"Will you ring me in the morning . . . promise?" She touched her hand to her lips and then turned to the key-hole.

Beaver hesitated a minute whether he should go back to the party, but decided not to. He was near home, and everyone at Polly's would have settled down by now; so he gave his address in Sussex Gardens, and went up to bed.

Just as he was undressed he heard the telephone ring-ing downstairs. It was his telephone. He went down, two flights in the cold. It was Brenda's voice.

"Darling, I was just going to ring off. I thought you must have gone back to Polly's. Is the telephone not by your bed?"

"No, it's on the ground floor."

"Oh dear, then it wasn't a very good idea to ring up, was it?"

"Oh, I don't know. What is it?"

"Just to say 'goodnight.' "

"Oh, I see, well—goodnight."

"And you'll ring me in the morning?"

"Yes."

"Early, before you've made any plans."

"Yes."

"Then goodnight, bless you."

Beaver went up the two flights of stairs again, and got into bed.

". . . going away in the middle of the party."

"I can't tell you how innocent it was. He didn't even come in."

"No one is going to know that."

"And he was furious when I rang him up."

"What does he think of you?"

"Simply can't make me out at all . . . terribly puzzled, and rather bored in bits."

"Are you going to go on with it?"

"I shouldn't know." The telephone rang. "Perhaps that's him."

But it was not.

Brenda had come into Marjorie's room and they were having breakfast in bed. Marjorie was more than ever like an elder sister that morning. "But really, Brenda, he's such a *dreary* young man."

"I know it all. He's second rate and a snob and, I should think, as cold as a fish, but I happen to have a fancy for him, that's all . . . besides I'm not sure he's *altogether* awful . . . he's got that odious mother whom he adores . . . and he's always been very poor. I don't think he's had a fair deal. I heard all about it last night. He got engaged once but they couldn't get married because of money and since then he's never had a proper affaire with anyone decent . . . he's got to be taught a whole lot of things. That's part of his attraction."

"Oh dear, I see you're very serious."

The telephone rang.

"Perhaps *that's* him."

But a familiar voice rang out from the instrument so that Brenda too could hear it, "Good morning, darling, what's the diet today?"

"Oh, Polly, what a good party last night."

"Not so bad for the old girl was it? I say what about your sister and Mr. Beaver."

"What about them?"

"How long has *that* been on?"

"There's nothing doing there, Polly."

"Don't you tell me. They were well away last night. How's the boy managed it? That's what I want to know. He must have something we didn't know about . . ."

"So Polly's on to your story. She'll be telling everyone in London at this moment."

"How I wish there was anything to tell. The cub hasn't even rung me up . . . Well, I'll leave him in peace. If he doesn't do anything about me, I'll go down to Hetton this afternoon. Perhaps that's him." But it was only Allan from the Conservative Central Office, to say how sorry he had been not to get to the party the night before. "I hear Brenda disgraced herself," he said.

"Goodness," said Brenda. "People do think that young men are easily come by."

"I scarcely saw you at Polly's last night," said Mrs. Beaver. "What became of you?"

"We went early. Brenda Last was tired."

"She was looking lovely. I am so glad you've made friends with her. When are you going to see her again."

"I said I'd ring up."

"Well, why don't you?"

"Oh, mumsey, what's the use! I can't afford to start taking about women like Brenda Last. If I ring up she'll say, what are you doing, and I shall have to ask her to something, and it will be the same thing every day. I simply haven't the money."

"I know, my son. It's very difficult for you . . . and you're wonderful about money. I ought to be grateful that I haven't a son always coming to me with debts. Still, it doesn't do to deny yourself *everything* you know. You're getting to be an old bachelor already at twenty-five. I could see Brenda liked you, that evening she came here."

"Oh she likes me all right."

"I hope she makes up her mind about that flat. They're going like hot cakes. I shall have to look about for another suitable house to split up. You'd be surprised who've been taking them—quite a number of people with houses in London already . . . Well, I must be getting back to work. I'm away for two nights by the way. See that Chambers looks after you properly. There are some Australians Sylvia Newport discovered who want to take a house in the country, so I'm driving them around to one or two that might do for them. Where are you lunching?"

"Margot's."

By one o'clock when they came back from taking Djinn to the Park, Beaver had not rung up. "So that's that," said Brenda, "I expect I'm glad really." She sent a telegram to Tony to expect her by the afternoon train and, in a small voice, ordered her things to be packed. "I don't seem to have anywhere to lunch," she said.

"Why don't you come to Margot's. I know she'd love it."

"Well ring up and ask her."

So she met Beaver again.

He was sitting some way from her and they did not speak to each other until everyone was going. "I kept trying to get through to you this morning," he said, "but the line was always engaged."

"Oh come on," said Brenda, "I'll sock you a movie."

Later she wired to Tony: *Staying with Marjorie another day or two all love to you both.*

Four

"Is mummy coming back today?"

"I hope so."

"That monkey-woman's party has lasted a long time. Can I come in to the station and meet her?"

"Yes, we'll both go."

"She hasn't seen Thunderclap for four days. She hasn't seen me jump the new post and rail, has she daddy?"

She was coming by the 3.18. Tony and John Andrew were there early. They wandered about the station looking at things, and bought some chocolate from a slot machine. The stationmaster came out to talk to them. "Her ladyship coming back today?" He was an old friend of Tony's.

"I've been expecting her every day. You know what it is when ladies get to London."

"Sam Brace's wife went to London and he couldn't get her back. Had to go up and fetch her himself. And then she give him a hiding."

Presently the train came in and Brenda emerged exquisitely from her third class carriage. "You've *both come*. What angels you are. I don't at all deserve it."

"Oh, mummy, have you brought the monkey-lady?"

"What *does* the child mean?"

"He's got it into his head that your chum Polly has a tail."

"Come to think of it, I shouldn't be surprised if she had."

Two little cases held all her luggage. The chauffeur strapped them on behind the car, and they drove to Hetton.

"What's all the news?"

"Ben's put the rail up ever so high and Thunderclap and I jumped it six times yesterday and six times again today and two more of the fish in the little pond are dead, floating upside down all swollen and nanny burnt her finger on the kettle yesterday and daddy and I saw a fox just as near as anything and he sat quite still and then went away into the wood and I began drawing a picture of a battle only I couldn't finish it because the paints weren't right and the grey carthorse the one that had worms is quite well again."

"Nothing much has happened," said Tony. "We've missed you. What did you find to do in London all this time?"

"Me? Oh I've been behaving rather badly to tell you the truth."

"Buying things?"

"Worse. I've been carrying on madly with young men and I've spent heaps of money and I've enjoyed it very much indeed. But there's one awful thing."

"What's that?"

"No, I think it had better keep. It's something you won't like at all."

"You've bought a Pekingese."

"Worse, far worse. Only I haven't done it yet. But I *want* to dreadfully."

"Go on."

"Tony, I've found a flat."

"Well you'd better lose it again quick."

"All right. I'll attack you about it again later. Meanwhile try not to brood about it."

"I shan't give it another thought."

"What's a flat, daddy?"

Brenda wore pyjamas at dinner, and afterwards sat close to Tony on the sofa and ate some sugar out of his coffee cup.

"I suppose all this means that you're going to start again about your flat?"

"Mmmm."

"You haven't signed any papers yet have you."

"Oh no." Brenda shook her head emphatically.

"Then no great harm's done." Tony began to fill his pipe.

Brenda knelt on the sofa, sitting back on her heels. "Listen, you haven't been brooding?"

"No."

"Because, you see, when you say 'flat' you're thinking of something quite different to me. *You* mean by a flat, a lift and a man in uniform, and a big front door with knobs, and an entrance hall and doors opening in all directions, with kitchens and sculleries and dining rooms and drawing rooms and servants' bathrooms . . . don't you, Tony?"

"More or less."

"Exactly. Now *I* mean just a bedroom and a bath and a telephone. You see the difference? Now a woman I know—"

"Who?"

"Just a woman—has fixed up a whole house like that off Belgrave Square and they are three pounds a week, no rates and taxes, constant hot water and central heating, woman comes in to make bed when required, what d'you think of that?"

"I see."

"Now this is how I look at it. What's three pounds a week? Less than nine bob a night. Where could one stay for less than nine bob a night with all those advantages. You're always going to the club and that costs more and I can't stay often with Marjorie because it's hell for her having me and anyway she's got that dog, and you're always saying when I come back in the evenings after shopping, 'Why didn't you stay the night,' you say, 'instead of killing yourself?' Time and again you say it. I'm sure we spend much more than three pounds a week through not having a flat. Tell you what, I'll give up Mr. Cruttwell. How's that?"

"D'you really want this thing?"

"Mmm."

"Well, I'll have to see. We *might* manage it, but it'll mean putting off the improvements down here."

"I don't really deserve it," she said, clinching the matter. "I've been carrying on *anyhow* this week."

Brenda's stay at Hetton lasted only for three nights. Then she returned to London saying that she had to see about the flat. It did not, however, require very great attention. There was only the colour of the paint to choose and some few articles of furniture. Mrs. Beaver had them ready for her inspection, a bed, a carpet, a dressing table and chair—there was not room for more. Mrs. Beaver tried to sell her a set of needlework pictures for the walls, but these she refused, also an electric bed warmer, a miniature weighing machine for the bathroom, a frigidaire, an antique grandfather clock, a backgammon set of looking-glass and synthetic ivory, a set of prettily bound French eighteenth century poets, a massage apparatus, and a wireless set fitted in a case of Regency lacquer, all of which had been grouped in the shop for her as a 'suggestion.' Mrs. Beaver bore Brenda no ill will for the modesty of her requirements; she was doing very well on the floor above with a Canadian lady who was having her walls covered with chromium plating at immense expense.

Meanwhile Brenda stayed with Marjorie, on terms which gradually became acrimonious. "I'm sorry to be pompous," she said one morning, "but I just don't want your Mr. Beaver hanging about the house all day and calling me Marjorie."

"Oh well, the flat won't be long now."

"And I shall go on saying that I think you're making a ridiculous mistake."

"It's just that you don't like Mr. Beaver."

"It isn't only that. I think it's hard cheese on Tony."

"Oh, Tony's all right."

"And if there's a row—"

"There won't be a row."

"You never know. If there is, I don't want Allan to think I've been helping to arrange things."

"I wasn't so disagreeable to you about Robin Beaseley."

"There was never much in that," said Marjorie.

But with the exception of her sister's, opinion was greatly in favour of Brenda's adventure. The morning telephone buzzed with news of her; even people with whom she had the barest acquaintance were delighted to relate that they had seen her and Beaver the evening before at restaurant or cinema. It had been an autumn of very sparse and meagre romance; only the most obvious people had parted or come together, and Brenda was filling a want long felt by those whose simple, vicarious pleasure it was to discuss the subject in bed over the telephone. For them her circumstances shed peculiar glamour; for five years she had been a legendary, almost ghostly name, the imprisoned princess of fairy story, and now that she had emerged there was more enchantment in the occurrence, than in the mere change of habit of any other circumspect wife. Her very choice of partner gave the affair an appropriate touch of fantasy; Beaver, the joke figure they had all known and despised, suddenly caught up to her among the luminous clouds of deity. If, after seven years looking neither to right nor left, she had at last broken away with Jock Grant-Menzies or Robin Beaseley or any other young buck with whom nearly everyone had had a crack one time or another, it would have been thrilling no doubt, but straightforward, drawing-room comedy. The choice of Beaver raised the whole escapade into a realm of poetry for Polly and Daisy and Angela and all the gang of gossips.

Mrs. Beaver made no bones about her delight. "Of course the subject has not been mentioned between John and myself, but if what I hear is true, I think it will do the boy a world of good. Of course he's always been very much in demand and had a great number of friends, but *that isn't the same thing*. I've felt for a long time a lack of something in him, and I think that a charming and experienced woman like Brenda Last is just the person to help him. He's got a *very* affectionate nature, but he's so sensitive that he hardly ever lets it appear . . . to tell you the truth I felt something of the kind was in the air last week, so I made an excuse to go away for a few days. If I had been there things might never have come to anything. He's very shy and reserved even to me. I'll have the chess-men done up and sent round to you this afternoon. Thank you so much."

And Beaver, for the first time in his life, found himself a person of interest and, almost of consequence. Women studied him with a new scrutiny, wondering what they had missed in him; men treated him as an equal, even as a successful fellow competitor. "How on earth has *he* got away with it?" they may have asked themselves, but now, when he came into Brat's, they made room for him at the bar and said, "Well, old boy, how about one?"

Brenda rang Tony up every morning and evening. Sometimes John Andrew spoke to her, too, as shrill as Polly Cockpurse; quite unable to hear her replies. She went to Hetton for the week-end, and then back to London, this time to the flat where the paint was already dry, though the hot water was not yet in perfect working order; everything smelt very new—walls, sheets, curtains—and the new radiators gave off a less agreeable reek of hot iron.

That evening she telephoned to Hetton. "I'm talking from the flat."

"Oh, ah."

"*Darling*, do try to sound interested. It's very exciting for me."

"What's it like?"

"Well there are a good many smells at present and the bath makes odd sounds and when you turn on the hot tap there's just a rush of air and that's all, and the cold tap keeps dripping and the water is rather brown and the cupboard doors are jammed and the curtains won't pull right across so that the street lamp shines in all night . . . but it's *lovely*."

"You don't say so."

"Tony, you must be nice about it. It's all so exciting—front door and a latch key and all . . . And someone sent me a lot of flowers today—so many that there's hardly room for them and I've had to put them in the basin on account of having no pots. It wasn't you, was it?"

"Yes . . . as a matter of fact."

"Darling, I did so hope it was . . . how like you."

"Three minutes please."

"Must stop now."

"When are you coming back?"

"Almost at once. Goodnight, my sweet."

"What a lot of talk," said Beaver.

All the time that she was speaking, she had been kept busy with one hand warding him off the telephone, which he threatened playfully to disconnect.

"Wasn't it sweet of Tony to send those flowers?"

"I'm awfully fond of Tony."

"Don't let that worry you, my beauty, he doesn't like you *at all*."

"*Doesn't* he? Why not?"

"No one does except me. You must get that clear . . . it's very odd that *I* should."

Beaver and his mother were going to Ireland for Christmas, to stay with cousins. Tony and Brenda had a family party at Hetton; Marjorie and Allan, Brenda's mother, Tony's Aunt Frances and two families of impoverished Lasts, humble and uncomplaining victims of primogeniture, to whom Hetton meant as much as it did to Tony. There was a little Christmas tree in the nursery for John Andrew and a big one downstairs in the central hall which was decorated by the impoverished Lasts and lit up for half an hour after tea (two footmen standing by with wet sponges on the end of poles, to extinguish the candles which turned turtle and threatened to start a fire). There were presents for all the servants, of value strictly graded according to their rank, and for all the guests (cheques for the impoverished Lasts). Allan always brought a large croûte of foie gras, a delicacy of which he was particularly fond. Everyone ate a great deal and became slightly torpid towards Boxingday evening; silver ladles of burning brandy went around the table, crackers were pulled and opened; paper hats, indoor fireworks, mottoes. This year, everything happened in its accustomed way; nothing seemed to menace the peace and stability of the house. The choir came up and sang carols in the pitch pine gallery, and later devoured hot punch and sweet biscuits. The vicar preached his usual Christmas sermon. It was one to which his parishioners were particularly attached. "How difficult it is for us," he began, blandly surveying his congregation, who coughed into their mufflers and chafed their chilblains under their woollen gloves, "to realize that this is indeed Christmas. Instead of the glowing log fire and windows tight shuttered against the drifting snow, we have only the harsh glare of the alien sun; instead of the happy circle of loved faces, of home and family, we have the uncomprehending stares of the subjugated, though no doubt grateful, heathen. Instead of the placid ox and ass of Bethlehem," said the vicar, slightly losing the thread of his comparisons, "we have for companions the ravening tiger and the exotic camel, the furtive jackal and the ponderous elephant . . ." And so on, through the pages of faded manuscript. The words had temporarily touched the heart of many an obdurate trooper, and hearing them again, as he had heard them year after year since Mr. Tendril had come to the parish, Tony and most of Tony's guests felt that it was an integral part of their Christmas festivities; one with which they would find it very hard to dispense. "The ravening tiger and the exotic camel' had long been bywords in the family, of frequent recurrence in all their games.

These games were the hardest part for Brenda. They did not amuse her and she still could not see Tony dressed up for charades without a feeling of shyness. Moreover she was tortured by the fear that any lack of gusto on her part might be construed by the poor Lasts as superiority. These scruples, had she known it, were quite superfluous for it never occurred to her husband's relatives to look on her with anything but cousinly cordiality and a certain tolerance, for, as Lasts, they considered they had far more right in Hetton than herself. Aunt Frances, with acid mind, quickly discerned the trouble and attempted to re-assure her, saying, "Dear child, all these feelings of deli-cacy are valueless; only the rich realize the gulf that sepa-rates them from the poor," but the uneasiness persisted and night after night she found herself being sent out of the room, asking or answering questions, performing actions in uncouth manners, paying forfeits, drawing pic-tures, writing verses, dressing herself up and even being chased about the house, and secluded in cupboards, at the will of her relatives. Christmas was on a Friday that year, so the party was a long one from Thursday until Monday.

She had forbidden Beaver to send her a present or to write to her; in self-protection, for she knew that whatever he said would hurt her by its poverty, but in spite of this she awaited the posts nervously, hoping that he might have disobeyed her. She had sent him to Ireland a ring of three interlocked hoops of gold and platinum. An hour after ordering it she regretted her choice. On Tues-day a letter came from him thanking her. *Darling Brenda,* he wrote. *Thank you so very much for the charming Christ-mas present. You can imagine my delight when I saw the pink leather case and my surprise at opening it. It really was sweet of you to send me such a charming present. Thank you again very much for it. I hope your party is being a success. It is rather dull here. The others went hunting yesterday. I went to the meet. They did not have a good day. Mother is here too and sends you her love. We shall be leaving tomorrow or the day after. Mother has got rather a cold.*

It ended there at the bottom of a page. Beaver had been writing it before dinner and later had put it in the envelope without remembering to finish it.

He wrote a large, schoolgirlish hand with wide spaces between the lines.

Brenda showed it to Marjorie who was still at Hetton. "I can't complain," she said. "He's never pretended to like me much. And anyway it was a damned silly present."

Tony had become fretful about his visit to Angela's. He always hated staying away.

"Don't come, darling. I'll make it all right with them."

"No, I'll come. I haven't seen so much of you in the last three weeks."

They had the whole of Wednesday alone together. Brenda exerted herself and Tony's fretfulness subsided. She was particularly tender to him at this time and scarcely teased him at all.

On Thursday they went North to Yorkshire. Beaver was there. Tony discovered him in the first half hour and brought the news to Brenda upstairs.

"I'll tell you something very odd," he said. "Who do you think is here?"

"Who?"

"Our old friend Beaver."

"Why's that odd particularly?"

"Oh I don't know. I'd forgotten all about him, hadn't you? D'you think he sent Angela a telegram as he did to us?"

"I daresay."

Tony supposed Beaver must be fairly lonely and took pains to be agreeable to him. He said, "All kinds of changes since we saw you last. Brenda's taken a flat in London."

"Yes, I know."

"How?"

"Well, my mother let it to her, you know."

Tony was greatly surprised and taxed Brenda with this. "You never told me who was behind your flat. I might not have been so amiable if I'd known."

"No, darling, that's why."

Half the house party wondered why Beaver was there; the other half knew. As a result of this he and Brenda saw each other very little, less than if they had been casual acquaintances, so that Angela remarked to her husband, "I daresay it was a mistake to ask him. It's so hard to know."

Brenda never started the subject of the half finished letter, but she noticed that Beaver was wearing his ring, and had already acquired a trick of twisting it as he talked.

On New Year's Eve there was a party at a neighbouring house. Tony went home early and Beaver and Brenda returned together in the back of a car. Next morning, while they were having breakfast, she said to Tony, "I've made a New Year resolution."

"Anything to do with spending more time at home?"

"Oh no, *quite* the reverse. Listen, Tony, it's serious. I think I'll take a course of something."

"Not bone setters again. I thought that was over."

"No, something like economics. You see I've been thinking. I don't really *do* anything at all at present. It's absurd to pretend I'm any use to John, the house runs itself. It seemed to me time I *took* to something. Now you're always talking about going into Parliament. Well if I had done a course of economics I could be some use canvassing and writing speeches and things—you know, the way Marjorie did when Allan was standing on the Clydeside. There are all sorts of lectures in London, to do with the University, where girls go. Don't you think it's rather a good idea?"

"It's one better than the bone setters," Tony admitted.

That was how the New Year began.

CHAPTER THREE

Hard Cheese on Tony

IT IS not uncommon at Brat's Club, between nine and ten in the evening, to find men in white ties and tail coats sitting by themselves and eating, in evident low spirits, large and extravagant dinners. They are those who have been abandoned at the last minute by their women. For twenty minutes or so they have sat in the foyer of some restaurant, gazing expectantly towards the revolving doors and alternately taking out their watches and ordering cocktails, until at length a telephone message has been brought them that their guests are unable to come. Then they go to Brat's half hoping to find friends but, more often than not, taking a melancholy satisfaction in finding the club deserted or peopled by strangers. So they sit there, round the walls, morosely regarding the mahogany tables before them, and eating and drinking heavily.

It was in this mood and for this reason that, one evening towards the middle of February, Jock Grant-Menzies arrived at the club.

"Anyone here?"

"Very quiet tonight, sir. Mr. Last is in the dining room."

Jock found him seated in a corner; he was in day clothes; the table and the chair at his side were littered with papers and magazines; one was propped up in front of him. He was half way through dinner and three quarters of the way through a bottle of Burgundy. "Hullo," he said. "Chucked? Come and join me."

It was some time since Jock had seen Tony; the meeting embarrassed him slightly, for like all his friends, he was wondering how Tony felt and how much he knew about

Brenda and John Beaver. However, he sat down at Tony's table.

"Been chucked?" asked Tony again.

"Yes, it's the last time I ask that bitch out."

"Better have a drink. I've been drinking a whole lot. Much the best thing."

They took what was left of the Burgundy and ordered another bottle.

"Just come up for the night," said Tony. "Staying here."

"You've got a flat now haven't you?"

"Well Brenda has. There isn't really room for two . . . we tried it once and it wasn't a success."

"What's she doing tonight?"

"Out somewhere. I didn't let her know I was coming . . . silly not to, but you see I got fed up with being alone at Hetton and thought I'd like to see Brenda so I came up suddenly on the spur of the moment, just like that. Damned silly thing to do. Might have known she'd be going out somewhere . . . she's very high principled about chucking . . . so there it is. She's going to ring me up here later, if she can get away."

They drank a lot. Tony did most of the talking. "Extraordinary idea of hers, taking up economics," he said. "I never thought it would last but she seems really keen on it . . . I suppose it's a good plan. You know there wasn't really much for her to do all the time at Hetton. Of course she'd rather die than admit it, but I believe she got a bit bored there sometimes. I've been thinking it over and that's the conclusion I came to. Brenda must have been bored . . . Daresay she'll get bored with economics some time . . . Anyway she seems cheerful enough now. We've had parties every week-end lately . . . I wish you'd come down sometimes, Jock. I don't seem to get on with Brenda's new friends."

"People from the school of economics?"

"No, but ones I don't know. I believe I bore them. Thinking it over that's the conclusion I've come to. I bore them. They talk about me as 'the old boy.' John heard them."

"Well, that's friendly enough."

"Yes, that's friendly."

They finished the Burgundy and drank some port. Presently Tony said, "I say, come next week-end, will you?"

"I think I'd love to."

"Wish you would. I don't see many old friends . . . Sure to be lots of people in the house, but you won't mind that will you? . . . sociable chap, Jock . . . doesn't mind people about. *I* mind it like hell." They drank some more port. Tony said, "Not enough bathrooms, you know . . . but of course you know. You've been there before, often. Not like the new friends who think me a bore. You don't think I'm a bore, do you?"

"No, old boy."

"Not even when I'm tight, like this? . . . There would have been bathrooms. I had the plans out. Four new ones. A chap down there made the plans . . . but then Brenda wanted the flat so I had to postpone them as an economy . . . I say, that's funny. We had to economize because of Brenda's economics."

"Yes, that's funny. Let's have some port."

Tony said, "You seem pretty low tonight."

"I am rather. Worried about the Pig Scheme. Constituents keep writing."

"*I* felt low, *bloody* low, but I'm all right again now. The best thing is to get tight. That's what I did and I don't feel low any more . . . discouraging to come to London and find you're not wanted. Funny thing, *you* feel low because your girl's chucked, and *I* feel low because mine won't chuck."

"Yes, that's funny."

"But you know I've felt low for weeks now . . . bloody low . . . how about some brandy?"

"Yes, why not? After all there are other things in life besides women and pigs."

They had some brandy and after a time Jock began to cheer up.

Presently a page came to their table to say, "A message from Lady Brenda, sir."

"Good, I'll go and speak to her."

"It's not her ladyship speaking. Someone was sending a message."

"I'll come and speak to her."

He went to the telephone in the lobby outside. "Darling," he said.

"Is that Mr. Last? I've got a message here, from Lady Brenda."

"Right, put me through to her."

"She can't speak herself, but she asked me to give you this message, that she's very sorry but she cannot join you tonight. She's very tired and has gone home to bed."

"Tell her I want to speak to her."

"I can't I'm afraid, she's gone to bed. She's very tired."

"She's very tired and she's gone to bed?"

"That's right."

"Well, I want to speak to her."

"Goodnight," said the voice.

"The old boy's plastered," said Beaver as he rang off.

"Oh dear. I feel rather awful about him. But what *can* he expect, coming up suddenly like this. He's got to be taught not to make surprise visits."

"Is he often like that?"

"No, it's quite new."

The telephone bell rang. "D'you suppose that's him again? I'd better answer it."

"I want to speak to Lady Brenda Last."

"Tony, darling, this *is* me, Brenda."

"Some damn fool said I couldn't speak to you."

"I left a message from where I was dining. Are you having a lovely evening?"

"Hellish. I'm with Jock. He's worried about the Pig Scheme. Shall we come around and see you?"

"No, not now, darling, I'm terribly tired and just going to bed."

"We'll come and see you."

"Tony, are you a tiny bit tight?"

"Stinking. Jock and I'll come and see you."

"*Tony,* you're *not* to. D'you hear? I can't have you making a brawl. The flats are getting a bad name anyhow."

"Their name'll be mud when Jock and I come."

"Tony, listen, will you please not come, not tonight. Be a good boy and stay at the club. Will you *please* not?"

"Shan't be long." He rang off.

"Oh God," said Brenda. "This isn't the least like Tony. Ring up Brat's and get on to Jock. He'll have more sense."

"That was Brenda."

"So I gathered."

"She's at the flat. I said that we'll go round."

"Splendid. Haven't seen her for weeks. Very fond of Brenda."

"So am I. Grand girl."

"Grand girl."

"A lady on the telephone for you, Mr. Grant-Menzies."

"Who?"

"She didn't give a name."

"All right. I'll come."

Brenda said to him, "Jock, what *have* you been doing to my husband."

"He's a bit tight, that's all."

"He's roaring. Look here he threatens to come round. I simply can't face him tonight in that mood, I'm tired out. You understand, don't you?"

"Yes, I understand."

"So, will you, *please,* keep him away. Are you tight too?"

"A little bit."

"Oh dear, can I trust you?"

"I'll try."

"Well, it doesn't sound too good. Goodbye" ... "John, you've got to go. Those hooligans may turn up at any moment. Have you got your taxi fare? You'll find some change in my bag."

"Was that your girl?"

"Yes."

"Made it up?"

"Not exactly."

"Far better to make it up. Shall we have some more brandy and go round to Brenda straight away?"

"Let's have some more brandy."

"Jock, you aren't still feeling low are you? Doesn't do to feel low. *I'm* not feeling low. I *was*, but I'm not any more."

"Then we'll have some brandy and then go to Brenda's."

"All right."

Half an hour later they got into Jock's car. "Tell you what, I shouldn't drive if I were you."

"Not drive?"

"No, I shouldn't drive. They'd say you were drunk."

"Who would?"

"Anyone you ran over. They'd say you were drunk."

"Well, so I am."

"Then I shouldn't drive."

"Too far to walk."

"We'll take a taxi."

"Oh hell, I can drive."

"Or let's not go to Brenda's at all."

"We'd better go to Brenda's" said Jock. "She's expecting us."

"Well I can't walk all that way. Besides I don't think she really wanted us to come."

"She'll be pleased when she sees us."

"Yes, but it's a long way. Let's go some other place."

"I'd like to see Brenda," said Jock. "I'm very fond of Brenda."

"She's a grand girl."

"She's a grand girl."

"Well let's take a taxi to Brenda's."

But half way Jock said, "Don't let's go there. Let's go some other place. Let's go to some low joint."

"All the same to me. Tell him to go to some low joint."

"Go to some low joint," said Jock, putting his head through the window.

The cab wheeled round and made towards Shaftesbury Avenue.

"We can always ring Brenda from the low joint."

"Yes, I think we ought to do that. She's a grand girl."

"Grand girl."

The cab turned down Wardour Street and then into Sink Street, a dingy little place inhabited for the most part by Asiatics.

"D'you know, I believe he's taking us to the old Sixty-four."

"Can't still be open? Thought they closed it down years ago."

But the door was brightly illumined and a seedy figure in peaked cap and braided overcoat stepped out to open the taxi for them.

The Sixty-four has never been shut. For a generation, while other night clubs have sprung into being, with various names and managers, and various pretensions to respectability, have enjoyed a precarious and brief existence, and come to grief at the hands either of police or creditors, the Sixty-four has maintained a solid front against all adversity. It has not been immune from persecution; far from it. Times out of number, magistrates have struck it off, cancelled its license, condemned its premises; the staff and until her death, the proprietress, have been constantly in and out of prison; there have been questions in the House and committees of enquiry, but whatever Home Secretaries and Commissioners of Police have risen into eminence and retired discredited, the doors of the Sixty-four have always been open from nine in the evening until four at night, and inside there has been an unimpeded flow of dubious, alcoholic preparations. A kindly young lady admitted Tony and Jock to the ramshackle building.

"D'you mind signing in?" Tony and Jock inscribed fictitious names at the foot of a form which stated, *I have been invited to a Bottle Party at 64 Sink Street given by Mr. Charles Weybridge.* "That's five bob each please."

It is not an expensive club to run, because none of the

staff, except the band, receive any wages; they make what they can by going through the overcoat pockets and giving the wrong change to drunks. The young ladies get in free but they have to see to it that their patrons spend money.

"Last time I was here, Tony, was the bachelor party before your wedding."

"Tight that night."

"Stinking."

"I'll tell you who else was tight that night—Reggie. Broke a fruit gum machine."

"Reggie was stinking."

"I say, you don't still feel low about that girl?"

"I don't feel low."

"Come on, we'll go downstairs."

The dance room was fairly full. An elderly man had joined the band and was trying to conduct it. "I like this joint," said Jock. "What'll we drink?"

"Brandy." They had to buy a whole bottle. They filled in an order form to the Montmorency Wine Company and paid two pounds. When it came it had a label saying *Very Old Liquor Fine Champagne. Imported by the Montmorency Wine Co.* The waiter brought ginger ale and four glasses. Two young ladies came and sat with them. They were called Milly and Babs. Milly said, "Are you in town for long?" Babs said, "Have you got such a thing as a cigarette?"

Tony danced with Babs. She said, "Are you fond of dancing?"

"No, are you?"

"So-so."

"Well, let's sit down."

The waiter said, "Will you buy a ticket in a raffle for a box of chocolates?"

"No."

"Buy one for me," said Babs.

Jock began to describe the specifications of the Basic Pig.

. . . Milly said, "You're married, aren't you?"

"No," said Jock.

"Oh I can always tell," said Milly. "Your friend is too."

"Yes, *he* is."

"You'd be surprised how many gentlemen come here just to talk about their wives."

"He hasn't."

Tony was leaning across the table and saying to Babs, "You see the trouble is my wife is studious. She's taking a course in economics."

Babs said, "I think it's nice for a girl to be interested in things."

The waiter said, "What will you be taking for supper?"

"Why we've only just had dinner."

"How about a nice haddock?"

"I tell you what I must do, is to telephone. Where is it?"

"D'you mean really the telephone or the gentlemen's?"

"No, the telephone."

"U'stairs in the office."

Tony rang up Brenda. It was some time before she answered, then, "Yes, who is it?"

"I have a message here from Mr. Anthony Last and Mr. Jocelyn Grant-Menzies."

"Oh, it's you Tony. Well, what do you want?"

"You recognized my voice?"

"I did."

"Well, I only wanted to give a message but as I am speaking to you I can give it myself, can't I?"

"Yes."

"Well Jock and I are terribly sorry but we can't come round this evening after all."

"Oh."

"You don't think it very rude I hope, but we have a lot to attend to."

"That's all right, Tony."

"Did I wake you up by any chance?"

"That's all right, Tony."

"Well, goodnight."

"Goodnight."

Tony went down to the table. "I've been talking to

Brenda. She sounded rather annoyed. D'you think we *ought* to go round there."

"We promised we would," said Jock.

"You should never disappoint a lady," said Milly.

"Oh it's too late now."

Babs said, "You two are officers, aren't you?"

"No, why?"

"I thought you were."

Milly said, "I like business gentlemen best, myself. They've more to say."

"What d'you do?"

"I design postman's hats," said Jock.

"Oh, go on."

"And my friend here trains sea lions."

"Tell us another."

Babs said, "I got a gentleman friend who works on a newspaper."

After a time Jock said, "I say, ought we to do something about Brenda?"

"You told her we weren't coming, didn't you?"

"Yes . . . but she might still be *hoping*."

"I tell you what, you go and ring her up and find out if she really wants us."

"All right." He came back ten minutes later. "*I* thought she sounded rather annoyed," he reported. "But I said in the end we wouldn't come."

"She may be tired," said Tony. "Has to get up early to do economics. Now I come to think of it someone *did* say she was tired, earlier on in the evening."

"I say what's this frightful piece of fish?"

"The waiter said you ordered it."

"Perhaps I did."

"I'll give it to the club cat," said Babs, "she's a dear called Blackberry."

They danced once or twice. Then Jock said, "D'you think we ought to ring up Brenda again?"

"Perhaps we ought. She sounded annoyed with us."

"Let's go now and ring her up on the way out."

"Aren't you coming home with us?" said Babs.

"Not tonight, I'm afraid."

"Be a sport," said Milly.

"No, we can't really."

"All right. Well how about a little present? We're professional dancing partners, you know," said Babs.

"Oh yes, sorry, how much?"

"Oh, we leave that to the gentlemen."

Tony gave them a pound. "You might make it a bit more," said Babs. "We've sat with you two hours."

Jock gave another pound. "Come and see us again one evening when you've more time," said Milly.

"I'm feeling rather ill," said Tony on the way upstairs. "Don't think I shall bother to ring up Brenda."

"Send a message."

"That's a good idea . . . Look here," he said to the seedy commissionaire. "Will you ring up this Sloane number and speak to her ladyship and say Mr. Grant-Menzies and Mr. Last are very sorry but they cannot call this evening. Got that?" He gave the man half a crown and they sauntered out into Sink Street. "Brenda can't expect us to do more than that," he said.

"I tell you what I'll do. I go almost past her door so I'll ring the bell a bit just in case she's awake and still waiting up for us."

"Yes, you do that. What a good friend you are, Jock."

"Oh I'm fond of Brenda . . . a grand girl."

"Grand girl . . . I wish I didn't feel ill."

Tony was awake at eight next morning, miserably articulating in his mind the fragmentary memories of the preceding night. The more he remembered, the baser his conduct appeared to him. At nine he had his bath and some tea. At ten he was wondering whether he should ring Brenda up when the difficulty was solved by her ringing him.

"Well, Tony, how do you feel?"

"Awful. I *was* tight."

"You were."

"I'm feeling pretty guilty too."

"I'm not surprised."

"I don't remember everything very clearly but I have the impression that Jock and I were rather bores."

"You were."

"Are you in a rage?"

"Well, I was last night. What made you do it, Tony, grown up men like you two?"

"We felt low."

"I bet you feel lower this morning . . . A box of white roses has just arrived from Jock."

"I wish I'd thought of that."

"You're such infants both of you."

"You aren't really in a rage?"

"Of course I'm not, darling. Now just you go straight back to the country. You'll feel all right again tomorrow."

"Am I not going to see you?"

"Not today I'm afraid. I've got lectures all the morning and I'm lunching out. But I'll be coming down on Friday evening or anyway Saturday morning."

"I see. You couldn't possibly chuck lunch or one of the lectures."

"Not possibly, darling."

"I see. You are an angel to be so sweet about last night."

"Nothing could have been more fortunate," Brenda said. "If I know Tony he'll be tortured with guilt for weeks to come. It was maddening last night but it was worth it. He's put himself so much in the wrong now that he won't dare to *feel* resentful, let alone say anything, whatever I do. And he hasn't really enjoyed himself at all, the poor sweet, so *that's* a good thing too. He had to learn not to make surprise visits."

"You are one for making people learn things," said Beaver.

Tony emerged from the 3.18 feeling cold, tired, and heavy with guilt. John Andrew had come in with the car to meet him. "Hullo, daddy, had a good time in London? You didn't mind me coming to the station did you? I *made* nanny let me."

"Very pleased to see you, John."

"How was mummy?"

"She sounded very well. I didn't see her."

"But you *said* you were going to see her."

"Yes, I thought I was, but I turned out to be wrong. I talked to her several times on the telephone."

"But you can telephone her from here, can't you, daddy? Why did you go all the way to London to telephone her? . . . *Why,* daddy?"

"It would take too long to explain."

"Well, tell me some of it . . . *Why,* daddy?"

"Look here I'm tired. If you don't stop asking questions I shan't let you ever come and meet the trains again."

John Andrew's face began to pucker. "I thought you'd *like* me to come and meet you."

"If you cry I shall put you in front with Dawson. It's absurd to cry at your age."

"I'd *sooner* go in front with Dawson," said John Andrew between his tears.

Tony picked up the speaking tube to tell the chauffeur to stop, but he could not make him hear. So he hitched the mouthpiece back on its hook and they drove on in silence, John Andrew leaning against the window and snivelling slightly. When they got to the house, he said, "Nanny, I don't want John to come to the station in future unless her ladyship or I specially say he can."

"No, sir, I wouldn't have him come today only he went on so. Come along now, John, and take off your coat. Goodness, child, where's your handkerchief."

Tony went and sat alone in front of the library fire. "Two men of thirty," he said to himself, "behaving as if they were up for the night from Sandhurst—getting drunk and ringing people up and dancing with tarts at the Sixty-four . . . And it makes it all the worst that Brenda was so nice about it." He dozed a little; then he went up to change. At dinner he said, "Ambrose, when I'm alone I think in future I'll have dinner at a table in the library."

Afterwards he sat with a book in front of the fire, but he was unable to read. At ten o'clock he scattered the logs in the fireplace before going upstairs. He fastened the library windows and turned out the lights. That night he went into Brenda's empty room to sleep.

Two

That was Wednesday; on Thursday Tony felt well again. He had a meeting of the County Council in the morning. In the afternoon he went down to the home farm and discussed a new kind of tractor with his agent. From then onwards he was able to say to himself, "Tomorrow this time Brenda and Jock will be here." He dined in front of the fire in the library. He had given up the diet some weeks ago. "Ambrose, when I am alone I don't really need a long dinner. In future I'll just have two courses." He looked over some accounts his agent had left for him and then went to bed, saying to himself, "When I wake up it will be the week-end."

But there was a telegram for him next morning from Jock saying, *Week end impossible have to go to constituency how about one after next*. He wired back, *Delighted any time always here*. "I suppose he's made it up with that girl," Tony reflected.

There was also a note from Brenda, written in pencil:

Coming Sat. with Polly, and a friend of Polly's called Veronica in P.'s car. Maids and luggage on 3.18. Will you tell Ambrose and Mrs. Massop. We had better open Lyonesse for Polly you know what she is about comfort. Veronica can go anywhere—not Galahad. Polly says she's v. amusing. Also Mrs. Beaver coming, please don't mind it is only on business, she thinks she can do something to morning room. Only Polly bringing maid. Also chauffeur. By the way I'm leaving Grimshawe at Hetton next week tell Mrs. Massop. It's a bore and expense boarding her out in London. In fact I think I might do without her altogether what do you think? except she's useful for sew-

ing. Longing to see John again. All going back Sunday
evening. Keep sober, darling. Try.

x x x x x x

B.

Tony found very little to occupy his time on Friday.
His letters were all finished by ten o'clock. He went down
to the farm but they had no business for him there. The
duties which before had seemed so multifarious, now
took up a very small part of his day; he had not realized
how many hours he used to waste with Brenda. He
watched John riding in the paddock. The boy clearly
bore him ill will for their quarrel on Wednesday; when
he applauded a jump, John said, "She usually does better
than this." Later, "When's mummy coming down?"

"Not till tomorrow."

"Oh."

"I've got to go over to Little Bayton this afternoon.
Would you like to come too and perhaps we could see
the kennels?"

John had for weeks past been praying for this expedition. "No, thank you," he said. "I want to finish a picture
I am painting."

"You can do that any time."

"I want to do it this afternoon."

When Tony had left them Ben said, "Whatever made
you speak to your dad like that for? You've been going on
about seeing the kennels since Christmas."

"Not with *him*," said John.

"You ungrateful little bastard, that's a lousy way to
speak of your dad."

"And you ought not to say bastard or lousy in front of
me, nanny says not."

So Tony went over alone to Little Bayton where he
had some business to discuss with Colonel Brink. He
hoped they would asked him to say on, but the Colonel
and his wife were themselves going out to tea, so he drove
back in the dusk to Hetton.

A thin mist lay breast high over the park; the turrets

and battlements of the abbey stood grey and flat; the
boiler man was hauling down the flag on the main tower.

"My poor Brenda, it's an appalling room," said Mrs.
Beaver.

"It's not one we use a great deal," said Tony very
coldly.

"I should think not," said the one they called Veronica.

"I can't see much wrong with it," said Polly, "except
it's a bit mouldy."

"You see," Brenda explained, not looking at Tony.
"What I thought was that I must have *one* habitable
room downstairs. At present there's only the smoking
room and the library. The drawing room is vast and quite
out of the question. I thought what I needed was a small
sitting room more or less to myself. Don't you think it has
possibilities?"

"But, my angel, the *shape's* all wrong," said Daisy. "And
that chimney piece—what is it made of, pink granite, and
all the plaster work and the dado. *Everything's* horrible.
It's so *dark*."

"I know exactly what Brenda wants," said Mrs. Beaver
more moderately. "I don't think it will be impossible. I
must think about it. As Veronica says, the structure does
rather limit one . . . you know I think the only thing to
do would be to disregard it altogether and find some treatment so definite that it *carried* the room if you see what
I mean . . . supposing we covered the walls with white
chromium plating and had natural sheepskin carpet . . . I
wonder if that would be running you in for more than
you meant to spend."

"I'd blow the whole thing sky-high," said Veronica.

Tony left them to their discussion.

"D'you really want Mrs. Beaver to do up the morning
room?"

"Not if you don't, sweet."

"But can you imagine it—white chromium plating?"

"Oh, that was just an idea."

Tony walked in and out between Mordred and Guinevere as he always did while they were dressing. "I say," he said, returning with his waistcoat. "You aren't going away tomorrow too, are you?"

"Must."

He went back to Mordred for his tie and bringing it to Brenda's room again, sat by her side at the dressing table to fasten it.

"By the way," said Brenda, "what did you think about keeping on Grimshawe?—it seems rather a waste."

"You used always to say you couldn't get on without her."

"Yes, but now I'm living at the flat everything's so simple."

"*Living?* Darling, you talk as though you had settled there for good."

"D'you mind moving a second, sweet? I can't see properly."

"Brenda, how long are you going on with this course of economics?"

"Me? I don't know."

"But you must have some idea?"

"Oh it's surprising what a lot there is to learn . . . I was so backward when I started . . ."

"Brenda . . ."

"Now run and put on your coat. They'll all be downstairs waiting for us."

That evening Polly and Mrs. Beaver played backgammon. Brenda and Veronica sat together on the sofa sewing and talking about their needlework; occasionally there were bursts of general conversation between the four women; they had the habit of lapsing into a jargon of their own which Tony did not understand; it was a thieves' slang, by which the syllables of each word were transposed. Tony sat just outside the circle, reading under another lamp.

That night when they went upstairs, the three guests came to sit in Brenda's room and talk to her while she went to bed. Tony could hear their low laughter through the dressing-room door. They had boiled water in an electric kettle and were drinking Sedobrol together.

Presently, still laughing, they left and Tony went into Brenda's room. It was in darkness, but hearing him come and seeing the square of light in the doorway, she turned on the little lamp by the bedside.

"Why, Tony," she said.

She was lying on the dais with her head deep back in the pillows; her face was shining with the grease she used for cleaning it; one bare arm on the quilted eiderdown, left there from turning the switch. "Why, Tony," she said, "I was almost asleep."

"Very tired?"

"Mm."

"Want to be left alone?"

"So tired . . . and I've just drunk a lot of that stuff of Polly's."

"I see . . . well goodnight."

"Goodnight . . . don't mind do you? . . . so tired."

He crossed to the bed and kissed her; she lay quite still, with closed eyes. Then he turned out the light and went back to the dressing room.

"Lady Brenda not ill, I hope?"

"No, nothing serious, thank you very much. She gets rather done up in London, you know, during the week, and likes to take Sunday quietly."

"And how are the great studies progressing?"

"Very well, I gather. She seems keen on it still."

"Splendid. We shall all be coming to her soon to solve our economic problems. But I daresay you and John miss her?"

"Yes, we do rather."

"Well please give her my kindest regards."

"I will indeed. Thank you so much."

Tony left the church porch and made his accustomed way to the hot houses; a gardenia for himself; four almost black carnations for the ladies. When he reached the room where they were sitting there was a burst of laughter. He paused on the threshold rather bewildered.

"Come in, darling, it isn't anything. It's only we had a bet on what coloured button-hole you'd be wearing and none of us won."

They still giggled a little as they pinned on the flowers he had brought them; all except Mrs. Beaver who said, "Any time you are buying cuttings or seeds do get them through me. I've made quite a little business of it, perhaps you didn't know . . . all kinds of rather unusual flowers. I do everything like that for Sylvia Newport and all sorts of people."

"You must talk to my head man about it."

"Well to tell you the truth I *have*—this morning while you were in church. He seems quite to understand."

They left early, so as to reach London in time for dinner. In the car Daisy said, "Golly what a house."

"Now you can see what I've been through all these years."

"My poor Brenda," said Veronica, unpinning her carnation and throwing it from the window into the side of the road.

"You know," Brenda confided next day, "I'm not *absolutely* happy about Tony."

"What's the old boy been up to?" asked Polly.

"Nothing much yet, but I do see it's pretty boring for him at Hetton all this time."

"I shouldn't worry."

"Oh, I'm not *worrying*. It's only, supposing he took to drink or something. It would make everything very difficult."

"I shouldn't have said that was his thing . . . We must get him interested in a girl."

"If only we could . . . Who is there?"

"There's always old Sybil."

"Darling, he's known her all his life."

"Or Souki de Foucauld-Esterhazy."

"He isn't his best with Americans."

"Well we'll find him someone."

"The trouble is that I've become such a habit with him—he won't take easily to a new one . . . ought she to be like me, or quite different?"

"I'd say, different, but it's hard to tell."

They discussed this problem in all its aspects.

Three

Brenda wrote:

Darling Tony,

Sorry not to have written or rung up but I've had such a busy time with bimetallism v. complicated.

Coming down Saturday with Polly again. Good her coming twice—Lyonesse can't be as beastly as most of the rooms can it.

Also charming girl I have taken up with who I want us to be kind to. She'd had a terrible life and she lives in one of these flats called Jenny Abdul Akbar. Not black but married one. Get her to tell you. She'll come by train 3.18 I expect. Must stop now and go to lecture.

Keep away from the Demon Rum.

x x x x x
Brenda.

Saw Jock last night at Café de Paris with shameless blonde. Who?

Cin no Djinñ how? has rheumatism and Marjorie is v. put out about it. She thinks his pelvis is out of place and Cruttwell won't do him which is pretty mean considing all the people she has brought there.

"Are you *certain* Jenny will be Tony's tea?"

"You can't ever be certain," said Polly. "She bores my pants off, but she's a good trier."

"Is mummy coming down today, daddy?"

"Yes."

"Who else?"

"Someone called Abdul Akbar."

"What a silly name. Is she foreign?"

"I don't know."

"Sounds foreign, doesn't she, daddy? D'you think she won't be able to talk any English? Is she black?"

"Mummy says not."

"Oh . . . who else?"

"Lady Cockpurse."

"The monkey woman. You know she wasn't a bit like a monkey except perhaps her face and I don't think she had a tail because I looked as close as anything . . . unless perhaps she has it rolled up between her legs. D'you think she has, daddy?"

"I shouldn't be surprised."

"*Very* uncomfortable."

Tony and John were friends again; but it had been a leaden week.

It was part of Polly Cockpurse's plan to arrive late at Hetton. "Give the girl a chance to get down to it," she said. So she and Brenda did not leave London until Jenny was already on her way from the station. It was a day of bitter cold and occasional rain. The resolute little figure huddled herself in the rugs until they reached the gates. Then she opened her bag, tucked up her veil, shook out her powder puff and put her face to rights. She licked the rouge from her finger with a sharp red tongue.

Tony was in the smoking room when she was announced; the library was now too noisy during the daytime for there were men at work on the walls of the morning room next door, tearing down the plaster tracery.

"Princess Abdul Akbar."

He rose to greet her. She was preceded by a heavy odour of musk.

"Oh, Mr. Last," she said, "what a sweet old place this is."

"I'm afraid it's been restored a great deal," said Tony.

"Ah, but its *atmosphere*. I always think that's what

counts in a house. Such dignity, and repose, but of course you're used to it. When you've been very unhappy as I have, you appreciate these things."

Tony said, "I'm afraid Brenda hasn't arrived yet. She's coming by car with Lady Cockpurse."

"Brenda's been *such* a friend to me." The Princess took off her furs and sat down on the stool before the fire, looking up at Tony. "D'you mind if I take off my hat?"

"No, no . . . of course."

She threw it on to the sofa and shook out her hair, which was dead black and curled. "D'you know, Mr. Last, I'm going to call you Teddy right away. You don't think that very fresh of me? And you must call me Jenny. Princess is so formal, isn't it, and suggests tight trousers and gold braid . . . Of course," she went on, stretching out her hands to the fire and letting her hair fall forwards a little across her face, "my husband was not called 'Prince' in Morocco; his title was Moulay—but there's no proper equivalent for a woman so I've always called myself Princess in Europe . . . Moulay is *far* higher really . . . my husband was a descendant of the Prophet. Are you interested in the East?"

"No . . . yes. I mean I know very little about it."

"It has an uncanny fascination for me. You must go there, Teddy. I know you'd like it. I've been saying the same to Brenda."

"I expect you'd like to see your room," said Tony. "They'll bring tea soon."

"No, I'll stay here. I like just to curl up like a cat in front of the fire, and if you're nice to me I'll purr, and if you're cruel I shall pretend not to notice—just like a cat . . . Shall I purr, Teddy?"

"Er . . . yes . . . do, please, if that's what you like doing."

"Englishmen are so gentle and considerate. It's wonderful to be back among them . . . mine own people. Sometimes when I look back at my life, especially at times like this among lovely old English things and kind people, I think the whole thing must be a frightful nightmare . . . then I remember my *scars* . . ."

"Brenda tells me you've taken one of the flats in the same house as hers. They must be very convenient."

"How English you are, Teddy—so shy of talking about personal things, intimate things . . . I like you for that, you know. I love everything that's solid and homely and *good* after . . . after all I've been through."

"You're not studying economics too, are you, like Brenda?"

"No; is Brenda? She never told me. What a wonderful person she is. When *does* she find the time?"

"Ah, here comes tea at last," said Tony. "I hope you allow yourself to eat muffins. So many of our guests nowadays are on a diet. I think muffins one of the few things that make the English winter endurable."

"Muffins stand for so much," said Jenny.

She ate heartily; often she ran her tongue over her lips, collecting crumbs that had become embedded there and melted butter from the muffin. One drop of butter fell on her chin and glittered there unobserved except by Tony. It was a relief to him when John Andrew was brought in.

"Come and be introduced to Princess Abdul Akbar."

John Andrew had never before seen a Princess; he gazed at her fascinated.

"Aren't you going to give me a kiss?"

He walked over to her and she kissed him on the mouth.

"Oh," he said, recoiling and rubbing away the taste of the lipstick; and then "What a beautiful smell."

"It's my last link with the East," she said.

"You've got butter on your chin."

She reached for her bag, laughing. "Why so I have. Teddy, you *might* have told me."

"Why do you call daddy, Teddy?"

"Because I hope we are going to be great friends."

"What a funny reason."

John stayed with them for an hour and all the time watched her fascinated. "Have you got a crown?" he asked. "How did you learn to speak English? What is that big ring made of? Did it cost much? Why are your nails that colour? Can you ride?"

She answered all his questions, sometimes enigmatically with an eye on Tony. She took out a little heavily scented handkerchief and showed John the monogram. "That is my only crown . . . now," she said. She told him about the horses she used to have—glossy black, with arched necks; foam round their silver bits; plumes tossing on their foreheads; silver studs on the harness, crimson saddle-cloths, "On the Moulay's birthday—"

"What's the Moulay?"

"A beautiful and a very bad man," she said gravely, "and on his birthday all his horsemen used to assemble round a great square, with all their finest clothes and trappings and jewels, with long swords in their hands. The Moulay used to sit on a throne under a great crimson canopy."

"What's a canopy?"

"Like a tent," she said more sharply, and then resuming her soft voice, "and all the horsemen used to gallop across the plain, in a great cloud of dust, waving their swords, straight towards the Moulay. And everyone used to hold their breath, thinking the horsemen were bound to ride right on top of the Moulay, but when they were a few feet away, as near as I am to you, galloping at full speed, they used to rein their horses back, up on to their hind legs and salute—"

"Oh but they *shouldn't*," said John. "It's *very* bad horsemanship indeed. Ben says so."

"They're the most wonderful horsemen in the world. Everyone knows that."

"Oh no, they can't be, if they do *that*. It's one of the *worst* things. Were they natives?"

"Yes, of course."

"Ben says natives aren't humans at all really."

"Ah but he's thinking of Negroes I expect. These are pure Semitic type."

"What's that?"

"The same as Jews."

"Ben says Jews are worse than natives."

"Oh dear, what a very severe boy you are. I was like that once. Life teaches one to be tolerant."

"It hasn't taught Ben," said John. "When's mummy coming? I thought she'd be here, otherwise I wouldn't have stopped painting my picture."

But when nanny came to fetch him, John, without invitation, went over and kissed Jenny goodnight. "Goodnight, Johnny-boy," she said.

"What did you call me?"

"Johnny-boy."

"You are funny with names."

Upstairs, meditatively splashing his spoon in the bread and milk, he said, "Nanny, I do think that Princess is beautiful, don't you?"

Nanny sniffed. "It would be a dull world if we all thought alike," she said.

"She's more beautiful than Miss Tendril, even. I think she's the most beautiful lady I've ever seen ... D'you think she'd like to watch me have my bath?"

Downstairs, Jenny said, "What a heavenly child ... I love children. That has been my great tragedy. It was when he found I couldn't have children that the Moulay first showed the Other Side of his Nature. It wasn't my fault ... you see my womb is out of place ... I don't know why I'm telling you all this, but I feel you'll understand. It's such a *waste of time,* isn't it, when one knows one is going to like someone and one goes on *pretending* ... I know at once if someone is going to be a real friend ..."

Polly and Brenda arrived just before seven. Brenda went straight up to the nursery. "Oh, mummy," said John. "There's such a beautiful lady downstairs. Do ask her to come and say goodnight. Nanny doesn't think she'd want to."

"Did daddy seem to like her?"

"He didn't talk much ... She doesn't know anything about horses or natives but she *is* beautiful. Please tell her to come up."

Brenda went downstairs and found Jenny with Polly and Tony in the smoking room. "You've made a wild success with John Andrew. He won't go to sleep until he's seen you again."

They went up together, and Jenny said, "They're both such dears."

"Did you and Tony get on? I was so sorry not to be here when you arrived."

"He was *so* sympathetic and gentle . . . and so wistful."

They sat on John's small bed in the night-nursery. He threw the clothes back and crawled out, nestling against Jenny. "Back to bed," she said, "or I shall spank you."

"Would you do it hard? I shouldn't mind."

"Oh dear,' said Brenda, "what a terrible effect you seem to have. He's never like this as a rule."

When they had gone nanny threw open another window. "Poof!" she said, "making the whole place stink."

"Don't you like it? *I* think it's lovely."

Brenda took Polly up to Lyonesse. It was a large suite, fitted up with satinwood for King Edward when, as Prince of Wales, he was once expected at a shooting party; he never came.

"How's it going?" she asked anxiously.

"Too soon to tell. I'm sure it will be all right."

"She's got the wrong chap. John Andrew's mad about her . . . quite embarrassing."

"I should say Tony was a slow starter. It's a pity she's got his name wrong. Ought we to tell her?"

"No, let's leave it."

When she was dressing Tony said, "Brenda, who *is* this joke-woman?"

"Darling, don't you like her?"

The disappointment and distress in her tone were so clear that Tony was touched. "I don't know about not liking her exactly. She's just a joke, isn't she?"

"Is she . . . oh dear . . . She's had a terrible life you know."

"So I gathered."

"Be nice to her, Tony please."

"Oh, I'll be nice to her. Is she Jewish?"

"I don't know. I never thought. Perhaps she is."

Soon after dinner Polly said she was tired and asked Brenda to come with her while she undressed. "Leave the young couple to it," she whispered outside the door.

"My dear, I don't believe it's going to be any good . . . the poor boy's got *some* taste you know, and a sense of humour."

"She didn't show up too well at dinner, did she?"

"She will *go on* so . . . and after all Tony's been used to me for seven years. It's rather a sudden change."

"Tired?"

"Mmm. Little bit."

"You gave me a pretty long bout of Abdul Akbar."

"I know. I'm sorry, darling, but Polly takes so long to get to bed . . . Was it awful? I wish you liked her more."

"She's awful."

"One has to make allowances . . . she's got the most terrible scars."

"So she told me."

"I've seen them."

"Besides I hoped to see something of you."

"Oh."

"Brenda, you aren't angry still about my getting tight that night and waking you up?"

"No, sweet, do I seem angry?"

". . . I don't know. You do rather . . . Has it been an amusing week?"

"Not amusing, very hard work. Bimetallism you know."

"Oh yes . . . well, I suppose you want to go to sleep."

"Mm . . . so tired. Goodnight, darling."

"Goodnight."

"Can I go and say good morning to the Princess, mummy?"

"I don't expect she's awake yet."

"Please, mummy, may I go and see. I'll just peep and if she's asleep, go away."

"I don't know what room she's in."

"Galahad, my lady," said Grimshawe who was putting out her clothes.

"Oh dear, why was she put there."

"It was Mr. Last's orders, my lady."

"Well, she's probably awake then."

John slipped out of the room and trotted down the passage to Galahad. "May I come in?"

"Hullo, Johnny-boy. Come in."

He swung on the handles of the door, half in, half out of the room. "Have you had breakfast? Mummy said you wouldn't be awake."

"I've been awake a long time. You see I was once very badly hurt, and now I don't always sleep well. Even the softest beds are too hard for me now."

"Ooh. What did you do? Was it a motor car accident?"

"Not an accident, Johnny-boy, not an accident . . . but come. It's cold with the door open. Look there are some grapes here. Would you like to eat them?"

John climbed on to the bed. "What are you going to do today?"

"I don't know yet. I haven't been told."

"Well I'll tell you. We'll go to church in the morning because I have to and then we'll go and look at Thunder-clap and I'll show you the place we jump and then you can come with me while I have dinner because I have it early and afterwards we can go down to Bruton wood and we needn't take nanny because it makes her so muddy and you can see where they dug out a fox in the drain just outside the wood, he nearly got away and then you can come and have tea in the nursery and I've got a little gramophone Uncle Reggie gave me for Christmas and it plays 'When Father Papered the Parlour,' do you know that song. Ben can sing it, and I've got some books to show you and a picture I did of the battle of Marston Moor."

"I think that sounds a lovely day. But don't you think I ought to spend some time with daddy and mummy and Lady Cockpurse?"

"Oh, *them* . . . besides it's all my foot about Lady Cock-purse having a tail. Please you *will* spend the day with me?"

"Well, we'll see."

"She's gone to church with him. That's a good sign isn't it?"

"Well, not really, Polly. He likes going alone, or with me. It's the time he gossips to the village."

"She won't stop him."

"I'm afraid you don't understand the old boy altogether. He's much odder than you'd think."

"I could see from your sermon that you knew the East, rector."

"Yes, yes, most of my life."

"It has an uncanny fascination, hasn't it?"

"Oh come on," said John, pulling at her coat. "We must go and see Thunderclap."

So Tony returned alone with the button-holes.

After luncheon Brenda said, "Why don't you show Jenny the house?"

"Oh yes, *do*."

When they reached the morning room he said, "Brenda's having it done up."

There were planks and ladders and heaps of plaster about.

"Oh, Teddy, what a shame. I do hate seeing things modernized."

"It isn't a room we used very much."

"No, but still . . ." she stirred the mouldings of fleur-de-lis that littered the floor, fragments of tarnished gilding and dusty stencil-work. "You know, Brenda's been a wonderful friend to me. I wouldn't say anything against her . . . but ever since I came here I've been wondering whether she really understands this beautiful place and all it means to you."

"Tell me more about your terrible life," said Tony, leading her back to the central hall.

"You are shy of talking about yourself, aren't you,

Teddy? It's a mistake, you know, to keep things bottled up. I've been very unhappy too."

Tony looked about him desperately in search of help; and help came. "Oh there you are," said a firm, child's voice. "Come on. We're going down to the woods now. We must hurry, otherwise it will be dark."

"Oh, Johnny-boy, must I really? I was just talking to daddy."

"*Come on.* It's all arranged. And afterwards you're to be allowed to have tea with me upstairs."

Tony crept into the library, habitable today, since the workmen were at rest. Brenda found him there two hours later. "*Tony,* here all alone? We thought you were with Jenny. What have you done with her?"

"John took her off . . . just in time before I said something rude."

"Oh dear . . . well there's only me and Polly in the smoking room. Come and have some tea. You look all funny—have you been asleep?"

"We must write it down a failure, definitely."

"What *does* the old boy expect? It isn't as though he was everybody's money."

"I daresay it would all have been all right, if she hadn't got his name wrong."

"Anyway, this lets you out. You've done far more than most wives would to cheer the old boy up."

"Yes, that's certainly true," said Brenda.

Four

Another five days; then Brenda came to Hetton again. "I shan't be here next week-end," she said, "I'm going to stay with Veronica."

"Am I asked?"

"Well you *were,* of course, but I refused for you. You know you always hate staying away."

"I wouldn't mind coming."

"Oh, darling, I wish I'd known. Veronica would have loved it so . . . but I'm afraid it will be too late now. She's only got a tiny house . . . to tell you the truth I didn't think you liked her much."

"I hated her like hell."

"Well then . . . ?"

"Oh, it doesn't matter. I suppose you must go back on Monday? The hounds are meeting here on Wednesday, you know."

"Are we giving them a lawner?"

"Yes, darling, you know we do every year."

"So we do."

"You couldn't stay down till then?"

"Not possibly, darling. You see if I miss one lecture I get right behind and can't follow the next. Besides I am not mad keen to see the hounds."

"Ben was asking if we'd let John go out."

"Oh, he's far too young."

"Not to hunt. But I thought he might bring his pony to the meet and ride with them to the first covert. He'd love it so."

"Is it quite safe?"

"Oh, yes, surely?"

"Bless his heart, I wish I could be here to see him."

"Do change your mind."

"Oh no, that's quite out of question. Don't make a thing about it, Tony."

That was when she first arrived; later everything got better. Jock was there that week-end, also Allan and Marjorie and another married couple whom Tony had known all his life. Brenda had arranged the party for him and he enjoyed it. He and Allan went out with rook rifles and shot rabbits in the twilight; after dinner the four men played billiard fives while one wife watched. "The old boy's happy as a lark," said Brenda to Marjorie. "He's settling down wonderfully to the new régime."

They came in breathless and rather hurried for whisky and soda.

"Tony nearly had one through the window," said Jock.

That night Tony slept in Guinevere.

"Everything *is* all right, isn't it," he said once.

"Yes of course, darling."

"I get depressed down here all alone and imagine things."

"You aren't to *brood*, Tony. You know that's one of the things that aren't allowed."

"I won't brood any more," said Tony.

Next day Brenda came to church with him. She had decided to devote the week-end wholly to him; it would be the last for some time.

"And how are the abstruse sciences, Lady Brenda?"

"Absorbing."

"We shall all be coming to you for advice about our overdraft."

"Ha, ha."

"And how's Thunderclap?" asked Miss Tendril.

"I'm taking her out hunting on Wednesday," said John. He had forgotten Princess Abdul Akbar in the excitement of the coming meet. "Please God make there be a good scent. Please God make me see the kill. Please God don't let me do anything wrong. God bless Ben and Thunderclap. Please God make me jump an enormous great oxer," he had kept repeating throughout the service.

Brenda did the round with Tony of cottages and hot houses; she helped him choose his button-hole.

Tony was in high spirits at luncheon. Brenda had begun to forget how amusing he could be. Afterwards he changed into other clothes and went with Jock to play golf. They stayed some time at the club house. Tony said, "We've got the hounds meeting at Hetton on Wednesday. Couldn't you stay down till then?"

"Must be back. There's going to be a debate on the Pig Scheme."

"I wish you'd stay. Look here why don't you ask that girl down. Everyone goes tomorrow. You could ring her up, couldn't you."

"I *could*."

"Would she hate it? She could have Lyonesse—Polly slept there two week-ends running so it can't be too uncomfortable."

"She'd probably love it. I'll ring up and ask her."

"Why don't you hunt too? There's a chap called Brink-well who's got some quite decent hirelings I believe."

"Yes, I might."

"Jock's staying on. He's having the shameless blonde down. You don't mind?"

"Me? Of course not."

"This has been a jolly week-end."

"I thought you were enjoying it."

"Just like old times—before the economics began."

Marjorie said to Jock, "D'you think Tony knows about Mr. Beaver?"

"Not a thing."

"I haven't mentioned it to Allan. D'you suppose he knows?"

"I doubt it."

"Oh, Jock, how d'you think it'll end?"

"She'll get bored with Beaver soon enough."

"The trouble is that he doesn't care for her in the least. If he did, it would soon be over . . . What an ass she is being."

"I should say she was managing it unusually well, if you asked me."

The other married couples said to each other, "D'you think Marjorie and Allan know about Brenda?"

"I'm sure they don't."

Brenda said to Allan, "Tony's as happy as a sand-boy, isn't he?"

"Full of beans."

"I was getting worried about him . . . You don't think he's got any idea about my goings on."

"Lord no. It's the last thing that would come into his head."

Brenda said, "I don't want him to be unhappy you know . . . Marjorie's been frightfully governessy about the whole thing."

"Has she? I haven't discussed it with her."

"How did *you* hear?"

"My dear girl, until this minute I didn't know you had any goings on. And I'm not asking any questions about them now."

"Oh . . . I thought everyone knew."

"That's always the trouble with people when they have affaires. They either think no one knows, or everybody. The truth is that a few people like Polly and Sybil make a point of finding out about everyone's private life; the rest of us just aren't interested."

"Oh."

Later he said to Marjorie, "Brenda tried to be confidential about Beaver this evening."

"I didn't know you knew."

"Oh I knew all right. But I wasn't going to let her feel important by talking about it."

"I couldn't disapprove more of the whole thing. Do you know Beaver?"

"I've seen him about. Anyway, it's her business and Tony's, not ours."

Five

Jock's blonde was called Mrs. Rattery. Tony had conceived an idea of her from what he overheard of Polly's gossip and from various fragments of information let fall by Jock. She was a little over thirty. Somewhere in the Cottesmore country there lived a long-legged, slightly discredited Major Rattery, to whom she had once been married. She was American by origin, now totally denationalized, rich, without property or possessions, except those that would pack in five vast trunks. Jock had had his eye on her last summer at Biarritz and had fallen in with her again in London where she played big bridge, very ably, for six or seven hours a day and changed her hotel, on an average, once every three weeks. Periodically she was liable to bouts of morphine; then she gave up her bridge and remained for several days at a time alone in her hotel suite, refreshed at intervals with glasses of cold milk.

She arrived by air on Monday afternoon. It was the first time that a guest had come in this fashion and the household was appreciably excited. Under Jock's direction the boiler man and one of the gardeners pegged out a dust sheet in the park to mark a landing for her and lit a bonfire of damp leaves to show the direction of the wind. The five trunks arrived in the ordinary way by train, with an elderly, irreproachable maid. She brought her own sheets with her in one of the trunks; they were neither silk nor coloured, without lace or ornament of any kind, except small, plain monograms.

Tony, Jock and John went out to watch her land. She climbed out of the cockpit, stretched, unbuttoned the flaps of her leather helmet, and came to meet them. "Forty-two minutes," she said, "not at all bad with the wind against me."

She was tall and erect, almost austere in helmet and overalls; not at all as Tony had imagined her. Vaguely, at the back of his mind he had secreted the slightly absurd expectation of a chorus girl, in silk shorts and brassière, popping out of an immense beribboned Easter Egg with a cry of "Whooppee, boys." Mrs. Rattery's greetings were deft and impersonal.

"Are you going to hunt on Wednesday?" asked John. "They're meeting here you know."

"I might go out for half the day, if I can find a horse. It'll be the first time this year."

"It's my first time too."

"We shall both be terribly stiff." She spoke to him exactly as though he were a man of her own age. "You'll have to show me the country."

"I expect they'll draw Bruton wood first. There's a big fox there, daddy and I saw him."

When they were alone together, Jock said, "It's delightful your coming down. What d'you think of Tony?"

"Is he married to that rather lovely woman we saw at the Café de Paris?"

"Yes."

"The one you said was in love with that young man?"

"Yes."

"Funny of her . . . What's this one's name again?"

"Tony Last. It's a pretty ghastly house, isn't it?"

"Is it? I never notice houses much."

She was an easy guest to entertain. After dinner on Monday she produced four packs of cards and laid out for herself on the smoking room table a very elaborate patience, which kept her engrossed all the evening. "Don't wait up for me," she said. "I shall stay here until it comes out. It often takes several hours."

They showed her where to put the lights out and left her to it.

Next day Jock said, "Have you got any pigs at the farm?"

"Yes."

"Would you mind if I went to see them?"

"Not the least—but why?"

"And is there a man who looks after them, who will be able to explain about them?"

"Yes."

"Well, I think I'll spend the morning with him. I've got to make a speech about pigs, fairly soon."

They did not see Mrs. Rattery until luncheon. Tony assumed she was asleep until she appeared in overalls from the morning room. "I was down early," she explained, "and found the men at work stripping the ceiling. I couldn't resist joining in. I hope you don't mind."

In the afternoon they went to a neighbouring livery stables to look for hirelings. After tea Tony wrote to Brenda; he had taken to writing letters in the past few weeks.

How enjoyable the week-end was, he wrote. *Thank you a thousand times for all your sweetness. I wish you were coming down next week-end, or that you had been able to stay on a little, but I quite understand.*

The Shameless Blonde is not the least what we expected —very serene and distant. Not at all like Jock's usual taste.

I am sure she hasn't any idea where she is or what my name is.

The work in the morning room is going on well. The foreman told me today he thought he would begin on the chromium plating by the end of the week. You know what I think about that.

John can talk of nothing except his hunting tomorrow. I hope he doesn't break his neck. Jock and his S.B. are going out too.

Hetton lay near the boundary of three packs; the Pigstanton, who hunted it, had in the division of territory come off with the worst country and they cherished a permanent resentment about some woods near Bayton. They were a somewhat ill-tempered lot, contemptuous of each other's performance, hostile to strangers, torn by internal rancour; united only in their dislike of the Master. In the case of Colonel Inch this unpopularity, traditional to the hunt, was quite undeserved; he was a timid, inconspicuous man who provided the neighbourhood with sport of a kind at great personal expense. He himself was seldom in sight of hounds and could often be found in another part of the country morosely nibbling ginger nut biscuits in a lane or towards the end of the day cantering heavily across country, quite lost, a lonely scarlet figure against the ploughed land, staring about him in the deepening twilight and shouting at yokels for information. The only pleasure he gained from his position, but that a substantial one, was in referring to it casually at Board Meetings of the various companies he directed.

The Pigstanton met twice a week. There was seldom a large field on Wednesdays, but the Hetton meet was popular; it lay in their best country and the prospect of stirrup cups had drawn many leathery old ladies from the neighbouring packs. There were also followers on foot and in every kind of vehicle, some hanging back diffidently, others, more or less known to Tony, crowding round the refreshment table. Mr. Tendril had a niece staying with him, who appeared on a motor bicycle.

John stood beside Thunderclap, solemn with excitement. Ben had secured a powerful, square-headed mare from a neighbouring farmer; he hoped to have a hunt after John had been taken home; at John's earnest entreaty nanny was confined indoors, among the housemaids whose heads obtruded at the upper windows; it was not her day. She had been out of temper while dressing him. "If I'm in at the death I expect Colonel Inch will blood me."

"You won't see any death," said nanny.

Now she stood with her eyes at a narrow slit gazing rather resentfully at the animated scene below. "It's all a lot of nonsense of Ben Hacket's," she thought. She deplored it all, hounds, Master, field, huntsman and whippers-in, Miss Tendril's niece in her mackintosh, Jock in rat-catcher, Mrs. Rattery in tall hat and cutaway coat oblivious of the suspicious glances of the subscribers, Tony smiling and chatting to his guests, the crazy old man with the terriers, the Press photographer, pretty Miss Ripon in difficulties with a young horse, titapping sideways over the lawn, the grooms and second horses, the humble, unknown followers in the background—it was all a lot of nonsense of Ben Hacket's. "It was after eleven before the child got to sleep last night," she reflected, "he was that over-excited."

Presently they moved off towards Bruton wood. The way lay down the South drive through Compton Last, along the main road for half a mile, and then through fields. "He can ride with them as far as the covert," Tony had said.

"Yes, sir, and there'd be no harm in his staying a bit to see hounds working, would there?"

"No, I suppose not."

"And if he breaks away towards home, there'd be no harm in our following a bit, if we keeps to the lanes and gates, would there, sir?"

"No, but he's not to stay out more than an hour."

"You wouldn't have me take him home with hounds running, would you, sir?"

"Well he's got to be in before one."

"I'll see to that, sir." "Don't you worry, my beauty," he said to John, "you'll get a hunt right enough."

They waited until the end of the line of horses and then trotted soberly behind them. Close at their heels followed the motor-cars, at low gear, in a fog of exhaust gas. John was breathless and slightly dizzy. Thunderclap was tossing her head and worrying at her snaffle. Twice while the field was moving off, she had tried to get away and had taken John round in a little circle, so that Ben had said, "Hold on to her, son" and had come up close beside him so as to be able to catch the reins if she looked like bolting. Once boring forwards with her head she took John by surprise and pulled him forwards out of his balance; he caught hold of the front of the saddle to steady himself and looked guiltily at Ben. "I'm afraid I'm riding very badly today. D'you think anyone has noticed?"

"That's all right, son. You can't keep riding-school manners when you're hunting."

Jock and Mrs. Rattery trotted side by side. "I rather like this absurd horse," she said; she rode astride and it was evident from the moment she mounted that she rode extremely well.

The members of the Pigstanton noted this with ill-concealed resentment for it disturbed their fixed opinion according to which, though all fellow members of the hunt were clowns and poltroons, strangers were without exception mannerless lunatics, and a serious menace to anyone within quarter of a mile of them.

Half way through the village Miss Ripon had difficulties in getting past a stationary baker's van. Her horse plunged and reared, trembling all over, turning about, and slipping frantically over the tarmac. They rode round her giving his heels the widest berth, scowling ominously and grumbling about her. They all knew that horse. Miss Ripon's father had been trying to sell him all the season, and had lately come down to eighty pounds. He was a good jumper on occasions but a beast of a horse to ride. Did Miss Ripon's father really imagine he was improving his chances of a sale by letting Miss Ripon make an exhibition of herself? It was like that skinflint Miss Ripon's father, to risk Miss Ripon's neck for eighty pounds. And anyway Miss Ripon had no business out on *any* horse . . .

Presently she shot past them at a canter; she was flushed in the face and her bun was askew; she leant back, pulling with all her weight. "That girl will come to no good," said Jock.

They encountered her later at the covert. Her horse was sweating and lathered at the bridle but temporarily at rest cropping the tufts of sedge that lay round the woods. Miss Ripon was much out of breath, and her hands shook as she fiddled with veil, bun and bowler. John rode up to Jock's side.

"What's happening, Mr. Grant-Menzies?"

"Hounds are drawing the covert."

"Oh."

"Are you enjoying yourself?"

"Oh yes. Thunderclap's terribly fresh. I've never known her like this."

There was a long wait as the horn sounded in the heart of the wood. Everyone stood at the corner of the big field, near a gate. Everyone, that is to say, except Miss Ripon who some minutes ago had disappeared suddenly, indeed in the middle of a sentence, at full gallop towards Hetton hills. After half an hour Jock said, "They're calling hounds off."

"Does that mean it's a blank?"

"I'm afraid so."

"I hate this happening in *our* woods," said Ben. "Looks bad."

Indeed the Pigstantons were already beginning to forget their recent hospitality and to ask each other what did one expect when Last did not hunt himself, and to circulate dark reports of how one of the keepers had been observed last week burying Something late in the evening.

They moved off again, away from Hetton. Ben began to

feel his responsibility. "D'you think I ought to take the young gentleman home, sir?"

"What did Mr. Last say?"

"He said he could go as far as the covert. He didn't say which, sir."

"I'm afraid it sounds as if he ought to go."

"*Oh, Mr. Grant-Menzies.*"

"Yes, come along, Master John. You've had enough for today."

"But I haven't had *any*."

"If you come back in good time today your dad will be all the more willing to let you come out another day."

"But there mayn't *be* another day. The world may come to an end. *Please*, Ben. *Please*, Mr. Grant-Menzies."

"It is a shame they shouldn't have found," said Ben. "He's been looking forward to it."

"Still I think Mr. Last would want him to go back," said Jock.

So John's fate was decided; hounds went in one direction, he and Ben in another. John was very near tears as they reached the main road.

"Look," said Ben, to encourage him. "Here comes Miss Ripon on that nappy bay. Seems as if she's going in, too. Had a fall by the looks of her."

Miss Ripon's hat and back were covered with mud and moss. She had had a bad twenty minutes since her disappearance. "I'm taking him away," she said. "I can't do anything with him this morning." She jogged along beside them towards the village. "I thought perhaps Mr. Last would let me come up to the house and telephone for the car. I don't feel like hacking him home in his present state. I can't think what's come over him," she added loyally. "He was out on Saturday. I've never known him like this before."

"He wants a man up," said Ben.

"Oh, he's no better with the groom and daddy won't go near him," said Miss Ripon, stung to indiscretion. "At least . . . I mean . . . I don't think that they'd be any better with him in this state."

He was quiet enough at that moment, keeping pace with
the other horses. They rode abreast, she on the outside
with John's pony between her and Ben.

Then this happened: they reached a turn in the road
and came face to face with one of the single decker, country buses that covered that neighbourhood. It was not
going fast and, seeing the horses, the driver slowed down
still further and drew into the side. Miss Tendril's niece
who had also despaired of the day's sport was following
behind them at a short distance on her motor bicycle; she
too slowed down and, observing that Miss Ripon's horse
was likely to be difficult, stopped.

Ben said, "Let me go first, miss. He'll follow. Don't hold
too hard on his mouth and just give him a tap."

Miss Ripon did as she was told; everyone in fact behaved with complete good-sense.

They drew abreast of the omnibus. Miss Ripon's horse
did not like it, but it seemed as though he would get by.
The passengers watched with amusement. At that moment
the motor bicycle, running gently in neutral gear, fired
back into the cylinder with a sharp detonation. For a second the horse stood rigid with alarm; then, menaced in
front and behind, he did what was natural to him and
shied sideways, cannoning violently into the pony at his
side. John was knocked from the saddle and fell on the
road while Miss Ripon's bay, rearing and skidding, continued to plunge away from the bus.

"Take a hold of him, miss. Use your whip," shouted
Ben. "The boy's down."

She hit him and the horse collected himself and bolted
up the road into the village, but before he went one of his
heels struck out and sent John into the ditch, where he lay
bent double, perfectly still.

Everyone agreed that it was nobody's fault.

It was nearly an hour before the news reached Jock and
Mrs. Rattery, where they were waiting beside another
blank covert. Colonel Inch stopped hunting for the day
and sent the hounds back to the kennels. The voices were

hushed which, five minutes before, had been proclaiming that they knew it for a fact, Last had given orders to shoot every fox on the place. Later, after their baths, they made up for it in criticism of Miss Ripon's father, but at the moment everyone was shocked and silent. Someone lent Jock and Mrs. Rattery a car to get home in, and a groom to see to the hirelings.

"It's the most appalling thing," said Jock in the borrowed car. "What on earth are we going to say to Tony?"

"I'm the last person to have about on an occasion like this," said Mrs. Rattery.

They passed the scene of the accident; there were still people hanging about, talking.

There were people hanging about, talking, in the hall at the house. The doctor was buttoning up his coat, just going.

"Killed instantly," he said. "Took it full on the base of the skull. Very sad, awfully fond of the kid. No one to blame though."

Nanny was there in tears; also Mr. Tendril and his niece; a policeman and Ben and two men who had helped bring up the body were in the servants' hall. "It wasn't the kid's fault," said Ben.

"It wasn't anyone's fault," they said.

"He'd had a lousy day too poor little bastard," said Ben. "If it was anyone's fault it was Mr. Grant-Menzie's making him go in."

"It wasn't anyone's fault," they said.

Tony was alone in the library. The first thing he said, when Jock came in was, "We've got to tell Brenda."

"D'you know where to get her?"

"She's probably at that school . . . But we can't tell her over the telephone . . . Anyway Ambrose has tried there and the flat but he can't get through . . . What on earth are we going to say to her?"

Jock was silent. He stood in the fireplace with his hands in the pockets of his breeches, with his back to Tony.

Presently Tony said, "You weren't anywhere near were you?"

"No, we'd gone on to another covert."

"That niece of Mr. Tendril's told me first . . . then we met them coming up, and Ben told me all that happened . . . It's awful for the girl."

"Miss Ripon?"

"Yes, she's just left . . . she had a nasty fall too, just after. Her horse slipped up in the village . . . she was in a terrible state, poor child, what with that and . . . John. She didn't know she'd hurt him until quite a time afterwards . . . she was in the chemist's shop having a bandage put on her forehead, when they told her. She cut it falling. She was in a terrible state. I sent her back in the car . . . it wasn't her fault."

"No, it wasn't anybody's fault. It just happened."

"That's it," said Tony. "It just happened . . . how are we going to tell Brenda?"

"One of us will have to go up."

"Yes . . . I think I shall have to stay here. I don't know why really, but there will be things to see to. It's an awful thing to ask anyone to do . . ."

"I'll go," said Jock.

"There'll be things to see to here . . . there's got to be an inquest the doctor says. It's purely formal of course, but it will be ghastly for that Ripon girl. She'll have to give evidence . . . she was in a terrible state. I hope I was all right to her. They'd just brought John in and I was rather muddled. She looked awful. I believe her father's bloody to her . . . I wish Brenda had been here. She's so good with everyone. I get in a muddle."

The two men stood in silence. Tony said, "Can you really face going up and seeing Brenda?"

"Yes, I'll go," said Jock.

Presently Mrs. Rattery came in. "Colonel Inch has been here," she said. "I talked to him. He wanted to give you his sympathy."

"Is he still here?"

"No, I told him you'd probably prefer to be left alone. He thought you'd be glad to hear he stopped the hunt."

"Nice of him to come . . . Were you having a good day?"

"No."

"I'm sorry. We saw a fox in Bruton wood last week, John and I . . . Jock's going up to London to fetch Brenda."

"I'll take him in the aeroplane. It'll be quicker."

"Yes that will be quicker."

"My maid can follow with the luggage by train . . . I'll go and change now. I won't be ten minutes."

"I'll change too," said Jock.

When he was alone Tony rang the bell. A young footman answered; he was quite young and had not been long at Hetton.

"Will you tell Mr. Ambrose that Mrs. Rattery is leaving today. She is flying up with Mr. Grant-Menzies. Her ladyship will probably be coming by the evening train."

"Very good, sir."

"They had better have some luncheon before they go. Something cold in the dining room. I will have it with them . . . And will you put a call through to Colonel Inch and thank him for coming. Say I will write. And to Mr. Ripon's to enquire how Miss Ripon is. And to the vicarage and ask Mr. Tendril if I can see him this evening. He's not here still?"

"No, sir, he left a few minutes ago."

"Tell him I shall have to discuss arrangements with him."

"Very good, sir."

Mr. Last was very matter of fact about everything, the footman reported later.

It was perfectly quiet in the library for the workmen in the morning room had laid aside their tools for the day.

Mrs. Rattery was ready first.

"They're just getting luncheon."

"We shan't want any," she said. "You forget we were going hunting."

"Better have something," said Tony, and then, "It's

awful for Jock, having to tell Brenda. I wonder how long it will be before she arrives."

There was something in Tony's voice as he said this which made Mrs. Rattery ask, "What are you going to do while you're waiting?"

"I don't know. I suppose there will be things to see to."

"Look here," said Mrs. Rattery, "Jock had better go up by car. I'll stay here until Lady Brenda comes."

"It would be awful for you."

"No, I'll stay."

Tony said, "I suppose it's ridiculous of me, but I wish you would . . . I mean won't it be awful for you? I am all in a muddle. It's so hard to believe yet, that it really happened."

"It happened all right."

The footman came to say that Mr. Tendril would call after tea that day; that Miss Ripon had gone straight to bed and was asleep.

"Mr. Grant-Menzies is going up in his car. He may be back tonight," said Tony. "Mrs. Rattery is waiting until her ladyship arrives."

"Very good, sir. And Colonel Inch wanted to know whether you would care to have the huntsman blow 'Gone Away' at the funeral."

"Say that I'll write to him," and when the footman had left the room Tony said, "An atrocious suggestion."

"Oh, I don't know. He's very anxious to be helpful."

"They don't like him much as Master."

Jock left soon after half past two. Tony and Mrs. Rattery had coffee in the library.

"I'm afraid this is a very difficult situation," said Tony. "After all we scarcely know each other."

"You don't have to think about me."

"But it must be awful for you."

"And you must stop thinking that."

"I'll try . . . the absurd thing is that I'm not thinking it, just saying it . . . I keep thinking of other things all the time."

"I know. You don't have to say anything."

Presently Tony said, "It's going to be so much worse for Brenda. You see she's got nothing else, much, except John. I've got her, and I love the house . . . but with Brenda John always came first . . . naturally . . . And then you know she's seen so little of John lately. She's been in London such a lot. I'm afraid that's going to hurt her."

"You can't ever tell what's going to hurt people."

"But, you see, I know Brenda so well."

Six

The library windows were open and the clock, striking the hour, high overhead among its crockets and finials, was clearly audible in the quiet room. It was some time since they had spoken. Mrs. Rattery sat with her back to Tony; she had spread out her intricate four pack patience on a card table; he was in front of the fire, in the chair he had taken after lunch.

"Only four o'clock?" he said.

"I thought you were asleep."

"No, just thinking . . . Jock will be more than half way there by now, about Aylesbury or Tring."

"It's a slow way to travel."

"It's less than four hours ago that it happened . . . it's odd to think that this is the same day; that it's only five hours ago they were all here at the meet having drinks." There was a pause in which Mrs. Rattery swept up the cards and began to deal them again. "It was twenty eight minutes past twelve when I heard. I looked at my watch . . . It was ten to one when they brought John in . . . just over three hours ago . . . It's almost incredible, isn't it, everything becoming absolutely different, suddenly like that?"

"It's always that way," said Mrs. Rattery.

"Brenda will hear in an hour now . . . if Jock finds her in. Of course she may very likely be out. He won't know where to find her because there's no one else in the flat. She leaves it locked up, empty, when she goes out . . . and she's out half the day. I know because I sometimes ring up

and can't get an answer. He may not find her for hours
... It may be as long again as the time since it happened.
That would only make it eight o'clock. It's quite likely
she won't come in until eight ... Think of it, all the time
between now and when it happened, before Brenda hears.
It's scarcely credible, is it? And then she's got to get down
here. There's a train that leaves at nine something. She
might get that. I wonder if I ought to have gone up too
... I didn't like to leave John."

(Mrs. Rattery sat intent over her game, moving little
groups of cards adroitly backward and forwards about the
table like shuttles across a loom; under her fingers order
grew out of chaos; she established sequence and precedence; the symbols before her became coherent, inter-
related.)

". . . Of course she may be at home when he arrives. In
that case she can get the evening train, she used always to
come by, when she went to London for the day, before
she got the flat ... I'm trying to see it all, as it's going to
happen, Jock coming and her surprise at seeing him, and
then his telling her ... It's awful for Jock ... She may
know at half past five or a bit earlier."

"It's a pity you don't play patience," said Mrs. Rattery.

"In a way I shall feel happier when she knows ... it
feels all wrong as it is at present, having it as a secret that
Brenda doesn't know ... I'm not sure how she fits in her
day. I suppose her last lecture is over at about five ... I
wonder if she goes home first to change if she's going out to
tea or cocktails. She can't sit about much in the flat, it's so
small."

Mrs. Rattery brooded over her chequer of cards and
then drew them towards her into a heap, haphazard once
more and without meaning; it had nearly come to a solu-
tion that time, but for a six of diamonds out of place, and
a stubbornly congested patch at one corner, where nothing could be made to move. "It's a heartbreaking game,"
she said.

The clock struck again.

"Is that only quarter past? . . . You know I think I should have gone off my head if I were alone. It's nice of you to stay with me."

"Do you play bezique?"

"I'm afraid not."

"Or piquet?"

"No. I've never been able to learn any card game except animal snap."

"Pity."

"There's Marjorie and several people I ought to wire to, but I'd better wait until I know that Jock has seen Brenda. Suppose she was with Marjorie when the telegram arrived."

"You've got to try and stop thinking about things. Can you throw craps?"

"No."

"That's easy; I'll show you. There'll be some dice in the backgammon board."

"I'm all right, really. I'd sooner not play."

"You get the dice and sit up here at the table. We've got six hours to get through."

She showed him how to throw craps. He said, "I've seen it on the cinema—pullman porters and taxi men."

"Of course you have, it's easy . . . there you see you've won, you take all."

Presently Tony said, "I've just thought of something."

"Don't you ever take a rest from thinking?"

"Suppose the evening papers have got hold of it already. Brenda may see it on a placard, or just pick up a paper casually and there it will be . . . perhaps with a photograph."

"Yes, I thought of that just now, when you were talking about telegraphing."

"But it's quite likely, isn't it? They get hold of everything so quickly. What can we do about it?"

"There isn't anything we can do. We've just got to wait . . . Come on, boy, throw up."

"I don't want to play any more. I'm worried."

"I know you're worried. You don't have to tell me . . .

you aren't going to give up playing just when the luck's running your way?"

"I'm sorry . . . it isn't any good."

He walked about the room, first to the window, then to the fireplace. He began to fill his pipe. "At least we can find out whether the evening papers have got it in. We can ring up and ask the hall porter at my club."

"That's not going to prevent your wife reading it. We've just got to wait. What was the game you said you knew? Animal something?"

"Snap."

"Well you come show me that."

"It's just a child's game. It would be ridiculous with two."

"I'll learn it."

"Well each of us chooses an animal."

"All right, I'm a hen and you're a dog. Now what?"

Tony explained.

"I'd say it was one of those games that you have to feel pretty good first, before you can enjoy them," said Mrs. Rattery. "But I'll try anything."

They each took a pack and began dealing. Soon a pair of eights appeared. "Bow-wow," said Mrs. Rattery, scooping in the cards.

Another pair. "Bow-wow," said Mrs. Rattery. "You know you aren't putting your heart into this."

"Oh," said Tony. "Coop-coop-coop."

Presently he said again, "Coop-coop-coop."

"Don't be dumb," said Mrs. Rattery, "that isn't a pair . . ."

They were still playing when Albert came in to draw the curtains. Tony had only two cards left which he turned over regularly; Mrs. Rattery was obliged to divide hers, they were too many to hold. They stopped playing when they found that Albert was in the room.

"What must that man have thought?" said Tony, when he had gone out.

("Sitting there clucking like a 'en," Albert reported, "and the little fellow lying dead upstairs.")

"We'd better stop."

"It wasn't a very good game. And to think it's the only one you know."

She collected the cards and began to deal them into their proper packs. Ambrose and Albert brought in tea. Tony looked at his watch. "Five o'clock. Now that the shutters are up we shan't hear the chimes. Jock must be in London by now."

Mrs. Rattery said, "I'd rather like some whisky."

Jock had not seen Brenda's flat. It was in a large, feature-less house, typical of the district. Mrs. Beaver deplored the space wasted by the well staircase and empty, paved hall. There was no porter; a woman came three mornings a week with bucket and mop. A board painted with the names of the tenants informed Jock that Brenda was IN. But he put little reliance on this information, knowing that Brenda was not one to remember as she came in and out, to change the indicator. He found her front door on the second floor. After the first flight the staircase changed from marble to a faded carpet that had been there before Mrs. Beaver undertook the reconstruction. Jock pressed the bell and heard it ringing just inside the door. Nobody came to open it. It was ten past five, and he had not ex-pected to find Brenda at home. He had decided on the road up that after trying the flat, he would go to his club and ring up various friends of Brenda's who might know where she was. He rang again, from habit, and waited a little; then turned to go. But at that moment the door next to Brenda's opened and a dark lady in a dress of crimson velvet looked out at him; she wore very large earrings of oriental filigree, set with bosses of opaque, valueless stone.

"Are you looking for Lady Brenda Last?"

"I am. Is she a friend of yours?"

"Oh *such* a friend," said Princess Abdul Akbar.

"Then perhaps you can tell me where I can find her?"

"I think she's bound to be at Lady Cockpurse's. I'm just going there myself. Can I give her any message?"

"I had better come and see her."

"Well wait five minutes and you can go with me. Come inside."

The Princess's single room was furnished promiscuously and with truly Eastern disregard of the right properties of things; swords meant to adorn the state robes of a Moorish caid were swung from the picture rail; mats made for prayer were strewn on the divan; the carpet on the floor had been made in Bokhara as a wall covering; while over the dressing table was draped a shawl made in Yokohama for sale to cruise-passengers; an octagonal table from Port Said held a Thibetan Buddha of pale soapstone; six ivory elephants from Bombay stood along the top of the radiator. Other cultures, too, were represented by a set of Lallique bottles and powder boxes, a phallic fetish from Senegal, a Dutch copper bowl, a wastepaper basket made of varnished aquatints, a golliwog presented at the gala dinner of a seaside hotel, a dozen or so framed photographs of the Princess, a garden scene ingeniously constructed in pieces of coloured wood, and a radio set in fumed oak, Tudor style. In so small a room the effect was distracting. The Princess sat at the looking glass, Jock behind her on the divan.

"What's your name?" she asked over her shoulder. He told her. "Oh, yes, I've heard them mention you. I was at Hetton the week-end before last . . . such a quaint old place."

"I'd better tell you. There's been a frightful accident there this morning."

Jenny Abdul Akbar spun round on the leather stool; her eyes were wide with alarm, her hand pressed to her heart. "Quick," she whispered. *"Tell me.* I can't bear it. Is it *death?"*

John nodded. "Their little boy . . . kicked by a horse."

"Little Jimmy."

"John."

"John . . . *dead.* It's *too* horrible."

"It wasn't anybody's fault."

"Oh yes," said Jenny. "It was. It was *my* fault. I ought never to have gone there . . . a terrible curse hangs over me. Wherever I go I bring nothing but sorrow . . . if only it was *I* that was dead . . . I shall never be able to face them again. I feel like a murderess . . . that brave little life snuffed out."

"I say you know, really, I shouldn't take that line about it."

"It isn't the first time it's happened . . . always, any-where, I am hunted down . . . without remorse. O God," said Jenny Abdul Akbar. "What have I done to deserve it?"

She rose to leave him; there was nowhere she could go except the bathroom. Jock said, through the door, "Well I must go along to Polly's and see Brenda."

"Wait a minute and I'll come too." She had brightened a little when she emerged. "Have you got a car here," she asked, "or shall I ring up a taxi?"

After tea Mr. Tendril called. Tony saw him in his study and was away half an hour. When he returned he went to the tray, which, on Mrs. Rattery's instructions, had been left in the library, and poured himself out whisky and ginger ale. Mrs. Rattery had resumed her patience. "Bad interview?" she asked without looking up.

"Awful." He drank the whisky quickly and poured out some more.

"Bring me one too, will you?"

Tony said, "I only wanted to see him about arrange-ments. He tried to be comforting. It was very painful . . . after all the last thing one wants to talk about at a time like this is religion."

"Some like it," said Mrs. Rattery.

"Of course," Tony began, after a pause, "when you haven't got children yourself—"

"I've got two sons," said Mrs. Rattery.

"Have you? I'm so sorry. I didn't realize . . . we know each other so little. How very impertinent of me."

"That's all right. People are always surprised. I don't see them often. They're at school somewhere. I took them to the cinema last summer. They're getting quite big.

One's going to be good looking I think. His father is."

"Quarter past six," said Tony. "He's bound to have told her by now."

There was a little party at Lady Cockpurse's, Veronica and Daisy and Sybil, Sòuki de Foucauld-Esterhazy, and four or five others, all women. They were there to consult a new fortune-teller called Mrs. Northcote. Mrs. Beaver had discovered her and for every five guineas that she earned at her introduction Mrs. Beaver took a commission of two pounds twelve and sixpence. She told fortunes in a new way, by reading the soles of the feet. They waited their turn impatiently. "What a time she is taking over Daisy."

"She is very thorough," said Polly, "and it tickles rather."

Presently Daisy emerged. "What was she like?" they asked.

"I mustn't tell or it spoils it all," said Daisy.

They had dealt cards for precedence. It was Brenda's turn now. She went next door to Mrs. Northcote, who was sitting at a stool beside an armchair. She was a dowdy, middle-aged woman with a slightly genteel accent. Brenda sat down and took off her shoe and stocking. Mrs. Northcote laid the foot on her knee and gazed at it with great solemnity; then she picked it up and began tracing the small creases of the sole with the point of a silver pencil case. Brenda wriggled her toes luxuriously and settled down to listen.

Next door they said, "Where's her Mr. Beaver today?"

"He's flown over to France with his mother to see some new wall papers. She's been worrying all day thinking he's had an accident."

"It's all very touching, isn't it? Though I can't see his point myself . . ."

"You must never do anything on Thursdays," said Mrs. Northcote.

"Nothing?"

"Nothing important. You are intellectual, imaginative, sympathetic, easily led by others, impulsive, affectionate.

You are highly artistic and are not giving full scope to your capabilities."

"Isn't there anything about love?"

"I am coming to love. All these lines from the great toe to the instep represent lovers."

"Yes, go on some more about that . . ."

Princess Abdul Akbar was announced.

"Where's Brenda?" she said. "I thought she'd be here."

"Mrs. Northcote's doing her now."

"Jock Grant-Menzies wants to see her. He's downstairs."

"Darling Jock . . . Why on earth didn't you bring him up."

"No, it's something terribly important. He's got to see Brenda alone."

"My dear, how mysterious. Well she won't be long now. We can't disturb them. It would upset Mrs. Northcote."

Jenny told them her news.

On the other side of the door, Brenda's leg was beginning to feel slightly chilly. "Four men dominate your fate," Mrs. Northcote was saying, "one is loyal and tender but he has not yet disclosed his love, one is passionate and overpowering, you are a little afraid of him."

"Dear me," said Brenda. "How very exciting. Who *can* they be?"

"One you must avoid; he bodes no good for you, he is steely hearted and rapacious."

"I bet that's my Mr. Beaver, bless him."

Downstairs Jock sat waiting in the small front room where Polly's guests usually assembled before luncheon. It was five past six.

Soon Brenda pulled on her stocking, stepped into her shoe, and joined the ladies. "*Most* enjoyable," she pronounced. "Why how odd you all look."

"Jock Grant-Menzies wants to see you downstairs."

"Jock? How very extraordinary. It isn't anything awful is it?"

"You better go and see him."

Suddenly Brenda became frightened by the strange air of the room and the unfamiliar expression in her friends' faces. She ran downstairs to the room where Jock was waiting.

"What is it, Jock? Tell me quickly, I'm scared. It's nothing awful is it?"

"I'm afraid it is. There's been a very serious accident."

"John?"

"Yes."

"Dead?"

He nodded.

She sat down on a hard little Empire chair against the wall, perfectly still with her hands folded in her lap, like a small well-brought-up child introduced into a room full of grown-ups. She said, "Tell me what happened? Why do you know about it first?"

"I've been down at Hetton since the week-end."

"Hetton?"

"Don't you remember? John was going hunting today."

She frowned, not at once taking in what he was saying. "John . . . John Andrew . . . I . . . Oh thank God . . ." Then she burst into tears.

She wept helplessly, turning round in the chair and pressing her forehead against its gilt back.

Upstairs Mrs. Northcote had Souki de Foucauld-Esterhazy by the foot and was saying, "There are four men dominating your fate. One is loyal and tender but has not yet disclosed his love . . ."

In the silence of Hetton, the telephone rang near the housekeeper's room and was switched through to the library. Tony answered it.

"This is Jock speaking. I've just seen Brenda. She's coming down by the seven o'clock train."

"Is she terribly upset?"

"Yes, naturally."

"Where is she now?"

"She's with me. I'm speaking from Polly's."

"Shall I talk to her?"

"Better not."

"All right . . . I'll meet that train. Are you coming too?"

"No."

"Well you've been wonderful. I don't know what I should have done without you and Mrs. Rattery."

"Oh, that's all right. I'll see Brenda off."

She had stopped crying and sat crouched in the chair. She did not look up while Jock telephoned. Then she said, "Yes, I'll go by that train."

"We ought to start. I suppose you will have to get some things from the flat."

"My bag . . . upstairs. You get it. I can't go in there again."

She did not speak on the way to her flat. She sat beside Jock as he drove, looking straight ahead. When they arrived she unlocked her door and led him in. The room was extremely empty of furniture. She sat down in the only chair. "There's plenty of time really. Tell me exactly what happened."

Jock told her.

"Poor little boy," she said. "Poor little boy."

Then she opened her cupboard and began to put a few things into a suitcase; she went in and out from the bathroom once or twice. "That's everything," she said. "There's still too much time."

"Would you like anything to eat?"

"Oh no, nothing to eat." She sat down again and looked at herself in the glass. She did not attempt to do anything to her face. "When you first told me," she said, "I didn't understand. I didn't know what I was saying."

"I know."

"I didn't say anything, did I?"

"You know what you said."

"Yes, I know . . . I didn't mean . . . I don't think it's any good trying to explain."

Jock said, "Are you sure you've got everything?"

"Yes, that's everything," she nodded towards the little case on the bed. She looked quite hopeless.

"Well, we'd better go to the station."

"All right. It's early. But it doesn't matter."

Jock took her to the train. As it was Wednesday the carriages were full of women returning after their day's shopping.

"Why not go first class?"

"No, no. I always go third."

She sat in the middle of a row. The women on either side looked at her curiously wondering if she were ill.

"Don't you want anything to read?"

"Nothing to read."

"Or eat?"

"Or eat."

"Then I'll say goodbye."

"Goodbye."

Another woman pushed past Jock into the carriage, laden with light parcels.

When the news became known Marjorie said to Allan, "Well, anyway, this will mean the end of Mr. Beaver."

But Polly Cockpurse said to Veronica, "That's the end of Tony so far as Brenda is concerned."

The impoverished Lasts were stunned by the telegram. They lived on an extensive but unprofitable chicken farm near Great Missenden. It did not enter the heads of any of them that now, if anything happened, they were the heirs to Hetton. Had it done so, their grief would have been just as keen.

Jock drove from Paddington to Brat's. One of the men by the bar said, "Ghastly thing about Tony Last's boy."

"Yes, I was there."

"No, were you? What a ghastly thing."

Later a telephone message came: "Princess Abdul Akbar wishes to know whether you are in the club."

"No, no, tell her I'm not here," said Jock.

Seven

The inquest was held at eleven o'clock next morning; it was soon over. The doctor, the bus-driver, Ben and Miss Ripon gave evidence. Miss Ripon was allowed to remain seated. She was very white and spoke in a trembling voice; her father glared at her from a near-by seat; under her hat was a small bare patch, where they had shaved off the hair to clean her cut. In his summary the coroner remarked that it was clear from the evidence that nobody was in any way to blame for the misadventure; it only remained to express the deep sympathy of the court to Mr. Last and Lady Brenda in their terrible loss. The people fell back to allow Tony and Brenda to reach their car. Colonel Inch and the hunt secretary were both present. Everything was done with delicacy and to show respect for their sorrow.

Brenda said, "Wait a minute. I must just speak to that poor Ripon girl."

She did it charmingly. When they were in the car, Tony said, "I wish you had been here yesterday. There were so many people about and I didn't know what to say to them."

"What did you do all day?"

"There was the shameless blonde . . . we played animal snap some of the time."

"Animal snap? Was that any good?"

"Not much . . . It's odd to think that yesterday this time it hadn't happened."

"Poor little boy," said Brenda.

They had scarcely spoken to each other since Brenda's arrival. Tony had driven to the station to meet her; by the time they reached the house Mrs. Rattery had gone to bed; that morning she left in her aeroplane without seeing either of them. They heard the machine pass over the house, Brenda in her bath, Tony downstairs in his study attending to the correspondence that had become necessary.

A day of fitful sunshine and blustering wind; white and grey clouds were scarcely moving, high overhead, but the bare trees round the house swayed and shook and there were swift whirlpools of straw in the stable yard. Ben changed from the Sunday suit he had worn at the inquest and went about his duties. Thunderclap, too, had been kicked yesterday and was very slightly lame in the off fore.

Brenda took off her hat and threw it down on a chair in the hall. "Nothing to say, is there?"

"There's no need to talk."

"No. I suppose there'll have to be a funeral."

"Well, of course."

"Yes; tomorrow?"

She looked into the morning room. "They've done quite a lot, haven't they?"

All Brenda's movements were slower than usual and her voice was flat and expressionless. She sank down into one of the armchairs in the centre of the hall, which nobody ever used. She sat there doing nothing. Tony put his hand on her shoulder but she said "Don't," not impatiently or nervously but without any expression. Tony said, "I'll go and finish those letters."

"Yes."

"See you at luncheon."

"Yes."

She rose, looked round listlessly for her hat, found it and went very slowly upstairs, the sunlight through the stained glass windows glowing and sparkling all about her.

In her room she sat on the window seat, looking out across the meadows and dun ploughland, the naked tossing trees, the church towers, the maelstroms of dust and leaf which eddied about the terrace below; she still held her hat and fidgeted with her fingers on the brooch which was clipped to one side of it.

Nanny knocked at the door and came in, red eyed. "If you please, my lady, I've been going through John's things. There's this handkerchief doesn't belong to him."

The heavy scent and crowned cypher at its corner proclaimed its origin.

"I know whose it is. I'll send it back to her."

"Can't think how it came to be there," said nanny.

"Poor little boy. Poor little boy," said Brenda to herself, when nanny had left her, and gazed out across the troubled landscape.

"I was thinking about the pony, sir."

"Oh yes, Ben."

"Will you want to be keeping her now?"

"I hadn't thought . . . no, I suppose not."

"Mr. Westmacott over at Restall was asking about her. He thought she might do for his little girl."

"Yes."

"How much shall we be asking?"

"Oh, I don't know . . . whatever you think is right."

"She's a good little pony and she's always been treated well. I don't think she ought to go under twenty-five quid, sir."

"All right, Ben, you see about it."

"I'll ask thirty, shall I, sir, and come down a bit."

"Do just what you think best."

"Very good, sir."

At luncheon Tony said, "Jock rang up. He wanted to know if there was anything he could do."

"How sweet of him. Why don't you have him down for the week-end?"

"Would you like that?"

"I shan't be here. I'm going to Veronica's."

"You're going to Veronica's?"

"Yes, don't you remember?"

There were servants in the room so that they said nothing more until later, when they were alone in the library. Then, "Are you really going away?"

"Yes. I can't stay here. You understand that, don't you?"

"Yes, of course. I was thinking we might both go away, abroad somewhere."

Brenda did not answer him but continued in her own line. "I couldn't stay here. It's all over, don't you see, our life down here."

"Darling, what *do* you mean?"

"Don't ask me to explain . . . not just now."

"But, Brenda, sweet, I don't understand. We're both young. Of course we can never forget John. He'll always be our eldest son but . . ."

"Don't go on, Tony, please don't go on."

So Tony stopped and after a time said, "So you're going to Veronica's tomorrow?"

"Mmmm."

"I think I will ask Jock to come."

"Yes, I should."

"And we can think about plans later when we've got more used to things."

"Yes, later."

Next morning.

"A sweet letter from mother," said Brenda, handing it across. Lady St. Cloud had written:

. . . I shall not come down to Hetton for the funeral, but I shall be thinking of you both all the time and my dear grandson. I shall think of you as I saw you all three, together, at Christmas. Dear children, at a time like this only yourselves can be any help to each other. Love is the only thing that is stronger than sorrow . . .

"I got a telegram from Jock," said Tony, "he *can* come."

"It's really rather embarrassing for us all, Brenda coming," said Veronica. "I do think she might have chucked. I shan't in the least know what to say to her."

Tony said to Jock, as they sat alone after dinner, "I've been trying to understand, and I think I do now. It's not how I feel myself but Brenda and I are quite different in lots of ways. It's *because* they were strangers and didn't know John, and were never in our life here, that she wants to be with them. That's it, don't you think? She wants to be absolutely alone and away from everything that reminds her of what has happened . . . all the same I feel awful about letting her go. I can't tell you what she was like here . . . quite mechanical. It's so much worse for her than it is for me, I see that. It's so terrible not being able to do anything to help."

Jock did not answer.

Beaver was staying at Veronica's. Brenda said to him, "Until Wednesday, when I thought something had happened to you, I had no idea that I loved you."

"Well you've said it often enough."

"I'm going to make you understand," said Brenda. "You clod."

On Monday morning Tony found this letter on his breakfast tray.

Darling Tony,

I am not coming back to Hetton. Grimshawe can pack everything and bring it to the flat. Then I shan't want her any more.

You must have realized for some time that things were going wrong.

I am in love with John Beaver and I want to have a divorce and marry him. If John Andrew had not died things might not have happened like this. I can't tell. As it is, I simply can't begin over again. Please do not mind too much. I suppose we shan't be allowed to meet while the case is on but I hope afterwards we shall be great friends. Anyway I shall always look on you as one whatever you think of me.

Best love from

Brenda.

When Tony read this his first thought was that Brenda had lost her reason. "She's only seen Beaver twice to my knowledge," he said.

But later he showed the letter to Jock who said, "I'm sorry it should have happened like this."

"But it's not true, is it?"

"Yes, I'm afraid it is. Everyone has known for some time."

But it was several days before Tony fully realized what it meant. He had got into a habit of loving and trusting Brenda.

CHAPTER FOUR

English Gothic—II

"How's the old boy taking it?"

"Not so well. It makes me feel rather a beast," said Brenda. "I'm afraid he minds a lot."

"Well you wouldn't like it if he didn't," said Polly to console her.

"No, I suppose not."

"I shall stick by you whatever happens," said Jenny Abdul Akbar.

"Oh everything is going quite smoothly now," said Brenda. "There was a certain amount of gêne with relatives."

Tony had been living with Jock for the last three weeks. Mrs. Rattery had gone to California and he was grateful for company. They dined together most evenings. They had given up going to Brat's; so had Beaver; they were afraid of meeting each other. Instead they went to Brown's where Beaver was not a member. Beaver was continually with Brenda nowadays, at one of half a dozen houses.

Mrs. Beaver did not like the turn things had taken; her workmen had been sent back from Hetton with their job unfinished.

In the first week Tony had had several distasteful interviews. Allan had attempted to act as peacemaker.

"You just wait a few weeks," he had said. "Brenda will come back. She'll soon get sick of Beaver."

"But I don't want her back."

"I know just how you feel, but it doesn't do to be medieval about it. If Brenda hadn't been upset at John's death this need never have come to a crisis. Why last year

Marjorie was going everywhere with that ass Robin Beaseley. She was mad about him at the time but I pretended not to notice and it all blew over. If I were you I should refuse to recognize that anything has happened."

Marjorie had said, "Of *course* Brenda doesn't love Beaver. How could she? . . . And if she thinks she does at the moment, I think it's your duty to prevent her making a fool of herself. You must refuse to be divorced—anyway until she has found someone more reasonable."

Lady St. Cloud had said, "Brenda has been very, very foolish. She always was an excitable girl, but I am sure there was never anything *wrong,* quite sure. *That* wouldn't be like Brenda at all. I haven't met Mr. Beaver and I do not wish to. I understand he is unsuitable in every way. Brenda would never want to marry anyone like that. I will tell you exactly how it happened, Tony. Brenda must have felt a tiny bit neglected—people often do at that stage of marriage. I have known countless cases—and it was naturally flattering to her to find a young man to beg and carry for her. That's all it was, nothing *wrong.* And then the terrible shock of little John's accident unsettled her and she didn't know what she was saying or writing. You'll both laugh over this little fracas in years to come."

Tony had not set eyes on Brenda since the afternoon of the funeral. Once he spoke to her over the telephone.

It was during the second week when he was feeling most lonely and bewildered by various counsels. Allan had been with him urging a reconciliation. "I've been talking to Brenda," he had said. "She's sick of Beaver already. The one thing she wants is to go back to Hetton and settle down with you again."

While Allan was there, Tony resolutely refused to listen but later the words, and the picture they evoked, would not leave his mind. So he rang her up and she answered him calmly and gravely.

"Brenda, this is Tony."

"Hullo, Tony, what is it?"

"I've been talking to Allan. He's just told me about your change of mind."

"I'm not sure I know what you mean."

"That you want to leave Beaver and come back to Hetton."

"Did Allan say that?"

"Yes, isn't it true?"

"I'm afraid it's not. Allan is an interfering ass. I had him here this afternoon. He told me that you didn't want a divorce but that you were willing to let me stay on alone in London and do as I liked provided there was no public scandal. It seemed a good idea and I was going to ring you up about it. But I suppose that's just his diplomacy too. Anyway I'm afraid there's no prospect of my coming back to Hetton just at present."

"Oh I see. I didn't think it was likely . . . I just rang you up."

"That's all right. How are you, Tony?"

"All right, thanks."

"Good, so am I. Goodbye."

That was all he had heard of her. Both avoided places where there was a likelihood of their meeting.

It was thought convenient that Brenda should appear as the plaintiff. Tony did not employ the family solicitors in the matter but another, less reputable firm who specialized in divorce. He had steeled himself to expect a certain professional gusto, even levity, but found them instead disposed to melancholy and suspicion.

"I gather Lady Brenda is being far from discreet. It is quite likely that the King's Proctor may intervene . . . Moreover there is the question of money. You understand that by the present arrangement since she is the innocent and injured party she will be entitled to claim substantial alimony from the courts."

"Oh that's all right," said Tony. "I've been into all that with her brother-in-law and have decided to make a settlement of five hundred a year. She has four hundred of her own and I understand Mr. Beaver has something."

"It's a pity we can't put it in writing," said the solicitor, "but that might constitute Conspiracy."

"Lady Brenda's word is quite good enough," said Tony.

"We like to protect our clients against even the most remote contingencies," said the lawyer with an air of piety, for he had not had Tony's opportunities to contract the habit of loving and trusting Brenda.

The fourth week-end after Brenda's departure from Hetton was fixed for Tony's infidelity. A suite was engaged at a seaside hotel ("We always send our clients there. The servants are well accustomed to giving evidence") and private detectives were notified. "It only remains to select a partner," said the solicitor; no hint of naughtiness lightened his gloom. "We have on occasions been instrumental in accommodating our clients but there have been frequent complaints, so we find it best to leave the choice to them. Lately we had a particularly delicate case involving a man of very rigid morality and a certain diffidence. In the end his own wife consented to go with him and supply the evidence. She wore a red wig. It was quite successful."

"I don't think that would do in this case."

"No. Exactly. I was merely quoting it as a matter of interest."

"I expect I shall be able to find someone," said Tony.

"I have no doubt of it," said the solicitor, bowing politely.

But when he came to discuss the question later with Jock, it did not seem so easy. "It's not a thing one can ask every girl to do," he said, "whichever way you put it. If you say it is merely a legal form it is rather insulting, and if you suggest going the whole hog it's rather fresh—suddenly, I mean, if you've never paid any particular attention to her before and don't propose to carry on with it afterwards . . . Of course there's always old Sybil."

But even Sybil refused. "I'd do it like a shot any other time," she said, "but just at the moment it wouldn't suit my book. There's a certain person who might hear about it and take it wrong . . . There's an awfully pretty girl called Jenny Abdul Akbar. I wonder if you've met her."

"Yes, I've met her."

"Well won't she do?"

"No."

"Oh dear, I don't know who to suggest."

"We'd better go and study the market at the Sixty-four," said Jock.

They dined at Jock's house. Lately they had found it a little gloomy at Brown's for people tended to avoid anyone they knew to be unhappy. Though they drank a magnum of champagne they could not recapture the light-hearted mood in which they had last visited Sink Street. And then Tony said, "Is it any good going there yet?"

"We may as well try. After all we aren't going there for enjoyment."

"No, indeed."

The doors were open at 64 Sink Street and the band was playing to an empty ballroom. The waiters were eating at a little table in the corner. Two or three girls were clustered round the Jack-Pot machine losing shillings hard and complaining about the cold. They ordered a bottle of the Montmorency Wine Company's brandy and sat down to wait.

"Any of those do?" asked Jock.

"I don't much care."

"Better get someone you like. You've got to put in a lot of time with her."

Presently Milly and Babs came downstairs.

"How are the postman's hats?" said Milly.

They could not recognize the allusion.

"You are the two boys who were here last month, aren't you?"

"Yes. I'm afraid we were rather tight."

"You don't say?" It was very seldom that Milly and Babs met anyone who was quite sober during their business hours.

"Well come and sit down. How are you both?"

"I think I'm starting a cold," said Babs. "I feel awful. Why can't they heat this hole, the mean hounds?"

Milly was more cheerful and swayed in her chair to the music. "Care to dance?" she said, and she and Tony began to shuffle across the empty floor.

"My friend is looking for a lady to take to the seaside," said Jock.

"What, this weather? That'll be a nice treat for a lonely girl." Babs sniffed into a little ball of handkerchief.

"It's for a divorce."

"Oh, I see. Well, why doesn't he take Milly? She doesn't catch cold easy. Besides she knows how to behave at a hotel. Lots of the girls here are all right to have a lark with in town but you have to have a *lady* for a divorce."

"D'you often get asked to do that?"

"Now and then. It's a nice rest—but it means so much *talking* and the gentlemen will always go on so about their wives."

While they were dancing Tony came straight to business. "I suppose you wouldn't care to come away for the week-end?" he asked.

"Shouldn't mind," said Milly. "Where?"

"I thought of Brighton."

"Oh. . . Is it for a divorce?"

"Yes."

"You wouldn't mind if I brought my little girl with us? She wouldn't be any trouble."

"Yes."

"You mean you wouldn't mind?"

"I mean I should mind."

"Oh . . . You wouldn't think I had a little girl of eight, would you?"

"No."

"She's called Winnie. I was only sixteen when I had her. I was the youngest of the family and our stepfather wouldn't leave any of us girls alone. That's why I have to work for a living. She lives with a lady at Finchley. Twenty-eight bob a week it costs me, not counting her clothes. She does like the seaside."

"No," said Tony. "I'm sorry but it would be quite impossible. We'll get a lovely present for you to take back to her."

"All right . . . One gentleman gave her a fairy bicycle

for Christmas. She fell off and cut her knee . . . When do
we start?"

"Would you like to go by train or car?"

"Oh train. Winnie's sick if she goes in a car."

"Winnie's not coming."

"No, but let's go by train anyway."

So it was decided that they should meet at Victoria on
Saturday afternoon.

Jock gave Babs ten shillings and he and Tony went
home. Tony had not slept much lately. He could not prevent himself, when alone, from rehearsing over and over
in his mind all that had happened since Beaver's visit to
Hetton; searching for clues he had missed at the time;
wondering where something he had said or done might
have changed the course of events; going back further
to his earliest acquaintance with Brenda to find indica-
tions that should have made him more ready to understand the change that had come over her; reliving scene
after scene in the last eight years of his life. All this kept
him awake.

Two

There was a general rendezvous at the first class book-
ing office. The detectives were the first, ten minutes before
their time. They had been pointed out to Tony at the
solicitor's office so that he should not lose them. They
were cheerful middle-aged men in soft hats and heavy
overcoats. They were looking forward to their week-end,
for most of their daily work consisted in standing about
at street corners watching front doors and a job of this
kind was eagerly competed for in the office. In more modest divorces the solicitors were content to rely on the evidence of the hotel servants. The detectives were a luxury
and proposed to treat themselves as such.

There was a slight fog in London that day. The station
lamps were alight prematurely.

Tony came next, with Jock at his side, loyally there to
see him off. They bought the tickets and waited. The de-

tectives, sticklers for professional etiquette, made an attempt at self-effacement, studying the posters on the walls and peering from behind a pillar.

"This is going to be hell," said Tony.

It was ten minutes before Milly came. She emerged from the gloom with a porter in front carrying her suitcase and a child dragging back on her arm behind her. Milly's wardrobe consisted mainly of evening dresses, for during the day she usually spent her time sitting before a gas-fire in her dressing gown. She made an insignificant and rather respectable appearance. "Sorry if I'm late," she said. "Winnie here couldn't find her shoes. I brought her along too. I knew you wouldn't really mind. She travels on a half ticket."

Winnie was a plain child with large gold-rimmed spectacles. When she spoke she revealed that two of her front teeth were missing.

"I hope you don't imagine she's coming with us."

"Yes, that's the idea," said Milly. "She won't be any trouble—she's got her puzzle."

Tony bent down to speak to the little girl. "Listen," he said. "You don't want to come to a nasty big hotel. You go with this kind gentleman here. He'll take you to a shop and let you choose the biggest doll you can find and then he'll drive you back in his motor to your home. You'll like that, won't you?"

"No," said Winnie. "I want to go to the seaside. I won't go with that man. I don't want a doll. I want to go to the seaside with my mummy."

Several people besides the detectives were beginning to take notice of the oddly assorted group.

"Oh God!" said Tony, "I suppose she's got to come."

The detectives followed at a distance down the platform. Tony settled his companions in a pullman car. "Look," said Milly, "we're travelling first class. Isn't that fun? We can have tea."

"Can I have an ice?"

"I don't expect they've got an ice. But you can have some nice tea."

"But I want an ice."

"You shall have an ice when you get to Brighton. Now be a good girl and play with your puzzle or mother won't take you to the seaside again."

"The Awful Child of popular fiction," said Jock as he left Tony.

Winnie sustained the part throughout the journey to Brighton. She was not inventive but she knew the classic routine thoroughly, even to such commonplace but alarming devices as breathing heavily, grunting and complaining of nausea.

Room at the hotel had been engaged for Tony by the solicitors. It was therefore a surprise to the reception clerk when Winnie arrived. "We have reserved in your name double and single communicating rooms, bathroom and sitting room," he said. "We did not understand you were bringing your daughter. Will you require a further room?"

"Oh Winnie can come in with me," said Milly.

The two detectives who were standing nearby at the counter, exchanged glances of disapproval.

Tony wrote *Mr. and Mrs. Last* in the Visitors' Book.

"And daughter," said the clerk with his finger on the place.

Tony hesitated. "She is my niece," he said, and inscribed her name on another line, as *Miss Smith*.

The detective, registering below, remarked to his colleague, "He got out of that all right. Quite smart. But I don't like the look of this case. Most irregular. Sets a nasty, respectable note bringing a kid into it. We've got the firm to consider. It doesn't do them any good to get mixed up with the King's Proctor."

"How about a quick one?" said his colleague indifferently.

Upstairs, Winnie said, "Where's the sea?"

"Just there across the street."

"I want to go and see it."

"But it's dark now, pet. You shall see it tomorrow."

"I want to see it tonight."

"You take her to see it now," said Tony.

"Sure you won't be lonely?"

"Quite sure."

"We won't be long."

"That's all right. You let her see it properly."

Tony went down to the bar where he was pleased to find the two detectives. He felt the need of male company. "Good evening," he said.

They looked at him askance. Everything in this case seemed to be happening as though with deliberate design to shock their professional feelings. "Good evening," said the senior detective. "Nasty, raw evening."

"Have a drink."

Since Tony was paying their expenses in any case, the offer seemed superfluous but the junior detective brightened instinctively and said, "Don't mind if I do."

"Come and sit down. I feel rather lonely."

They took their drinks to a table out of hearing of the bar man. "Mr. Last, sir, this is all *wrong*," said the senior detective. "You haven't no business to recognize us at all. I don't know what they'd say at the office."

"Best respects," said the junior detective.

"This is Mr. James, my colleague," said the senior detective. "My name is Blenkinsop. James is new to this kind of work."

"So am I," said Tony.

"A pity we've such a nasty week-end for the job," said Blenkinsop, "very damp and blowy. Gets me in the joints."

"Tell me," said Tony. "Is it usual to bring children on an expedition of this kind?"

"It is *not*."

"I thought it couldn't be."

"Since you ask me, Mr. Last, I regard it as most irregular and injudicious. It looks wrong, and cases of this kind depend very much on making the right impression. Of course as far as James and I are concerned, the matter is O.K. There won't be a word about it in our evidence. But you can't trust the servants. You might very likely happen to strike one who was new to the courts, who'd blurt it out, and then where would we be? I don't like it, Mr. Last, and that's the truth."

"You can't feel more strongly about it than I do."

"Fond of kids myself," said James, who was new to this kind of work. "How about one with us."

"Tell me," said Tony, when they had been at their table some little time. "You must have observed numerous couples in your time, qualifying for a divorce; tell me, how do they get through their day?"

"It's easier in the summer," said Blenkinsop, "the young ladies usually bathe and the gentlemen read the papers on the esplanade; some goes for motor drives and some just hangs around the bar. They're mostly glad when Monday comes."

Milly and her child were in the sitting room when Tony came up.

"I've ordered an ice," said Milly.

"Quite right."

"I want late dinner. I want late dinner."

"No, dear, not late dinner. You have an ice up here."

Tony returned to the bar. "Mr. James," he said. "Did I understand you to say you were fond of children?"

"Yes, in their right place."

"You wouldn't I suppose consider dining tonight with the little girl who has accompanied me? I should take it as a great kindness."

"Oh no, sir, hardly that."

"You would not find me ungrateful."

"Well, sir, I don't like to appear unobliging, but it's not part of my duties."

He seemed to be wavering but Blenkinsop interposed. "Quite out of the question, sir."

When Tony left them Blenkinsop spoke from the depth of his experience; it was the first job that he and James had been on together, and he felt under some obligation to put his junior wise. "Our trouble is always the same— to make the clients realize that divorce is a serious matter."

Eventually extravagant promises for the morrow, two or three ices and the slight depression induced by them, persuaded Winnie to go to bed.

"How are we going to sleep?" asked Milly.

"Oh, just as you like."

"Just as *you* like."

"Well perhaps Winnie would be happier with you . . . she'll have to go into the other room tomorrow morning when they bring in breakfast, of course."

So she was tucked up in a corner of the double bed and to Tony's surprise was asleep before they went down to dinner.

A change of clothes brought to both Tony and Milly a change of temper. She, in her best evening frock, backless and vermilion, her face newly done and her bleached curls brushed out, her feet in high red shoes, some bracelets on her wrists, a dab of scent behind the large sham pearls in her ears, shook off the cares of domesticity and was once more in uniform, reporting for duty, a legionary ordered for active service after the enervating restraints of a winter in barracks; and Tony, filling his cigar case before the mirror, and slipping it into the pocket of his dinner jacket, reminded himself that phantasmagoric, and even gruesome as the situation might seem to him, he was nevertheless a host, so that he knocked at the communicating door and passed with a calm manner into his guest's room; for a month now he had lived in a world suddenly bereft of order; it was as though the whole reasonable and decent constitution of things, the sum of all he had experienced or learned to expect, were an inconspicuous, inconsiderable object mislaid somewhere on the dressing table; no outrageous circumstance in which he found himself, no new mad thing brought to his notice could add a jot to the all-encompassing chaos that shrieked about his ears. He smiled at Milly from the doorway. "Charming," he said, "perfectly charming. Shall we go down to dinner?"

Their rooms were on the first floor. Step by step, with her hand on his arm, they descended the staircase into the bright hall below.

"Cheer up," said Milly. "You have a tongue sandwich. That'll make you talk."

"Sorry, am I being a bore?"

"I was only joking. You are a serious boy, aren't you?"

In spite of the savage weather the hotel seemed full of week-end visitors. More were arriving through the swing doors, their eyes moist and their cheeks rigid from the icy cold outside.

"Yids," explained Milly superfluously. "Still it's nice to get a change from the club once in a while."

One of the new arrivals was a friend of Milly's. He was supervising the collection of his luggage. Anywhere else he would have been a noticeable figure, for he wore a large fur coat and a beret; under the coat appeared tartan stockings and black and white shoes. "Take 'em up and get 'em unpacked and quick about it," he said. He was a stout little young man. His companion, also in furs, was staring resentfully at one of the showcases that embellished the hall.

"Oh for Christ's sake," she said.

Milly and the young man greeted each other. "This is Dan," she said.

"Well, well, well," said Dan, "what next."

"Do I get a drink?" said Dan's girl.

"Baby, you do, if I have to get it myself. Won't you two join us, or are we de trop?"

They went together into the glittering lounge. "I'm cold like hell," said Baby.

Dan had taken off his greatcoat and revealed a suit of smooth, purplish plus fours, and a silk shirt of a pattern Tony might have chosen for pyjamas. "We'll soon warm you up," he said.

"This place stinks of yids," said Baby.

"I always think that's the sign of a good hotel, don't you?" said Tony.

"Like hell," said Baby.

"You mustn't mind Baby, she's cold," Dan explained.

"Who wouldn't be in your lousy car?"

They had some cocktails. Then Dan and Baby went to

their room; they must doll up, they explained, as they
were going to a party given by a friend of Dan's, at a place
of his near there. Tony and Milly went in to dinner.
"He's a very nice boy," she said, "and comes to the club
a lot. We get all sorts there, but Dan's one of the decent
ones. I was going to have gone abroad with him once but
in the end he couldn't get away."

"His girl didn't seem to like us much."

"Oh, she was cold."

Tony did not find conversation easy at dinner. At first
he commented on their neighbours as he would have done
if he had been dining with Brenda at Espinosa's. "That's
a pretty girl in the corner."

"I wonder you don't go and join her, dear," said Milly
testily.

"Look at that woman's diamonds. Do you think they
can be real?"

"Why don't you ask her, if you're so interested?"

"That's an interesting type—the dark woman dancing."

"I'm sure she'd be delighted to hear it."

Presently Tony realized that it was not etiquette in
Milly's world, to express interest in women, other than
the one you were with.

They drank champagne. So, Tony noticed with dis-
pleasure, did the two detectives. He would have something to say about that when their bill for expenses came
in. It was not as though they had been accommodating
in the matter of Winnie. All the time, at the back of his
mind, he was worrying with the problem of what they
could possibly do after dinner, but it was solved for him,
just as he was lighting his cigar, by the appearance of
Dan from the other side of the dining room. "Look here,"
he said, "if you two aren't doing anything special why
don't you join up with us and come to the party at my
friend's place. You'll like it. He always gives one the best
of everything."

"Oh do let's," said Milly.

Dan's evening clothes were made of blue cloth that

was supposed to appear black in artificial light; for some reason, however, they remained very blue.

So Milly and Tony went to Dan's friend's place and had the best of everything. There was a party of twenty or thirty people, all more or less like Dan. Dan's friend was most hospitable. When he was not fiddling with the wireless, which gave trouble off and on throughout the evening, he was sauntering among his guests refilling their glasses. "This stuff's all right," he said, showing the label, "it won't hurt you. It's the right stuff."

They had a lot of the right stuff.

Quite often Dan's friend noticed that Tony seemed to be out of the party. Then he would come across and put his hand on Tony's shoulder. "I'm so glad Dan brought you," he would say. "Hope you're getting all you want. Delighted to see you. Come again when there isn't a crowd and see over the place. Interested in roses?"

"Yes, I like them very much."

"Come when the roses are out. You'd like that if you're interested in roses. Damn that radio, it's going wonky again."

Tony wondered whether he was as amiable when people he did not know were brought over unexpectedly to Hetton.

At one stage in the evening he found himself sitting on a sofa with Dan. "Nice kid Milly," he said.

"Yes."

"I'll tell you a thing I've noticed about her. She attracts quite a different type from the other girls. People like you and me."

"Yes."

"You wouldn't think she had a daughter of eight, would you."

"No, it's very surprising."

"I didn't know for ages. Then I was taking her to Dieppe for the week-end and she wanted to bring the child along too. Of course that put the kybosh on it, but I've always liked Milly just the same. You can trust her to behave anywhere." He said this with a sour glance towards Baby who was full of the right stuff and showing it.

It was after three before the party broke up. Dan's friend renewed his invitation to come again when the roses were out. "I doubt if you'll find a better show of roses anywhere in the south of England," he said.

Dan drove them back to the hotel. Baby sat beside him in front, disposed to be quarrelsome. "Where were you?" she kept asking. "Never saw you all the evening. Where did you get to? Where were you hiding? I call it a lousy way to take a girl out."

Tony and Milly sat at the back. From habit and exhaustion she put her head on his shoulder and her hand in his. When they reached their rooms, however, she said, "Go quietly. We don't want to wake Winnie."

For an hour or so Tony lay in the warm little bedroom, reviewing over and over again the incidents of the last three months; then he too fell asleep.

He was awakened by Winnie. "Mother's still asleep," she said.

Tony looked at his watch. "So I should think," he said. It was quarter past seven. "Go back to bed."

"No, I'm dressed. Let's go out."

She went to the window and pulled back the curtains, filling the room with glacial morning light. "It's hardly raining at all," she said.

"What do you want to do?"

"I want to go on the pier."

"It won't be open yet."

"Well I want to go down to the sea. Come on."

Tony knew that he would not get to sleep again that morning. "All right. You go and wait while I dress."

"I'll wait here. Mother snores so."

Twenty minutes later they went downstairs into the hall where aproned waiters were piling up the furniture and brushing the carpets. A keen wind met them as they emerged from the swing door. The asphalt promenade was wet with spray and rain. Two or three female figures were scudding along, bowed to the wind, prayer books clutched in their gloved hands. Four or five rugged old men were hobbling down to bathe, hissing like ostlers. "Oh come on," said Winnie.

They went down to the beach and stumbled painfully across the shingle to the margin of the sea. Winnie threw some stones. The bathers were in the water now; some of them had dogs who swam snorting beside them. "Why don't you bathe?" asked Winnie.

"Far too cold."

"But *they're* bathing. I want to."

"You must ask your mother."

"I believe you're afraid. Can you swim?"

"Yes."

"Well why don't you? Bet you can't."

"All right. I can't."

"Then why did you say you could. Fibber."

They walked along the shingle. Winnie slithered about astride a backwater. "Now I'm all wet," she said.

"Better come back and change."

"It feels horrible. Let's go and have breakfast."

The hotel did not, as a rule, cater for guests who breakfasted downstairs at eight o'clock on Sunday morning. It took a long time before anything could be got ready. There were no ices, much to Winnie's annoyance. She ate grapefruit and kippers and scrambled eggs on toast, complaining fitfully about her wet clothing. After breakfast Tony sent her upstairs to change and, himself, smoked a pipe in the lounge and glanced over the Sunday papers. Here at nine o'clock he was interrupted by the arrival of Blenkinsop. "We missed you last night," he said.

"We went to a party."

"You shouldn't have done that—not strictly, but I daresay no harm will come of it. Have you had your breakfast?"

"Yes, in the dining room with Winnie."

"But, Mr. Last, what are you thinking of? You've got to get evidence from the hotel servants."

"Well, I didn't like to wake Milly."

"She's paid for it, isn't she? Come, come, Mr. Last, this won't do at all. You'll never get your divorce if you don't give your mind to it more."

"All right," said Tony. "I'll have breakfast again."

"In bed mind."

"In bed." And he went wearily upstairs to his rooms.

Winnie had drawn the curtains but her mother was still asleep. "She woke up once and then turned over. Do get her to come out. I want to go on the pier."

"Milly," said Tony firmly. "Milly."

"Oh," she said. "What time is it?"

"We've got to have breakfast."

"Don't want any breakfast. I think I'll sleep a little."

"You have had breakfast," said Winnie.

"Come on," said Tony. "Plenty of time to sleep afterwards. This is what we came for."

Milly sat up in bed. "O.K.," she said. "Winnie darling, give mother her jacket off the chair." She was a conscientious girl, ready to go through with her job however unattractive it might seem. "But it's early."

Tony went into his room and took off his shoes, collar and tie, coat and waistcoat, and put on a dressing gown.

"You are greedy," said Winnie, "eating two breakfasts."

"When you're a little older you'll understand these things. It's the Law. Now I want you to stay in the sitting room for quarter of an hour very quietly. Promise? And afterwards you can do exactly what you like."

"Can I bathe?"

"Yes certainly, if you're quiet now."

Tony got into bed beside Milly and pulled the dressing gown tight round his throat. "Does that look all right?"

"Love's young dream," said Milly.

"All right then. I'll ring the bell."

When the tray had been brought Tony got out of bed and put on his things. "So much for my infidelity," he said. "It is curious to reflect that this will be described in the papers as 'intimacy.'"

"Can I bathe now?"

"Certainly."

Milly turned over to sleep again. Tony took Winnie to the beach. The wind had got up and a heavy sea was pounding on the shingle.

"This little girl would like to bathe," said Tony.

"No bathing for children today," said the beach attendant.

"The very idea," said various onlookers. "Does he want to drown the child?" "He's no business to be trusted with children." "*Unnatural* beast."

"But I *want* to bathe," said Winnie. "You said I could bathe if you had two breakfasts."

The people who had clustered round to witness Tony's discomfort, looked at one another askance. "Two breakfasts? Wanting to let the child bathe? The man's balmy."

"Never mind," said Tony. "We'll go on the pier."

Several of the crowd followed them round the slots, curious to see what new enormity this mad father might attempt. "There's a man who's eaten two breakfasts and tries to drown his little girl," they informed other spectators, sceptically observing his attempts to amuse Winnie with skee-ball. Tony's conduct confirmed the view of human nature derived from the weekly newspapers which they had all been reading that morning.

"Well," said Brenda's solicitor. "We have our case now, all quite regular and complete. I don't think it can come on until next term—there's a great rush at the moment, but there's no harm in you having your own evidence ready. I've got it typed out for you. You'd better keep it by you and get it clear in your mind."

"*. . . My marriage was an ideally happy one,*" she read, "*until shortly before Christmas last year when I began to suspect that my husband's attitude had changed towards me. He always remained in the country when my studies took me to London. I realized that he no longer cared for me as he used to. He began to drink heavily and on one occasion made a disturbance at our flat in London, constantly ringing up when drunk and sending a drunken friend round to knock on the door. Is that necessary?*"

"Not strictly, but it is advisable to put it in. A great
deal depends on psychological impression. Judges in their
more lucid moments sometimes wonder why perfectly respectable, happily married men go off for week-ends to
the seaside with women they do not know. It is always
helpful to offer evidence of general degeneracy."

"I see," said Brenda. *"From then onwards I had him
watched by private agents and as a result of what they
told me, I left my husband's house on April 5th.* Yes, that
all seems quite clear."

Three

Lady St. Cloud preserved an atavistic faith in the authority and preternatural good judgment of the Head of
the Family; accordingly her first act, on learning from
Marjorie of Brenda's wayward behaviour, was to cable
for Reggie's return from Tunisia where he was occupied
in desecrating some tombs. His departure, like all his
movements, was leisurely. He did not take the first available boat or the second, but eventually he arrived in London on the Monday after Tony's visit to Brighton. He
held a family conclave in his library consisting of his
mother, Brenda, Marjorie, Allan and the solicitor; later
he discussed the question fully with each of them sever-
ally; he took Beaver out to luncheon; he dined with Jock;
he even called on Tony's Aunt Frances. Finally on Thursday evening he arranged to meet Tony for dinner at
Brown's.

He was eight years older than Brenda; very occasionally
a fugitive, indefinable likeness was detectable between
him and Marjorie, but both in character and appearance
he was as different from Brenda as it was possible to imagine. He was prematurely, unnaturally stout, and he carried his burden of flesh as though he were not yet used
to it; as though it had been buckled on to him that morning for the first time and he were still experimenting for
its better adjustment; there was an instability in his gait
and in his eyes, a furtive look as though he were at any

moment liable to ambush and realized that he was unfairly handicapped for flight. This impression, however, was made solely by his physical appearance; it was the deep bed of fat in which his eyes lay, which gave them this look of suspicion; the caution of his movements resulted from the exertion of keeping his balance and not from any embarrassment at his own clumsiness, for it had never occurred to him that he looked at all unusual.

Rather more than half Reggie St. Cloud's time and income was spent abroad in modest archaeological expeditions. His house in London was full of their fruit—fragmentary amphoras, corroded bronze axe-heads, little splinters of bone and charred stick, a Graeco-Roman head in marble, its features obliterated and ground smooth with time. He had written two little monographs about his work, privately printed and both dedicated to members of the royal family. When he came to London he was regular in attendance at the House of Lords; all his friends were well over forty and for some years now he had established himself as a member of their generation; few mothers still regarded him as a possible son-in-law.

"This whole business of Brenda is *very* unfortunate," said Reggie St. Cloud.

Tony agreed.

"My mother is extremely upset about it, naturally. I'm upset myself. I don't mind admitting, perfectly frankly, that I think she has behaved very foolishly, foolishly and wrongly. I can quite understand your being upset about it too."

"Yes," said Tony.

"But all the same, making every allowance for your feelings, I do think that you are behaving rather vindictively in the matter."

"I'm doing exactly what Brenda wanted."

"My dear fellow, she doesn't know what she wants. I saw this chap Beaver yesterday. I didn't like him *at all*. Do you?"

"I hardly know him."

"Well I can assure you I didn't like him. Now you're just throwing Brenda into his arms. That's what it amounts to, as I see it, and I call it vindictive. Of course at the moment Brenda's got the idea that she's in love with him. But it won't last. It couldn't with a chap like Beaver. She'll want to come back in a year, just you see. Allan says the same."

"I've told Allan. I don't want her back."

"Well, that's vindictive."

"No, I just couldn't feel the same about her again."

"Well, why feel *the same*? One has to change as one gets older. Why, ten years ago I couldn't be interested in anything later than the Sumerian age and I assure you that now I find even the Christian era full of significance."

For some time he spoke about some *tabulae execrationum* that he had lately unearthed. "Almost every grave had them," he said, "mostly referring to the circus factions, scratched on lead. They used to be dropped in through a funnel. We had found forty-three up to date, before this wretched business happened, and I had to come back. Naturally I'm upset."

He sat for a little eating silently. This last observation had brought the conversation back to its point of departure. He clearly had more to say on the subject and was meditating the most convenient approach. He ate in a ruthless manner, champing his food (it was his habit, often, without noticing it, to consume things that others usually left on their plates, the heads and tails of whiting, whole mouthfuls of chicken bone, peach stones and apple cores, cheese rinds and the fibrous parts of the artichoke). "Besides, you know," he said, "it isn't as though it was all Brenda's fault."

"I haven't been thinking particularly whose fault it is."

"Well that's all very well but you seem rather to be taking the line of the injured husband—saying you can't feel the same again, and all that. I mean to say, it takes two to make a quarrel and I gather things had been going wrong for some time. For instance you'd been drinking a lot—have some more burgundy by the way."

"Did Brenda say that?"

"Yes. And then you'd been going round a bit with other girls yourself. There was some woman with a Moorish name you had to stay at Hetton while Brenda was there. Well that's a bit thick you know. I'm all for people going their own way but if they do, they can't blame others, if you see what I mean."

"Did Brenda say that?"

"Yes. Don't think I'm trying to lecture you or anything, but all I feel is that you haven't any right to be vindictive to Brenda, as things are."

"She said I drank and was having an affair with the woman with a Moorish name."

"Well I don't know she actually said that, but she said you'd been getting tight lately and that you were certainly interested in that girl."

The fat young man opposite Tony ordered prunes and cream. Tony said he had finished dinner.

He had imagined during the preceding week-end that nothing could now surprise him.

"So that really explains what I want to say," continued Reggie blandly. "It's about money. I understand that when Brenda was in a very agitated state just after the death of her child, she consented to some verbal arrangement with you about settlements."

"Yes, I'm allowing her five hundred a year."

"Well you know I don't think that you have any right to take advantage of her generosity in that way. It was most imprudent of her to consider your proposal—she admits now that she was not really herself when she did so."

"What does she suggest instead?"

"Let's go outside and have coffee."

When they were settled in front of the fire in the empty smoking room, he answered, "Well I've discussed it with the lawyers and with the family and we decided that the sum should be increased to two thousand."

"That's quite out of the question. I couldn't begin to afford it."

"Well, you know, I have to consider Brenda's interests. She has very little of her own and there will be no more coming to her. My mother's income is an allowance which I pay under my father's will. I shan't be able to give her anything. I am trying to raise everything I can for an expedition to one of the oases in the Lybian desert. This chap Beaver has got practically nothing and doesn't look like earning any. So you see—"

"But, my dear Reggie, you know as well as I do that it's out of the question."

"It's rather less than a third of your income."

"Yes but almost every penny goes on the estate. Do you realize that Brenda and I together haven't spent half the amount a year on our personal expenses. It's all I can do to keep things going as it is."

"I didn't expect you'd take this line, Tony. I think its extremely unreasonable of you. After all it's absurd to pretend in these days that a single man can't be perfectly comfortable on four thousand a year. It's more than I've ever had."

"It would mean giving up Hetton."

"Well I gave up Brakeleigh, and I assure you, my dear fellow, I never regret it. It was a nasty wrench at the time of course, old association and everything like that, but I can tell you this, that when the sale was finally through I felt a different man, free to go where I liked . . ."

"But I don't happen to want to go anywhere else except Hetton."

"There's a lot in what these labour fellows say, you know. Big houses are a thing of the past in England I'm afraid."

"Tell me, did Brenda realize when she agreed to this proposal that it meant my leaving Hetton."

"Yes, it was mentioned I think. I daresay you'll find it quite easy to sell to a school or something like that. I remember the agent said when I was trying to get rid of Brakeleigh that it was a pity it wasn't Gothic because schools and convents always go for Gothic. I daresay you'll get a very comfortable price and find yourself better off in the end than you are now."

"No. It's impossible," said Tony.

"You're making things extremely awkward for everyone," said Reggie. "I can't understand why you are taking up this attitude."

"What is more I don't believe that Brenda ever expected or wanted me to agree."

"Oh yes, she did, my dear fellow. I assure you of that."

"It's inconceivable."

"Well," said Reggie, puffing at his cigar. "There's more to it than just money. Perhaps I'd better tell you everything. I hadn't meant to. The truth is that Beaver is cutting up nasty. He says he can't marry Brenda unless she's properly provided for. Not fair on her, he says. I quite see his point on a way."

"Yes, I see his point," said Tony. "So what your proposal really amounts to is that I should give up Hetton in order to buy Beaver for Brenda."

"It's not how I should have put it," said Reggie.

"Well I'm not going to and that's the end of it. If that's all you wanted to say, I may as well leave you."

"No, it isn't quite all I wanted to say. In fact I think I must have put things rather badly. It comes from trying to respect people's feelings too much. You see I wasn't so much asking you to agree to anything as explaining what our side propose to do. I've tried to keep everything on a friendly basis but I see it's not possible. Brenda will ask for alimony of two thousand a year from the Court and on our evidence we shall get it. I'm sorry you oblige me to put it so bluntly."

"I hadn't thought of that."

"No, nor had we to be quite frank. It was Beaver's idea."

"You seem to have got me in a fairly hopeless position."

"It's not how I should have put it."

"I should like to make absolutely sure that Brenda is in on this. D'you mind if I ring her up."

"Not at all, my dear fellow. I happen to know she's at Marjorie's tonight."

"Brenda, this is Tony . . . I've just been dining with Reggie."

"Yes, he said something about it."

"He tells me that you are going to sue for alimony. Is that so?"

"Tony, don't be so bullying. The lawyers are doing everything. It's no use coming to me."

"But did you know that they proposed to ask for two thousand?"

"Yes. They did say that. I know it sounds a lot but . . ."

"And you know exactly how my money stands don't you? You know it means selling Hetton, don't you? . . . hullo, are you still there?"

"Yes, I'm here."

"You know it means that?"

"Tony, don't make me feel a beast. Everything has been so difficult."

"You do know just what you are asking?"

"Yes . . . I suppose so."

"All right, that's all I wanted to know."

"Tony, how odd you sound . . . don't ring off."

He hung up the receiver and went back to the smoking room. His mind had suddenly become clearer on many points that had puzzled him. A whole Gothic world had come to grief . . . there was now no armour, glittering in the forest glades, no embroidered feet on the greensward; the cream and dappled unicorns had fled . . .

Reggie sat expanded in his chair. "Well?"

"I got on to her. You were quite right. I'm sorry I didn't believe you. It seemed so unlikely at first."

"That's all right, my dear fellow."

"I've decided exactly what's going to happen."

"Good."

"Brenda is not going to get her divorce. The evidence I provided at Brighton isn't worth anything. There happens to have been a child there all the time. She slept both nights in the room I am supposed to have occupied. If you care to bring the case I shall defend it and win, but I think when you have seen my evidence you will drop it. I am

going away for six months or so. When I come back, if
she wishes it, I shall divorce Brenda without settlements
of any kind. Is that clear?"

"But look here, my dear fellow."

"Goodnight. Thank you for dinner. Good luck to the
excavations."

On his way out of the club he noticed that John Beaver
of Brat's Club was up for election.

"Who on earth would have expected the old boy to
turn up like that?" asked Polly Cockpurse.

"Now I understand why they keep going on in the
papers about divorce law reform," said Veronica. "It's
too monstrous that he should be allowed to get away with
it."

"The mistake they made was in telling him first," said
Souki.

"It's so like Brenda to trust everyone," said Jenny.

"I do think Tony comes out of this pretty poorly," said
Marjorie.

"Oh I don't know," said Allan. "I expect your ass of
a brother put the thing wrong."

CHAPTER FIVE

In Search of a City

"Any idea how many times round the deck make a mile?"

"None, I'm afraid," said Tony. "But I should think
you must have walked a great distance."

"Twenty-two times. One soon gets out of sorts at sea
if you're used to an active life. She's not much of a boat.
Travel with this line often?"

"Never before."

"Ah. Thought you might have been in business in the islands. Not many tourists going out this time of year. Just the other way about. All coming home, if you see what I mean. Going far?"

"Demerara."

Ah. Looking for minerals perhaps?"

"No, to tell you the truth I am looking for a city."

The genial passenger was surprised and then laughed. "Sounded just like you said you were looking for a city."

"Yes."

"That *was* what you said?"

"Yes."

"I thought it sounded like that ... well, so long. I must do another few rounds before dinner."

He paced off up the deck, straddling slightly in order to keep his balance and occasionally putting out a hand to the rail for support.

Regularly every three minutes for the last hour or so, this man had come by. At first Tony had looked up at his approach and then turned away again out to sea. Presently the man had taken to nodding, then to saying "Hullo" or "Bit choppy" or "Here we are again"; finally he had stopped and begun a conversation.

Tony went aft to break this rather embarrassing recurrence. He descended the companion-way which led to the lower deck. Here, in crates lashed to the side, was a variety of livestock—some stud bulls, a heavily blanketed race-horse, a couple of beagles, being exported to various West Indian islands. Tony threaded a way between them and the hatches to the stern, where he sat against a winch watching the horizon mount above the funnels, then fall until they stood out black against the darkening sky. The pitch was more sensible here than it had been amidships; the animals shifted restlessly in their cramped quarters; the beagles whined intermittently. A lascar took down from a line some washing which had been flapping there all day.

The wash of the ship was quickly lost in the high waves.

They were steaming westward down the Channel. As it grew to be night, lighthouses appeared flashing from the French coast. Presently a steward walked round the bright, upper deck striking chimes on a gong of brass cylinders and the genial passenger went below to prepare himself for dinner in hot sea water which splashed from side to side of the bath and dissolved the soap in a thin, sticky scum. He was the only man to dress that evening. Tony sat in the mustering darkness until the second bell. Then he left his greatcoat in the cabin and went down to dinner.

It was the first evening at sea.

Tony sat at the captain's table, but the captain was on the bridge that evening. There were empty chairs on either side of him. It was not rough enough for the fiddles to be out, but the stewards had removed the flower vases and damped the table-cloth to make it adhesive. A coloured archdeacon sat facing him. He ate with great refinement but his black hands looked immense on the wet, whitish cloth. "I'm afraid our table is not showing up very well tonight," he said. "I see you are not a sufferer. My wife is in her cabin. *She* is a sufferer."

He was returning from a Congress, he told Tony.

At the top of the stairs was a lounge named the Music and Writing Room. The light here was always subdued, in the day by the stained glass of the windows, at night by pink silk shades which hid the electric candles. Here the passengers assembled for their coffee, sitting on bulky, tapestry covered chesterfields or on swivel chairs irremovably fastened before the writing tables. Here too the steward for an hour every day presided over the cupboardful of novels which constituted the ship's library.

"It's not much of a boat," said the genial passenger, sitting himself beside Tony. "But I expect things will look brighter when we get into the sun."

Tony lit a cigar and was told by a steward that he must not smoke in this room. "That's all right," said the genial passenger, "we're just going down to the bar." "You know," he said a few minutes later, "I feel I owe you an apology. I thought you were potty just now before dinner.

Honestly I did, when you said you were going to Demerara to look for a city. Well it sounded pretty potty. Then the purser—I'm at his table. Always get the cheeriest crowd at the purser's table *and* the best attention—the purser told me about you. You're the explorer aren't you?"

"Yes, come to think of it, I suppose I am," said Tony.

It did not come easily to him to realize that he was an explorer. It was barely a fortnight ago that he had become one. Even the presence in the hold of two vast crates, bearing his name and labelled *NOT WANTED ON THE VOYAGE*—crates containing such new and unfamiliar possessions as a medicine chest, an automatic shot gun, camping equipment, pack saddles, a cinema camera, dynamite, disinfectants, a collapsible canoe, filters, tinned butter and, strangest of all, an assortment of what Dr. Messinger called 'trade goods'—failed to convince him fully of the serious nature of his expedition. Dr. Messinger had arranged everything. It was he who chose the musical boxes and mechanical mice, the mirrors, combs, perfumery, pills, fish-hooks, axe-heads, coloured rockets, and rolls of artificial silk, which were packed in the box of 'trade goods.' And Dr. Messinger himself was a new acquaintance who, prostrate now in his bunk with what the Negro clergyman would have called 'suffering,' that day, for the first time since Tony had met him, seemed entirely human.

Tony had spent very little of his life abroad. At the age of eighteen, before going to the University, he had been boarded for the summer with an elderly gentleman near Tours, with the intention that he should learn the language. (. . . a grey stone house surrounded by vines. There was a stuffed spaniel in the bathroom. The old man had called it 'Stop' because it was chic at that time to give dogs an English name. Tony had bicycled along straight, white roads to visit the châteaux; he carried rolls of bread and cold veal tied to the back of the machine, and the soft dust seeped into them through the paper and gritted against his teeth. There were two other English boys there, so he had learned little French. One of them fell

in love and the other got drunk for the first time on
sparkling Vouvray at a fair that had been held in the
town. That evening Tony won a live pigeon at a tom-
bola; he set it free and later saw it being recaptured by
the proprietor of the stall with a butterfly net . . .) Later
he had gone to central Europe for a few weeks with a
friend from Balliol. (They had found themselves suddenly rich with the falling mark and had lived in unaccustomed grandeur in the largest hotel suites. Tony had
bought a fur for a few shillings and given it to a girl in
Munich who spoke no English.) Later still his honeymoon
with Brenda in a villa, lent to them, on the Italian Riviera. (. . . cypress and olive trees, a domed church half
way down the hill, between the villa and the harbour, a
café where they sat out in the evening, watching the fishing boats and the lights reflected in the quiet water, waiting for the sudden agitation of sound and motion as the
speed boat came in. It had been owned by a dashing young
official, who called it *JAZZ GIRL*. He seemed to spend
twenty hours a day running in and out of the little harbour . . .) Once Brenda and he had gone to Le Touquet
with Brat's golf team. That was all. After his father died
he had not left England. They could not easily afford it;
it was one of the things they postponed until death duties
were paid off; besides that, he was never happy away from
Hetton and Brenda did not like leaving John Andrew.

Thus Tony had no very ambitious ideas about travel,
and when he decided to go abroad his first act was to call
at a tourist agency and come away laden with a sheaf of
brightly coloured prospectuses, which advertised commo-
dious cruises among palm trees, Negresses and ruined
arches. He was going away because it seemed to be the
conduct expected of a husband in his circumstances, because the associations of Hetton were for the time poisoned for him, because he wanted to live for a few months
away from people who would know him or Brenda, in
places where there was no expectation of meeting her or
Beaver or Reggie St. Cloud at every corner he frequented,
and with this feeling of evasion dominant in his mind, he

took the prospectuses to read at the Greville Club. He had been a member there for some years, but rarely used it; his resignation was only postponed by his recurrent omission to cancel the banker's order for his subscription. Now that Brat's and Brown's were distasteful to him he felt thankful that he had kept on with the Greville. It was a club of intellectual flavour, composed of dons, a few writers and the officials of museums and learned societies. It had a tradition of garrulity so that he was not surprised when, seated in an armchair and surrounded with his illustrated folders, he was addressed by a member unknown to him who asked if he were thinking of going away. He was more surprised when he looked up and studied the questioner.

Dr. Messinger, though quite young, was bearded, and Tony knew few young men with beards. He was also very small, very sunburned and prematurely bald; the ruddy brown of his face and hands ended abruptly along the line of his forehead, which rose in a pale dome; he wore steel-rimmed spectacles and there was something about his blue serge suit which suggested that the wearer found it uncomfortable.

Tony admitted that he was considering taking a cruise.

"I am going away shortly," said Dr. Messinger, "to Brazil. At least it may be Brazil or Dutch Guiana. One cannot tell. The frontier has never been demarcated. I ought to have started last week only my plans were upset. Do you by any chance know a Nicaraguan calling himself alternately Ponsonby and Fitz Clarence?"

"No, I don't think I do."

"You are fortunate. That man has just robbed me of two hundred pounds and some machine guns."

"Machine guns?"

"Yes, I travel with one or two, mostly for show you know, or for trade, and they are not easy to buy nowadays. Have you ever tried?"

"No."

"Well you can take it from me that it's not easy. You can't just walk into a shop and order machine guns."

"No, I suppose not."

"Still at a pinch I can do without them. But I can't do without the two hundred pounds."

Tony had open on his knee a photograph of the harbour at Agadir. Dr. Messinger looked over his shoulder at it. "Ah yes," he said, "interesting little place. I expect you know Zingerman there?"

"No, I've not been there yet."

"You'd like him—a very straight fellow. He used to do quite a lot, selling ammunition to the Atlas caids before the pacification. Of course it was easy money with the capitulations, but he did it better than most of them. I believe he's running a restaurant now in Mogador." Then he continued dreamily, "The pity is I can't let the R.G.S. in on this expedition. I've got to find the money privately."

It was one o'clock and the room was beginning to fill up; an Egyptologist was exhibiting a handkerchief-ful of scarabs to the editor of a church weekly.

"We'd better go up and lunch," said Dr. Messinger.

Tony had not intended to lunch at the Greville but there was something compelling about the invitation; moreover, he had no other engagement.

Dr. Messinger lunched off apples and a rice pudding. ("I have to be very careful what I eat," he said.) Tony ate cold steak and kidney pie. They sat at a window in the big dining room upstairs. The places round them were soon filled with members, who even carried the tradition of general conversation so far as to lean back in their chairs and chat over their shoulders from table to table— a practice which greatly hindered the already imperfect service. But Tony remained oblivious to all that was said, absorbed in what Dr. Messinger was telling him.

". . . You see there has been a continuous tradition about the City since the first explorers of the sixteenth century. It has been variously allocated, sometimes down in Matto Grosso, sometimes on the upper Orinoco in what is now Venezuela. I myself used to think it lay somewhere on the Uraricuera. I was out there last year and it was then that I established contact with the Pie-wie Indians;

no white man had ever visited them and got out alive. And it was from the Pie-wies that I learned where to look. None of them had ever visited the City, of course, but they *knew about it*. Every Indian between Ciudad Bolívar and Para knows about it. But they won't talk. Queer people. But I became blood-brother with a Pie-wie—interesting ceremony. They buried me up to the neck in mud and all the women of the tribe spat on my head. Then we ate a toad and a snake and a beetle and after that I was a blood-brother—well, he told me that the City lies between the head waters of the Courantyne and the Takutu. There's a vast tract of unexplored country there. I've often thought of visiting it.

"I've been looking up the historical side too, and I more or less know how the City got there. It was the result of a migration from Peru at the beginning of the fifteenth century when the Incas were at the height of their power. It is mentioned in all the early Spanish documents as a popular legend. One of the younger princes rebelled and led his people off into the forest. Most of the tribes have a tradition in one form or another of a strange race passing through their territory."

"But what do you suppose this city will be like?"

"Impossible to say. Every tribe has a different word for it. The Pie-wies call it the 'Shining' or 'Glittering,' the Arekuna the 'Many Watered,' the Patamonas the 'Bright Feathered,' the Warau oddly enough, use the same word for it that they use for a kind of aromatic jam they make. Of course one can't tell how a civilization may have developed or degenerated in five hundred years of isolation . . ."

Before Tony left the Greville that day, he tore up his sheaf of cruise prospectuses, for he had arranged to join Dr. Messinger in his expedition.

"Done much of that kind of thing?"

"No, to tell you the truth it is the first time."

"Ah. Well I daresay it's more interesting than it

sounds," conceded the genial passenger, "else people wouldn't do it so much."

The ship, so far as any consideration of comfort had contributed to her design, was planned for the tropics. It was slightly colder in the smoking room than on deck. Tony went to his cabin and retrieved his cap and greatcoat; then he went aft again, to the place where he had sat before dinner. It was a starless night and nothing was visible beyond the small luminous area round the ship, save for a single lighthouse that flashed short-long, short-long, far away on the port bow. The crests of the waves caught the reflection from the promenade deck and shone for a moment before plunging away into the black depths behind. The beagles were awake, whining.

For some days now Tony had been thoughtless about the events of the immediate past. His thoughts were occupied with the City, the Shining, the Many Watered, the Bright Feathered, the Aromatic Jam. He had a clear picture of it in his mind. It was Gothic in character, all vanes and pinnacles, gargoyles, battlements, groining and tracery, pavilions and terraces, a transfigured Hetton, pennons and banners floating on the sweet breeze, everything luminous and translucent; a coral citadel crowning a green hill top sewn with daisies, among groves and streams; a tapestry landscape filled with heraldic and fabulous animals and symmetrical, disproportionate blossom.

The ship tossed and tunnelled through the dark waters towards this radiant sanctuary.

"I wonder if anyone is doing anything about those dogs," said the genial passenger, arriving at his elbow. "I'll ask the purser tomorrow. We might exercise them a bit. Kind of mournful the way they go on."

Next day they were in the Atlantic. Ponderous waves rising over murky, opaque depths. Dappled with foam at the crests, like downland where on the high, exposed places, snow has survived the thaw. Lead-grey and slate in the sun, olive, field-blue and khaki like the uniforms of a battlefield; the sky overhead was neutral and steely with swollen clouds scudding across it, affording rare half hours of sunlight. The masts swung slowly across this sky and the bows heaved and wallowed below the horizon. The man who had made friends with Tony paraded the deck with the two beagles. They strained at the end of their chains, sniffing the scuppers; the man lurched behind them unsteadily. He wore a pair of race glasses with which he occasionally surveyed the seas; he offered them to Tony whenever they passed each other.

"Been talking to the wireless operator," he said. "We ought to pass quite near the *Yarmouth Castle* at about eleven."

Few of the passengers were on their feet. Those who had come on deck lay in long chairs on the sheltered side, pensive, wrapped in tartan rugs. Dr. Messinger kept to his cabin. Tony went to see him and found him torpid, for he was taking large doses of chloral. Towards evening the wind freshened and by dinner time was blowing hard; portholes were screwed up and all destructible objects disposed on the cabin floors; a sudden roll broke a dozen coffee cups in the music and reading room. That night there was little sleep for anyone on board; the plating creaked, luggage shifted from wall to wall. Tony wedged himself firm in his bunk with the lifebelt and thought of the City.

. . . Carpet and canopy, tapestry and velvet, portcullis and bastion, water fowl on the moat and kingcups along its margin, peacocks trailing their finery across the lawns; high overhead in a sky of sapphire and swansdown silver bells chiming in a turret of alabaster.

Days of shadow and exhaustion, salt wind and wet mist, foghorn and the constant groan and creak of straining metal. Then they were clear of it, after the Azores. Awnings were out and passengers moved their chairs to windward. High noon and an even keel; the blue water lapping against the sides of the ship, rippling away be-

hind her to the horizon; gramophones and deck tennis;
bright arcs of flying fish ("Look, Ernie, come quick, there's
a shark." "That's not a shark, it's a dolphin." "Mr. Brink
said it was a porpoise." "There he is again. Oh if I had
my camera."), clear, tranquil water and the regular turn
and tread of the screw; there were many hands to caress
the beagles as they went loping by. Mr. Brink amid laughter suggested that he should exercise the race-horse, or,
with a further burst of invention, the bull. Mr. Brink sat
at the purser's table with the cheery crowd.

Dr. Messinger left his cabin and appeared on deck
and in the dining saloon. So did the wife of the archdeacon; she was very much whiter than her husband. On
Tony's other side at table sat a girl named Thérèse de
Vitré. He had noticed her once or twice during the grey
days, a forlorn figure almost lost among furs and cushions
and rugs; a colourless little face with wide dark eyes. She
said, "The last days have been terrible. I saw you walking
about. How I envied you."

"It ought to be calm all the way now," and inevitably,
"are you going far?"

"Trinidad. That is my home . . . I tried to decide who
you were from the passenger list."

"Who was I?"

"Well . . . someone called Colonel Strapper."

"Do I look so old?"

"Are colonels old? I didn't know. It's not a thing we
have much in Trinidad. Now I know who you are because
I asked the head steward. Do tell me about your explor-
ing."

"You'd better ask Doctor Messinger. He knows more
about it than I do."

"No, *you* tell me."

She was eighteen years old; small and dark, with a face
that disappeared in a soft pointed chin so that attention
was drawn to the large, grave eyes and the high forehead;
she had not long outgrown her schoolgirl plumpness and
she moved with an air of exultance, as though she had

lately shed an encumbrance and was not yet fatigued by the other burdens that would succeed it. For two years she had been at school in Paris.

". . . Some of us used to keep lipstick and rouge secretly in our bedrooms and try it on at night. One girl called Antoinette came to Mass on Sunday wearing it. There was a terrible row with Madame de Supplice and she left after that term. It was awfully brave. We all envied her . . . But she was an ugly girl, always eating chocolates . . .

". . . Now I am coming home to be married . . . No, I am not yet affiancée but you see there are so few young men I can marry. They must be Catholic and of an island family. It would not do to marry an official and go back to live in England. But it will be easy because I have no brothers or sisters and my father has one of the best houses in Trinidad. You must come and see it. It is a stone house, outside the town. My family came to Trinidad in the French Revolution. There are two or three other rich families and I shall marry one of them. Our son will have the house. It will be easy . . ."

She wore a little coat, of the kind that were then fashionable, and no ornament except a string of pearls. ". . . There was an American girl at Madame de Supplice who was engaged. She had a ring with a big diamond but she could never wear it except in bed. Then one day she had a letter from her young man saying he was going to marry another girl. How she cried. We all read the letter and most of us cried too . . . But in Trinidad it will be quite easy."

Tony told her about the expedition; of the Peruvian emigrants in the middle age and their long caravan working through the mountains and forests, llamas packed with works of intricate craftsmanship; of the continual rumours percolating to the coast and luring adventurers up into the forests; of the route they would take up the rivers, then cutting through the bush along Indian trails and across untravelled country; of the stream they might strike higher up and how, Dr. Messinger said, they would make woodskin canoes and take to the water again; how

finally they would arrive under the walls of the city like
the Vikings at Byzantium. "But of course," he added,
"there may be nothing in it. It ought to be an interesting
journey in any case."

"How I wish I was a man," said Thérèse de Vitré.

After dinner they danced to the music of an amplified
gramophone and the girl drank lemon squash on the
bench outside the deck bar, sucking it through two straws.

A week of blue water that grew clearer and more tranquil daily, of sun that grew warmer, radiating the ship and
her passengers, filling them with good humour and ease;
blue water that caught the sun in a thousand brilliant
points, dazzling the eyes as they searched for porpoises
and flying fish; clear blue water in the shallows revealing
its bed of silver sand and smooth pebble, fathoms down;
soft warm shade on deck under the awnings; the ship
moved amid unbroken horizons on a vast blue disc of blue,
sparkling with sunlight.

Tony and Miss de Vitré played quoits and shuffleboard;
they threw rope rings into a bucket from a short distance.
("We'll go in a small boat," Dr. Messinger had said, "so
as to escape all that hideous nonsense of deck games.")
Twice consecutively Tony won the sweepstake on the
ship's run; the prize was eighteen shillings. He bought
Miss de Vitré a woollen rabbit at the barber's shop.

It was unusual for Tony to use 'Miss' in talking to anyone. Except Miss Tendril he could think of no one he
addressed in that way. But it was Thérèse who first called
him 'Tony,' seeing it engraved in Brenda's handwriting
in his cigarette case. "How funny," she said, "that was
the name of the man who didn't marry the American girl
at Madame de Supplice's"; and after that they used each
other's Christian names to the great satisfaction of the
other passengers who had little to interest them on board
except the flowering of this romance.

"I can't believe this is the same ship as in those cold,
rough days," said Thérèse.

They reached the first of the islands; a green belt of

palm trees with wooded hills rising beyond them and a small town heaped up along the shores of a bay. Thérèse and Tony went ashore and bathed. Thérèse swam badly with her head ridiculously erect out of the water. There was practically no bathing in Trinidad, she explained. They lay for some time on the firm, silver beach; then drove back into the town in the shaky, two-horse carriage he had hired, past ramshackle cabins from which little black boys ran out to beg or swing behind on the axle, in the white dust. There was nowhere in the town to dine so they returned to the ship at sundown. She lay out at some distance but from where they stood after dinner, leaning over the rail, they could just hear in the intervals when the winch was not working, the chatter and singing in the streets. Thérèse put her arm through Tony's, but the decks were full of passengers and agents and swarthy little men with lists of cargo. There was no dancing that night. They went above on to the boat deck and Tony kissed her.

Dr. Messinger came on board by the last launch. He had met an acquaintance in the town. He had observed the growing friendship between Tony and Thérèse with the strongest disapproval and told him of a friend of his who had been knifed in a back street of Smyrna, as a warning of what happened if one got mixed up with women.

In the islands the life of the ship disintegrated. There were changes of passengers; the black archdeacon left after shaking hands with everyone on board; on their last morning his wife took round a collecting box in aid of an organ that needed repairs. The captain never appeared at meals in the dining saloon. Even Tony's first friend no longer changed for dinner; the cabins were stuffy from being kept locked all day.

Tony and Thérèse bathed again at Barbados and drove round the island visiting castellated churches. They dined at an hotel high up out of town and ate flying fish.

"You must come to my home and see what real creole cooking is like," said Thérèse. "We have a lot of old recipes that the planters used to use. You must meet my father and mother."

They could see the lights of the ship from the terrace where they were dining; the bright decks with figures moving about and the double line of portholes.

"Trinidad the day after tomorrow," said Tony.

They talked of the expedition and she said it was sure to be dangerous. "I don't like Doctor Messinger at all," she said. "Not anything about him."

"And you will have to choose your husband."

"Yes. There are seven of them. There was one called Honoré I liked but of course I haven't seen him for two years. He was studying to be an engineer. There's one called Mendoza who's very rich but he isn't really a Trinidadian. His grandfather came from Dominica and they say he has coloured blood. I expect it will be Honoré. Mother always brought in his name when she wrote to me and he sent me things at Christmas and on my fête. Rather silly things because the shops aren't good in Port of Spain."

Later she said, "You'll be coming back by Trinidad, won't you? So I shall see you then. Will you be a long time in the bush?"

"I expect you'll be married by then."

"Tony, why haven't you ever got married?"

"But I am."

"Married?"

"Yes."

"You're teasing me."

"No, honestly I am. At least I was."

"Oh."

"Are you surprised?"

"I don't know. Somehow I didn't think you were. Where is she?"

"In England. We had a row."

"Oh . . . What's the time?"

"Quite early."

"Let's go back."

"D'you want to?"

"Yes, please. It's been a delightful day."

"You said that as if you were saying goodbye."

"Did I? I don't know."

The Negro chauffeur drove them at great speed into the town. Then they sat in a rowing boat and bobbed slowly out to the ship. Earlier in the day in good spirts they had bought a stuffed fish. Thérèse found she had left it behind at the hotel. "It doesn't matter," she said.

Blue water came to an end after Barbados. Round Trinidad the sea was opaque and colourless, full of the mud which the Orinoco brought down from the mainland. Thérèse spent all that day in her cabin, doing her packing.

Next day she said goodbye to Tony in a hurry. Her father had come out to meet her in the tender. He was a wiry bronzed man with a long grey moustache. He wore a panama hat and smart silk clothes, and smoked a cheroot; the complete slave-owner of the last century. Thérèse did not introduce him to Tony. "He was someone on the ship," she explained, obviously.

Tony saw her once next day in the town, driving with a lady who was obviously her mother. She waved but did not stop. "Reserved lot, these real old creoles," remarked the passenger who had first made friends with Tony and had now attached himself again. "Poor as church mice most of them but stinking proud. Time and again I've palled up with them on board and when we got to port it's been goodbye. Do they ever so much as ask you to their houses? Not they."

Tony spent the two days with this first friend who had business connections in the place. On the second day it rained heavily and they could not leave the terrace of the hotel. Dr. Messinger was engaged on some technical enquiries at the Agricultural Institute.

Muddy sea between Trinidad and Georgetown; and the ship lightened of cargo rolled heavily in the swell. Dr. Messinger took to his cabin once more. Rain fell contin-

uously and a slight mist enclosed them so that they
seemed to move in a small puddle of brown water; the
foghorn sounded regularly through the rain. Scarcely a
dozen passengers remained on board and Tony prowled
disconsolately about the deserted decks or sat alone in
the music room, his mind straying back along the path
he had forbidden it, to the tall elm avenue at Hetton and
the budding copses.

Next day they arrived at the mouth of the Demarara.
The customs sheds were heavy with the reek of sugar and
loud with the buzzing of bees. There were lengthy formali-
ties in getting their stores ashore. Dr. Messinger saw to it
while Tony lit a cigar and strayed out on to the quay.
Small shipping of all kinds lay round them; on the further bank a low, green fringe of mangrove; behind, the
tin roofs of the town were visible among feathery palm
trees; everything steamed from the recent rain. Black
stevedores grunted rhythmically at their work; East Indians trotted to and fro busily with invoices and bills of
lading. Presently Dr. Messinger pronounced that everything was in order and that they could go into the town
to their hotel.

Two

The storm lantern stood on the ground between the two
hammocks, which in their white sheaths of mosquito net,
looked like the cocoons of gigantic silkworms. It was eight
o'clock, two hours after sundown; river and forest were
already deep in night. The howler monkeys were silent but
tree frogs near at hand set up a continuous, hoarse chorus;
birds were awake, calling and whistling, and far in the
depths about them came the occasional rending and re-
verberation of dead wood falling among the trees.

The six black boys who manned the boat squatted at a
distance round their fire. They had collected some cobs of
maize, three days back in a part of the bush, deserted now,
choked and overrun with wild growth, that had once been
a farm. (The gross second growth at that place had been

full of alien plants, fruit and cereals, all rank now, and reverting to earlier type.) The boys were roasting their cobs in the embers.

Fire and storm lantern together shed little light; enough only to suggest the dilapidated roof about their heads, the heap of stores, disembarked and overrun by ants and, beyond, the undergrowth that had invaded the clearing and the vast columns of treetrunk that rose beyond it, disappearing out of sight in the darkness.

Bats like blighted fruit hung in clusters from the thatch and great spiders rode across it astride their shadows. This place had once been a ballata station. It was the furthest point of commercial penetration from the coast. Dr. Messinger marked it on his map with a triangle and named it in red 'First Base Camp.'

The first stage of the journey was over. For ten days they had been chugging up-stream in a broad, shallow boat. Once or twice they had passed rapids (there the outboard engine had been reinforced by paddles; the men strained in time to the captain's count; the bosun stood in the bows with a long pole warding them off the rocks). They had camped at sundown on patches of sand bank or in clearings cut from the surrounding bush. Once or twice they came to a 'house' left behind by ballata bleeders or gold washers.

All day Tony and Dr. Messinger sprawled amidships among their stores, under an improvised canopy of palm thatch; sometimes in the hot hours of the early afternoon they fell asleep. They ate in the boat, out of tins, and drank rum mixed with the water of the river which was mahogany brown but quite clear. The nights seemed interminable to Tony; twelve hours of darkness, noisier than a city square with the squealing and croaking and trumpeting of the bush denizens. Dr. Messinger could tell the hours by the succession of sounds. It was not possible to read by the light of the storm lantern. Sleep was irregular and brief after the days of lassitude and torpor. There was little to talk about; everything had been said during the day, in the warm shade among the stores. Tony lay awake, scratching.

Since they had left Georgetown there had not been any part of his body that was ever wholly at ease. His face and neck were burned by the sun reflected from the water; the skin was flaking off them so that he was unable to shave. The stiff growth of beard pricked him between chin and throat. Every exposed part of his skin was also bitten by cabouri fly. They had found a way into the button-holes of his shirt and the laces of his breeches; mosquitoes had got him at the ankles when he changed into slacks for the evening. He had picked up bêtes rouges in the bush and they were crawling and burrowing under his skin; the bitter oil which Dr. Messinger had given him as protection, had set up a rash of its own wherever he had applied it. Every evening after washing he had burned off a few ticks with a cigarette end but they had left irritable little scars behind them; so had the djiggas which one of the black boys had dug out from under his toe nails and the horny skin on his heels and the balls of his feet. A marabunta had left a painful swelling on his left hand.

As Tony scratched he shook the framework from which the hammocks hung. Dr. Messinger turned over and said, "Oh, for God's sake." He tried not to scratch; then he tried to scratch quietly; then in a frenzy he scratched as hard as he could, breaking the skin in a dozen places. "Oh, for God's sake," said Dr. Messinger.

'Half past eight,' thought Tony. 'In London they are just beginning to collect for dinner.' It was the time of year in London when there were parties every night. (Once, when he was trying to get engaged to Brenda, he had gone to them all. If they had dined in different houses, he would search the crowd for Brenda and hang about by the stairs waiting for her to arrive. Later he would hang about to take her home. Lady St. Cloud had done everything to make it easy for him. Later, after they were married, in the two years they had spent in London before Tony's father died, they had been to fewer parties, one or two a week at the most, except for a very gay month just when Brenda was well again, after John Andrew's birth.) Tony began to imagine a dinner party assembling at that moment in London, with Brenda there and the surprised look with which she greeted each new arrival. If there was a fire she would be as near it as she could get. Would there be a fire at the end of May? He could not remember. There were nearly always fires at Hetton in the evening, whatever the season.

Then after another bout of scratching it occurred to Tony that it was not half past eight in England. There was five hours difference in time. They had altered their watches daily on the voyage out. Which way? It ought to be easy to work out. The sun rose in the east. England was east of America so they got the sun later. It came to them at second hand and slightly soiled after Polly Cockpurse and Mrs. Beaver and Princess Abdul Akbar had finished with it . . . Like Polly's dresses which Brenda used to buy for ten or fifteen pounds each . . . he fell asleep.

He woke an hour later to hear Dr. Messinger cursing and to see him sitting astride his hammock working with bandages, iodine and his great toe.

"A vampire bat got it. I must have gone to sleep with my foot against the netting. God knows how long he had been at it, before I woke up. That lamp ought to keep them off but it doesn't seem to."

The black boys were still awake, munching over the fire. "Vampires plenty bad this side, chief," they said. "Dat why for us no leave de fire."

"It's just the way to get sick, blast it," said Dr. Messinger. "I may have lost pints of blood."

Brenda and Jock were dancing together at Anchorage House. It was late, the party was thinning, and now for the first time that evening, it was possible to dance with pleasure. The ballroom was hung with tapestry and lit by candles. Lady Anchorage had lately curtsied her farewell to the last royalty.

"How I hate staying up late," Brenda said, "but it seems

a shame to take my Mr. Beaver away. He's so thrilled to be here, bless him, and it was a great effort to get him asked . . . Come to think of it," she added later, "I suppose that this is the last year *I* shall be able to go to this kind of party."

"You're going through with it?"

"I don't know, Jock. It doesn't really depend on me. It's all a matter of holding down Mr. Beaver. He's getting very restive. I have to feed him a bit of high life every week or so, and I suppose that'll all stop if there's a divorce. Any news of Tony?"

"Not for some time now. I got a cable when he landed. He's gone off on some expedition with a crook doctor."

"Is it *absolutely* safe?"

"Oh, I imagine so. The whole world is civilized now isn't it—charabancs and Cook's offices everywhere."

"Yes, I suppose it is . . . I hope he's not *brooding*. I shouldn't like to think of him being unhappy."

"I expect he's getting used to things."

"I do hope so. I'm very fond of Tony, you know, in spite of the monstrous way he behaved."

There was an Indian village a mile or two distant from the camp. It was here that Tony and Dr. Messinger proposed to recruit porters for the two hundred mile march that lay between them and the Pie-wie country. The niggers were river men and could not be taken into Indian territory. They would go back with the boat.

At dawn Tony and Dr. Messinger drank a mug each of hot cocoa and ate some biscuits and what was left over from the bully beef opened the night before. Then they set out for the village. One of the blacks went in front with cutlass to clear the trail. Dr. Messinger and Tony followed one behind the other; another black came behind them carrying samples of trade goods—a twenty dollar Belgian gun, some rolls of printed cotton, hand-mirrors in coloured celluloid frames, some bottles of highly scented pomade.

It was a rough, unfrequented trail, encumbered by

numerous fallen trunks; they waded knee-deep through two streams that ran to feed the big river; underfoot there was sometimes a hard network of bare root, sometimes damp and slippery leaf mould.

Presently they reached the village. They came into sight of it quite suddenly, emerging from the bush into a wide clearing. There were eight or nine circular huts of mud and palm thatch. No one was visible but two or three columns of smoke, rising straight and thin into the morning air, told them that the place was inhabited.

"Dey people all afeared," said the black boy.

"Go and find someone to speak to us," said Dr. Messinger.

The nigger went to the low door of the nearest house and peered in.

"Dere ain't no one but women dere," he reported. "Dey dressing deirselves. Come on out dere," he shouted into the gloom. "De chief want talk to you."

At last, very shyly, a little old woman emerged, clad in the filthy calico gown that was kept for use in the presence of strangers. She waddled towards them on bandy legs. Her ankles were tightly bound with blue beads. Her hair was lank and ragged; her eyes were fixed on the earthenware bowl of liquid which she carried. When she was a few feet from Tony and Dr. Messinger she set the bowl on the ground, and still with downcast eyes, shook hands with them. Then she stooped, picked up the bowl once more and held it to Dr. Messinger.

"Cassiri," he explained, "the local drink made of fermented cassava."

He drank some and handed the bowl to Tony. It contained a thick, purplish liquid. When Tony had drunk a little, Dr. Messinger explained, "It is made in an interesting way. The women chew the root up and spit it into a hollow tree-trunk."

He then addressed the woman in Wapishiana. She looked at him for the first time. Her brown, Mongol face was perfectly blank, devoid alike of comprehension and curiosity. Dr. Messinger repeated and amplified his question. The woman took the bowl from Tony and set it on the ground.

Meanwhile other faces were appearing at the doors of the huts. Only one woman ventured out. She was very stout and she smiled confidently at the visitors.

"Good morning," she said. "How do you do? I am Rosa. I speak English good. I live bottom-side two years with Mr. Forbes. You give me cigarette."

"Why doesn't this woman answer?"

"She no speak English."

"But I was speaking Wapishiana."

"She Macushi woman. All these people Macushi people."

"Oh. I didn't know. Where are the men?"

"Men all go hunting three days."

"When will they be back?"

"They go after bush pig."

"When will they be back?"

"No, bush pig. Plenty bush pig. Men all go hunting. You give me cigarette."

"Listen, Rosa, I want to go to the Pie-wie country."

"No, this Macushi. All the people Macushi."

"But we want to go Pie-wie."

"No, *all* Macushi. You give me cigarette."

"It's hopeless," said Dr. Messinger. "We shall have to wait till the men come back." He took a packet of cigarettes from his pocket. "Look," he said, "cigarettes."

"Give me."

"When men come back from hunting you come to river and tell me. Understand?"

"No, men hunting bush pig. You give me cigarettes."

Dr. Messinger gave her the cigarettes.

"What else you got?" she said.

Dr. Messinger pointed to the load which the second nigger had laid on the ground.

"Give me," she said.

"When men come back, I give you plenty things if men come with me to Pie-wies."

"No, *all* Macushi here."

"We aren't doing any good," said Dr. Messinger. "We'd better go back to camp and wait. The men have been away three days. It's not likely they will be much longer . . . I wish I could speak Macushi."

They turned about, the four of them, and left the village. It was ten o'clock by Tony's wrist watch when they reached their camp.

Ten o'clock on the river Waurupang was question time at Westminster. For a long time now Jock had had a question which his constituents wanted him to ask. It came up that afternoon.

"I should like to ask the Minister of Agriculture whether in view of the dumping in this country of Japanese pork pies, the right honourable member is prepared to consider a modification of the eight and a half score basic pig from two and a half inches of thickness round the belly as originally specified, to two inches."

Replying for the Minister, the under-secretary said: "The matter is receiving the closest attention. As the honourable member is no doubt aware the question of the importation of pork pies is a matter for the Board of Trade, not for the Board of Agriculture. With regard to the specifications of the basic pig, I must remind the honourable member that, as he is doubtless aware, the eight and a half score pig is modelled on the requirements of the bacon curers and has no direct relation to pig meat for sale in pies. That is being dealt with by a separate committee who have not yet made their report."

"Would the honourable member consider an increase of the specified maximum of fatness on the shoulders?"

"I must have notice of that question."

Jock left the House that afternoon with the comfortable feeling that he had at last done something tangible in the interest of his constituents.

Two days later the Indians returned from hunting. It was tedious waiting. Dr. Messinger put in some hours daily in checking the stores. Tony went into the bush with his gun but the game had all migrated from that part of the river bank. One of the black boys was badly injured in the foot and calf by a sting-ray; after that they stopped bathing and washed in a zinc pail. When the news of the Indians' return reached camp, Tony and Dr. Messinger went to the village to see them but a feast had already started and everyone in the place was drunk. The men lay in their hammocks and the women trotted between them carrying calabashes of cassiri. Everything reeked of roast pork.

"It will take them a week to get sober," said Dr. Messinger.

All that week the black boys lounged in camp; sometimes they washed their clothes and hung them out on the bulwarks of the boat to dry in the sun; sometimes they went fishing and came back with a massive catch, speared on a stick (the flesh was tasteless and rubbery); usually in the evenings they sang songs round the fire. The fellow who had been stung kept to his hammock, groaning loudly and constantly asking for medicine.

On the sixth day the Indians began to appear. They shook hands all round and then retired to the margin of the bush where they stood gazing at the camp equipment. Tony tried to photograph them but they ran away giggling like schoolgirls. Dr. Messinger spread out on the ground the goods he had brought for barter.

They retired at sundown but on the seventh day they came again, greatly reinforced. The entire population of the village was there. Rosa sat down on Tony's hammock under the thatch roof.

"Give me cigarettes," she said.

"You tell them I want men to go Pie-wie country," said Dr. Messinger.

"Pie-wie bad people. Macushi people no go with Pie-wie people."

"You say I want the men. I give them guns."

"You give me cigarettes . . ."

Negotiations lasted for two days. Eventually twelve men agreed to come; seven of them insisted on bringing their wives with them. One of these was Rosa. When everything was arranged there was a party in the village and all the Indians got drunk again. This time, however, it was a shortér business as the women had not had time to prepare much cassiri. In three days the caravan was able to set out.

One of the men had a long, single-barrelled, muzzle-loading gun; several others carried bows and arrows; they were naked except for red cotton cloths round their loins. The women wore grubby calico dresses—they had been issued to them years back by an itinerant preacher and kept for occasions of this kind; they had wicker panniers on their shoulders, supported by a band across the forehead. All the heaviest luggage was carried by the women in these panniers, including the rations for themselves and their men. Rosa had, in addition, an umbrella with a dented, silver crook, a relic of her association with Mr. Forbes.

The Negroes returned down-stream to the coast. A dump of provisions, in substantial tin casing, was left in the ruinous shelter by the bank.

"There's no one to touch it. We can send back for it in case of emergency from the Pie-wie country," said Dr. Messinger.

Tony and Dr. Messinger walked immediately behind the man with the gun who was acting as guide; behind them the file straggled out for half a mile or more through the forest.

"From now onwards the map is valueless to us," said Dr. Messinger with relish.

(Roll up the map—you will not need it again for how many years, said William Pitt . . . memories of Tony's private school came back to him at Dr. Messinger's words, of inky little desks and a coloured picture of a Viking raid, of Mr. Trotter who had taught him history and wore very vivid ties.)

Three

"Mumsey, Brenda wants a job."
"Why?"

"Just like everybody else, short of money and nothing to do. She wondered if she could be any use to you at the shop."

"Well . . . It's hard to say. At any other time she is exactly the kind of saleswoman I am always looking for . . . but I don't know. *As things are* I'm not sure it would be wise."

"I said I'd ask you, that's all."

"John, you never tell me *anything* and I don't like to seem interfering; but what *is* going to happen between you and Brenda."

"I don't know."

"You never tell me *anything*," repeated Mrs. Beaver. "And there are so many rumours going round. Is there going to be a divorce?"

"I don't know."

Mrs. Beaver sighed. "Well I must get back to work. Where are you lunching?"

"Brat's."

"Poor John. By the way, I thought you were joining Brown's."

"I haven't heard anything from them. I don't know whether they've had an election yet."

"Your father was a member."

"I've an idea I shan't get in . . . anyway I couldn't really afford it."

"I'm not happy about you, John. I'm not sure that things are working out as well as I hoped about Christmas time."

"There's my telephone. Perhaps it's Margot. She hasn't asked me to anything for weeks."

But it was only Brenda.

"I'm afraid mother's got nothing for you at the shop," he said.

"Oh well. I expect something will turn up. I could do with a little good luck just at the moment."

"So could I. Have you asked Allan about Brown's?"

"Yes, I did. He says they elected about ten chaps last week."

"Oh, does that mean I've been black balled?"

"I shouldn't know. Gentlemen are so odd about their clubs."

"I thought that you were going to make Allan and Reggie support me."

"I asked them. What does it matter anyway? D'you want to come to Veronica's for the week-end?"

"I'm not sure that I do."

"I'd like it."

"It's a beastly little house—and I don't think Veronica likes me. Who'll be there?"

"I shall be."

"Yes . . . well, I'll let you know."

"Am I seeing you this evening?"

"I'll let you know."

"Oh dear," said Brenda as she rang off. "Now he's taken against me. It isn't my fault he can't get in to Brown's. As a matter of fact I believe Reggie *did* try to help."

Jenny Abdul Akbar was in the room with her. She came across every morning now in her dressing gown and they read the newspaper together. The dressing gown was of striped Berber silk.

"Let's go and have a cosy lunch at the Ritz," she said.

"The Ritz isn't cosy at lunch time and it costs eight and six. I daren't cash a cheque for three weeks, Jenny. The lawyers are so disagreeable. I've never been like this before."

"What wouldn't I do to Tony? Leaving you stranded like this."

"Oh, what's the good of knocking Tony? I don't suppose he's having a packet of fun himself in Brazil or wherever it is."

"I hear they are putting in bathrooms at Hetton—while you are practically starving. And he hasn't even gone to Mrs. Beaver for them."

"Yes, I *do* think that was mean."

Presently Jenny went back to dress. Brenda telephoned to a delicatessen store round the corner for some sandwiches. She would spend that day in bed, as she spent two or three days a week at this time. Perhaps, if Allan was making a speech somewhere, as he usually was, Marjorie would have her to dinner. The Helm-Hubbards had a supper party that night but Beaver had not been asked. "If I went there without him it would be a major bust-up . . . Come to think of it, Marjorie's probably going. Well I can always have sandwiches for dinner here. They make all kinds. Thank God for the little shop round the corner." She was reading a biography of Thiers that had lately appeared; it was very long and would keep her going well into the night.

At one o'clock Jenny came in to say goodbye (she had a latch key of Brenda's) dressed for a cosy lunch. "I got Polly and Souki," she said. "We're going to Daisy's joint. I *wish* you were coming."

"Me? Oh, I'm all right," said Brenda and she thought, 'It might occur to her to sock a girl a meal once in a way.'

They walked for a fortnight, averaging about fifteen miles a day. Sometimes they would do much more and sometimes much less; the Indian who went in front decided the camping places; they depended on water and evil spirits.

Dr. Messinger made a compass traverse of their route. It gave him something to think about. He took readings every hour from an aneroid. In the evening, if they had halted early enough, he employed the last hours of daylight in elaborating a chart. *'Dry water course, three deserted huts, stony ground . . .'*

"We are now in the Amazon system of rivers," he announced with satisfaction one day. "You see, the water is running South." But almost immediately they crossed a stream flowing in the opposite direction. "Very curious," said Dr. Messinger. "A discovery of genuine scientific value."

Next day they waded through four streams at intervals of two miles, running alternately North and South. The chart began to have a mythical appearance.

"Is there a name for any of these streams," he asked Rosa.

"Macushi people called him Waurupang."

"No, not river where we first camped. *These rivers.*"

"Yes, Waurupang."

"This river here."

"Macushi people call him all Waurupang."

"It's hopeless," said Dr. Messinger.

"Don't you think that possibly we *have* struck the upper waters of the Waurupang?" suggested Tony, "and have crossed and recrossed the stream as it winds down the valley."

"It is a hypothesis," said Dr. Messinger.

When they were near water they forced their way through blind bush; the trail there was grown over and barred by timber; only Indian eyes and Indian memory could trace its course; sometimes they crossed little patches of dry savannah, dun grass growing in tufts from the baked earth; thousands of lizards scampered and darted before their feet and the grass rustled like newspaper; it was burning hot in these enclosed spaces. Sometimes they climbed up into the wind, over loose red pebbles that bruised their feet; after these painful ascents they would lie in the wind till their wet clothes grew cold against their bodies; from these low eminences they could see other hill tops and the belts of bush through which they had travelled, and the file of porters trailing behind them. As each man and woman arrived he sank on to the dry grass and rested against his load; when the last of them came up with the party Dr. Messinger would give the word and they would start off again, descending into the green heart of the forest before them.

Tony and Dr. Messinger seldom spoke to one another, either when they were marching or at the halts for they were constantly strained and exhausted. In the evenings after they had washed and changed into clean shirts and flannel trousers, they talked a little, mostly about the number of miles they had done that day, their probable position and the state of their feet. They drank rum and water after their bath; for supper there was usually bully beef stewed with rice and flour dumplings. The Indians ate farine, smoked hog and occasional delicacies picked up by the way—armadillo, iguana, fat white grubs from the palm trees. The women had some dried fish with them that lasted for eight days; the smell grew stronger every day until the stuff was eaten, then it still hung about them and the stores but grew fainter until it merged into the general indefinable smell of the camp.

There were no Indians living in this country. In the last five days of the march they suffered from lack of water. They had left the Waurupang behind and the streams they came to were mostly dry; they had to reconnoitre up and down their beds in search of tepid, stagnant puddles. But after two weeks they came to a river once more, flowing deep and swift to the Southeast. This was the border of the Pie-wie country and Dr. Messinger marked the place where they stopped, Second Base Camp. The cabouri fly infested this stream in clouds.

"John, I think it's time you had a holiday."

"A holiday what from, mumsey?"

"A change . . . I'm going to California in July. To the Fischbaums—Mrs. Arnold Fischbaum, not the one who lives in Paris. I think it would do you good to come with me."

"Yes, mumsey."

"You *would* like it, wouldn't you?"

"Me? Yes, I'd like it."

"You've picked up that way of talking from Brenda. It sounds ridiculous in a man."

"Sorry, mumsey."

"All right then, that's settled."

At sunset the cabouri fly disappeared. Until then, through the day, it was necessary to keep covered; they settled on any exposed flesh like house-flies upon jam; it was only when they were gorged that their bite was perceptible; they left behind a crimson, smarting circle with

a black dot at its centre. Tony and Dr. Messinger wore
cotton gloves which they had brought for the purpose,
and muslin veils, hanging down under their hats. Later
they employed two women to squat beside their hammocks
and fan them with leafy boughs; the slightest breeze was
enough to disperse the flies, but soon as Tony and Dr.
Messinger dozed the women would lay aside their work,
and they woke instantly, stung in a hundred places. The
Indians bore the insects as cows bear horse-flies; passively
with occasional fretful outbursts when they would slap
their shoulders and thighs.

After dark there was some relief for there were few mosquitoes at this camp but they could hear the vampire bats
all night long nuzzling and flapping against their netting.

The Indians would not go hunting in this forest. They
said there was no game, but Dr. Messinger said it was because they were afraid of the evil spirits of the Pie-wie
people. Provisions were not lasting as well as Dr. Messinger had calculated. During the march it had been difficult
to keep a proper guard over the stores. There was a bag of
farine, half a bag of sugar and a bag of rice short. Dr. Messinger instituted careful rationing; he served them himself, measuring everything strictly in an enamel cup; even
so the women managed to get to the sugar behind his back.
He and Tony had finished the rum except for one bottle
which was kept in case of emergency.

"We can't go on breaking into tinned stores," said Dr.
Messinger peevishly. "The men must go out and shoot
something."

But they received the orders with expressionless, downcast faces and remained in camp.

"No birds, no animals here," explained Rosa. "All gone.
May be they get some fish."

But the Indians could not be persuaded to exert themselves. They could see the sacks and bales of food heaped
on the bank; it would be plenty of time to start hunting
and fishing when that had been exhausted.

Meanwhile there were canoes to be built.

"This is clearly Amazon water," said Dr. Messinger. "It

probably flows into the Rio Branco or the Rio Negro. The Pie-wies live along the bank and the City must from all accounts be down-stream of us, up one of the tributaries. When we reach the first Pie-wie village we will be able to get guides."

The canoes were made of woodskin. Three days were spent in finding trees of suitable age and straightness and in felling them. They cut four trees and worked on them where they lay, clearing the brush for a few feet round them. They stripped the bark with their broad-bladed knives; that took another week. They worked patiently but clumsily; one woodskin was split in getting it off the trunk. There was nothing Tony and Dr. Messinger could do to help. They spent that week guarding the sugar from the women. As the men moved about the camp and the surrounding bush, their steps were soundless; their bare feet seemed never to disturb the fallen leaves, their bare shoulders made no rustle in the tangled undergrowth; their speech was brief and scarcely audible, they never joined in the chatter and laughing of their women; sometimes they gave little grunts as they worked; only once they were merry, when one of them let his knife slip as he was working on the tree-trunk and cut deeply into the ball of his thumb. Dr. Messinger dressed the wound with iodine, lint and bandages. After that the women constantly solicited him, showing him little scratches on their arms and legs and asking for iodine.

Two of the trees were finished on one day, then another next day (that was the one which split) and the fourth two days after that; it was a larger tree than the others. When the last fibre was severed four men got round the trunk and lifted the skin clear. It curled up again at once making a hollow cylinder, which the men carried down to the water-side and set afloat, fastening it to a tree with a loop of vine-rope.

When all the woodskins were ready it was an easy matter to make canoes of them. Four men held them open while two others fixed the struts. The ends were left open, and curled up slightly so as to lift them clear (when the craft was fully laden it drew only an inch or two of water). Then the men set about fashioning some single-bladed paddles; that, too, was an easy matter.

Every day Dr. Messinger asked Rosa, "When will the boats be ready? Ask the men," and she replied, "Just now."

"How many days—four?—five?—how many?"

"No, not many. Boats finish just now."

At last when it was clear that the work was nearly complete, Dr. Messinger busied himself with arrangements. He sorted out the stores, dividing the necessary freight into two groups; he and Tony were to sit in separate boats and each had with him a rifle and ammunition, a camera, tinned rations, trade goods and his own luggage. The third canoe which would be manned solely by Indians was to hold the flour and rice, sugar and farine, and the rations for the men. The canoes would not hold all the stores and an 'emergency dump' was made a little way up the bank.

"We shall take eight men with us. Four can stay behind with the women to guard the camp. Once we are among the Pie-wies everything will be easy. These Macushis can go home then. I don't think they will rob the stores. There is nothing here that would be much use to them."

"Hadn't we better keep Rosa with us to act as interpreter with the Macushis?"

"Yes, perhaps we had. I will tell her."

That evening everything was finished except the paddles. In the first exhilarating hour of darkness, when Tony and Dr. Messinger were able to discard the gloves and veils that had been irking them all day, they called Rosa across to the part of the camp where they ate and slept.

"Rosa, we have decided to take you down the river with us. We need you to help us talk to the men. Understand?"

Rosa said nothing; her face was perfectly blank, lit from below by the storm lantern that stood on a box between them; the shadow of her high cheek bones hid her eyes; lank, ragged hair, a tenuous straggle of tattooing along forehead and lip, rotund body in its filthy cotton gown, bandy brown legs.

"Understand?"

But still she said nothing; she seemed to be looking over their heads into the dark forest, but her eyes were lost in shadow.

"Listen, Rosa, all women and four men stay here in camp. Six men come in boats to Pie-wie village. You come with boats. When we reach Pie-wie village, you and eight men and boats go back to camp to other women and men. Then back to Macushi country. Understand?"

At last Rosa spoke. "Macushi people no go with Pie-wie people."

"I am not asking you to *go with* Pie-wie people. You and men take us as far as Pie-wies, then you go back to Macushi people. Understand?"

Rosa raised her arm in an embracing circle which covered the camp and the road they had travelled and the broad savannahs behind them. "Macushi peoples there," she said. Then she raised the other arm and waved it down-stream towards the hidden country. "Pie-wie peoples there," she said. "Macushi peoples no go with Pie-wie peoples."

"Now listen, Rosa. You are sensible woman. You lived two years with black gentleman, Mr. Forbes. You like cigarettes—"

"Yes, give me cigarettes."

"You come with men in boats, I give you plenty, plenty cigarettes."

Rosa looked stolidly ahead of her and said nothing.

"Listen. You will have your man and seven others to protect you. How can we talk with men without you?"

"Men no go," said Rosa.

"Of course the men will go. The only question is, will you come too?"

"Macushi peoples no go with Pie-wie peoples," said Rosa.

"Oh God," said Dr. Messinger wearily. "All right we'll talk about it in the morning."

"You give me cigarette . . ."

"It's going to be awkward if that woman doesn't come."

"It's going to be much more awkward if none of them come," said Tony.

Next day the boats were ready. By noon they were launched and tied in to the bank. The Indians went silently about the business of preparing their dinner. Tony and Dr. Messinger ate tongue, boiled rice and some tinned peaches.

"We're all right for stores," said Dr. Messinger. "There's enough for three weeks at the shortest and we are bound to come across the Pie-wies in a day or two. We will start tomorrow."

The Indians' wages, in rifles, fish-hooks and rolls of cotton, had been left behind for them at their village. There were still half a dozen boxes of 'trade' for use during the later stages of the journey. A leg of bushpig was worth a handful of shot or twenty gun caps in that currency; a fat game bird cost a necklace.

When dinner was over, at about one o'clock, Dr. Messinger called Rosa over to them. "We start tomorrow," he said.

"Yes, just now."

"Tell the men what I told you last night. Eight men to come in boats, others wait here. You come in boats. All these stores stay here. All these stores go in boats. You tell men that."

Rosa said nothing.

"Understand?"

"No peoples go in boats," she said. "All peoples go this way," and she extended her arm towards the trail that they had lately followed. "Tomorrow or next day all people go back to village."

There was a long pause; at last Dr. Messinger said, "You tell the men to come here . . . It's no use threatening them," he remarked to Tony when Rosa had waddled back to the fireside. "They are a queer, timid lot. If you threaten them they take fright and disappear leaving you stranded. Don't worry, I shall be able to persuade them."

They could see Rosa talking at the fireside but none of

the group moved. Presently, having delivered her message, she was silent and squatted down among them with the head of one of the women between her knees. She had been searching it for lice when Dr. Messinger's summons had interrupted her.

"We'd better go across and talk to them."

Some of the Indians were in hammocks. The others were squatting on their heels; they had scraped earth over the fire and extinguished it. They gazed at Tony and Dr. Messinger with slit, pig eyes. Only Rosa seemed incurious; her head was averted; all her attention went to her busy fingers as she picked and crunched the lice from her friend's hair.

"What's the matter?" asked Dr. Messinger. "I told you to bring the men here."

Rosa said nothing.

"So Macushi people are cowards. They are afraid of Pie-wie people."

"It's the cassava field," said Rosa. "We must go back to dig the cassava. Otherwise it will be bad."

"Listen. I want the men for one, two weeks. No more. After that, all finish. They can go home."

"It is the time to dig the cassava. Macushi people dig cassava before the big rains. All people go home just now."

"It's pure blackmail," said Dr. Messinger. "Let's get out some trade goods."

He and Tony together prised open one of the cases and began to spread out the contents on a blanket. They had chosen these things together at a cheap store in Oxford Street. The Indians watched the display in unbroken silence. There were bottles of scent and pills, bright celluloid combs set with glass jewels, mirrors, pocket knives with embossed aluminum handles, ribbons and necklaces and barter of more solid worth in the form of axe-heads, brass cartridge cases and flat, red flasks of gunpowder.

"You give me this," said Rosa picking out a pale blue rosette, that had been made as a boat-race favour. "Give me this," she repeated, rubbing some drops of scent into the palm of her hands and inhaling deeply.

"Each man can choose three things from this box if he comes in the boats."

But Rosa replied monotonously, "Macushi people dig cassava field just now."

"It's no good," said Dr. Messinger after half an hour's fruitless negotiation. "We shall have to try with the mice. I wanted to keep them till we reached the Pie-wies. It's a pity. But they'll fall for the mice, you see. I *know* the Indian mind."

These mice were comparatively expensive articles; they had cost three and sixpence each, and Tony remembered vividly the embarrassment with which he had witnessed their demonstration on the floor of the toy department.

They were of German manufacture; the size of large rats but conspicuously painted in spots of green and white; they had large glass eyes, stiff whiskers and green and white ringed tails; they ran on hidden wheels, and inside them were little bells that jingled as they moved. Dr. Messinger took one out of their box, unwrapped the tissue paper and held it up to general scrutiny. There was no doubt that he had captured his audience's interest. Then he wound it up. The Indians stirred apprehensively at the sound.

The ground where they were camping was hard mud, inundated at flood time. Dr. Messinger put the toy down at his feet and set it going; tinkling merrily it ran towards the group of Indians. For a moment Tony was afraid that it would turn over, or become stuck against a root but the mechanism was unimpaired and by good chance there was a clear course. The effect exceeded anything that he had expected. There was a loud intake of breath, a series of horrified, small grunts, a high wail of terror from the women, and a sudden stampede; a faint patter of bare brown feet among the fallen leaves, bare limbs, quiet as bats, pushed through the undergrowth, ragged cotton gowns caught and tore in the thorn bushes. Before the toy had run down, before it had jingled its way to the place where the nearest Indian had been squatting, the camp was empty.

"Well I'm damned," said Dr. Messinger, "that's better than I expected."

"More than you expected anyway."

"Oh it's all right. They'll come back. I know them."

But by sundown there was still no sign. Throughout the hot afternoon Tony and Dr. Messinger, shrouded from cabouri fly, sprawled in their hammocks. The empty canoes lay in the river; the mechanical mouse had been put away. At sundown Dr. Messinger said, "We'd better make a fire. They'll come back when it is dark."

They brushed the earth away from the old embers, brought new wood and made a fire; they lit the storm lantern.

"We'd better get some supper," said Tony.

They boiled water and made some cocoa, opened a tin of salmon and finished the peaches that were left over from midday. They lit their pipes and drew the sheaths of mosquito netting across their hammocks. Most of this time they were silent. Presently they decided to go to sleep.

"We shall find them all here in the morning," said Dr. Messinger. "They're an odd bunch."

All round them the voices of the bush whistled and croaked, changing with the hours as the night wore on to morning.

Dawn broke in London, clear and sweet, dove-grey and honey, with promise of good weather; the lamps in the streets paled and disappeared; the empty streets ran with water, and the rising sun caught it as it bubbled round the hydrants; the men in overalls swung the nozzles of their hoses from side to side and the water jetted and cascaded in a sparkle of light.

"Let's have the window open," said Brenda. "It's stuffy in here."

The waiter drew back the curtains, opened the windows.

"It's quite light," she added.

"After five. Oughtn't we to go to bed."

"Yes."

"Only another week and then all the parties will be over," said Beaver.

"Yes."

"Well let's go."

"All right. Can you pay? I just haven't any money."

They had come on after the party, for breakfast at a club Daisy had opened. Beaver paid for the kippers and tea. "Eight shillings," he said. "How does Daisy expect to make a success of the place when she charges prices like that?"

"It does seem a lot . . . So you really *are* going to America?"

"I must. Mother has taken the tickets."

"Nothing I've said tonight makes any difference?"

"Darling, don't go on. We've been through all that. You know it's the only thing that *can* happen. Why spoil the last week?"

"You *have* enjoyed the summer, haven't you."

"Of course . . . well, shall we go?"

"Yes. You needn't bother to see me home."

"Sure you don't mind? It *is* miles out of the way and it's late."

"There's no knowing what I mind."

"Brenda, darling, for heaven's sake . . . It isn't like you to go on like this."

"I never was one for making myself expensive."

The Indians returned during the night, while Tony and Dr. Messinger were asleep; without a word spoken the little people crept out of hiding; the women had removed their clothes and left them at a distance so that no twig should betray their movements; their naked bodies moved soundlessly through the undergrowth; the glowing embers of the fire and the storm lantern twenty yards away were their only light; there was no moon. They collected their wicker baskets and their rations of farine, their bows and arrows, the gun and their broad-bladed knives; they rolled up their hammocks into compact cylinders. They took nothing with them that was not theirs. Then they crept back through the shadows, into the darkness.

When Tony and Dr. Messinger awoke it was clear to them what had happened.

"The situation is grave," said Dr. Messinger. "But not desperate."

Four

For four days Tony and Dr. Messinger paddled downstream. They sat, balancing themselves precariously, at the two ends of the canoe; between them they had piled the most essential of their stores; the remainder, with the other canoes, had been left at the camp, to be called for when they had recruited help from the Pie-wies. Even the minimum which Dr. Messinger had selected overweighted the craft so that it was dangerously low; and movement brought the water to the lip of the gunwale and threatened disaster; it was heavy to steer and they made slow progress, contenting themselves for the most part, with keeping end on, and drifting with the current.

Twice they came to the stretches of cataract, and here they drew in to the bank, unloaded, and waded beside the boat, sometimes plunging waist deep, sometimes clambering over the rocks, guiding it by hand until they reached clear water again. Then they tied up to the bank and carried their cargo down to it through the bush. For the rest of the way the river was broad and smooth; a dark surface which reflected in fine detail the walls of forest on either side, towering up from the undergrowth to their flowering crown a hundred or more feet above them. Sometimes they came to a stretch of water scattered with fallen petals and floated among them, moving scarcely less slowly than they, as though resting in a blossoming meadow. At night they spread their tarpaulin on stretches of dry beach, and hung their hammocks in the bush. Only the cabouri fly and rare, immobile alligators menaced the peace of their days.

They kept a constant scrutiny of the banks but saw no sign of human life.

Then Tony developed fever. It came on him quite suddenly, during the fourth afternoon. At their midday halt he was in complete health and had shot a small deer that came down to drink on the opposite bank; an hour later he was shivering so violently that he had to lay down his paddle; his head was flaming with heat, his body and limbs frigid; by sunset he was slightly delirious.

Dr. Messinger took his temperature and found that it was a hundred and four degrees, Fahrenheit. He gave him twenty-five grains of quinine and lit a fire so close to his hammock that by morning it was singed and blacked with smoke. He told Tony to keep wrapped up in his blanket, but at intervals throughout that night he woke from sleep to find himself running with sweat; he was consumed with thirst and drank mug after mug of river water. Neither that evening nor next morning was he able to eat anything.

But next morning his temperature was down again. He felt weak and exhausted but he was able to keep steady in his place and paddle a little.

"It was just a passing attack, wasn't it?" he said. "I shall be perfectly fit tomorrow, shan't I?"

"I hope so," said Dr. Messinger.

At midday Tony drank some cocoa and ate a cupful of rice. "I feel grand," he said.

"Good."

That night the fever came on again. They were camping on a sand bank. Dr. Messinger heated stones and put them under Tony's feet and in the small of his back. He was awake most of the night fuelling the fire and refilling Tony's mug with water. At dawn Tony slept for an hour and woke feeling slightly better; he was taking frequent doses of quinine and his ears were filled with a muffled sound as though he were holding those shells to them in which, he had been told in childhood, one could hear the beat of the sea.

"We've got to go on," said Dr. Messinger. "We can't be far from a village now."

"I feel awful. Wouldn't it be better to wait a day till I am perfectly fit again."

"It's no good waiting. We've got to get on. D'you think you can manage to get into the canoe?"

Dr. Messinger knew that Tony was in for a long bout.

For the first few hours of that day Tony lay limp in the bows. They had shifted the stores so that he could lie full length. Then the fever came on again and his teeth chattered. He sat up and crouched with his head in his knees, shaking all over; only his forehead and cheeks were burning hot under the noon sun. There was still no sign of a village.

It was late in the afternoon when he first saw Brenda. For some time he had been staring intently at the odd shape amidships where the stores had been piled; then he realized that it was a human being.

"So the Indians came back?" he said.

"Yes."

"I knew they would. Silly of them to be scared by a toy. I suppose the others are following."

"Yes, I expect so. Try and sit still."

"Damned fool, being frightened of a toy," Tony said derisively to the woman amidships. Then he saw that it was Brenda. "I'm sorry," he said. "I didn't see it was you. *You* wouldn't be frightened of a toy."

But she did not answer him. She sat as she used often to sit when she came back from London, huddled over her bowl of bread and milk.

Dr. Messinger steered the boat in to the side. They nearly capsized as he helped Tony out. Brenda got ashore without assistance. She stepped out in her delicate, competent way, keeping the balance of the boat.

"That's what poise means," said Tony. "D'you know I once saw a questionnaire that people had to fill in when they applied for a job in an American firm, and one of the things they had to answer was 'Have you poise?'"

Brenda was at the top of the bank waiting for him. "What was so absurd about the question was that they had only the applicant's word for it," he explained laboriously. "I mean—is it a sign of poise to think you have it."

"Just sit quiet here while I sling your hammock."

"Yes, I'll sit here with Brenda. I am so glad she could come. She must have caught the three-eighteen."

She was with him all that night and all the next day. He talked to her ceaselessly but her replies were rare and enigmatic. On the succeeding evening he had another fit of sweating. Dr. Messinger kept a large fire burning by the hammock and wrapped Tony in his own blanket. An hour before dawn Tony fell asleep and when he awoke Brenda had gone.

"You're down to normal again."

"Thank God. I've been pretty ill, haven't I? I can't remember much."

Dr. Messinger had made something of a camp. He had chopped a square clear of undergrowth, the size of a small room. Their two hammocks hung on opposite sides of it. The stores were all ashore, arranged in an orderly pile on the tarpaulin.

"How d'you feel?"

"Grand," said Tony, but when he got out of his hammock he found he could not stand without help. "Of course, I haven't eaten anything. I expect it will be a day or two before I'm really well."

Dr. Messinger said nothing, but strained the tea clear of leaves by pouring it slowly from one mug into another; he stirred into it a large spoonful of condensed milk.

"See if you can drink this."

Tony drank it with pleasure and ate some biscuits.

"Are we going on today?" he asked.

"We'll think about it." He took the mugs down to the bank and washed them in the river. When he came back he said, "I think I'd better explain things. It's no use your thinking you are cured because you are out of fever for one day. That's the way it goes. One day fever and one day normal. It may take a week or it may take much longer. That's a thing we've got to face. I can't risk taking you in

the canoe. You nearly upset us several times the day before yesterday."

"I thought there was someone there I knew."

"You thought a lot of things. It'll go on like that. Meanwhile we've provisions for about ten days. There's no immediate anxiety there but it's a thing to remember. Besides
what you need is a roof over your head and constant nursing. If only we were at a village . . ."

"I'm afraid I'm being a great nuisance."

"That's not the point. The thing is to find what is best
for us to do."

But Tony felt too tired to think; he dozed for an hour or
so. When he awoke Dr. Messinger was cutting back the
bush further. "I'm going to fix up the tarpaulin as a roof."

(He had marked this place on his map *Temporary
Emergency Base Camp*.)

Tony watched him listlessly. Presently he said, "Look
here, why don't you leave me here and go down the river
for help?"

"I thought of that. It's too big a risk."

That afternoon Brenda was back at Tony's side and he
was shivering and tossing in his hammock.

When he was next able to observe things, Tony noted
that there was a tarpaulin over his head, slung to the tree-
trunks. He asked, "How long have we been here?"

"Only three days."

"What time is it now?"

"Getting on for ten in the morning."

"I feel awful."

Dr. Messinger gave him some soup. "I am going down-
stream for the day," he said, "to see if there's any sign of a
village. I hate leaving you but it's a chance worth taking.
I shall be able to get a long way in the canoe now it's
empty. Lie quiet. Don't move from the hammock. I shall
be back before night. I hope with some Indians to help."

"All right," said Tony and fell asleep.

Dr. Messinger went down to the river's edge and untied
the canoe; he brought with him a rifle, a drinking cup and

a day's provisions. He sat in the stern and pushed out from the bank; the current carried the bow down and in a few strokes of the paddle he was in midstream.

The sun was high and its reflection in the water dazzled and scorched him; he paddled on with regular, leisurely strokes; he was travelling fast. For a mile's stretch the river narrowed and the water raced so that all he had to do was to trail the blade of the paddle as a rudder; then the walls of forest on either side of him fell back and he drifted into a great open lake, where he had to work heavily to keep in motion; all the time he watched keenly to right and left for the column of smoke, the thatched domes, the sly brown figure in the undergrowth, the drinking cattle, that would disclose the village he sought. But there was no sign. In the open water he took up his field glasses and studied the whole wooded margin. But there was no sign.

Later the river narrowed once more and the canoe shot forward in the swift current. Ahead of him the surface was broken by rapids; the smooth water seethed and eddied; a low monotone warned him that beyond the rapids was a fall. Dr. Messinger began to steer for the bank. The current was running strongly and he exerted his full strength; ten yards from the beginning of this rapids his bow ran in under the bank. There was a dense growth of thorn here, overhanging the river; the canoe slid under them and bit into the beach; very cautiously Dr. Messinger knelt forward in his place and stretched up to a bough over his head. It was at that moment he came to grief; the stern swung out downstream and as he snatched at the paddle the craft was swept broadside into the troubled water; there it adopted an eccentric course, spinning and tumbling to the falls. Dr. Messinger was tipped into the water; it was quite shallow in places and he caught at the rocks but they were worn smooth as ivory and afforded no hold for his hands; he rolled over twice, found himself in deep water and attempted to swim, found himself among boulders again and attempted to grapple with them. Then he reached the falls.

They were unspectacular as falls in that country go—a

drop of ten feet or less—but they were enough for Dr. Messinger. At their foot the foam subsided into a great pool, almost still, and strewn with blossoms from the forest trees that encircled it. Dr. Messinger's hat floated very slowly towards the Amazon and the water closed over his bald head.

Brenda went to see the family solicitors.

"Mr. Graceful," she said, "I've got to have some more money."

Mr. Graceful looked at her sadly. "I should have thought that was really a question for your bank manager. I understand that your securities are in your own name and that the dividends are paid into your account."

"They never seem to pay dividends nowadays. Besides it's really very difficult to live on so little."

"No doubt. No doubt."

"Mr. Last left you with power of attorney, didn't he?"

"With strictly limited powers, Lady Brenda. I am instructed to pay the wage bill at Hetton and all expenses connected with the upkeep of the estate—he is putting in new bathrooms and restoring some decorations in the morning room which had been demolished. But I am afraid that I have no authority to draw on Mr. Last's account for other charges."

"But, Mr. Graceful, I am sure he didn't intend to stay abroad so long. He can't possibly have meant to leave me stranded like this, can he? . . . Can he?"

Mr. Graceful paused and fidgeted a little. "To be quite frank, Lady Brenda, I fear that was his intention. I raised this particular point shortly before his departure. He was quite resolved on the subject."

"But is he *allowed* to do that? I mean haven't I got any rights under the marriage settlement or anything?"

"Nothing which you can claim without application to the Courts. You *might* find solicitors who would advise you to take action. I cannot say that I should be one of them. Mr. Last would oppose any such order to the utmost and I think that, in the present circumstances, the Courts would undoubtedly find for him. In any case it would be a prolonged, costly and slightly undignified proceeding."

"Oh, I see . . . well, that's that, isn't it?"

"It certainly looks as though it were."

Brenda rose to go. It was high summer and through the open windows she could see the sun-bathed gardens of Lincoln's Inn.

"There's one thing. Do you know, I mean, can you tell me whether Mr. Last made another will?"

"I'm afraid that is a thing I cannot discuss."

"No, I suppose not. I'm sorry if it was wrong to ask. I just wanted to know how I am with him."

She still stood between the door and the table looking lost, in her bright summer clothes. "Perhaps I can say as much as this to guide you. The heirs presumptive to Hetton are now his cousins, the Richard Lasts at Princes Risborough. I think that your knowledge of Mr. Last's character and opinions will tell you that he would always wish his fortune to go with the estate, in order that it may be preserved in what he holds to be its right condition."

"Yes," said Brenda, "I ought to have thought of that. Well, goodbye."

And she went out alone into the sunshine.

All that day Tony lay alone, fitfully oblivious of the passage of time. He slept a little; once or twice he left his hammock and found himself weak and dizzy. He tried to eat some of the food which Dr. Messinger had left out for him, but without success. It was not until it grew dark that he realized the day was over. He lit the lantern and began to collect wood for the fire, but the sticks kept slipping from his fingers and each time that he stooped he felt giddy, so that after a few fretful efforts he left them where they had fallen and returned to his hammock. And lying there, wrapped in his blanket, he began to cry.

After some hours of darkness the lamp began to burn low; he leant painfully over, and shook it. It needed refilling. He knew where the oil was kept, crept to it, supporting himself first on the hammock rope and then on a pile of boxes. He found the keg, pulled out the bung and began to refill the lamp, but his hand trembled and the oil spilled over the ground, then his head began to swim again so that he shut his eyes; the keg rolled over on its side and emptied itself with slow gurglings. When he realized what had happened he began to cry again. He lay down in his hammock and in a few minutes the light sank, flickered and went out. There was a reek of kerosene on his hands and on the sodden earth. He lay awake in the darkness crying.

Just before dawn the fever returned and a constant company of phantoms perplexed his senses.

Brenda awoke in the lowest possible spirits. The evening before she had spent alone at a cinema. Afterwards she felt hungry—she had had no proper meal that day—but she had not the strength to go alone into any of the supper restaurants. She bought a meat pie at a coffee stall and took it home. It looked delicious but, when she came to eat she found that she had lost her appetite. The remains of that pie lay on the dressing table when she awoke.

It was August and she was entirely alone. Beaver was that day landing in New York. (He had cabled her from mid-ocean that the crossing was excellent.) It was for her the last of Beaver. Parliament was over and Jock Grant-Menzies was paying his annual visit to his elder brother in Scotland; Marjorie and Allan at the last moment had made Lord Monomark's yacht and were drifting luxuriously down the coast of Spain attending bull-fights (they had even asked her to look after Djinn). Her mother was at the chalet Lady Anchorage always lent her on the lake of Geneva. Polly was everywhere. Even Jenny Abdul Akbar was cruising in the Baltic.

Brenda opened her newspaper and read an article by a young man who said that the London Season was a thing of the past; that everyone was too busy in those days to keep up the pre-war routine; that there were no more formal dances but a constant round of more modest entertaining; that August in London was the gayest time of all (he rewrote this annually in slightly different words). It did not console Brenda to read that article.

For weeks past she had attempted to keep a fair mind towards Tony and his treatment of her; now at last she broke down and turning over buried her face in the pillow, in an agony of resentment and self-pity.

In Brazil she wore a ragged cotton gown of the same pattern as Rosa's. It was not unbecoming. Tony watched her for some time before he spoke. "Why are you dressed like that?"

"Don't you like it? I got it from Polly."

"It looks so dirty."

"Well, Polly travels about a lot. You must get up now to go to the County Council Meeting."

"But it isn't Wednesday?"

"No, but time is different in Brazil, surely you remember."

"I can't get as far as Pigstanton. I've got to stay here until Messinger comes back. I'm ill. He told me to be quiet. He's coming this evening."

"But all the County Council are here. The Shameless Blonde brought them in her aeroplane."

Sure enough they were all there. Reggie St. Cloud was chairman. He said, "I strongly object to Milly being on the committee. She is a woman of low repute."

Tony protested. "She has a daughter. She has as much right here as Lady Cockpurse."

"Order," said the Mayor. "I must ask you gentlemen to confine your remarks to the subject under discussion. We have to decide about the widening of the Bayton-Pigstanton road. There have been several complaints that it's impossible for the Green Line Buses to turn the corner safely at Hetton Cross."

"Green Line *rats*."

"I said Green Line rats. Mechanical green line rats. Many of the villagers have been scared by them and have evacuated their cottages."

"I evacuated," said Reggie St. Cloud. "I was driven out of my house by mechanical green rats."

"Order," said Lady Cockpurse. "I move that Mr. Last address the meeting."

"Hear, hear."

"Ladies and gentlemen," said Tony. "I beg you to understand that I am ill and must not move from the hammock. Dr. Messinger has given the clearest instructions."

"Winnie wants to bathe."

"No bathing in Brazil. No bathing in Brazil." The meeting took up the cry. "No bathing in Brazil."

"But you had two breakfasts."

"Order," said the Mayor. "Lord St. Cloud, I suggest you put the question to the vote."

"The question is whether the contract for the widening of the corner at Hetton Cross shall be given to Mrs. Beaver. Of the tenders submitted hers was by far the most expensive but I understand that her plans included a chromium plated wall on the south side of the village . . ."

". . . and two breakfasts," prompted Winnie.

". . . and two breakfasts for the men engaged on the work. Those in favour of the motion will make a clucking sound in imitation of hens, those against will say bow-wow."

"A most improper proceeding," said Reggie. "What will the servants think?"

"We have got to do something until Brenda has been told."

". . . Me? I'm all right."

"Then I take it the motion is carried."

"Oh, I *am* glad Mrs. Beaver got the job," said Brenda. "You see I'm in love with John Beaver, I'm in love with John Beaver, I'm in love with John Beaver."

"Is that the decision of the committee?"

"Yes, she is in love with John Beaver."

"Then that is carried unanimously."

"No," said Winnie. "He ate two breakfasts."

". . . by an overwhelming majority."

"Why are you all changing your clothes?" asked Tony for they were putting on hunting coats."

"For the lawn meet. Hounds are meeting here today."

"But you can't hunt in summer."

"Time is different in Brazil and there is no bathing."

"I saw a fox yesterday in Bruton wood. A mechanical green fox with a bell inside him that jingled as he ran. It frightened them so much that they ran away and the whole beach was deserted and there was no bathing except for Beaver. He can bathe every day for the time is different in Brazil."

"I'm in love with John Beaver," said Ambrose.

"Why, I didn't know you were here."

"I came to remind you that you were ill, sir. You must on no account leave your hammock."

"But how can I reach the City if I stay here?"

"I will serve it directly, sir, in the library."

"Yes, in the library. There is no point in using the dining hall now that her ladyship has gone to live in Brazil."

"I will send the order to the stables, sir."

"But I don't want the pony. I told Ben to sell her."

"You will have to ride to the smoking room, sir. Dr. Messinger has taken the canoe."

"Very well, Ambrose."

"Thank you, sir."

The committee had moved off down the avenue; all except Colonel Inch who had taken the other drive and was trotting towards Compton Last. Tony and Mrs. Rattery were all alone.

"Bow-wow," she said, scooping in the cards. "That carries the motion."

Looking up from the card table, Tony saw beyond the trees the ramparts and battlements of the City; it was quite near him. From the turret of the gatehouse a heraldic banner floated in the tropic breeze. He struggled into an upright position and threw aside his blankets. He was stronger and steadier when the fever was on him. He picked his way through the surrounding thorn-scrub; the sound of music rose from the glittering walls; some pro-

cession or pageant was passing along them. He lurched
into tree-trunks and became caught up in roots and hanging tendrils of bush-vine; but he pressed forward uncon-
scious of pain and fatigue.

At last he came into the open. The gates were open before him and trumpets were sounding along the walls,
saluting his arrival; from bastion to bastion the message
ran to the four points of the compass; petals of almond
and apple blossom were in the air; they carpeted the way,
as, after a summer storm, they lay in the orchards at Hetton. Gilded cupolas and spires of alabaster shone in the
sunlight.

Ambrose announced, "The City is served."

CHAPTER SIX

Du Côté de Chez Todd

ALTHOUGH Mr. Todd had lived in Amazonas for nearly
sixty years, no one except a few families of Pie-wie Indians
was aware of his existence. His house stood in a small
savannah, one of those little patches of sand and grass that
crop up occasionally in that neighbourhood, three miles
or so across, bounded on all sides by forest.

The stream which watered it was not marked on any
map; it ran through rapids, always dangerous and at most
seasons of the year impassable, to join the upper waters
of the river where Dr. Messinger had come to grief. None
of the inhabitants of the district, except Mr. Todd, had
ever heard of the governments of Brazil or Dutch Guiana,
both of which, from time to time claimed its possession.

Mr. Todd's house was larger than those of his neighbours, but similar in character—a palm thatch roof, breast
high walls of mud and wattle, and a mud floor. He owned

the dozen or so head of puny cattle which grazed in the savannah, a plantation of cassava, some banana and mango trees, a dog and, unique in the neighbourhood, a single-barrelled breech-loading shot gun. The few commodities which he employed from the outside world came to him through a long succession of traders, passed from hand to hand, bartered for in a dozen languages at the extreme end of one of the longest threads in the web of commerce that spreads from Manáos into the remote fastness of the forest.

One day while Mr. Todd was engaged in filling some cartridges, a Pie-wie came to him with the news that a white man was approaching through the forest, alone and very sick. He closed the cartridge and loaded his gun with it, put those that were finished into his pocket and set out in the direction indicated.

The man was already clear of the bush when Mr. Todd reached him, sitting on the ground, clearly in a very bad way. He was without hat or boots, and his clothes were so torn that it was only by the dampness of his body that they adhered to it; his feet were cut and grossly swollen; every exposed surface of skin was scarred by insect and bat bites; his eyes were wild with fever. He was talking to himself in delirium but stopped when Todd approached and addressed him in English.

"You're the first person who's spoken to me for days," said Tony. "The others won't stop. They keep bicycling by . . . I'm tired . . . Brenda was with me at first but she was frightened by a mechanical mouse, so she took the canoe and went off. She said she would come back that evening but she didn't. I expect she's staying with one of her new friends in Brazil . . . You haven't seen her have you?"

"You are the first stranger I have seen for a very long time."

"She was wearing a top hat when she left. You can't miss her." Then he began talking to someone at Mr. Todd's side, who was not there.

"Do you see that house over there? Do you think you

can managed to walk to it? If not I can send some Indians to carry you."

Tony squinted across the savannah at Mr. Todd's hut.

"Architecture harmonizing with local character," he said, "indigenous material employed throughout. Don't let Mrs. Beaver see it or she will cover it with chromium plating."

"Try and walk." Mr. Todd hoisted Tony to his feet and supported him with a stout arm.

"I'll ride your bicycle. It *was* you I passed just now on a bicycle wasn't it? . . . except that your beard is a different colour. His was green . . . green as mice."

Mr. Todd led Tony across the hummocks of grass towards the house.

"It is a very short way. When we get there I will give you something to make you better."

"Very kind of you . . . rotten thing for a man to have his wife go away in a canoe. That was a long time ago. Nothing to eat since." Presently he said, "I say, you're English. I'm English too. My name is Last."

"Well, Mr. Last, you aren't to bother about anything more. You're ill and you've had a rough journey. I'll take care of you."

Tony looked round him. "Are you all English?"

"Yes, all of us."

"That dark girl married a Moor . . . It's very lucky I met you all. I suppose you're some kind of cycling club?"

"Yes."

"Well, I feel too tired for bicycling . . . never liked it much . . . you fellows ought to get motor bicycles you know, much faster and noisier . . . Let's stop here."

"No, you must come as far as the house. It's not very much further."

"All right . . . I suppose you would have some difficulty getting petrol here."

They went very slowly, but at length reached the house.

"Lie there in the hammock."

"That's what Messinger said. He's in love with John Beaver."

"I will get something for you."

"Very good of you. Just my usual morning tray—coffee, toast, fruit. And the morning papers. If her ladyship has been called I will have it with her . . ."

Mr. Todd went into the back room of the house and dragged a tin canister from under a heap of skins. It was full of a mixture of dried leaf and bark. He took a handful and went outside to the fire. When he returned his guest was bolt upright astride the hammock, talking angrily.

". . . You would hear better and it would be more polite if you stood still when I addressed you instead of walking round in a circle. It is for your own good that I am telling you . . . I know you are friends of my wife and that is why you will not listen to me. But be careful. She will say nothing cruel, she will not raise her voice, there will be no hard words. She hopes you will be great friends afterwards as before. But she will leave you. She will go away quietly during the night. She will take her hammock and her rations of farine . . . Listen to me. I know I am not clever but that is no reason why we should forget courtesy. Let us kill in the gentlest manner. I will tell you what I have learned in the forest, where time is different. There is no City. Mrs. Beaver has covered it with chromium plating and converted it into flats. Three guineas a week with a separate bathroom. Very suitable for base love. And Polly will be there. She and Mrs. Beaver under the fallen battlements . . ."

Mr. Todd put a hand behind Tony's head and held up the concoction of herbs in the calabash. Tony sipped and turned away his head.

"Nasty medicine," he said, and began to cry.

Mr. Todd stood by him holding the calabash. Presently Tony drank some more, screwing up his face and shuddering slightly at the bitterness. Mr. Todd stood beside him until the draught was finished; then he threw out the dregs on to the mud floor. Tony lay back in the hammock sobbing quietly. Soon he fell into a deep sleep.

Tony's recovery was slow. At first, days of lucidity alternated with delirium; then his temperature dropped and he was conscious even when most ill. The days of fever grew less frequent, finally occurring in the normal system of the tropics, between long periods of comparative health. Mr. Todd dosed him regularly with herbal remedies.

"It's very nasty," said Tony, "but it does do good."

"There is medicine for everything in the forest," said Mr. Todd; "to make you well and to make you ill. My mother was an Indian and she taught me many of them. I have learned others from time to time from my wives. There are plants to cure you and give you fever, to kill you and send you mad, to keep away snakes, to intoxicate fish so that you can pick them out of the water with your hands like fruit from a tree. There are medicines even I do not know. They say that it is possible to bring dead people to life after they have begun to stink, but I have not seen it done."

"But surely you are English?"

"My father was—at least a Barbadian. He came to Guiana as a missionary. He was married to a white woman but he left her in Guiana to look for gold. Then he took my mother. The Pie-wie women are ugly but very devoted. I have had many. Most of the men and women living in this savannah are my children. That is why they obey—for that reason and because I have the gun. My father lived to a great age. It is not twenty years since he died. He was a man of education. Can you read?"

"Yes, of course."

"It is not everyone who is so fortunate. I cannot."

Tony laughed apologetically. "But I suppose you haven't much opportunity here."

"Oh yes, that is just it. I have a *great* many books. I will show you when you are better. Until five years ago there was an Englishman—at least a black man, but he was well educated in Georgetown. He died. He used to read to me every day until he died. You shall read to me when you are better."

"I shall be delighted to."

"Yes, you shall read to me," Mr. Todd repeated, nodding over the calabash.

During the early days of his convalescence Tony had little conversation with his host; he lay in the hammock staring up at the thatched roof and thinking about Brenda. The days, exactly twelve hours each, passed without distinction. Mr. Todd retired to sleep at sundown, leaving a little lamp burning—a hand-woven wick drooping from a pot of beef fat—to keep away vampire bats.

The first time that Tony left the house Mr. Todd took him for a little stroll around the farm.

"I will show you the black man's grave," he said, leading him to a mound between the mango trees. "He was very kind. Every afternoon until he died, for two hours, he used to read to me. I think I will put up a cross—to commemorate his death and your arrival—a pretty idea. Do you believe in God?"

"I suppose so. I've never really thought about it much."

"I have thought about it a *great* deal and I still do not know . . . Dickens did."

"I suppose so."

"Oh yes, it is apparent in all his books. You will see."

That afternoon Mr. Todd began the construction of a headpiece for the Negro's grave. He worked with a large spokeshave in a wood so hard that it grated and rang like metal.

At last when Tony had passed six or seven consecutive nights without fever, Mr. Todd said, "Now I think you are well enough to see the books."

At one end of the hut there was a kind of loft formed by a rough platform erected in the eaves of the roof. Mr. Todd propped a ladder against it and mounted. Tony followed, still unsteady after his illness. Mr. Todd sat on the platform and Tony stood at the top of the ladder looking over. There was a heap of small bundles there, tied up with rag, palm leaf and raw hide.

"It has been hard to keep out the worms and ants. Two are practically destroyed. But there is an oil the Indians make that is useful."

He unwrapped the nearest parcel and handed down a

calf bound book. It was an early American edition of *Bleak House*.

"It does not matter which we take first."

"You are fond of Dickens?"

"Why, yes, of course. More than fond, far more. You see, they are the only books I have ever heard. My father used to read them and then later the black man . . . and now you. I have heard them all several times by now but I never get tired; there is always more to be learned and noticed, so many characters, so many changes of scene, so many words . . . I have all Dickens books here except those that the ants devoured. It takes a long time to read them all—more than two years."

"Well," said Tony lightly, "they will well last out my visit."

"Oh, I hope not. It is delightful to start again. Each time I think I find more to enjoy and admire."

They took down the first volume of *Bleak House* and that afternoon Tony had his first reading.

He had always rather enjoyed reading aloud and in the first year of marriage had shared several books in this way with Brenda, until one day, in a moment of frankness, she remarked that it was torture to her. He had read to John Andrew, late in the afternoon, in winter, while the child sat before the nursery fender eating his supper. But Mr. Todd was a unique audience.

The old man sat astride his hammock opposite Tony, fixing him throughout with his eyes, and following the words, soundlessly, with his lips. Often when a new character was introduced he would say, "Repeat the name, I have forgotten him," or "Yes, yes, I remember her well. She dies, poor woman." He would frequently interrupt with questions; not as Tony would have imagined about the circumstances of the story—such things as the procedure of the Lord Chancellor's Court or the social conventions of the time, though they must have been unintelligible, did not concern him—but always about the characters. "Now why does she say that? Does she really mean it? Did she feel faint because of the heat of the fire or of something in that paper?" He laughed loudly at all the jokes and at some passages which did not seem humorous to Tony, asking him to repeat them two or three times; and later at the description of the sufferings of the outcasts in "Tom-all-alones" tears ran down his cheeks into his beard. His comments on the story were usually simple. "I think that Dedlock is a very proud man," or, "Mrs. Jellyby does not take enough care of her children."

Tony enjoyed the readings almost as much as he did.

At the end of the first day the old man said, "You read beautifully, with a far better accent than the black man. And you explain better. It is almost as though my father were here again." And always at the end of a session he thanked his guest courteously. "I enjoyed that *very* much. It was an extremely distressing chapter. But, if I remember rightly, it will all turn out well."

By the time that they were in the second volume however, the novelty of the old man's delight had begun to wane, and Tony was feeling strong enough to be restless. He touched more than once on the subject of his departure, asking about canoes and rains and the possibility of finding guides. But Mr. Todd seemed obtuse and paid no attention to these hints.

One day, running his thumb through the pages of *Bleak House* that remained to be read, Tony said, "We still have a lot to get through. I hope I shall be able to finish it before I go."

"Oh yes," said Mr. Todd. "Do not disturb yourself about that. You will have time to finish it, my friend."

For the first time Tony noticed something slightly menacing in his host's manner. That evening at supper, a brief meal of farine and dried beef, eaten just before sundown, Tony renewed the subject.

"You know, Mr. Todd, the time has come when I must be thinking about getting back to civilization. I have already imposed myself on your hospitality for too long."

Mr. Todd bent over the plate, crunching mouthfuls of farine, but made no reply.

"How soon do you think I shall be able to get a boat? . . . I said how soon do you think I shall be able to get a boat? I appreciate all your kindness to me more than I can say but . . ."

"My friend, any kindness I may have shown is amply repaid by your reading of Dickens. Do not let us mention the subject again."

"Well I'm very glad you have enjoyed it. I have, too. But I really must be thinking of getting back . . ."

"Yes," said Mr. Todd. "The black man was like that. He thought of it all the time. But he died here . . ."

Twice during the next day Tony opened the subject but his host was evasive. Finally he said, "Forgive me, Mr. Todd, but I really must press the point. When can I get a boat?"

"There is no boat."

"Well, the Indians can build one."

"You must wait for the rains. There is not enough water in the river now."

"How long will that be?"

"A month . . . two months . . ."

They had finished *Bleak House* and were nearing the end of *Dombey and Son* when the rain came.

"Now it is time to make preparations to go."

"Oh, that is impossible. The Indians will not make a boat during the rainy season—it is one of their superstitions."

"You might have told me."

"Did I not mention it? I forgot."

Next morning Tony went out alone while his host was busy, and, looking as aimless as he could, strolled across the savannah to the group of Indian houses. There were four or five Pie-wies sitting in one of the doorways. They did not look up as he approached them. He addressed them in the few words of Macushi he had acquired during the journey but they made no sign whether they understood him or not. Then he drew a sketch of a canoe in the sand, he went through some vague motions of carpentry,

pointed from them to him, then made motions of giving
something to them and scratched out the outlines of a gun
and a hat and a few other recognizable articles of trade.
One of the women giggled but no one gave any sign of
comprehension, and he went away unsatisfied.

At their midday meal Mr. Todd said, "Mr. Last, the
Indians tell me that you have been trying to speak with
them. It is easier that you say anything you wish through
me. You realize, do you not, that they would do nothing
without my authority. They regard themselves, quite
rightly in many cases, as my children."

"Well, as a matter of fact, I was asking them about a
canoe."

"So they gave me to understand . . . and now if you have
finished your meal perhaps we might have another chapter. I am quite absorbed in the book."

They finished *Dombey and Son;* nearly a year had
passed since Tony had left England, and his gloomy fore-
boding of permanent exile became suddenly acute when,
between the pages of *Martin Chuzzlewit,* he found a doc-
ument written in pencil in irregular characters.

Year 1919.

*I James Todd of Brazil do swear to Barnabas Washing-
ton of Georgetown that if he finish this book in fact Martin Chuzzlewit I will let him go away back as soon as finished.*

There followed a heavy pencil X and after it: *Mr. Todd
made this mark signed Barnabas Washington.*

"Mr. Todd," said Tony, "I must speak frankly. You
saved my life, and when I get back to civilization I will reward you to the best of my ability. I will give you anything
within reason. But at present you are keeping me here
against my will. I demand to be released."

"But, my friend, what is keeping you? You are under
no restraint. Go when you like."

"You know very well that I can't get away without your
help."

"In that case you must humour an old man. Read me
another chapter."

"Mr. Todd, I swear by anything you like that when I get to Manáos I will find someone to take my place. I will pay a man to read to you all day."

"But I have no need of another man. You read so well."

"I have read for the last time."

"I hope not," said Mr. Todd politely.

That evening at supper only one plate of dried meat and farine was brought in and Mr. Todd ate alone. Tony lay without speaking, staring at the thatch.

Next day at noon a single plate was put before Mr. Todd but with it lay his gun, cocked, on his knee, as he ate. Tony resumed the reading of *Martin Chuzzlewit* where it had been interrupted.

Weeks passed hopelessly. They read *Nicholas Nickleby* and *Little Dorrit* and *Oliver Twist*. Then a stranger arrived in the savannah, a half-caste prospector, one of that lonely order of men who wander for a lifetime through the forests, tracing the little streams, sifting the gravel and, ounce by ounce, filling the little leather sack of gold dust, more often than not dying of exposure and starvation with five hundred dollars' worth of gold hung around their necks. Mr. Todd was vexed at his arrival, gave him farine and *tasso* and sent him on his journey within an hour of his arrival, but in that hour Tony had time to scribble his name on a slip of paper and put it into the man's hand.

From now on there was hope. The days followed their unvarying routine; coffee at sunrise, a morning of inaction while Mr. Todd pottered about on the business of the farm, farine and *tasso* at noon, Dickens in the afternoon, farine and *tasso* and sometimes some fruit for supper, silence from sunset to dawn with the small wick glowing in the beef fat and the palm thatch overhead dimly discernible; but Tony lived in quiet confidence and expectation.

Sometime, this year or the next, the prospector would arrive at a Brazilian village with news of his discovery. The disasters of the Messinger expedition would not have passed unnoticed. Tony could imagine the headlines that must have appeared in the popular press; even now probably there were search parties working over the country he had crossed; any day English voices must sound over the savannah and a dozen friendly adventurers come crashing through the bush. Even as he was reading, while his lips mechanically followed the printed pages, his mind wandered away from his eager, crazy host opposite, and he began to narrate to himself incidents of his homecoming— the gradual re-encounters with civilization (he shaved and bought new clothes at Manáos, telegraphed for money, received wires of congratulation; he enjoyed the leisurely river journey to Belem, the big liner to Europe; savoured good claret and fresh meat and spring vegetables; he was shy at meeting Brenda and uncertain how to address her . . . "*Darling*, you've been much longer than you said. I quite thought you were lost . . .")

And then Mr. Todd interrupted. "May I trouble you to read that passage again? It is one I particularly enjoy."

The weeks passed; there was no sign of rescue but Tony endured the day for hope of what might happen on the morrow; he even felt a slight stirring of cordiality towards his jailer and was therefore quite willing to join him when, one evening after a long conference with an Indian neighbour, he proposed a celebration.

"It is one of the local feast days," he explained, "and they have been making *piwari*. You may not like it but you should try some. We will go across to this man's home tonight."

Accordingly after supper they joined a party of Indians that were assembled round the fire in one of the huts at the other side of the savannah. They were singing in an apathetic, monotonous manner and passing a large calabash of liquid from mouth to mouth. Separate bowls were brought for Tony and Mr. Todd, and they were given hammocks to sit in.

"You must drink it all without lowering the cup. That is the etiquette."

Tony gulped the dark liquid, trying not to taste it. But it was not unpleasant, hard and muddy on the palate like most of the beverages he had been offered in Brazil, but with a flavour of honey and brown bread. He leant back in the hammock feeling unusually contented. Perhaps at that very moment the search party was in camp a few hours' journey from them. Meanwhile he was warm and drowsy. The cadence of song rose and fell interminably, liturgically. Another calabash of *piwari* was offered him and he handed it back empty. He lay full length watching the play of shadows on the thatch as the Pie-wies began to dance. Then he shut his eyes and thought of England and Hetton and fell asleep.

He awoke, still in the Indian hut, with the impression that he had outslept his usual hour. By the position of the sun he knew it was late afternoon. No one else was about. He looked for his watch and found to his surprise that it was not on his wrist. He had left it in the house, he supposed, before coming to the party.

"I must have been tight last night," he reflected. "Treacherous drink that." He had a headache and feared a recurrence of fever. He found when he set his feet to the ground that he stood with difficulty; his walk was unsteady and his mind confused as it had been during the first weeks of his convalescence. On the way across the savannah he was obliged to stop more than once, shutting his eyes and breathing deeply. When he reached the house he found Mr. Todd sitting there.

"Ah, my friend, you are late for the reading this afternoon. There is scarcely another half hour of light. How do you feel?"

"Rotten. That drink doesn't seem to agree with me."

"I will give you something to make you better. The forest has remedies for everything; to make you awake and to make you sleep."

"You haven't seen my watch anywhere?"

"You have missed it?"

"Yes. I thought I was wearing it. I say, I've never slept so long."

"Not since you were a baby. Do you know how long? Two days."

"Nonsense. I can't have."

"Yes, indeed. It is a long time. It is a pity because you missed our guests."

"Guests?"

"Why, yes. I have been quite gay while you were asleep. Three men from outside. Englishmen. It is a pity you missed them. A pity for them, too, as they particularly wished to see you. But what could I do? You were so sound asleep. They had come all the way to find you, so— I thought you would not mind—as you could not greet them yourself I gave them a little souvenir, your watch. They wanted something to take back to England where a reward is being offered for news of you. They were very pleased with it. And they took some photographs of the little cross I put up to commemorate your coming. They were pleased with that, too. They were very easily pleased. But I do not suppose they will visit us again, our life here is so retired . . . no pleasures except reading . . . I do not suppose we shall ever have visitors again . . . well, well, I will get you some medicine to make you feel better. Your head aches, does it not? . . . We will not have any Dickens today . . . but tomorrow, and the day after that, and the day after that. Let us read *Little Dorrit* again. There are passages in that book I can never hear without the temptation to weep."

CHAPTER SEVEN

English Gothic—III

A LIGHT breeze in the dewy orchards; brilliant, cool sunshine over meadows and copses; the elms were all in bud in the avenue; everything was early that year for it had been a mild winter. High overhead among its gargoyles and crockets the clock chimed for the hour and solemnly struck fourteen. It was half past eight. The clock had been irregular lately. It was one of the things that Richard Last intended to see to when death duties were paid and silver foxes began to show a profit.

Molly Last bowled up the drive on her two-stroke motor-cycle; there was bran mash on her breeches and in her hair. She had been feeding the Angora rabbits.

On the gravel in front of the house the new memorial stood, shrouded in a flag. Molly propped the motor-cycle against the wall of the drawbridge and ran in to breakfast.

Life at Hetton was busier but simpler since Richard Last's succession. Ambrose remained but there were no longer any footmen; he and a boy and four women servants did the work of the house. Richard Last called them his 'skeleton staff.' When things were easier he would extend the household; meanwhile the dining hall and the library were added to the state apartments which were kept locked and shuttered; the family lived in the morning room, the smoking room and what had been Tony's study. Most of the kitchen quarters, too, were out of use; an up-to-date and economical range had been installed in one of the pantries.

The family all appeared downstairs by half past eight, except Agnes who took longer to dress and was usually some minutes late; Teddy and Molly had been out for an hour, she among the rabbits, he to the silver foxes. Teddy was twenty-two and lived at home. Peter was still at Oxford.

They breakfasted together in the morning room. Mrs. Last sat at one end of the table; her husband at the other; there was a constant traffic from hand to hand to and fro between them of cups, plate, honey jars and correspondence.

Mrs. Last said, "Molly, you have rabbit feed on your head again."

"Oh well, I shall have to tidy up anyway before the jamboree."

Mr. Last said, "*Jamboree.* Is nothing sacred to you children?"

Teddy said, "Another casualty at the stinkeries. That little vixen we bought from the people at Oakhampton got her brush bitten off during the night. Must have got it through the wire into the next cage. Tricky birds, foxes."

Agnes came next; she was a neat, circumspect child of twelve, with large, grave eyes behind her goggles. She kissed her father and mother and said, "I'm sorry if I'm late."

"*If* you're late . . ." said Mr. Last tolerantly.

"How long will the show last?" asked Teddy. "I've got to run over to Bayton and get some more rabbits for the foxes. Chivers says he's got about fifty waiting for me. We can't shoot enough here. Greedy little beggars."

"It will be all over by half past eleven. Mr. Tendril isn't going to preach a sermon. It's just as well really. He's got it into his head that cousin Tony died in Afghanistan."

"There's a letter here from Cousin Brenda. She's very sorry but she can't get down for the dedication."

"Oh."

There was a general silence.

"She says that Jock has a three line whip for this afternoon."

"Oh."

"She could have come without him," said Molly.

"She sends her love to us all and to Hetton."

There was another pause.

"Well I think it's a jolly good thing," said Molly. "*She* couldn't show much widowly grief. It didn't take *her* long to get hitched up again."

"*Molly.*"

"And you know you think the same."

"I will not allow you to talk like that about Cousin Brenda, whatever we think. She had a perfect right to marry again and I hope she and Mr. Grant-Menzies are very happy."

"She was always jolly decent to us when she used to live here," said Agnes.

"Well I should hope so," said Teddy. "After all it's *our* place."

The day was still fine at eleven o'clock, though the wind had got up, fluttering the papers on which the order of the service was printed and once threatening to unveil the memorial prematurely. Several relatives were present, Lady St. Cloud, Aunt Frances, and the family of impoverished Lasts who had not profited by Tony's disappearance. All the household and estate servants were there, several tenants and most of the village; there were also a dozen or so neighbours, among them Colonel Inch—Richard Last and Teddy had hunted regularly that season with the Pigstanton. Mr. Tendril conducted the brief service in his clear, resonant voice that was clearly audible above the blustering wind. When he pulled the cord the flag fell away from the memorial without mishap.

It was a plain monolith of local stone, inscribed:

ANTHONY LAST OF HETTON
EXPLORER
BORN AT HETTON, 1902
DIED IN BRAZIL, 1934

When the local visitors had left and the relatives had gone into the house to be shown the new labour saving arrangements, Richard Last and Lady St. Cloud remained for a short time on the gravel.

"I'm glad we put that up," he said. "You know, I should have never thought of it, if it had not been for a Mrs. Beaver. She wrote to me as soon as the news of Tony's death was published. I didn't know her at the time. Of course we knew very few of Tony's friends."

"It was her suggestion?"

"Yes, she said that as one of Tony's closest friends she knew he would wish to have some monument at Hetton. She was most considerate—even offering to arrange with

the contractors for it. Her own plans were more ambitious. She proposed that we should have the Chapel re-
decorated as a chantry. But I think this is what he would
have preferred. The stone comes from one of our own
quarries and was cut by the estate workmen."

"Yes, I think he would have preferred this," said Lady
St. Cloud.

Teddy had chosen Galahad for his bedroom. He dis-
engaged himself from the family and hurried up to change
out of his dark clothes. Within ten minutes he was in his
car driving to Chivers' farm. Before luncheon he was back
with the rabbits. They were skinned and tied round the
feet into four bundles.

"Coming to the stinkeries?" he asked Agnes.

"No, I'm looking after Cousin Frances. She got rather
on mother's nerves through crabbing the new boiler."

The silver fox farm was behind the stables; a long
double row of wire cages; they had wire floors covered
with earth and cinders to prevent the animals digging
their way out. They lived in pairs; some were moderately
tame but it was unwise to rely upon them. Teddy and
Ben Hacket—who helped with them—had been badly bitten more than once that winter. They ran up to the doors
when they saw Teddy come with the rabbits. The vixen
who had lost her brush seemed little the worse for her
accident.

Teddy surveyed his charges with pride and affection. It
was by means of them that he hoped one day to restore
Hetton to the glory that it had enjoyed in the days of his
Cousin Tony.

DECLINE
AND
FALL

Prelude

MR. SNIGGS, the Junior Dean, and Mr. Postlethwaite, the Domestic Bursar, sat alone in Mr. Sniggs's room overlooking the garden quad at Scone College. From the rooms of Sir Alastair Digby-Vaine-Trumpington, two staircases away, came a confused roaring and breaking of glass. They alone of the senior members of Scone were at home that evening, for it was the night of the annual dinner of the Bollinger Club. The others were all scattered over Boar's Hill and North Oxford at gay, contentious little parties, or at other senior common rooms, or at the meetings of learned societies, for the annual Bollinger dinner is a difficult time for those in authority.

It is not accurate to call this an annual event, because quite often the Club is suspended for some years after each meeting. There is tradition behind the Bollinger; it numbers reigning kings among its past members. At the last dinner, three years ago, a fox had been brought in in a cage and stoned to death with champagne bottles. What an evening that had been! This was the first meeting since then, and from all over Europe old members had rallied for the occasion. For two days they had been pouring into Oxford: epileptic royalty from their villas of exile; uncouth peers from crumbling country seats; smooth young men of uncertain tastes from embassies and legations; illiterate lairds from wet granite hovels in the Highlands; ambitious young barristers and Conservative candidates torn from the London season and the indelicate advances of debutantes; all that was most sonorous of name and title was there for the beano.

"The fines!" said Mr. Sniggs, gently rubbing his pipe along the side of his nose. "Oh, my! the fines there'll be after this evening!"

There is some highly prized port in the senior common-room cellars that is only brought up when the College fines have reached £50.

"We shall have a week of it at least," said Mr. Postle-thwaite, "a week of Founder's port."

A shriller note could now be heard rising from Sir Ala-stair's rooms; any who have heard that sound will shrink at the recollection of it; it is the sound of the English county families baying for broken glass. Soon they would all be tumbling out into the quad, crimson and roaring in their bottle-green evening coats, for the real romp of the evening.

"Don't you think it might be wiser if we turned out the light?" said Mr. Sniggs.

In darkness the two dons crept to the window. The quad below was a kaleidoscope of dimly discernible faces.

"There must be fifty of them at least," said Mr. Pos-tlethwaite. "If only they were all members of the College! Fifty of them at ten pounds each. Oh, my!"

"It'll be more if they attack the Chapel," said Mr. Sniggs. "Oh, please God, make them attack the Chapel."

"I wonder who the unpopular undergraduates are this term. They always attack their rooms. I hope they have been wise enough to go out for the evening."

"I think Partridge will be one; he possesses a painting by Matisse or some such name."

"And I'm told he has black sheets in his bed."

"And Sanders went to dinner with Ramsay MacDon-ald once."

"And Rending can afford to hunt, but collects china instead."

"And smokes cigars in the garden after breakfast."

"Austen has a grand piano."

"They'll enjoy smashing that."

"There'll be a heavy bill for to-night; just you see! But I confess I should feel easier if the Dean or the Master were in. They can't see us from here, can they?"

It was a lovely evening. They broke up Mr. Austen's grand piano, and stamped Lord Rending's cigars into his carpet, and smashed his china, and tore up Mr. Partridge's sheets, and threw the Matisse into his water jug; Mr. Sanders had nothing to break except his windows, but they found the manuscript at which he had been working for the Newdigate Prize Poem, and had great fun with that. Sir Alastair Digby-Vaine-Trumpington felt quite ill with excitement, and was supported to bed by Lumsden of Strathdrummond. It was half-past eleven. Soon the evening would come to an end. But there was still a treat to come.

Paul Pennyfeather was reading for the Church. It was his third year of uneventful residence at Scone. He had come there after a creditable career at a small public school of ecclesiastical temper on the South Downs, where he had edited the magazine, been President of the Debating Society, and had, as his report said, "exercised a wholesome influence for good" in the House of which he was head boy. At home he lived in Onslow Square with his guardian, a prosperous solicitor who was proud of his progress and abysmally bored by his company. Both his parents had died in India at the time when he won the essay prize at his preparatory school. For two years he had lived within his allowance, aided by two valuable scholarships. He smoked three ounces of tobacco a week —John Cotton, Medium—and drank a pint and a half of beer a day, the half at luncheon and the pint at dinner, a meal he invariably ate in Hall. He had four friends, three of whom had been at school with him. None of the Bollinger Club had ever heard of Paul Pennyfeather, and he, oddly enough, had not heard of them.

Little suspecting the incalculable consequences that the evening was to have for him, he bicycled happily back from a meeting of the League of Nations Union. There had been a most interesting paper about plebiscites in Poland. He thought of smoking a pipe and reading another chapter of the *Forsyte Saga* before going to bed. He knocked at the gate, was admitted, put away his bicycle, and diffidently, as always, made his way across the quad towards his rooms. What a lot of people there seemed to

be about! Paul had no particular objection to drunken-
ness—he had read rather a daring paper to the Thomas
More Society on the subject—but he was consumedly shy
of drunkards.

Out of the night Lumsden of Strathdrummond swayed
across his path like a druidical rocking stone. Paul tried
to pass.

Now it so happened that the tie of Paul's old school
bore a marked resemblance to the pale blue and white of
the Bollinger Club. The difference of a quarter of an inch
in the width of the stripes was not one that Lumsden of
Strathdrummond was likely to appreciate.

"Here's an awful man wearing the Boller tie," said the
Laird. It is not for nothing that since pre-Christian times
his family has exercised chieftainship over uncharted
miles of barren moorland.

Mr. Sniggs was looking rather apprehensively at Mr.
Postlethwaite.

"They appear to have caught somebody," he said. "I
hope they don't do him any serious harm."

"Dear me, can it be Lord Rending? I think I ought
to intervene."

"No, Sniggs," said Mr. Postlethwaite, laying a hand on
his impetuous colleague's arm. "No, no, no. It would be
unwise. We have the prestige of the senior common room
to consider. In their present state they might not prove
amenable to discipline. We must at all costs avoid an
outrage."

At length the crowd parted, and Mr. Sniggs gave a sigh
of relief.

"But it's quite all right. It isn't Rending. It's Pennyfeather—some one of no importance."

"Well, that saves a great deal of trouble. I am glad,
Sniggs; I am, really. What a lot of clothes the young man
appears to have lost!"

Next morning there was a lovely College meeting.

"Two hundred and thirty pounds," murmured the Domestic Bursar ecstatically, "*not* counting the damage!

That means five evenings, with what we have already collected. Five evenings of Founder's port!"

"The case of Pennyfeather," the Master was saying, "seems to be quite a different matter altogether. He ran the whole length of the quadrangle, you say, *without his trousers*. It is unseemly. It is more: it is indecent. In fact, I am almost prepared to say that it is flagrantly indecent. It is *not* the conduct we expect of a scholar."

"Perhaps if we fined him really heavily?" suggested the Junior Dean.

"I very much doubt whether he could pay. I understand he is not well off. *Without trousers,* indeed! And at that time of night! I think we should do far better to get rid of him altogether. That sort of young man does the College no good."

Two hours later, while Paul was packing his three suits in his little leather trunk, the Domestic Bursar sent a message that he wished to see him.

"Ah, Mr. Pennyfeather," he said, "I have examined your rooms and notice two slight burns, one on the window sill and the other on the chimney piece, no doubt from cigarette ends. I am charging you five-and-sixpence for each of them on your battels. That is all, thank you."

As he crossed the quad Paul met Mr. Sniggs.

"Just off?" said the Junior Dean brightly.

"Yes, sir," said Paul.

And a little farther on he met the Chaplain.

"Oh, Pennyfeather, before you go, surely you have my copy of Dean Stanley's *Eastern Church?*"

"Yes. I left it on your table."

"Thank you. Well, good-bye, my dear boy. I suppose that after that reprehensible affair last night you will have to think of some other profession. Well, you may congratulate yourself that you discovered your unfitness for the priesthood before it was too late. If a parson does a thing of that sort, you know, all the world knows. And so many do, alas! What do you propose doing?"

"I don't really know yet."

"There is always commerce, of course. Perhaps you may be able to bring to the great world of business some of the ideals you have learned at Scone. But it won't be easy, you know. It is a thing to be lived down with courage. What did Dr. Johnson say about fortitude? . . . Dear, dear! *no trousers!*"

At the gates Paul tipped the porter.

"Well, good-bye, Blackall," he said. "I don't suppose I shall see you again for some time."

"No, sir, and very sorry I am to hear about it. I expect you'll be becoming a schoolmaster, sir. That's what most of the gentlemen does, sir, that gets sent down for indecent behaviour."

"God damn and blast them all to hell," said Paul meekly to himself as he drove to the station, and then he felt rather ashamed, because he rarely swore.

Part One

CHAPTER ONE

Vocation

"SENT down for indecent behaviour, eh?" said Paul Pennyfeather's guardian. "Well, thank God your poor father has been spared this disgrace. That's all I can say."

There was a hush in Onslow Square, unbroken except by Paul's guardian's daughter's gramophone playing Gilbert and Sullivan in her little pink boudoir at the top of the stairs.

"My daughter must know nothing of this," continued Paul's guardian.

There was another pause.

"Well," he resumed, "you know the terms of your father's will. He left the sum of five thousand pounds, the interest of which was to be devoted to your education and the sum to be absolutely yours on your twenty-first birthday. That, if I am right, falls in eleven months' time. In the event of your education being finished before that time, he left me with complete discretion to withhold this allowance should I not consider your course of life satisfactory. I do not think that I should be fulfilling the trust which your poor father placed in me if, in the present circumstances, I continued any allowance. Moreover, you will be the first to realize how impossible it would be for me to ask you to share the same home with my daughter."

"But what is to happen to me?" said Paul.

"I think you ought to find some work," said his guardian thoughtfully. "Nothing like it for taking the mind off nasty subjects."

"But what kind of work?"

"Just work, good healthy toil. You have led too sheltered a life, Paul. Perhaps I am to blame. It will do you the world of good to face facts for a bit—look at life in the raw, you know. See things steadily and see them whole, eh?" And Paul's guardian lit another cigar.

"Have I no legal right to any money at all?" asked Paul.

"None whatever, my dear boy," said his guardian quite cheerfully. . . .

That spring Paul's guardian's daughter had two new evening frocks and, thus glorified, became engaged to a well-conducted young man in the Office of Works.

"Sent down for indecent behaviour, eh?" said Mr. Levy, of Church and Gargoyle, scholastic agents. "Well, I don't think we'll say anything about that. In fact, officially, mind, you haven't told me. We call that sort of thing 'Education discontinued for personal reasons,' you understand." He picked up the telephone. "Mr. Swanson, have we any 'education discontinued' posts, male, on hand? . . . Right! . . . Bring it up, will you? I think," he added, turning again to Paul, "we have just the thing for you."

A young man brought in a slip of paper.

"What about that?"

Paul read it:

"Private and Confidential Notice of Vacancy.

"Augustus Fagan, Esquire, Ph.D., Llanabba Castle, N. Wales, requires immediately junior assistant master to teach Classics and English to University Standard with Subsidiary Mathematics, German, and French. Experience essential; first-class games essential.

"Status of School: School.

"Salary offered: £120 resident post.

"Reply promptly but carefully to Dr. Fagan ('Esq.,

Ph.D.,' on envelope), enclosing copies of testimonials and photograph, if considered advisable, mentioning that you have heard of the vacancy through us."

"Might have been made for you," said Mr. Levy.

"But I don't know a word of German, I've had no experience, I've got no testimonials, and I can't play cricket."

"It doesn't do to be too modest," said Mr. Levy. "It's wonderful what one can teach when one tries. Why, only last term we sent a man who had never been in a laboratory in his life as senior Science Master to one of our leading public schools. He came wanting to do private coaching in music. He's doing very well, I believe. Besides, Dr. Fagan can't expect *all* that for the salary he's offering. Between ourselves, Llanabba hasn't a good name in the profession. We class schools, you see, into four grades: Leading School, First-rate School, Good School, and School. Frankly," said Mr. Levy, "School is pretty bad. I think you'll find it a very suitable post. So far as I know, there are only two other candidates, and one of them is totally deaf, poor fellow."

Next day Paul went to Church and Gargoyle to interview Dr. Fagan. He had not long to wait. Dr. Fagan was already there interviewing the other candidates. After a few minutes Mr. Levy led Paul into the room, introduced him, and left them together.

"A most exhausting interview," said Dr. Fagan. "I am sure he was a very nice young man, but I could not make him understand a word I said. Can *you* hear me quite clearly?"

"Perfectly, thank you."

"Good; then let us get to business."

Paul eyed him shyly across the table. He was very tall and very old and very well dressed; he had sunken eyes and rather long white hair over jet-black eyebrows. His head was very long, and swayed lightly as he spoke; his voice had a thousand modulations, as though at some remote time he had taken lessons in elocution; the backs of his hands were hairy, and his fingers were crooked like claws.

"I understand you have had no previous experience?"

"No, sir, I am afraid not."

"Well, of course, that is in many ways an advantage. One too easily acquires the professional tone and loses vision. But of course we must be practical. I am offering a salary of one hundred and twenty pounds, but only to a man with experience. I have a letter here from a young man who holds a diploma in forestry. He wants an extra ten pounds a year on the strength of it, but it is vision I need, Mr. Pennyfeather, not diplomas. I understand, too, that you left your University rather suddenly. Now—why was that?"

This was the question that Paul had been dreading, and, true to his training, he had resolved upon honesty.

"I was sent down, sir, for indecent behaviour."

"Indeed, indeed? Well, I shall not ask for details. I have been in the scholastic profession long enough to know that nobody enters it unless he has some very good reason which he is anxious to conceal. But, again to be practical, Mr. Pennyfeather, I can hardly pay one hundred and twenty pounds to any one who has been sent down for indecent behaviour. Suppose that we fix your salary at ninety pounds a year to begin with? I have to return to Llanabba tonight. There are six more weeks of term, you see, and I have lost a master rather suddenly. I shall expect you to-morrow evening. There is an excellent train from Euston that leaves at about ten. I think you will like your work," he continued dreamily; "you will find that my school is built upon an ideal—an ideal of service and fellowship. Many of the boys come from the very best families. Little Lord Tangent has come to us this term, the Earl of Circumference's son, you know. Such a nice little chap, erratic, of course, like all his family, but he has *tone*." Dr. Fagan gave a long sigh. "I wish I could say the same for my staff. Between ourselves, Pennyfeather, I think I shall have to get rid of Grimes fairly soon. He is *not* out of the top drawer, and boys notice

these things. Now, your predecessor was a thoroughly
agreeable young man. I was sorry to lose him. But he used
to wake up my daughters coming back on his motor bicycle at all hours of the night. He used to borrow money
from the boys, too, quite large sums, and the parents ob-
jected. I had to get rid of him. . . . Still, I was very sorry.
He had tone."

Dr. Fagan arose, put on his hat at a jaunty angle, and
drew on a glove.

"Good-bye, my dear Pennyfeather. I think, in fact I
know, that we are going to work well together. I can always tell these things."

"Good-bye, sir," said Paul. . . .

"Five per cent, of ninety pounds is four pounds ten
shillings," said Mr. Levy cheerfully. "You can pay now
or on receipt of your first term's salary. If you pay now
there is a reduction of 15 per cent. That would be three
pounds six shillings and sixpence."

"I'll pay when I get my wages," said Paul.

"Just as you please," said Mr. Levy. "Only too glad to
have been of use to you."

CHAPTER TWO

Llanabba Castle

LLANABBA CASTLE presents two quite different aspects, according as you approach it from the Bangor or the coast
road. From the back it looks very much like any other
large country house, with a great many windows and a
terrace, and a chain of glass houses and the roofs of innumerable nondescript kitchen buildings disappearing
into the trees. But from the front—and that is how it is
approached from Llanabba station—it is formidably feudal; one drives past at least a mile of machicolated wall

before reaching the gates; these are towered and turreted and decorated with heraldic animals and a workable portcullis. Beyond them at the end of the avenue stands the Castle, a model of mediæval impregnability.

The explanation of this rather striking contrast is simple enough. At the time of the cotton famine in the 'sixties Llanabba House was the property of a prosperous Lancashire mill owner. His wife could not bear to think of their men starving; in fact, she and her daughters organized a little bazaar in their aid, though without any very substantial results. Her husband had read the Liberal economists and could not think of paying without due return. Accordingly "enlightened self-interest" found a way. An encampment of mill hands was settled in the park, and they were put to work walling the grounds and facing the house with great blocks of stone from a neighbouring quarry. At the end of the American war they returned to their mills, and Llanabba House became Llanabba Castle after a great deal of work had been done very cheaply.

Driving up from the station in a little closed taxi, Paul saw little of all this. It was almost dark in the avenue and quite dark inside the house.

"I am Mr. Pennyfeather," he said to the butler. "I have come here as a master."

"Yes," said the butler, "I know all about you. This way."

They went down a number of passages, unlit and smelling obscurely of all ghastly smells of school, until they reached a brightly lighted door.

"In there. That's the Common Room." Without more ado, the butler made off into the darkness.

Paul looked round. It was not a very big room. Even he felt that, and all his life he had been accustomed to living in constricted spaces.

"I wonder how many people live here," he thought, and with a sick thrust of apprehension counted sixteen pipes in a rack at the side of the chimney piece. Two gowns hung on a hook behind the door. In a corner were some golf clubs, a walking stick, an umbrella and two miniature rifles. Over the chimney piece was a green baize notice board covered with lists; there was a typewriter on the table. In a bookcase were a number of very old textbooks and some new exercise books. There were also a bicycle pump, two armchairs, a straight chair, half a bottle of invalid port, a boxing glove, a bowler hat, yesterday's *Daily News*, and a packet of pipe cleaners.

Paul sat down disconsolately on the straight chair.

Presently there was a knock at the door, and a small boy came in.

"Oh!" he said, looking at Paul intently.

"Hullo!" said Paul.

"I was looking for Captain Grimes," said the little boy.

"Oh!" said Paul.

The child continued to look at Paul with a penetrating impersonal interest.

"I suppose you're the new master?" he said.

"Yes," said Paul. "I'm called Pennyfeather."

The little boy gave a shrill laugh. "I think that's terribly funny," he said, and went away.

Presently the door opened again, and two more boys looked in. They stood and giggled for a time and then made off.

In the course of the next half hour six or seven boys appeared on various pretexts and stared at Paul.

Then a bell rang, and there was a terrific noise of whistling and scampering. The door opened, and a very short man of about thirty came into the Common Room. He had made a great deal of noise in coming because he had an artificial leg. He had a short red moustache, and was slightly bald.

"Hullo!" he said.

"Hullo!" said Paul.

"I'm Captain Grimes," said the newcomer, and "Come in, you," he added to some one outside.

Another boy came in.

"What do you mean," said Grimes, "by whistling when I told you to stop?"

"Every one else was whistling," said the boy.

"What's that got to do with it?" said Grimes.

"I should think it had a lot to do with it," said the boy.

"Well, just you do a hundred lines, and next time, remember, I shall beat you," said Grimes, "with this," waving the walking stick.

"That wouldn't hurt much," said the boy, and went out.

"There's no discipline in the place," said Grimes, and then he went out too.

"I wonder whether I'm going to enjoy being a schoolmaster," thought Paul.

Quite soon another and older man came into the room.

"Hullo!" he said to Paul.

"Hullo!" said Paul.

"I'm Prendergast," said the newcomer. "Have some port?"

"Thank you, I'd love to."

"Well, there's only one glass."

"Oh, well, it doesn't matter, then."

"You might get your tooth glass from your bedroom."

"I don't know where that is."

"Oh, well, never mind; we'll have some another night. I suppose you're the new master?"

"Yes."

"You'll hate it here. I know. I've been here ten years. Grimes only came this term. He hates it already. Have you seen Grimes?"

"Yes, I think so."

"He isn't a gentleman. Do you smoke?"

"Yes."

"A pipe, I mean."

"Yes."

"Those are my pipes. Remind me to show them to you after dinner."

At this moment the butler appeared with a message that Dr. Fagan wished to see Mr. Pennyfeather.

Dr. Fagan's part of the Castle was more palatial. He

stood at the end of a long room with his back to a rococo marble chimney piece; he wore a velvet dinner jacket.

"Settling in?" he asked.

"Yes," said Paul.

Sitting before the fire, with a glass bottle of sweets in her lap, was a brightly dressed woman in early middle age.

"That," said Dr. Fagan with some disgust, "is my daughter."

"Pleased to meet you," said Miss Fagan. "Now what I always tells the young chaps as comes here is, 'Don't let the dad overwork you.' He's a regular Tartar, is Dad, but then you know what scholars are—inhuman. Ain't you," said Miss Fagan, turning on her father with sudden ferocity—"ain't you inhuman?"

"At times, my dear, I am grateful for what little detachment I have achieved. But here," he added, "is my other daughter."

Silently, except for a scarcely perceptible jingling of keys, another woman had entered the room. She was younger than her sister, but far less gay.

"How do you do?" she said. "I do hope you have brought some soap with you. I asked my father to tell you, but he so often forgets these things. Masters are not supplied with soap or with boot polish or with washing over two shillings and sixpence weekly. Do you take sugar in your tea?"

"Yes, usually."

"I will make a note of that and have two extra lumps put out for you. Don't let the boys get them, though."

"I have put you in charge of the fifth form for the rest of this term," said Dr. Fagan. "You will find them delightful boys, quite delightful. Clutterbuck wants watching, by the way, a very delicate little chap. I have also put you in charge of the games, the carpentering class and the fire drill. And I forget, do you teach music?"

"No, I'm afraid not."

"Unfortunate, most unfortunate. I understood from Mr. Levy that you did. I have arranged for you to take

Beste-Chetwynde in organ lessons twice a week. Well, you must do the best you can. There goes the bell for dinner. I won't detain you. Oh, one other thing. Not a word to the boys, please, about the reasons for your leaving Oxford! We schoolmasters must temper discretion with deceit. There, I fancy I have said something for you to think about. Good night."

"Tootle-oo," said the elder Miss Fagan.

CHAPTER THREE

Captain Grimes

PAUL had very little difficulty in finding the dining hall. He was guided there by the smell of cooking and the sound of voices. It was a large, panelled room, far from disagreeable, with fifty or sixty boys of ages ranging from ten to eighteen settled along four long tables. The smaller ones wore Eton suits, the elder ones dinner jackets.

He was led to a place at the head of one of the tables. The boys on either side of him stood up very politely until he sat down. One of them was the boy who had whistled at Captain Grimes. Paul thought he rather liked him.

"I'm called Beste-Chetwynde," he said.

"I've got to teach you the organ, I believe."

"Yes, it's great fun: we play in the village church. Do you play terribly well?"

Paul felt this was not a moment for candour, and so, "tempering discretion with deceit," he said, "Yes, remarkably well."

"I say, do you really, or are you rotting?"

"Indeed, I'm not. I used to give lessons to the Master of Scone."

"Well, you won't be able to teach me much," said

Beste-Chetwynde cheerfully. "I only do it to get off gym. I say, they haven't given you a napkin. These servants are too awful. Philbrick," he shouted to the butler, "why haven't you given Mr. Pennyfeather a napkin?"

"Forgot," said Philbrick, "and it's too late now because Miss Fagan's locked the linen up."

"Nonsense!" said Beste-Chetwynde; "go and get one at once. That man's all right, really," he added, "only he wants watching."

In a few minutes Philbrick returned with the napkin.

"It seems to me that you're a remarkably intelligent boy," said Paul.

"Captain Grimes doesn't think so. He says I'm half-witted. I'm glad you're not like Captain Grimes. He's so common, don't you think?"

"You mustn't talk about the other masters like that in front of me."

"Well, that's what we all think about him, anyway. What's more, he wears combinations. I saw in his washing book one day when I was fetching him his hat. I think combinations are rather awful, don't you?"

There was a commotion at the end of the hall.

"I expect that's Clutterbuck being sick," said Beste-Chetwynde. "He's usually sick when we have mutton."

The boy on Paul's other side now spoke for the first time.

"Mr. Prendergast wears a wig," he said, and then became very confused and subsided into a giggle.

"That's Briggs," said Beste-Chetwynde, "only every one calls him Brolly, because of the shop, you know."

"They're silly rotters," said Briggs.

All this was a great deal easier than Paul had expected; it didn't seem so very hard to get on with boys, after all.

After a time they all stood up, and amid considerable noise Mr. Prendergast said grace. Some one called out "Prendy!" very loudly just by Paul's ear.

". . . *per Christum Dominum nostrum. Amen,*" said Mr. Prendergast. "Beste-Chetwynde, was that you who made that noise?"

"Me, sir? No, sir."

"Pennyfeather, did Beste-Chetwynde make that noise?"

"No, I don't think so," said Paul, and Beste-Chetwynde gave him a friendly look, because, as a matter of fact, he had.

Captain Grimes linked arms with him outside the dining hall.

"Filthy meal, isn't it, old boy?" he said.

"Pretty bad," said Paul.

"Prendy's on duty to-night. I'm off to the pub. How about you?"

"All right," said Paul.

"Prendy's not so bad in his way," said Grimes, "but he can't keep order. Of course, you know he wears a wig. Very hard for a man with a wig to keep order. I've got a false leg, but that's different. Boys respect that. Think I lost it in the war. Actually," said the Captain, "and strictly between ourselves, mind, I was run over by a tram in Stoke-on-Trent when I was one-over-the-eight. Still, it doesn't do to let that out to every one. Funny thing, but I feel I can trust you. I think we're going to be pals."

"I hope so," said Paul.

"I've been feeling the need of a pal for some time. The bloke before you wasn't bad—a bit stand-offish, though. He had a motor bike, you see. The daughters of the house didn't care for him. Have you met Miss Fagan?"

"I've met two."

"They're both bitches," said Grimes, and added moodily, "I'm engaged to be married to Flossie."

"Good God! Which is she?"

"The elder. The boys called them Flossie and Dingy. We haven't told the old boy yet. I'm waiting till I land in the soup again. Then I shall play that as my last card. I generally get into the soup sooner or later. Here's the pub. Not such a bad little place in its way. Clutterbuck's father makes all the beer round here. Not bad stuff, either. Two pints, please, Mrs. Roberts!"

In the farther corner sat Philbrick, talking volubly in Welsh to a shady-looking old man.

"Damned cheek his coming in here!" said Grimes.

Mrs. Roberts brought them their beer. Grimes took a long draught and sighed happily.

"This looks like being the first end of term I've seen for two years," he said dreamily. "Funny thing, I can always get on all right for about six weeks, and then I land in the soup. I don't believe I was ever meant by Nature to be a schoolmaster. Temperament," said Grimes, with a far-away look in his eyes—"that's been my trouble, temperament and sex."

"Is it quite easy to get another job after—after you've been in the soup?" asked Paul.

"Not at first, it isn't, but there 're ways. Besides, you see, I'm a public-school man. That means everything. There's a blessed equity in the English social system," said Grimes, "that insures the public-school man against starvation. One goes through four or five years of perfect hell at an age when life is bound to be hell anyway, and after that the social system never lets one down.

"Not that I stood four or five years of it, mind; I got the push soon after my sixteenth birthday. But my housemaster was a public-school man. He knew the system. 'Grimes,' he said, 'I can't keep you in the House after what has happened. I have the other boys to consider. But I don't want to be too hard on you. I want you to start again.' So he sat down there and then wrote me a letter of recommendation to any future employer, a corking good letter, too. I've got it still. It's been very useful at one time or another. That's the public-school system all over. They may kick you out, but they never let you down.

"I subscribed a guinea to the War Memorial Fund. I felt I owed it to them. I was really sorry," said Grimes, "that that cheque never got through.

"After that I went into business. Uncle of mine had a brush factory at Edmonton. Doing pretty well before the

war. That put the lid on the brush trade for me. You're
too young to have been in the war, I suppose? Those were
days, old boy. We shan't see the like of them again. I
don't suppose I was really sober for more than a few
hours for the whole of that war. Then I got into the soup
again, pretty badly that time. Happened over in France.
They said, 'Now, Grimes, you've got to behave like a gentleman. We don't want a court-martial in this regiment.
We're going to leave you alone for half an hour. There's
your revolver. You know what to do. Good-bye, old man,'
they said quite affectionately.

"Well, I sat there for some time looking at that revolver. I put it up to my head twice, but each time I
brought it down again. 'Public-school men don't end
like this,' I said to myself. It was a long half hour, but
luckily they had left a decanter of whisky in there with
me. They'd all had a few, I think. That's what made them
all so solemn. There wasn't much whisky left when they
came back, and, what with that and the strain of the situation, I could only laugh when they came in. Silly thing
to do, but they looked so surprised, seeing me there alive
and drunk.

" 'The man's a cad,' said the colonel, but even then I
couldn't stop laughing, so they put me under arrest and
called a court-martial.

"I must say I felt pretty low next day. A major came
over from another battalion to try my case. He came to
me first, and bless me if it wasn't a cove I'd known at
school!

" 'God bless my soul,' he said, 'if it isn't Grimes of Podg-
er's! What's all this nonsense about a court-martial?' So
I told him. 'H'm,' he said, 'pretty bad. Still, it's out of the
question to shoot an old Harrovian. I'll see what I can
do about it.' And next day I was sent to Ireland on a
pretty cushy job connected with postal service. That saw
me out as far as the war was concerned. You can't get into
the soup in Ireland, do what you like. I don't know if all
this bores you?"

"Not at all," said Paul. "I think it's most encouraging."

"I've been in the soup pretty often since then, but never quite so badly. Some one always turns up and says, 'I can't see a public-school man down and out. Let me put you on your feet again.' I should think," said Grimes, "I've been put on my feet more often than any living man."

Philbrick came across the bar parlour towards them.

"Feeling lonely?" he said. "I've been talking to the station master here, and if either of you wants an introduction to a young lady—"

"Certainly not," said Paul.

"Oh, all right," said Philbrick, making off.

"Women are an engima," said Grimes, "as far as Grimes is concerned."

CHAPTER FOUR

Mr. Prendergast

PAUL was awakened next morning by a loud bang on his door, and Beste-Chetwynde looked in. He was wearing a very expensive-looking Charvet dressing gown.

"Good morning, sir," he said. "I thought I'd come and tell you, as you wouldn't know: there's only one bathroom for the masters. If you want to get there before Mr. Prendergast, you ought to go now. Captain Grimes doesn't wash much," he added, and then disappeared.

Paul went to the bath and was rewarded some minutes later by hearing the shuffling of slippers down the passage and the door furiously rattled.

As he was dressing Philbrick appeared.

"Oh, I forgot to call you. Breakfast is in ten minutes."

After breakfast Paul went up to the Common Room. Mr. Prendergast was there polishing his pipes, one by one, with a chamois leather. He looked reproachfully at Paul.

"We must come to some arrangment about the bathroom," he said. "Grimes very rarely has a bath. I have one before breakfast."

"So do I," said Paul defiantly.

"Then I suppose I shall have to find some other time," said Mr. Prendergast, and he gave a deep sigh as he returned his attention to his pipes. "After ten years, too," he added, "but everything's like that. I might have known you'd want the bath. It was so easy when there was only Grimes and that other young man. He was never down in time for breakfast. Oh, dear! oh, dear! I can see that things are going to be very difficult."

"But surely we could both have one?"

"No, no, that's out of the question. It's all part of the same thing. Everything has been like this since I left the ministry."

Paul made no answer, and Mr. Prendergast went on breathing and rubbing.

"I expect you wonder how I came to be here?"

"No, no," said Paul soothingly. "I think it's very natural."

"It's not natural at all; it's most unnatural. If things had happened a little differently I should be a rector with my own house and bathroom. I might even have been a rural dean, only"—and Mr. Prendergast dropped his voice to a whisper—"only I had *Doubts*.

"I don't know why I'm telling you all this; nobody else knows. I somehow feel you'll understand.

"Ten years ago I was a clergyman of the Church of England. I had just been presented to a living in Worthing. It was such an attractive church, not old, but *very* beautifully decorated, six candles on the altar, Reservation in the Lady Chapel, and an excellent heating apparatus which burned coke in a little shed by the sacristy door; no graveyard, just a hedge of golden privet between the church and the rectory.

"As soon as I moved in my mother came to keep house for me. She bought some chintz, out of her own money, for the drawing-room curtains. She used to be 'at home' once a week to the ladies of the congregation. One of them, the dentist's wife, gave me a set of the *Encyclopædia Britannica* for my study. It was all very pleasant until my *Doubts* began."

"Were they as bad as all that?" asked Paul.

"They were insuperable," said Mr. Prendergast; "that is why I am here now. But I expect I am boring you?"

"No, do go on. That's to say, unless you find it painful to think about."

"I think about it all the time. It happened like this, quite suddenly. We had been there about three months, and my mother had made great friends with some people called Bundle—rather a curious name. I think he was an insurance agent until he retired. Mrs. Bundle used very kindly to ask us in to supper on Sundays after Evensong. They were pleasant informal gatherings, and I used quite to look forward to them. I can see them now as they sat there on this particular evening; there was my mother and Mr. and Mrs. Bundle, and their son, rather a spotty boy, I remember, who used to go in to Brighton College by train every day, and Mrs. Bundle's mother, a Mrs. Crump, rather deaf, but a very good Churchwoman, and Mrs. Abel—that was the name of the dentist's wife who gave me the *Encyclopædia Britannica*—and old Major Ending, the people's warden. I had preached two sermons that day besides taking the children's Bible class in the afternoon, and I had rather dropped out of the conversation. They were all talking away quite happily about the preparations that were being made on the pier for the summer season, when suddenly, for no reason at all, my *Doubts* began." He paused, and Paul felt constrained to offer some expression of sympathy.

"What a terrible thing!" he said.

"Yes, I've not known an hour's real happiness since. You see, it wasn't the ordinary sort of Doubt about Cain's wife or the Old Testament miracles or the consecration of Archbishop Parker. I'd been taught how to explain all those while I was at college. No, it was something deeper than all that. *I couldn't understand why God had made the world at all.* There was my mother and the Bundles and Mrs. Crump talking away quite unconcernedly while I sat there wrestling with this sudden assault of doubt. You see how fundamental that is. Once granted the first step, I can see that everything else follows—Tower of Babel, Babylonian captivity, Incarnation, Church, bishops, incense, everything—but what I couldn't see, and what I can't see now, is, *why* did it all begin?

"I asked my bishop; he didn't know. He said that he didn't think the point really arose as far as my practical duties as a parish priest were concerned. I discussed it with my mother. At first she was inclined to regard it as a passing phase. But it didn't pass, so finally she agreed with me that the only honourable thing to do was to resign my living; she never really recovered from the shock, poor old lady. It was a great blow after she had bought the chintz and got so friendly with the Bundles."

A bell began ringing down a distant passage.

"Well, well, we must go to prayers, and I haven't finished my pipes." He took his gown from the peg behind the door and slipped it over his shoulders.

"Perhaps one day I shall see Light," he said, "and then I shall go back to the ministry. Meanwhile—"

Clutterbuck ran past the door, whistling hideously.

"That's a nasty little boy," said Mr. Prendergast, "if ever there was one."

CHAPTER FIVE

Discipline

PRAYERS were held downstairs in the main hall of the Castle. The boys stood ranged along the panelled walls, each holding in his hands a little pile of books. Grimes sat on one of the chairs beside the baronial chimney piece.

"Morning," he said to Paul; "only just down, I'm afraid. Do I smell of drink?"

"Yes," said Paul.

"Comes of missing breakfast. Prendy been telling you about his Doubts?"

"Yes," said Paul.

"Funny thing," said Grimes, "but I've never been worried in that way. I don't pretend to be a particularly pious sort of chap, but I've never had any Doubts. When you've been in the soup as often as I have, it gives you a sort of feeling that everything's for the best, really. You know, God's in His heaven; all's right with the world. I can't quite explain it, but I don't believe one can ever be unhappy for long provided one does just exactly what one wants to and when one wants to. The last chap who put me on my feet said I was 'singularly in harmony with the primitive promptings of humanity.' I've remembered that phrase because somehow it seemed to fit me. Here comes the old man. This is where we stand up."

As the bell stopped ringing Dr. Fagan swept into the hall, the robes of a Doctor of Philosophy swelling and billowing about him. He wore an orchid in his buttonhole.

"Good morning, gentlemen," he said.

"Good morning, sir," chorused the boys.

The Doctor advanced to the table at the end of the room, picked up a Bible, and opening it at random, read a chapter of blood-curdling military history without any evident relish. From that he plunged into the Lord's Prayer, which the boys took up in a quiet chatter. Mr. Prendergast's voice led them in tones that testified to his ecclesiastical past.

Then the Doctor glanced at a sheet of notes he held in his hand. "Boys," he said, "I have some announcements to make. The Fagan cross-country running challenge cup will not be competed for this year, on account of the floods."

"I expect the old boy has popped it," said Grimes in Paul's ear.

"Nor will the Llanabba Essay Prize."

"On account of the floods," said Grimes.

"I have received my account for the telephone," proceeded Dr. Fagan, "and I find that during the past quarter there have been no less than twenty-three trunk calls to London, none of which was sent by me or by members of my family. I look to the prefects to stop this, unless of course they are themselves responsible, in which case I must urge them in my own interests to make use of the village post-office, to which they have access.

"I think that is everything, isn't it, Mr. Prendergast?"

"*Cigars,*" said Mr. Prendergast in a stage whisper.

"Ah, yes, cigars. Boys, I have been deeply distressed to learn that several cigar ends have been found—where have they been found?"

"*Boiler room.*"

"In the boiler room. I regard this as reprehensible. What boy has been smoking cigars in the boiler room?"

There was a prolonged silence, during which the Doctor's eye travelled down the line of boys.

"I will give the culprit until luncheon to give himself up. If I do not hear from him by then the whole school will be heavily punished."

"Damn!" said Grimes. "I gave those cigars to Clutterbuck. I hope the little beast has the sense to keep quiet."

"Go to your classes," said the Doctor.

The boys filed out.

"I should think, by the look of them, they were exceedingly cheap cigars," added Mr. Prendergast sadly. "They were a pale yellow colour."

"That makes it worse," said the Doctor. "To think of any boy under my charge smoking pale yellow cigars in a boiler room! It is *not* a gentlemanly fault."

The masters went upstairs.

"That's your little mob in there," said Grimes; "you let them out at eleven."

"But what am I to teach them?" said Paul in sudden panic.

"Oh, I shouldn't try to *teach* them anything, not just yet, anyway. Just keep them quiet."

"Now that's a thing I've never learned to do," sighed Mr. Prendergast.

Paul watched him amble into his class room at the end of the passage, where a burst of applause greeted his arrival. Dumb with terror, he went into his own class room.

Ten boys sat before him, their hands folded, their eyes bright with expectation.

"Good morning, sir," said the one nearest him.

"Good morning," said Paul.

"Good morning, sir," said the next.

"Good morning," said Paul.

"Good morning, sir," said the next.

"Oh, shut up," said Paul.

At this the boy took out a handkerchief and began to cry quietly.

"Oh, sir," came a chorus of reproach, "you've hurt his feelings. He's very sensitive; it's his Welsh blood you know: it makes people very emotional. Say 'Good morning' to him, sir, or he won't be happy all day. After all, it is a good morning, isn't it, sir?"

"Silence!" shouted Paul above the uproar, and for a few moments things were quieter.

"Please, sir," said a small voice—Paul turned and saw a grave-looking youth holding up his hand—"please, sir, perhaps he's been smoking cigars and doesn't feel well."

"Silence!" said Paul again.

The ten boys stopped talking and sat perfectly still, staring at him. He felt himself getting hot and red under this scrutiny.

"I suppose the first thing I ought to do is to get your names clear. What is your name?" he asked, turning to the first boy.

"Tangent, sir."

"And yours?"

"Tangent, sir," said the next boy. Paul's heart sank.

"But you can't both be called Tangent."

"No, sir, *I'm* Tangent. He's just trying to be funny."

"I like that. *Me* trying to be funny! Please, sir, I'm Tangent, sir; really I am."

"If it comes to that," said Clutterbuck from the back of the room, "there is only one Tangent here, and that is me. Any one else can jolly well go to blazes."

Paul felt desperate.

"Well, is there any one who isn't Tangent?"

Four or five voices instantly arose.

"I'm not, sir; I'm not Tangent. I wouldn't be called Tangent, not on the end of a barge pole."

In a few seconds the room had become divided into two parties: those who were Tangent and those who were not. Blows were already being exchanged, when the door opened and Grimes came in. There was a slight hush.

"I thought you might want this," he said, handing Paul a walking stick. "And if you take my advice, you'll set them something to do."

He went out; and Paul, firmly grasping the walking stick, faced his form.

"Listen," he said. "I don't care a damn what any of you are called, but if there's another word from any one I shall keep you all in this afternoon."

"You can't keep me in," said Clutterbuck; "I'm going for a walk with Captain Grimes."

"Then I shall very nearly kill you with this stick. Meanwhile you will all write an essay on 'Self-indulgence.' There will be a prize of half a crown for the longest essay, irrespective of any possible merit."

From then onward all was silence until break. Paul, still holding the stick, gazed despondently out of the window. Now and then there rose from below the shrill of the servants scolding each other in Welsh. By the time the bell rang Clutterbuck had covered sixteen pages, and was awarded the half crown.

"Did you find those boys difficult to manage?" asked Mr. Prendergast, filling his pipe.

"Not at all," said Paul.

"Ah, you're lucky. I find all boys utterly intractable. I don't know why it is. Of course my wig has a lot to do with it. Have you noticed that I wear a wig?"

"No, no, of course not."

"Well, the boys did as soon as they saw it. It was a great mistake my ever getting one. I thought when I left Worthing that I looked too old to get a job easily. I was only forty-one. It was very expensive, even though I chose the cheapest quality. Perhaps that's why it looks so like a wig. I don't know. I knew from the first that it was a mistake, but once they had seen it, it was too late to go back. They make all sorts of jokes about it."

"I expect they'd laugh at something else if it wasn't that."

"Yes, no doubt they would. I daresay it's a good thing to localize their ridicule as far as possible. Oh, dear! oh, dear! If it wasn't for my pipes, I don't know how I should manage to keep on. What made you come here?"

"I was sent down from Scone for indecent behaviour."

"Oh yes, like Grimes?"

"No," said Paul firmly, "not like Grimes."

"Oh, well, it's all much the same really. And there's the bell. Oh, dear! oh, dear! I believe that loathsome little man's taken my gown."

Two days later Beste-Chetwynde pulled out the *vox humana* and played *Pop Goes the Weasel*.

"D'you know, sir, you've made rather a hit with the fifth form?"

He and Paul were seated in the organ loft of the village church. It was their second music lesson.

"For goodness' sake, leave the organ alone. How d'you mean 'hit'?"

"Well, Clutterbuck was in the matron's room this morning. He'd just got a tin of pineapple chunks. Tangent said, 'Are you going to take that into Hall?' and he said, 'No, I'm going to eat them in Mr. Pennyfeather's hour.' 'Oh, no, you're not,' said Tangent. 'Sweets and biscuits are one thing, but pineapple chunks are going too far. It's little stinkers like you,' he said, 'who turn decent masters savage.' "

"Do you think that's so very complimentary?"

"I think it's one of the most complimentary things I ever heard said about a master," said Beste-Chetwynde; "would you like me to try that hymn again?"

"No," said Paul decisively.

"Well, then, I'll tell you another thing," said Beste-Chetwynde. "You know that man Philbrick. Well, I think there's something odd about him."

"I've no doubt of it."

"It's not just that he's such a bad butler. The servants are always ghastly here. But I don't believe he's a butler at all."

"I don't quite see what else he *can* be."

"Well, have you ever known a butler with a diamond tie pin?"

"No, I don't think I have."

"Well, Philbrick's got one, and a diamond ring too. He showed them to Brolly. Colossal great diamonds, Brolly says. Philbrick said he used to have bushels of diamonds and emeralds before the war, and that he used to eat off gold plate. We believe that he's a Russian prince in exile."

"Generally speaking, Russians are not shy about using their titles, are they? Besides, he looks very English."

"Yes, we thought of that, but Brolly said lots of Russians came to school in England before the war. And now I *am* going to play the organ," said Beste-Chetwynde. "After all, my mother does pay five guineas a term extra for me to learn."

CHAPTER SIX

Conduct

SITTING over the Common Room fire that afternoon waiting for the bell for tea, Paul found himself reflecting that on the whole the last week had not been quite as awful as he expected. As Beste-Chetwynde had told him, he was a distinct success with his form; after the first day an understanding had been established between them. It was tacitly agreed that when Paul wished to read or to write letters he was allowed to do so undisturbed while he left them to employ the time as they thought best; when Paul took it upon him to talk to them about their lessons they remained silent, and when he set them work to do some of it was done. It had rained steadily, so that there had been no games. No punishments, no reprisals, no exertion, and in the evenings the confessions of Grimes, any one of which would have glowed with outstanding shamelessness from the appendix to a treastise in psychoanalysis.

Mr. Prendergast came in with the post.

"A letter for you, two for Grimes, nothing for me," he said. "No one ever writes to me. There was a time when I used to get five or six letters a day, not counting circulars. My mother used to file them for me to answer—one heap of charity appeals, another for personal letters, another for marriages and funerals, another for baptisms and churchings and another for anonymous abuse. I wonder why it is the clergy always get so many letters of that sort, sometimes from quite educated people. I remember my father had great trouble in that way once, and he was forced to call in the police because they became so threatening. And, do you know, it was the curate's wife who had sent them—such a quiet little woman. There's your letter. Grimes's look like bills. I can't think why shops give that man credit at all. I always pay cash, or at least I should if I ever bought anything. But d'you know that, except for my tobacco and the *Daily News* and occasionally a little port when it's very cold, I don't think I've bought anything for two years. The last thing I bought was that walking stick. I got it at Shanklin, and Grimes uses it for beating the boys with. I hadn't really meant to buy one, but I was there for the day—two years this August—and I went into the tobacconist's to buy some tobacco. He hadn't the sort I wanted, and I felt I couldn't go out without getting something, so I bought that. It cost one-and-six," he added wistfully, "so I had no tea."

Paul took his letter. It had been forwarded from Onslow Square. On the flap were embossed the arms of Scone College. It was from one of his four friends.

Scone College J.C.R.,
Oxford.

My Dear Pennyfeather [it ran]:

I need hardly tell you how distressed I was when I heard of your disastrous misfortune. It seems to me that a real injustice has been done to you. I have not heard the full facts of the case, but I was confirmed in my opinion by a very curious incident last night. I was just going to bed when Digby-Vaine-Trumpington came into my rooms without knocking. He was smoking a cigar. I had never spoken to him before, as you know, and was very much surprised at his visit. He said: "I'm told you are a friend of Pennyfeather's." I said I was, and he said: "Well, I gather I've rather got him into a mess"; I said: "Yes," and he said: "Well, will you apologize to him for me when you write?" I said I would. Then he said: "Look here, I'm told he's rather poor. I thought of sending him some money—£20 for sort of damages, you know. It's all I can spare at the moment. Wouldn't it be a useful thing to do?" I fairly let him have it, I can tell you, and told him just what I thought of him for making such an insulting suggestion. I asked him how he dared treat a gentleman like that just because he wasn't in his awful set. He seemed rather taken aback and said: "Well, all my friends spend all their time trying to get money out of me," and went off.

I bicycled to St. Magnus's at Little Beckley and took some rubbings of the brasses there. I wished you had been with me.

Yours,
ARTHUR POTTS.

P. S.—I understand you are thinking of taking up educational work. It seems to me that the great problem of education is to train the moral perceptions, not merely to discipline the appetites. I cannot help thinking that it is in greater fastidiousness rather than in greater self-control that the future progress of the race lies. I shall be interested to hear what your experience has been over the matter. The chaplain does not agree with me in this. He says great sensibility usually leads to enervation of will. Let me know what you think.

"What do you think about that?" asked Paul, handing Mr. Prendergast the letter.

"Well," he said after studying it carefully, "I think your friend is wrong about sensibility. It doesn't do to rely on one's own feelings, does it, not in anything?"

"No, I mean about the money."

"Good gracious, Pennyfeather! I hope you are in no doubt about that. Accept it at once, of course."

"It's a temptation."

"My dear boy, it would be a sin to refuse. Twenty pounds! Why, it takes me half a term to earn that."

The bell rang for tea. In the dining hall Paul gave the letter to Grimes.

"Shall I take that twenty pounds?" he asked.

"Take it? My God! I should think you would."

"Well, I'm not sure," said Paul.

He thought about it all through afternoon school, all

the time he was dressing for dinner, and all through dinner. It was a severe struggle, but his early morning training was victorious.

"If I take that money," he said to himself, "I shall never know whether I have acted rightly or not. It would always be on my mind. If I refuse, I shall be sure of having done right. I shall look back upon my self-denial with exquisite self-approval. By refusing I can convince myself that, in spite of the unbelievable things that have been happening to me during the last ten days, I am still the same Paul Pennyfeather I have respected so long. It is a test case of the durability of my ideals."

He tried to explain something of what he felt to Grimes as they sat in Mrs. Roberts's bar parlour that evening.

"I'm afraid you'll find my attitude rather difficult to understand," he said. "I suppose it's largely a matter of upbringing. There is every reason why I should take this money. Digby-Vaine-Trumpington is exceedingly rich; and if he keeps it, it will undoubtedly be spent on betting or on some deplorable debauch. Owing to his party I have suffered irreparable harm. My whole future is shattered, and I have directly lost one hundred and twenty pounds a year in scholarships and two hundred and fifty pounds a year allowance from my guardian. By any ordinary process of thought, the money is justly mine. But," said Paul Pennyfeather, "there is my honour. For generations the British bourgeoisie have spoken of themselves as gentlemen, and by that they have meant, among other things, a self-respecting scorn of irregular perquisites. It is the quality that distinguishes the gentleman from both the artist and the aristocrat. Now I am a gentleman. I can't help it; it's born in me. I just can't take that money."

"Well, I'm a gentleman too, old boy," said Grimes, "and I was afraid you might feel like that, so I did my best for you and saved you from yourself."

"What d'you mean by that?"

"Dear old boy, don't be angry, but immediately after tea I sent off a wire to your friend Potts: *Tell Trumping-*

ton send money quick, and signed it 'Pennyfeather.' I
don't mind lending you the bob till it comes, either."

"Grimes, you wretch!" said Paul, but, in spite of himself, he felt a great wave of satisfaction surge up within
him. "We must have another drink on that."

"Good for you," said Grimes, "and it's on me this
round."

"To the durability of ideals!" said Paul as he got his
pint.

"My word, what a mouthful!" said Grimes; "I can't
say that. Cheerioh!"

Two days later came another letter from Arthur Potts:

DEAR PENNYFEATHER:

I enclose Trumpington's cheque for £20. I am glad that
my dealings with him are at an end. I cannot pretend
to understand your attitude in this matter, but no doubt
you are the best judge.

Stiggins is reading a paper to the O.S.C.U. on "Sex Repression and Religious Experience." Every one expects
rather a row, because you know how keen Walton is on
the mystical element, which I think Stiggins is inclined to
discount.

YOURS,
ARTHUR POTTS.

There is a most interesting article in the *Educational
Review* on the new methods that are being tried at the
Innesborough High School to induce co-ordination of
the senses. They put small objects into the children's
mouths and make them draw the shapes in red chalk.
Have you tried this with your boys? I must say I envy
you your opportunities. Are your colleagues enlightened?

"This same Potts," said Grimes as he read the letter,
"would appear to be something of a stinker. Still, we've
got the doings. How about a binge?"

"Yes," said Paul, "I think we ought to do something
about one. I should like to ask Prendy too."

"Why, of course. It's just what Prendy needs. He's been looking awfully down in the mouth lately. Why shouldn't we all go over to the Metropole at Cwmpryddyg for dinner one night? We shall have to wait until the old boy goes away, otherwise he'll notice that there's no one on duty."

Later in the day Paul suggested the plan to Mr. Prendergast.

"Really, Pennyfeather," he said, "I think that's uncommonly kind of you. I hardly know what to say. Of course, I should love it. I can't remember when I dined at an hotel last. Certainly not since the war. It *will* be a treat. My dear boy, I'm quite overcome."

And, much to Paul's embarrassment, a tear welled up in each of Mr. Prendergast's eyes, and coursed down his cheeks.

CHAPTER SEVEN

Philbrick

THAT morning just before luncheon the weather began to show signs of clearing, and by half-past one the sun was shining. The Doctor made one of his rare visits to the school dining hall. At his entry everybody stopped eating and laid down his knife and fork.

"Boys," said the Doctor, regarding them benignly, "I have an announcement to make. Clutterbuck, will you kindly stop eating while I am addressing the school. The boys' manners need correcting, Mr. Prendergast. I look to the prefects to see to this. Boys, the chief sporting event of the year will take place in the playing fields to-morrow. I refer to the Annual School Sports, unfortunately postponed last year owing to the General Strike. Mr. Penny-

feather, who, as you know, is himself a distinguished athlete, will be in charge of all arrangements. The preliminary heats will be run off to-day. All boys must compete
in all events. The Countess of Circumference has kindly
consented to present the prizes. Mr. Prendergast will act
as referee, and Captain Grimes as timekeeper. I shall myself be present to-morrow to watch the final competitions.
That is all, thank you. Mr. Pennyfeather, perhaps you
will favour me with an interview when you have finished
your luncheon?"

"Good God!" murmured Paul.

"I won the long jump at the last sports," said Briggs,
"but every one said that it was because I had spiked shoes.
Do you wear spiked shoes, sir?"

"Invariably," said Paul.

"Every one said it was taking an unfair advantage. You
see, we never know beforehand when there's going to be
sports, so we don't have time to get ready."

"My mamma's coming down to see me to-morrow," said
Beste-Chetwynde; "just my luck! Now I shall have to
stay here all the afternoon."

After luncheon Paul went to the morning room, where
he found the Doctor pacing up and down in evident
high excitement.

"Ah, come in, Pennyfeather! I am just making the arrangements for to-morrow's fête. Florence, will you get
on to the Clutterbucks on the telephone and ask them to
come over, and the Hope-Brownes. I think the Warring-
tons are too far away, but you might ask them, and of
course the Vicar and old Major Sidebotham. The more
guests the better, Florence!

"And, Diana, you must arrange the tea. Sandwiches,
foie gras sandwiches—last time, you remember, the liver
sausage you bought made Lady Bunyan ill—and cakes,
plenty of cakes, with coloured sugar! You had better take
the car into Llandudno and get them there.

"Philbrick, there must be champagne cup, and will you
help the men putting up the marquee? And flags, Diana!
There should be flags left over from last time."

"I made them into dusters," said Dingy.

"Well, we must buy more. No expense must be spared. Pennyfeather, I want you to get the results of the first heats out by four o'clock. Then you can telephone them to the printers, and we shall have the programmes by to-morrow. Tell them fifty will be enough; they must be decorated with the school colours and crest in gold. And there must be flowers, Diana, banks of flowers," said the Doctor with an expansive gesture. "The prizes shall stand among banks of flowers. Do you think there ought to be a bouquet for Lady Circumference?"

"No," said Dingy.

"Nonsense!" said the Doctor. "Of course there must be a bouquet. It is rarely that the scholarly calm of Llanabba gives place to festival, but when it does taste and dignity shall go unhampered. It shall be an enormous bouquet, redolent of hospitality. You are to procure the most expensive bouquet that Wales can offer; do you understand? Flowers, youth, wisdom, the glitter of jewels, music," said the Doctor, his imagination soaring to dizzy heights under the stimulus of the words, "music! There must be a band."

"I never heard of such a thing," said Dingy. "A band, indeed! You'll be having fireworks next."

"*And fireworks,*" said the Doctor, "and do you think it would be a good thing to buy Mr. Prendergast a new tie? I noticed how shabby he looked this morning."

"No," said Dingy with finality, "that is going too far. Flowers and fireworks are one thing, but I insist on drawing the line somewhere. It would be sinful to buy Mr. Prendergast a tie."

"Perhaps you are right," said the Doctor. "But there shall be music. I understand that the Llanabba Silver Band was third at the North Wales Eisteddfod last month. Will you get on to them, Florence? I think Mr. Davies at the station is the bandmaster. Can the Clutterbucks come?"

"Yes," said Flossie, "six of them."

"Admirable! And then there is the Press. We must

ring up the *Flint and Denbigh Herald* and get them to
send a photographer. That means whisky. Will you see to
that, Philbrick? I remember at one of our sports I omit-
ted to offer whisky to the Press, and the result was a *most*
unfortunate photograph. Boys do get into such indelicate
positions during the obstacle race, don't they?

"Then there are the prizes. I think you had better
take Grimes into Llandudno with you to help with the
prizes. I don't think there is any need for undue extrava-
gance with the prizes. It gives boys a wrong idea of sport.
I wonder whether Lady Circumference would think it
odd if we asked her to present parsley crowns. Perhaps she
would. Utility, economy, and apparent durability are the
qualities to be sought for, I think.

"And, Pennyfeather, I hope you will see that they are
distributed fairly evenly about the school. It doesn't do to
let any boy win more than two events; I leave you to arrange that. I think it would be only right if little Lord
Tangent won something, and Beste-Chetwynde—yes, his
mother is coming down, too.

"I am afraid all this has been thrown upon your
shoulders rather suddenly. I only learned this morning
that Lady Circumference proposed to visit us, and as
Mrs. Beste-Chetwynde was coming too, it seemed too good
an opportunity to be missed. It is not often that the visits
of two such important parents coincide. She is the Honourable Mrs. Beste-Chetwynde, you know—sister-in-law
of Lord Pastmaster—a very wealthy woman, South American. They always say that she poisoned her husband, but
of course little Beste-Chetwynde doesn't know that. It
never came into court, but there was a great deal of talk
about it at the time. Perhaps you remember the case?"

"No," said Paul.

"Powdered glass," said Flossie shrilly, "in his coffee."

"Turkish coffee," said Dingy.

"To work!" said the Doctor; "we have a lot to see to."

It was raining again by the time that Paul and Mr.
Prendergast reached the playing fields. The boys were

waiting for them in bleak little groups, shivering at the
unaccustomed austerity of bare knees and open necks.
Clutterbuck had fallen down in the mud and was crying
quietly behind a tree.

"How shall we divide them?" said Paul.

"I don't know," said Mr. Prendergast. "Frankly, I deplore the whole business."

Philbrick appeared in an overcoat and a bowler hat.

"Miss Fagan says she's very sorry, but she's burned the
hurdles and the jumping posts for firewood. She thinks
she can hire some in Llandudno for to-morrow. The Doctor says you must do the best you can till then. I've got
to help the gardeners put up the blasted tent."

"I think that, if anything, sports are rather worse than
concerts," said Mr. Prendergast. "They at least happen
indoors. Oh, dear! oh, dear! How wet I am getting. I
should have got my boots mended if I'd known this was
going to happen."

"Please, sir," said Beste-Chetwynde, "we're all getting
rather cold. Can we start?"

"Yes, I suppose so," said Paul. "What do you want to
do?"

"Well we ought to divide up into heats and then run a
race."

"All right! Get into four groups."

This took some time. They tried to induce Mr. Prendergast to run too.

"The first race will be a mile. Prendy, will you look
after them? I want to see if Philbrick and I can fix up anything for the jumping."

"But what am I to do?" said Mr. Prendergast.

"Just make each group run to the Castle and back and
take the names of the first two in each heat. It's quite
simple."

"I'll try," he said sadly.

Paul and Philbrick went into the pavilion together.

"Me, a butler," said Philbrick, "made to put up tents
like a blinking Arab!"

"Well, it's a change," said Paul.

"It's a change for me to be a butler," said Philbrick. "I wasn't made to be any one's servant."

"No, I suppose not."

"I expect you wonder how it is that I come to be here?" said Philbrick.

"No," said Paul firmly, "nothing of the kind. I don't in the least want to know anything about you; d'you hear?"

"I'll tell you," said Philbrick; "it was like this—"

"I don't want to hear your loathsome confessions; can't you understand?"

"It isn't a loathsome confession," said Philbrick. "It's a story of love. I think it is without exception the most beautiful story I know.

"I daresay you may have heard of Sir Solomon Philbrick?"

"No," said Paul.

"What, never heard of old Solly Philbrick?"

"No; why?"

"Because that's me. And I can tell you this. It's a pretty well known name across the river. You've only to say Solly Philbrick, of the 'Lamb and Flag' anywhere south of Waterloo Bridge to see what fame is. Try it."

"I will one day."

"Mind you, when I say *Sir* Solomon Philbrick, that's only a bit of fun, see? That's what the boys call me. Plain Mr. Solomon Philbrick I am, really, just like you or him," with a jerk of the thumb towards the playing fields, from which Mr. Prendergast's voice could be heard crying weakly: "Oh, do get into line, you beastly boys," "but *Sir* Solomon's what they call me. Out of respect, see?"

"When I say, 'Are you ready? Go!' I want you to go," Mr. Prendergast could be heard saying. "Are you ready? Go! Oh, why *don't* you go?" And his voice became drowned in shrill cries of protest.

"Mind you," went on Philbrick, "I haven't always been in the position that I am now. I was brought up rough, damned rough. Ever heard speak of 'Chick' Philbrick?"

"No, I'm afraid not."

"No, I suppose he was before your time. Useful little boxer, though. Not first class, on account of his drinking so much *and* being short in the arm. Still, he used to earn five pound a night at the Lambeth Stadium. Always popular with the boys, he was, even when he was so full he couldn't hardly fight. He was my dad, a good-hearted sort of fellow but rough, as I was telling you; he used to knock my poor mother about something awful. Got jugged for it twice, but my! he took it out of her when he got out. There aren't many left like him nowadays, what with education and whisky the price it is.

" 'Chick' was all for getting me on in the sporting world, and before I left school I was earning a few shillings a week holding the sponge at the Stadium on Saturday nights. It was there I met Toby Cruttwell. Perhaps you ain't never heard of him, neither?"

"No, I am terribly afraid I haven't. I'm not very well up in sporting characters."

"Sporting! What, Toby Cruttwell a sporting character! You make me laugh. Toby Cruttwell," said Philbrick with renewed emphasis, "what brought off the Buller diamond robbery of 1912, and the Amalgamated Steel Trust robbery of 1910, and the Isle of Wight burglaries in 1914! He wasn't no sporting character, Toby wasn't. Sporting character! D'you know what he done to Alf Larrigan, what tried to put it over on one of his girls? I'll tell you. Toby had a doctor in tow at the time, name of Peterfield; lives in Harley Street, with a swell lot of patients. Well, Toby knew a thing about him. He'd done in one of Toby's girls what went to him because she was going to have a kid. Well, Toby knew that, so he had to do what Toby told him, see?

"Toby didn't kill Alf; that wasn't his way. Toby never killed no one except a lot of blinking Turks the time they gave him the V.C. But he got hold of him and took him to Dr. Peterfield, and—" Philbrick's voice sank to a whisper.

"Second heat, get ready. Now, if you don't go when I

say 'Go,' I shall disqualify you all; d'you hear? Are you
ready? *Go!*"

". . . He hadn't no use for girls after that. Ha, ha, ha!
Sporting character's good. Well, me and Toby worked together for five years. I was with him in the Steel Trust
and the Buller diamonds, and we cleared a nice little
profit. Toby took 75 per cent., him being the older man,
but even with that I did pretty well. Just before the war
we split. He stuck to safecracking, and I settled down
comfortable at the 'Lamb and Flag,' Camberwell Green.
A very fine house that was before the war, and it's the
best in the locality now, though I says it. Things aren't
quite so easy as they was, but I can't complain. I've got
the picture house next to it, too. Just mention my name
there any day you like to have a free seat."

"That's very kind of you."

"You're welcome. Well, then there was the war. Toby
got the V.C. in the Dardanelles and turned respectable.
He's in Parliament now—Major Cruttwell, M.P., Conservative member for some potty town on the South
Coast. My old woman ran the pub for me. Didn't tell you
I was married, did I? Pretty enough bit of goods when
we was spliced, but she ran to fat. Women do in the pub-
lic-house business. After the war things were a bit slow,
and then my old woman kicked the bucket. I didn't
think I'd mind much, her having got so fat and all, nor I
didn't not at first, but after a time, when the excitement
of the funeral had died down and things were going on
just the same as usual, I began to get restless. You know
how things get, and I took to reading the papers. Before
that my old woman used to read out the bits she'd like,
and sometimes I'd listen and sometimes I wouldn't, but
anyhow they weren't the things that interested me. She
never took no interest in crime, not unless it was a murder. But I took to reading the police news, and I took
to dropping in at the pictures whenever they sent me a
crook film. I didn't sleep so well, neither, and I used to
lie awake thinking of old times. Of course I could have

married again: in my position I could have married pretty well who I liked; but it wasn't that I wanted.

"Then one Saturday night I came into the bar. I generally drop in on Saturday evenings and smoke a cigar and stand a round of drinks. It sets the right tone. I wear a buttonhole in the summer, too, and a diamond ring. Well, I was in the saloon when who did I see in the corner but Jimmy Drage—cove I used to know when I was working with Toby Cruttwell. I never see a man look more discouraged.

" 'Hullo, Jimmy!' I says. 'We don't see each other as often as we used. How are things with you?' I says it cordial, but careful like, because I didn't know what Jimmy was up to.

" 'Pretty bad,' says Jimmy. 'Just fooled a job.'

" 'What sort of job?' I says. 'Nobbling,' he says, meaning kidnapping.

" 'It was like this,' he says. 'You know a toff called Lord Utteridge?'

" 'The bloke what had them electric burglar alarms,' I says, 'Utteridge House, Belgrave Square?'

" 'That's the blinking bastard. Well, he's got a son—nasty little kid about twelve, just going off to college for the first time. I'd had my eye on him,' Jimmy said, 'for a long time, him being the only son and his father so rich, so when I'd finished the last job I was on I had a go at him. Everything went as easy as drinking,' Jimmy said. There was a garage just round the corner behind Belgrave Square where he used to go every morning to watch them messing about with the cars. Crazy about cars the kid was. Jimmy comes in one day with his motor bike and side car and asks for some petrol. He comes up and looks at it in the way he had.

" 'That bike's no good,' he says. 'No good?' says Jimmy. 'I wouldn't sell it not for a hundred quid, I wouldn't. This bike,' he says, 'won the Grand Prix at Boulogne.' 'Nonsense! the kid says; 'it wouldn't do thirty, not downhill.' 'Well, just you see,' Jimmy says. 'Come for a run? I bet you I'll do eighty on the road.' In he got, and away

they went till they got to a place Jimmy knew. Then
Jimmy shuts him up safe and writes to the father. The kid
was happy as blazes taking down the engine of Jimmy's
bike. It's never been the same since, Jimmy told me, but
then it wasn't much to talk of before. Everything had
gone through splendid till Jimmy got his answer from
Lord Utteridge. Would you believe it, that unnatural
father wouldn't stump up, him that owns ships and coal
mines enough to buy the blinking Bank of England. Said
he was much obliged to Jimmy for the trouble he had
taken, that the dearest wish of his life had been gratified
and the one barrier to his complete happiness removed,
but that, as the matter had been taken up without his
instructions, he did not feel called upon to make any
payment in respect of it, and remained his sincerely, Utteridge.

"That was a nasty one for Jimmy. He wrote once or
twice after that, but got no answer, so by the time the kid
had spread bits of the bike all over the room Jimmy let
him go.

" 'Did you try pulling out 'is teeth and sending them to
his pa?' I asks.

" 'No,' says Jimmy, 'I didn't do that.'

" 'Did you make the kid write pathetic, asking to be
let out?'

" 'No,' says Jimmy, 'I didn't do that.'

" 'Did you cut off one of his fingers and put it in the
letter box?'

" 'No,' he says.

" 'Well, man alive,' I says, 'you don't deserve to succeed. You just don't know your job.'

" 'Oh, cut that out,' he says; 'it's easy to talk. You've
been out of the business ten years. You don't know what
things are like nowadays.'

"Well, that rather set me thinking. As I say, I'd been
getting restless doing nothing but just pottering round
the pub all day. 'Look here,' I says, 'I bet you I can bring
off a job like that any day with any kid you like to mention.' 'Done!' says Jimmy. So he opens a newspaper. 'The

first toff we find what's got a only son,' he says. 'Right!'
says I. Well, about the first thing we found was a picture
of Lady Circumference with her only son, Lord Tangent,
at Warwick Races. 'There's your man,' says Jimmy. And
that's what brought me here."

"But, good gracious," said Paul, "why have you told
me this monstrous story? I shall certainly inform the police. I never heard of such a thing."

"That's all right," said Philbrick. "The job's off.
Jimmy's won his bet. All this was before I met Dina,
see?"

"Dina?"

"Miss Diana. Dina I calls her, after a song I heard.
The moment I saw that girl I knew the game was up. My
heart just stood still. There's a song about that, too.
That girl," said Philbrick, "could bring a man up from
the depths of hell itself."

"You feel as strongly as that about her?"

"I'd go through fire and water for that girl. She's not
happy here. I don't think her dad treats her proper. Sometimes," said Philbrick, "I think she's only marrying me
to get away from here."

"Good heavens! Are you going to get married?"

"We fixed it up last Thursday. We've been going together for some time. It's bad for a girl being shut away
like that, never seeing a man. She was in a state she'd
have gone with anybody until I came along, just housekeeping day in, day out. The only pleasure she ever got
was cutting down the bills and dismissing the servants.
Most of them leave before their month is up, anyway,
they're that hungry. She's got a head on her shoulders,
she has. Real business woman, just what I need at the
'Lamb.'

"Then she heard me on the 'phone one day giving instructions to our manager at the Picture Theatre. That
made her think a bit. A prince in disguise, as you might
say. It was she who actually suggested our getting married. I shouldn't have had the face to, not while I was butler. What I'd meant to do was to hire a car one day and

come down with my diamond ring and buttonhole and pop the question. But there wasn't any need for that. Love's a wonderful thing."

Philbrick stopped speaking and was evidently deeply moved by his recital. The door of the pavilion opened, and Mr. Prendergast came in.

"Well," asked Paul, "how are the sports going?"

"Not very well," said Mr. Prendergast; "in fact, they've gone."

"All over?"

"Yes. You see, none of the boys came back from the first race. They just disappeared behind the trees at the top of the drive. I expect they've gone to change. I don't blame them, I'm sure. It's terribly cold. Still, it was discouraging launching heat after heat and none coming back. Like sending troops into battle, you know."

"The best thing for us to do is to go back and change too."

"Yes, I suppose so. Oh, what a day!"

Grimes was in the Common Room.

"Just back from the gay metropolis of Llandudno," he said. "Shopping with Dingy is not a seemly occupation for a public-school man. How did the heats go?"

"There weren't any," said Paul.

"Quite right," said Grimes; "you leave this to me. I've been in the trade some time. These things are best done over the fire. We can make out the results in peace. We'd better hurry. The old boy wants them sent to be printed this evening."

And taking a sheet of paper and a small stub of pencil, Grimes made out the programme.

"How about that?" he said.

"Clutterbuck seems to have done pretty well," said Paul.

"Yes, he's a splendid little athlete," said Grimes. "Now just you telephone that through to the printers, and they'll get it done to-night. I wonder if we ought to have a hurdle race?"

"No," said Mr. Prendergast.

CHAPTER EIGHT

The Sports

HAPPILY enough, it did not rain next day, and after morn-ing school everybody dressed up to the nines. Dr. Fagan appeared in a pale gray morning coat and sponge-bag trousers, looking more than ever *jeune premier;* there was a spring in his step and a pronounced sprightliness of bearing that Paul had not observed before. Flossie wore a violet frock of knitted wool made for her during the preceding autumn by her sister. It was the colour of indelible ink on blotting paper, and was ornamented at the waist with flowers of emerald green and pink. Her hat, also home made, was the outcome of many winter evenings of ungrudged labour. All the trimmings of all her previous hats had gone to its adornment. Dingy wore a little steel brooch made in the shape of a bull dog. Grimes wore a stiff evening collar of celluloid.

"Had to do something to celebrate the occasion," he said, "so I put on a 'choker.' Phew, though, it's tight. Have you seen my fiancée's latest creation? Ascot ain't in it. Let's get down to Mrs. Roberts for a quick one before the happy throng rolls up."

"I wish I could, but I've got to go round the ground with the Doctor."

"Righto, old boy! See you later. Here comes Prendy in his coat of many colours."

Mr. Prendergast wore a blazer of faded stripes, which smelt strongly of camphor.

"I think Dr. Fagan encourages a certain amount of display on these occasions," he said. "I used to keep wicket for my college, you know, but I was too short-sighted to be much good. Still, I am entitled to the blazer," he said with a note of defiance in his voice, "and it is more appropriate to a sporting occasion than a stiff collar."

"Good old Prendy!" said Grimes. "Nothing like a change of clothes to bring out latent pep. I felt like that my first week in khaki. Well, so long. Me for Mrs. Roberts. Why don't you come too, Prendy?"

"D'you know," said Mr. Prendergast, "I think I will."

Paul watched them disappear down the drive in amazement. Then he went off to find the Doctor.

"Frankly," said the Doctor, "I am at a loss to understand my own emotions. I can think of no entertainment that fills me with greater detestation than a display of competitive athletics, none—except possibly folk dancing. If there are two women in the world whose company I abominate—and there are very many more than two— they are Mrs. Beste-Chetwynde and Lady Circumference. I have, moreover, had an extremely difficult encounter with my butler, who—will you believe it?—waited at luncheon in a mustard-coloured suit of plus fours and a diamond tie pin, and when I reprimanded him, attempted to tell me some ridiculous story about his being the proprietor of a circus or swimming bath or some such concern. And yet," said the Doctor, "I am filled with a wholly delightful exhilaration. I can't understand it. It is not as though this was the first occasion of the kind. During the fourteen years that I have been at Llanabba there have been six sports days and two concerts, all of them, in one way or another, utterly disastrous. Once Lady Bunyan was taken ill; another time it was the matter of the press photographers and the obstacle race; another time some quite unimportant parents brought a dog with them which bit two of the boys very severely and one of the masters, who swore terribly in front of every one. I could hardly blame him, but of course he had to go. Then there was the concert when the boys refused to sing 'God Save the King' because of the pudding they had had for luncheon. One way and another, I have been consistently unfortunate in my efforts at festivity. And yet I look forward to each new fiasco with the utmost relish. Perhaps, Pennyfeather, you will bring luck to Llanabba; in fact, I feel confident you have already done so. Look at the sun!"

Picking their way carefully among the dry patches in the water-logged drive, they reached the playing fields. Here the haphazard organization of the last twenty-four hours seemed to have been fairly successful. A large marquee was already in position, and Philbrick—still in plus fours—and three gardeners were at work putting up a smaller tent.

"That's for the Llanabba Silver Band," said the Doctor. "Philbrick, I required you to take off those loathsome garments."

"They were new when I bought them," said Philbrick, "and they cost eight pounds fifteen. Anyhow I can't do two things at once, can I? If I go back to change, who's going to manage all this, I'd like to know?"

"All right! Finish what you are doing first. Let us just review the arrangements. The marquee is for the visitors' tea. That is Diana's province. I expect we shall find her at work."

Sure enough, there was Dingy helping two servants to arrange plates of highly coloured cakes down a trestle table. Two other servants in the background were cutting sandwiches. Dingy, too, was obviously enjoying herself.

"Jane, Emily, remember that that butter has to do for three loaves. Spread it thoroughly, but don't waste it, and cut the crusts as thin as possible. Father, will you see to it that the boys who come in with their parents come in *alone*? You remember last time how Briggs brought in four boys with him, and they ate all the jam sandwiches before Colonel Loder had had any. Mr. Pennyfeather, the champagne cup is *not* for the masters. In fact, I expect you will find yourselves too much occupied helping the visitors to have any tea until they have left the tent. You had better tell Captain Grimes that, too. I am sure Mr. Prendergast would not think of pushing himself forward."

Outside the marquee were assembled several seats and

tubs of palms and flowering shrubs. "All this must be set in order," said the Doctor; "our guests may arrive in less than an hour." He passed on. "The cars shall turn aside from the drive here and come right into the ground. It will give a pleasant background to the photographs, and, Pennyfeather, if you would with tact direct the photographer so that more prominence was given to Mrs. Beste-Chetwynde's Hispano Suiza than to Lady Circumference's little motor car, I think it would be all to the good. All these things count, you know."

"Nothing seems to have been done about marking out the ground," said Paul.

"No," said the Doctor, turning his attention to the field for the first time, "nothing. Well, you must do the best you can. They can't do everything."

"I wonder if any hurdles have come?"

"They were ordered," said the Doctor. "I am certain of it. Philbrick, have any hurdles come?"

"Yes," said Philbrick with a low chuckle.

"Why, pray, do you laugh at the mention of hurdles?"

"Just you look at them!" said Philbrick. "They're behind the tea house there."

Paul and the Doctor went to look and found a pile of spiked iron railings in sections heaped up at the back of the marquee. They were each about five feet high and were painted green with gilt spikes.

"It seems to me that they have sent the wrong sort," said the Doctor.

"Yes."

"Well, we must do the best we can. What other things ought there to be?"

"Weight, hammer, javelin, long-jump pit, high-jump posts, low hurdles, eggs, spoon and greasy pole," said Philbrick.

"Previously competed for," said the Doctor imperturbably. "What else?"

"Somewhere to run," suggested Paul.

"Why, God bless my soul, they've got the whole park! How did you manage yesterday for the heats?"

"We judged the distance by eye."

"Then that is what we shall have to do to-day. Really, my dear Pennyfeather, it is quite unlike you to fabricate difficulties in this way. I am afraid you are getting un-nerved. Let them go on racing until it is time for tea; and remember," he added sagely, "the longer the race the more time it takes. I leave the details to you. I am concerned with *style*. I wish, for instance, we had a start-ing pistol."

"Would this be any use?" said Philbrick, producing an enormous service revolver. "Only take care; it's loaded."

"The very thing," said the Doctor. "Only fire into the ground, mind. We must do everything we can to avoid an accident. Do you always carry that about with you?"

"Only when I'm wearing my diamonds," said Phil-brick.

"Well, I hope that is not often. Good gracious! Who are these extraordinary-looking people?"

Ten men of revolting appearance were approaching from the drive. They were low of brow, crafty of eye and crooked of limb. They advanced huddled together with the loping tread of wolves, peering about them furtively as they came, as though in constant terror of ambush; they slavered at their mouths, which hung loosely over their receding chins, while each clutched under his ape-like arm a burden of curious and unaccountable shape. On seeing the Doctor they halted and edged back, those behind squinting and mouthing over their companions' shoulders.

"Crikey!" said Philbrick. "Loonies! This is where I shoot."

"I refuse to believe the evidence of my eyes," said the Doctor. "These creatures simply do not exist."

After brief preliminary shuffling and nudging, an eld-erly man emerged from the back of the group. He had a rough black beard and wore on his uneven shoulders a druidical wreath of brass mistletoe berries.

"Why, it's my friend the station master!" said Phil-brick.

"We are the silver band the Lord bless and keep you," said the station master in one breath, "the band that no one could beat whatever but two indeed in the Eisteddfod that for all North Wales was look you."

"I see," said the Doctor; "I see. That's splendid. Well, will you please go into your tent, the little tent over there."

"To march about you would not like us?" suggested the station master; "we have a fine yellow flag look you that embroidered for us was in silks."

"No, no. Into the tent!"

The station master went back to consult with his fellow musicians. There was a baying and growling and yapping as of the jungle at moonrise, and presently he came forward again with an obsequious, sidelong shuffle.

"Three pounds you pay us would you said indeed to at the sports play."

"Yes, yes, that's right, three pounds. Into the tent!"

"Nothing whatever we can play without the money first," said the station master firmly.

"How would it be," said Philbrick, "if I gave him a clout on the ear?"

"No, no, I beg you to do nothing of the kind. You have not lived in Wales as long as I have." He took a note case from his pocket, the sight of which seemed to galvanize the musicians into life; they crowded round, twitching and chattering. The Doctor took out three pound notes and gave them to the station master. "There you are, Davies!" he said. "Now take your men into the tent. They are on no account to emerge until after tea; do you understand?"

The band slunk away, and Paul and the Doctor turned back toward the Castle.

"The Welsh character is an interesting study," said Dr. Fagan. "I have often considered writing a little monograph on the subject, but I was afraid it might make me unpopular in the village. The ignorant speak of them as Celts, which is of course wholly erroneous. They are of pure Iberian stock—the aboriginal inhabitants of Europe who survive only in Portugal and the Basque district. Celts readily intermarry with their neighbours and absorb them. From the earliest times the Welsh have been looked upon as an unclean people. It is thus that they have preserved their racial integrity. Their sons and daughters rarely mate with humankind except their own blood relations. In Wales there was no need for legislation to prevent the conquering people intermarrying with the conquered. In Ireland that was necessary, for their intermarriage was a political matter. In Wales it was moral. I hope, by the way, you have no Welsh blood?"

"None whatever," said Paul.

"I was sure you had not, but one cannot be too careful. I once spoke of this subject to the sixth form and learned later that one of them had a Welsh grandmother. I am afraid it hurt his feelings terribly, poor little chap. She came from Pembrokeshire, too, which is of course quite a different matter. I often think," he continued, "that we can trace almost all the disasters of English history to the influence of Wales. Think of Edward of Carnarvon, the first Prince of Wales, a perverse life, Pennyfeather, and an unseemly death, then the Tudors and the dissolution of the Church, then Lloyd George, the temperance movement, Non-conformity and lust stalking hand in hand through the country, wasting and ravaging. But perhaps you think I exaggerate? I have a certain rhetorical tendency, I admit."

"No, no," said Paul.

"The Welsh," said the Doctor, "are the only nation in the world that has produced no graphic or plastic art, no architecture, no drama. They just sing," he said with disgust, "sing and blow down wind instruments of plated silver. They are deceitful because they cannot discern truth from falsehood, depraved because they cannot discern the consequences of their indulgence. Let us consider," he continued, "the etymological derivations of the Welsh language. . . ."

But here he was interrupted by a breathless little boy who panted down the drive to meet them. "Please, sir,

Lord and Lady Circumference have arrived, sir. They're
in the library with Miss Florence. She asked me to tell
you."

"The sports will start in ten minutes," said the Doctor.
"Run and tell the other boys to change and go at once
to the playing fields. I will talk to you about the Welsh
again. It is a matter to which I have given some thought,
and I can see that you are sincerely interested. Come in
with me and see the Circumferences."

Flossie was talking to them in the library.

"Yes, isn't it a sweet colour?" she was saying. "I do
like something bright myself. Diana made it for me; she
does knit a treat, does Diana, but of course I chose the
colour, you know, because, you see, Diana's taste is all for
wishy-washy grays and browns. Mournful, you know.
Well, here's the dad. Lady Circumference was just saying
how much she likes my frock what you said was vulgar,
so there!"

A stout elderly woman dressed in a tweed coat and skirt
and jaunty Tyrolean hat advanced to the Doctor.
"Hullo!" she said in a deep bass voice, "how are you?
Sorry if we're late. Circumference ran over a fool of a boy.
I've just been chaffing your daughter here about her frock.
Wish I was young enough to wear that kind of thing.
Older I get the more I like colour. We're both pretty long
in the tooth, eh?" She gave Dr. Fagan a hearty shake of
the hand that obviously caused him acute pain. Then she
turned to Paul.

"So you're the Doctor's hired assassin, eh? Well, I hope
you keep a firm hand on my toad of a son. How's he
doin'?"

"Quite well," said Paul.

"Nonsense!" said Lady Circumference. "The boy's a
dunderhead. If he wasn't he wouldn't be here. He wants
beatin' and hittin' and knockin' about generally, and
then he'll be no good. That grass is shockin' bad on the
terrace, Doctor; you ought to sand it down and resow it,
but you'll have to take that cedar down if you ever want
it to grow properly at the side. I hate cuttin' down a tree

—like losin' a tooth—but you have to choose, tree or grass; you can't keep 'em both. What d'you pay your head man?"

As she was talking Lord Circumference emerged from the shadows and shook Paul's hand. He had a long fair moustache and large watery eyes which reminded Paul a little of Mr. Prendergast.

"How do you do?" he said.

"How do you do?" said Paul.

"Fond of sport, eh?" he said. "I mean these sort of sports?"

"Oh, yes," said Paul. "I think they're so good for the boys."

"Do you? Do you think that?" said Lord Circumference very earnestly; "do you think they're good for the boys?"

"Yes," said Paul; "don't you?"

"Me? Yes, oh, yes. I think so, too. Very good for the boys."

"So useful in case of a war or anything," said Paul.

"D'you think so? D'you really and truly think so? That there's going to be another war, I mean?"

"Yes, I'm sure of it; aren't you?"

"Yes, of course, I'm sure of it too. And that awful bread, and people coming on to one's own land and telling one what one's to do with one's own butter and milk, and commandeering one's horses! Oh, yes, all over again! My wife shot her hunters rather than let them go to the army. And girls in breeches on all the farms! All over again! Who do you think it will be this time?"

"The Americans," said Paul stoutly.

"No, indeed, I hope not. We had German prisoners on two of the farms. That wasn't so bad, but if they start putting Americans on my land, I'll just refuse to stand it. My daughter brought an American down to luncheon the other day, and, do you know . . . ?"

"Dig it and dung it," said Lady Circumference. "Only it's got to be dug deep, mind. Now how did your calceolarias do last year?"

"I really have no idea," said the Doctor. "Flossie, how did our calceolarias do?"

"Lovely," said Flossie.

"I don't believe a word of it," said Lady Circumference. "Nobody's calceolarias did well last year."

"Shall we adjourn to the playing fields?" said the Doctor. "I expect they are all waiting for us."

Talking cheerfully, the party crossed the hall and went down the steps.

"Your drive's awful wet," said Lady Circumference. "I expect there's a blocked pipe somewhere. Sure it ain't sewage?"

"I was never any use at short distances," Lord Circumference was saying. "I was always a slow starter, but I was once eighteenth in the Crick at Rugby. We didn't take sports so seriously at the 'Varsity when I was up: everybody rode. What college were you at?"

"Scone."

"Scone, were you? Ever come across a young nephew of my wife's called Alastair Digby-Vaine-Trumpington?"

"I just met him," said Paul.

"That's very interesting. Greta, Mr. Pennyfeather knows Alastair."

"Does he? Well, that boy's doing no good for himself. Got fined twenty pounds the other day, his mother told me. Seemed proud of it. If my brother had been alive he'd have licked all that out of the young cub. It takes a man to bring up a man."

"Yes," said Lord Circumference meekly.

"Who else do you know at Oxford? Do you know Freddy French-Wise?"

"No."

"Or Tom Obblethwaite or that youngest Castleton boy?"

"No, I'm afraid not. I had a great friend called Potts."

"*Potts!*" said Lady Circumference, and left it at that.

All the school and several local visitors were assembled in the field. Grimes stood by himself, looking depressed. Mr. Prendergast, flushed and unusually vivacious, was talking to the Vicar. As the headmaster's party came into sight the Llanabba Silver Band struck up *Men of Harlech*.

"Shockin' noise," commented Lady Circumference graciously.

The head prefect came forward and presented her with a programme, beribboned and embossed in gold. Another prefect set a chair for her. She sat down with the Doctor next to her and Lord Circumference on the other side of him.

"Pennyfeather," cried the Doctor above the band, "start them racing."

Philbrick gave Paul a megaphone. "I found this in the pavilion," he said. "I thought it might be useful."

"Who's that extraordinary man?" asked Lady Circumference.

"He is the boxing coach and swimming professional," said the Doctor. "A finely developed figure, don't you think?"

"First race," said Paul through the megaphone, "under sixteen. Quarter mile!" He read out Grimes's list of starters.

"What's Tangent doin' in this race?" said Lady Circumference. "The boy can't run an inch."

The silver band stopped playing.

"The course," said Paul, "starts from the pavilion, goes round that clump of elms . . ."

"Beeches," corrected Lady Circumference loudly.

". . . and ends in front of the band stand. Starter, Mr. Prendergast; timekeeper, Captain Grimes."

"I shall say, 'Are you ready? one, two, three!' and then fire," said Mr. Prendergast. "Are you ready? One"—there was a terrific report. "Oh, dear! I'm sorry"—but the race had begun. Clearly Tangent was not going to win; he was sitting on the grass crying because he had been wounded in the foot by Mr. Prendergast's bullet. Philbrick carried him, wailing dismally, into the refreshment tent, where Dingy helped him off with his shoe. His heel was slightly grazed. Dingy gave him a large slice of cake, and he hobbled out surrounded by a sympathetic crowd.

"That won't hurt him," said Lady Circumference, "but I think some one ought to remove the pistol from that old man before he does anything serious."

"I knew that was going to happen," said Lord Circumference.

"A most unfortunate beginning," said the Doctor.

"Am I going to die?" said Tangent, his mouth full of cake.

"For God's sake, look after Prendy," said Grimes in Paul's ear. "The man's as tight as a lord, and on one whisky, too."

"First blood to me!" said Mr. Prendergast gleefully.

"The last race will be run again," said Paul down the megaphone. "Starter, Mr. Philbrick; timekeeper, Mr. Prendergast."

"On your marks! Get set." Bang went the pistol, this time without disaster. The six little boys scampered off through the mud, disappeared behind the beeches and returned rather more slowly. Captain Grimes and Mr. Prendergast held up a piece of tape.

"Well run, sir!" shouted Colonel Sidebotham. "Jolly good race."

"Capital," said Mr. Prendergast, and dropping his end of the tape, he sauntered over to the Colonel. "I can see you are a fine judge of a race, sir. So was I once. So's Grimes. A capital fellow, Grimes; a bounder, you know, but a capital fellow. Bounders can be capital fellows; don't you agree, Colonel Slidebottom? In fact, I'd go farther and say that capital fellows *are* bounders. What d'you say to that? I wish you'd stop pulling at my arm, Pennyfeather. Colonel Shybotham and I are just having a most interesting conversation about bounders."

The silver band struck up again, and Mr. Prendergast began a little jig, saying: "Capital fellow! capital fellow!" and snapping his fingers. Paul led him to the refreshment tent.

"Dingy wants you to help her in there," he said firmly, "and, for God's sake, don't come out until you feel better."

"I never felt better in my life," said Mr. Prendergast indignantly. "Capital fellow! capital fellow!"

"It is not my affair, of course," said Colonel Sidebotham, "but if you ask me I should say that man had been drinking."

"He was talking very excitedly to me," said the Vicar, "about some apparatus for warming a church in Worthing and about the Apostolic Claims of the Church of Abyssinia. I confess I could not follow him clearly. He seems deeply interested in Church matters. Are you quite sure he is right in the head? I have noticed again and again since I have been in the Church that lay interest in ecclesiastical matters is often a prelude to insanity."

"Drink, pure and simple," said the Colonel. "I wonder where he got it? I could do with a spot of whisky."

"Quarter Mile Open!" said Paul through his megaphone.

Presently the Clutterbucks arrived. Both the parents were stout. They brought with them two small children, a governess, and an elder son. They debouched from the car one by one, stretching their limbs in evident relief.

"This is Sam," said Mr. Clutterbuck, "just down from Cambridge. He's joined me in the business, and we've brought the nippers along for a treat. Don't mind, do you, Doc? And last, but not least, my wife."

Dr. Fagan greeted them with genial condescension and found them seats.

"I am afraid you have missed all the jumping events," he said. "But I have a list of the results here. You will see that Percy has done extremely well."

"Didn't know the little beggar had it in him. See that, Martha? Percy's won the high jump and the long jump and the hurdles. How's your young hopeful been doing, Lady Circumference?"

"My boy has been injured in the foot," said Lady Circumference coldly.

"Dear me! Not badly, I hope? Did he twist his ankle in the jumping?"

"No," said Lady Circumference, "he was shot at by one

of the assistant masters. But it is kind of you to inquire."

"Three Miles Open!" announced Paul. "The course of six laps will be run as before."

"On your marks! Get set." Bang went Philbrick's revolver. Off trotted the boys on another race.

"Father," said Flossie, "don't you think it's time for the tea interval?"

"Nothing can be done before Mrs. Beste-Chetwynde arrives," said the Doctor.

Round and round the muddy track trotted the athletes while the silver band played sacred music unceasingly.

"Last lap!" announced Paul.

The school and the visitors crowded about the tape to cheer the winner. Amid loud applause Clutterbuck breasted the tape well ahead of the others.

"Well run! Oh, good, jolly good, sir!" cried Colonel Sidebotham.

"Well run, Percy!" chorused the two little Clutterbucks, prompted by their governess.

"That boy cheated," said Lady Circumference. "He only went round five times. I counted."

"I think unpleasantness so mars the afternoon," said the Vicar.

"How dare you suggest such a thing?" asked Mrs. Clutterbuck. "I appeal to the referee. Percy ran the full course, didn't he?"

"Clutterbuck wins," said Captain Grimes.

"Fiddlesticks!" said Lady Circumference. "He deliberately lagged behind and joined the others as they went behind the beeches. The little toad!"

"Really, Greta," said Lord Circumference, "I think we ought to abide by the referee's decision."

"Well, they can't expect me to give away the prizes, then. Nothing would induce me to give that boy a prize."

"Do you understand, madam, that you are bringing a serious accusation against my son's honour?"

"Serious accusation fiddlesticks! What he wants is a jolly good hidin'."

"No doubt you judge other people's sons by your own. Let me tell you, Lady Circumference . . ."

"Don't attempt to browbeat me, sir. I know a cheat when I see one."

At this stage of the discussion the Doctor left Mrs. Hope-Browne's side, where he had been remarking upon her son's progress in geometry, and joined the group round the winning post.

"If there is a disputed decision," he said genially, "they shall race again."

"Percy has won already," said Mr. Clutterbuck. "He has been adjudged the winner."

"Splendid! splendid! A promising little athlete. I congratulate you, Clutterbuck."

"But he only ran five laps," said Lady Circumference.

"Then clearly he has won the five furlong race, a very exacting length."

"But the other boys," said Lady Circumference, almost beside herself with rage, "have run six lengths."

"Then they," said the Doctor imperturbably, "are first, second, third, fourth and fifth respectively in the Three Miles. Clearly there has been some confusion. Diana, I think we might now serve tea."

Things were not easy, but there was fortunately a distraction, for as he spoke an enormous limousine of dove-gray and silver stole soundlessly on to the field.

"But what could be more opportune? Here is Mrs. Beste-Chetwynde."

Three light skips brought him to the side of the car, but the footman was there before him. The door opened, and from the cushions within emerged a tall young man in a clinging dove-gray overcoat. After him, like the first breath of spring in the Champs Élysées came Mrs. Beste-Chetwynde—two lizard-skin feet, silk legs, chinchilla body, a tight little black hat pinned with platinum and diamonds, and the high invariable voice that may be heard in any Ritz Hotel from New York to Buda-Pesth.

"I hope you don't mind my bringing Chokey, Dr. Fagan?" she said. "He's just crazy about sport."

"I sure am that," said Chokey.

"Dear Mrs. Beste-Chetwynde!" said Dr. Fagan; "dear, dear, Mrs. Beste-Chetwynde! He pressed her glove, and for the moment was at a loss for words of welcome, for "Chokey," though graceful of bearing and irreproachably dressed, was a Negro.

CHAPTER NINE

The Sports (continued)

THE refreshment tent looked very nice. The long table across the centre was covered with a white cloth. Bowls of flowers were ranged down it at regular intervals, and between them plates of sandwiches and cakes and jugs of lemonade and champagne cup. Behind it against a background of palms stood the four Welsh housemaids in clean caps and aprons pouring out tea. Behind them again sat Mr. Prendergast, a glass of champagne cup in his hand, his wig slightly awry. He rose unsteadily to his feet at the approach of the guests, made a little bow, and then sat down again rather suddenly.

"Will you take round the *foie gras* sandwiches, Mr. Pennyfeather?" said Dingy. "They are not for the boys or Captain Grimes."

"One for little me!" said Flossie as he passed her.

Philbrick, evidently regarding himself as one of the guests, was engaged in a heated discussion on greyhound racing with Sam Clutterbuck.

"What price the coon?" he asked as Paul gave him a sandwich.

"It does my heart good to see old Prendy enjoying himself," said Grimes. "Pity he shot that kid, though."

"There's not much the matter with him to see the way

he's eating his tea. I say, this is rather a poor afternoon, isn't it?"

"Circulate, old boy, circulate. Things aren't going too smoothly."

Nor indeed were they. The sudden ebullition of ill-feeling over the Three-mile Race, though checked by the arrival of Mrs. Beste-Chetwynde, was by no means forgotten. There were two distinctly hostile camps in the tea tent. On one side stood the Circumferences, Tangent, the Vicar, Colonel Sidebotham and the Hope-Brownes, on the other the seven Clutterbucks, Philbrick, Flossie and two or three parents who had been snubbed already that afternoon by Lady Circumference. No one spoke of the race, but outraged sportsmanship glinted perilously in every eye. Several parents, intent on their tea, crowded round Dingy and the table. Eminently aloof from all these stood Chokey and Mrs. Beste-Chetwynde. Clearly the social balance was delicately poised, and the issue depended upon them. With or without her Negro, Mrs. Beste-Chetwynde was a woman of vital importance.

"Why, Dr. Fagan," she was saying, "it is too disappointing that we've missed the sports. We had just the slowest journey, stopping all the time to see the churches. You can't move Chokey once he's seen an old church. He's just crazy about culture, aren't you, darling?"

"I sure am that," said Chokey.

"Are you interested in music?" said the Doctor tactfully.

"Well, just you hear that, Baby," said Chokey; "am *I* interested in music? I should say I am."

"He plays just too divinely," said Mrs. Beste-Chetwynde.

"Has he heard my new records, would you say?"

"No, darling, I don't expect he has."

"Well, just you hear *them*, sir, and then you'll know— am I interested in music."

"Now, darling, don't get discouraged. I'll take you over and introduce you to Lady Circumference. It's his inferiority complex, the angel. He's just crazy to meet the aristocracy, aren't you, my sweet?"

"I sure am that," said Chokey.

"I think it's an insult bringing a nigger here," said Mrs. Clutterbuck. "It's an insult to our own women."

"Niggers are all right," said Philbrick. "Where I draw a line is a Chink, nasty inhuman things. I had a pal bumped off by a Chink once. Throat cut horrible, it was, from ear to ear."

"Good gracious!" said the Clutterbuck governess; "was that in the Boxer rising?"

"No," said Philbrick cheerfully. "Saturday night in the Edgware Road. Might have happened to any of us."

"What did the gentleman say?" asked the children.

"Never you mind, my dears. Run and have some more of the green cake."

They ran off obediently, but the little boy was later heard whispering to his sister as she knelt at her prayers, "cut horrible from ear to ear," so that until quite late in her life Miss Clutterbuck would feel a little faint when she saw a 'bus that was going to the Edgware Road.

"I've got a friend lives in Savannah," said Sam, "and he's told me a thing or two about niggers. Of course it's hardly a thing to talk about before the ladies, but, to put it bluntly, *they have uncontrollable passions*. See what I mean?"

"What a terrible thing!" said Grimes.

"You can't blame 'em, mind: it's just their nature. Animal, you know. Still, what I do say is, since they're like that, the less we see of them the better."

"Quite," said Mr. Clutterbuck.

"I had such a curious conversation just now," Lord Circumference was saying to Paul, "with your bandmaster over there. He asked me whether I should like to meet his sister-in-law; and when I said, 'Yes, I should be delighted to,' he said that it would cost a pound normally, but that he'd let me have special terms. What *can* he have meant, Mr. Pennyfoot?"

" 'Pon my soul," Colonel Sidebotham was saying to the Vicar, "I don't like the look of that nigger. I saw enough of Fuzzy-Wuzzy in the Soudan—devilish good enemy and

devilish bad friend. I'm going across to talk to Mrs. Clutterbuck. Between ourselves, I think Lady C. went a bit
far. I didn't see the race myself, but there are limits. . . ."

"Rain ain't doin' the turnip crop any good," Lady Circumference was saying.

"No, indeed," said Mrs. Beste-Chetwynde. "Are you in
England for long?"

"Why, I live in England, of course," said Lady Circumference.

"My dear, how divine! But don't you find it just too
expensive?"

This was one of Lady Circumference's favourite topics,
but somehow she did not feel disposed to enlarge on it to
Mrs. Beste-Chetwynde with the same gusto as when she
was talking to Mrs. Sidebotham and the Vicar's wife. She
never felt quite at ease with people richer than herself.

"Well, we all feel the wind a bit since the war," she said
briefly. "How's Bobby Pastmaster?"

"Dotty," said Mrs. Beste-Chetwynde, "terribly dotty,
and he and Chokey don't get on. You'll like Chokey. He's
just crazy about England, too. We've been round all the
cathedrals, and now we're going to start on the country
houses. We were thinking of running over to see you at
Castle Tangent one afternoon."

"That would be delightful, but I'm afraid we are in
London at present. Which did you like best of the cathedrals, Mr. Chokey?"

"Chokey's not really his name, you know. The angel's
called 'Mr. Sebastien Cholmondley.' "

"Well," said Mr. Cholmondley, "they were all fine, just
fine. When I saw the cathedrals my heart just rose up and
sang within me. I sure am crazy about culture. You folk
think because we're coloured we don't care about nothing
but jazz. Why, I'd give all the jazz in the world for just
one little stone from one of your cathedrals."

"It's quite true. He would."

"Well, that's most interesting, Mr. Cholmondley. I used
to live just outside Salisbury when I was a girl, but, little

as I like jazz, I never felt quite as strongly as that about it."

"Salisbury is full of historical interest, Lady Circumference, but in my opinion York Minster is the more refined."

"Oh, you angel!" said Mrs. Beste-Chetwynde. "I could eat you up every bit."

"And is this your first visit to an English school?" asked the Doctor.

"I should say not. Will you tell the Doctor the schools I've seen?"

"He's been to them all, even the quite new ones. In fact, he liked the new ones best."

"They were more spacious. Have you ever seen Oxford?"

"Yes; in fact, I was educated there."

"Were you, now? I've seen Oxford and Cambridge and Eton and Harrow. That's me all over. That's what I like, see? *I* appreciate art. There's plenty coloured people come over here and don't see nothing but a few night clubs. I read Shakespeare," said Chokey, "*Hamlet, Macbeth, King Lear*. Ever read them?"

"Yes," said the Doctor; "as a matter of fact, I have."

"My race," said Chokey, "is essentially an artistic race. We have the child's love of song and colour and the child's natural good taste. All you white folks despise the poor coloured man. . . ."

"No, no," said the Doctor.

"Let him say his piece, the darling," said Mrs. Beste-Chetwynde. "Isn't he divine!"

"You folks all think the coloured man hasn't got a soul. Anything's good enough for the poor coloured man. Beat him; put him in chains; load him with burdens. . . ." Here Paul observed a responsive glitter in Lady Circumference's eye. "But all the time that poor coloured man has a soul same as you have. Don't he breathe the same as you? don't he eat and drink? Don't he love Shakespeare and cathedrals and the paintings of the old masters same as you? Isn't he just asking for your love and help to raise him from the servitude into which your forefathers plunged him? Oh, say, white folks, why don't you stretch out a helping hand to the poor coloured man, that's as good as you are, if you'll only let him be?"

"My sweet," said Mrs. Beste-Chetwynde, "you mustn't get discouraged. They're all friends here."

"Is that so?" said Chokey. "Should I sing them a song?"

"No, don't do that, darling. Have some tea."

"I had a friend in Paris," said the Clutterbuck governess, "whose sister knew a girl who married one of the black soldiers during the war, and you wouldn't believe what he did to her. Joan and Peter, run and see if Daddy wants some more tea. He tied her up with a razor strop and left her on the stone floor for the night without food or covering. And then it was over a year before she could get a divorce."

"Used to cut the tent ropes," Colonel Sidebotham was saying, "and then knife the poor beggars through the canvas."

"You can see 'em in Shaftesbury Avenue and Charing Cross Road any night of the week," Sam Clutterbuck was saying. "The women just hanging on to 'em."

"The mistake was ever giving them their freedom," said the Vicar. "They were far happier and better looked after before."

"It's queer," said Flossie, "that a woman with as much money as Mrs. Beste-Chetwynde should wear such *dull* clothes."

"That ring didn't cost less than five hundred," said Philbrick.

"Let's go and talk to the Vicar about God," said Mrs. Beste-Chetwynde. "Chokey thinks religion is just divine."

"My race is a very spiritual one," said Chokey.

"The band has been playing *Men of Harlech* for over half an hour," said the Doctor. "Diana, do go and tell them to try something else."

"I sometimes think I'm getting rather bored with col-

oured people," Mrs. Beste-Chetwynde said to Lady Circumference. "Are you?"

"I have never had the opportunity."

"I daresay you'd be good with them. They take a lot of
living up to; they *are* so earnest. Who's that dear, dim,
drunk little man?"

"That is the person who shot my son."

"My dear, how too shattering for you. Not dead, I
hope? Chokey shot a man at a party the other night. He
gets gay at times, you know. It's only when he's on his best
behaviour that he's so class-conscious. I must go and rescue the Vicar."

The station master came into the tent, crab-like and
obsequious.

"Well, my good man?" said the Doctor.

"The young lady I have been telling that no other tunes
can we play whatever with the lady smoking at her cigarette look you."

"God bless my soul! Why not?"

"The other tunes are all holy tunes look you. Blasphemy it would be to play the songs of Sion while the lady
at a cigarette smokes whatever. *Men of Harlech* is good
music look you."

"This is most unfortunate. I can hardly ask Mrs. Beste-
Chetwynde to stop smoking. Frankly I regard this as im-
pertinence."

"But no man can you ask against his Maker to blas-
pheme whatever unless him to pay more you were. Three
pounds for the music is good and one for the blasphemy
look you."

Dr. Fagan gave him another pound. The station master
retired, and in a few minutes the silver band began a
singularly emotional rendering of *In Thy courts no more
are needed Sun by day and moon by night.*

CHAPTER TEN

Post Mortem

As THE last car drove away the Doctor and his daughters and Paul and Grimes walked up the drive together towards the Castle.

"Frankly the day has been rather a disappointment to me," said the Doctor. "Nothing seemed to go quite right in spite of all our preparations."

"And expense," said Dingy.

"I am sorry, too, that Mr. Prendergast should have had that unfortunate disagreement with Mrs. Beste-Chetwynde's coloured friend. In all the ten years during which we have worked together I have never known Mr. Prendergast so self-assertive. It was *not* becoming of him. Nor was it Philbrick's place to join in. I was seriously alarmed. They seemed so angry, and all about some minor point of ecclesiastical architecture.

"Mr. Cholmondley was very sensitive," said Flossie.

"Yes, he seemed to think that Mr. Prendergast's insistence on the late development of the rood screen was in some way connected with colour prejudice. I wonder why that was? To my mind it showed a very confused line of thought. Still, it would have been more seemly if Mr. Prendergast had let the matter drop, and what could Philbrick know of the matter?"

"Philbrick is not an ordinary butler," said Dingy.

"No, indeed not," said the Doctor. "I heartily deplore his jewellery."

"I didn't like Lady Circumference's speech," said Flossie. "Did you?"

"I did not," said the Doctor; "nor, I think, did Mrs.

Clutterbuck. I thought her reference to the Five Furlong race positively brutal. I was glad Clutterbuck had done so well in the jumping yesterday."

"She rather wanders from the point, doesn't she?" said Dingy. "All that about hunting, I mean."

"I don't think Lady Circumference is conscious of any definite divisions in the various branches of sport. I have often observed in women of her type a tendency to regard all athletics as inferior forms of foxhunting. It is *not* logical. Besides, she was nettled at some remark of Mr. Cholmondley's about cruelty to animals. As you say, it was irrelevant and rather unfortunate. I also resented the references to the Liberal party. Mr. Clutterbuck has stood three times, you know. Taken as a whole, it was *not* a happy speech. I was quite glad when I saw her drive away."

"What a pretty car Mrs. Beste-Chetwynde has got!" said Flossie, "but how ostentatious of her to bring a footman."

"I can forgive the footman," said Dingy, "but I can't forgive Mr. Cholmondley. He asked me whether I had ever heard of a writer called Thomas Hardy."

"He asked *me* to go to Reigate with him for the week end," said Flossie, ". . . in rather a sweet way, too."

"Florence, I trust you refused?"

"Oh, yes," said Flossie sadly, "I refused."

They went on up the drive in silence. Presently Dingy asked: "What are we going to do about those fireworks you insisted on buying? Every one has gone away."

"I don't feel in a mood for fireworks," said the Doctor. "Perhaps another time, but not now."

Back in the Common Room, Paul and Grimes subsided moodily into the two easy chairs. The fire, unattended since luncheon, had sunk to a handful of warm ashes.

"Well, old boy," said Grimes, "so that's over."

"Yes," said Paul.

"All the gay throng melted away?"

"Yes," said Paul.

"Back to the daily round and cloistral calm?"

"Yes," said Paul.

"As a beano," said Grimes, "I have known better."

"Yes," said Paul.

"Lady C.'s hardly what you might call bonhommous."

"Hardly."

"Old Prendy made rather an ass of himself?"

"Yes."

"Hullo, old boy! You sound a bit flat. Feeling the strain of the social vortex, a bit giddy after the gay whirl, eh?"

"I say, Grimes," said Paul, "what d'you suppose the relationship is between Mrs. Beste-Chetwynde and that nigger?"

"Well, I don't suppose she trots round with him just for the uplift of his conversation; do you?"

"No, I suppose not."

"In fact, I don't mind diagnosing a simple case of good old sex."

"Yes, I suppose you're right."

"I'm sure of it. Great Scott, what's that noise?"

It was Mr. Prendergast.

"Prendy, old man," said Grimes, "you've let down the morale of the Common Room a pretty good wollop."

"Damn the Common Room!" said Mr. Prendergast. "What does the Common Room know about rood screens?"

"That's all right, old boy. We're all friends here. What you say about rood screens goes."

"They'll be questioning the efficacy of infant baptism next. The Church has never countenanced lay opinion on spiritual matters. Now if it were a question of food and drink," said Mr. Prendergast, "if it were a question of drink— But not infant baptism. Just drink." And he sat down.

"A sad case, brother," said Grimes, "truly a sad case. Prendy, do you realize that in two minutes the bell will go for Prep. and you're on duty?"

"Ding, dong, dell! Pussy's in the well."

"Prendy, that's irrelevant."

"I know several songs about bells. Funeral bells, wedding bells, sacring bells, sheep bells, fire bells, door bells, dumb bells, and just plain bells."

Paul and Grimes looked at each other sadly.

"It seems to me," said Paul, "that one of us will have to take Prep. for him to-night."

"No, no, old boy; that'll be all right," said Grimes. "You and I are off to Mrs. Roberts. Prendy gives me a thirst."

"But we can't leave him like this."

"He'll be all right. The little beasts can't make any more noise than they do usually."

"You don't think the old man will find him?"

"Not a chance."

The bell rang. Mr. Prendergast jumped to his feet, straightened his wig, and steadied himself gravely against the chimney piece.

"There's a good chap," said Grimes gently. "Just you trot down the passage to the little boys and have a good nap."

Singing quietly to himself, Mr. Prendergast sauntered down the passage.

"I hope he's none the worse for this," said Grimes. "You know, I feel quite fatherly towards old Prendy. He did give it to that blackamoor about Church architecture, bless him."

Arm in arm they went down the main avenue towards the inn.

"Mrs. Beste-Chetwynde asked me to call on her in London," said Paul.

"Did she? Well, just you go. I've never been much of a one for society and the smart set myself, but if you like that sort of thing, Mrs. Beste-Chetwynde is the goods all right. Never open a paper but there's a photograph of her at some place or other."

"Does she photograph well?" asked Paul. "I should rather think that she would."

Grimes looked at him narrowly. "Fair to middling. Why the sudden interest?"

"Oh, I don't know. I was just wondering."

At Mrs. Roberts's they found the Llanabba Silver Band chattering acrimoniously over the division of the spoils.

"All the afternoon the band I have led in *Men of Harlech* and sacred music too look you and they will not give me a penny more than themselves whatever. The college gentleman whatever if it is right I ask," said the station master, "me with a sister-in-law to support too look you."

"Now don't bother, old boy," said Grimes, "because, if you do, I'll tell your pals about the extra pound you got out of the Doctor."

The discussion was resumed in Welsh, but it was clear that the station master was slowly giving way.

"That settled him all right. Take my tip, old boy: never get mixed up in a Welsh wrangle. It doesn't end in blows, like an Irish one, but goes on for ever. They'll still be discussing that three pounds at the end of term; just you see."

"Has Mr. Beste-Chetwynde been dead long?" asked Paul.

"I shouldn't say so; why?"

"I was just wondering."

They sat for some time smoking in silence.

"If Beste-Chetwynde is fifteen," said Paul, "that doesn't necessarily make her more than thirty-three, does it?"

"Old boy," said Grimes, "you're in love."

"Nonsense!"

"Smitten?" said Grimes.

"No, no."

"The tender passion?"

"No."

"Cupid's jolly little darts?"

"No."

"Spring fancies, love's young dream?"

"Nonsense!"

"Not even a quickening of the pulse?"

"No."

"A sweet despair?"

"Certainly not."

"A trembling hope?"

"No."

"A *frisson? a je ne sais quoi?*"

"Nothing of the sort."

"Liar!" said Grimes.

There was another long pause. "Grimes," said Paul at length, "I wonder if you can be right?"

"Sure of it, old boy. Just you go in and win. Here's to the happy pair! May all your troubles be little ones."

In a state of mind totally new to him, Paul accompanied Grimes back to the Castle. Prep. was over. Mr. Prendergast was leaning against the fireplace with a contented smile on his face.

"Hullo, Prendy, old wine skin! How are things with you?"

"Admirable," said Mr. Prendergast. "I have never known them better. I have just caned twenty-three boys."

CHAPTER ELEVEN

Philbrick (continued)

NEXT day Mr. Prendergast's self-confidence had evaporated.

"Head hurting?" asked Grimes.

"Well, as a matter of fact, it is rather."

"Eyes tired? Thirsty?"

"Yes, a little."

"Poor old Prendy! Don't I know? Still, it was worth it, wasn't it?"

"I don't remember very clearly all that happened, but I walked back to the Castle with Philbrick, and he told me all about his life. It appears he is really a rich man and not a butler at all."

"I know," said Paul and Grimes simultaneously.

"You both knew? Well, it came as a great surprise to me, although I must admit I had noticed a certain superiority in his manner. But I find almost every one like that. Did he tell you his whole story—about his shooting the Portuguese Count and everything?"

"No, he didn't tell me *that*," said Paul.

"Shooting a Portuguese Count? Are you sure you've got hold of the right end of the stick, old boy?"

"Yes, yes, I'm sure of it. It impressed me very much. You see Philbrick is really Sir Solomon Philbrick, the shipowner."

"The novelist, you mean," said Grimes.

"The retired burglar," said Paul.

The three masters looked at each other.

"Old boys, it seems to me some one's been pulling our legs."

"Well, this is the story that he told me," continued Mr. Prendergast. "It all started from our argument about Church architecture with the black man. Apparently Philbrick has a large house in Carlton House Terrace."

"Camberwell Green."

"Cheyne Walk."

"Well, I'm telling you what he told me. He has a house in Carlton House Terrace. I remember the address well because a sister of Mrs. Crump's was once governess in a house in the same row, and he used to live there with an actress who, I regret to say, was not his wife. I forget her name, but I know it is a particularly famous one. He was sitting in the Athenæum Club one day when the Archbishop of Canterbury approached him and said that the Government were anxious to make him a peer, but that it was impossible while he lived a life of such open irregularity. Philbrick turned down the offer. He is a Roman Catholic, I forgot to tell you. But all that doesn't really explain why he is here. It only shows how important he is. His ships weigh *hundreds* and *hundreds* of tons, he told me.

"Well, one evening he and this play actress were giving a party, and they were playing baccarat. There was a

Portuguese Count there—a very dark man from the Lega-
tion, Philbrick said. The game rapidly became a personal
contest between these two. Philbrick won over and over
again until the Count had no more money left and had
signed many I.O.U.'s. Finally very late in the night he
took from the Countess's hand—she was sitting beside him
with haggard eyes watching him play—an enormous emerald. As big as a golf ball, Philbrick said.

"'This has been an heirloom of my family since the
first Crusade,' said the Portuguese Count. 'It is the one
thing which I had hoped to leave to my poor, poor little
son.' And he tossed it on the table.

"'I will wager against it my new four-funnel, turbine-
driven liner called *The Queen of Arcady*,' said Philbrick.

"'That's not enough,' said the Portuguese Countess.

"'And my steam yacht *Swallow* and four tugs and a
coaling barge,' said Philbrick. All the party rose to ap-
plaud his reckless bid.

"The hand was played. Philbrick had won. With a low
bow he returned the emerald to the Portuguese Countess.
'For your son!' he said. Again the guests applauded, but
the Portuguese Count was livid with rage. 'You have in-
sulted my honour,' he said. 'In Portugal we have only one
way of dealing with such an occurrence.'

"There and then they went out into Hyde Park, which
was quite close. They faced each other and fired: it was
just dawn. At the feet of the Achilles statue Philbrick
shot the Portuguese Count dead. They left him with his
smoking revolver in his hand. The Portuguese Countess
kissed Philbrick's hand as she entered her car. 'No one
will ever know,' she said. 'It will be taken for suicide. It
is a secret between us.'

"But Philbrick was a changed man. The actress was
driven from his house. He fell into a melancholy and
paced up and down his deserted home at night, over-
powered by his sense of guilt. The Portuguese Countess
rang him up, but he told her it was the wrong number.
Finally he went to a priest and confessed. He was told
that for three years he must give up his house and

wealth and live among the lowest of the low. That," said
Mr. Prendergast simply, "is why he is here. Wasn't that
the story he told you?"

"No, it wasn't," said Paul.

"Not the shade of a likeness," said Grimes. "He told
me all about himself one evening at Mrs. Roberts's. It
was like this:

"Mr. Philbrick, senior, was a slightly eccentric sort of
a cove. He made a big pile out of diamond mines while
he was quite young and settled in the country and devoted his declining years to literature. He had two kids:
Philbrick and a daughter called Gracie. From the start
Philbrick was the apple of the old chap's eye, while he
couldn't stick Miss Gracie at any price. Philbrick could
spout Shakespeare and *Hamlet* and things by the yard before Gracie could read 'The cat sat on the mat.' When he
was eight he had a sonnet printed in the local paper.
After that Gracie wasn't in it anywhere. She lived with
the servants like Cinderella, Philbrick said, while he,
sensible little beggar, had the best of everything and
quoted classics and flowery language to the old boy upstairs. After he left Cambridge he settled down in London
and wrote away like blazes. The old man just loved that;
he had all Philbrick's books bound in blue leather and
put in a separate bookcase with a bust of Philbrick on
top. Poor old Gracie found things a bit thin, so she ran
off with a young chap in a motor trade who didn't know
one end of a book from the other, or of a car for that matter, as it turned out. When the old boy popped off he left
Philbrick everything, except a few books to Gracie. The
young man had only married her because he thought the
old boy was bound to leave her something, so he hopped
it. That didn't worry Philbrick. He lived for his art, he
said. He just moved into a bigger house and went on writing away fifteen to the dozen. Gracie tried to get some
money out of him more than once, but he was so busy
writing books, he couldn't bother about her. At last she
became a cook in a house at Southgate. Next year she
died. That didn't worry Philbrick at first. Then after a

week or so he noticed an odd thing. There was always a
smell of cooking all over the house, in his study, in his
bedroom, everywhere. He had an architect in who said
he couldn't notice any smell, and rebuilt the kitchen and
put in all sorts of ventilators. Still, the smell got worse. It
used to hang about his clothes so that he didn't dare go
out, a horrible fatty smell. He tried going abroad, but the
whole of Paris reeked of English cooking. That was bad
enough, but after a time plates began rattling round his
bed when he tried to sleep at nights and behind his chair
as he wrote his books. He used to wake up in the night
and hear the frizzling of fried fish and the singing of ket-
tles. Then he knew what it was: it was Gracie haunting
him. He went to the Society for Psychical Research, and
they got through a conversation to Gracie. He asked how
he could make reparation. She said that he must live
among servants for a year and write a book about them
that would improve their lot. He tried to go the whole
hog at first and started as *chef,* but of course that wasn't
really in his line, and the family he was with got so ill, he
had to leave. So he came here. He says the book is most
moving, and that he'll read me bits of it some day. Not
quite the same story as Prendy's."

"No, it's not. By the way, did he say anything about
marrying Dingy?"

"Not a word. He said that as soon as the smell of cooking wore off he was going to be the happiest man in the
world. Apparently he's engaged to a female poet in Chel-
sea. He's not the sort of cove I'd have chosen for a brother-
in-law. But then Flossie isn't really the sort of wife I'd
have chosen. These things happen, old boy."

Paul told them about the "Lamb and Flag" at Camberwell Green and about Toby Cruttwell. "D'you think that
story is true, or yours, or Prendy's?" he asked.

"No," said Mr. Prendergast.

CHAPTER TWELVE

The Agony of Captain Grimes

Two days later Beste-Chetwynde and Paul were in the organ loft of the Llanabba Parish Church.

"I don't think I played that terribly well, do you, sir?"

"No."

"Shall I stop for a bit?"

"I wish you would."

"Tangent's foot has swollen up and turned black," said Beste-Chetwynde with relish.

"Poor little brute!" said Paul.

"I had a letter from my mamma this morning," Beste-Chetwynde went on. "There's a message for you in it. Shall I read you what she says?"

He took out a letter written on the thickest possible paper. "The first part is all about racing and a row she's had with Chokey. Apparently he doesn't like the way she's rebuilt our house in the country. I think it was time she dropped that man, don't you?"

"What does she say about me?" asked Paul.

"She says:

" 'By the way, dear boy, I must tell you that the spelling in your last letters has been *just too shattering* for words. You know how terribly anxious I am for you to get on and go to Oxford, and everything, and I have been think-ing, don't you think it might be a good thing if we were to have a tutor next holidays? Would you think it *too* bor-ing? Some one young who would fit in. I thought, would that good-looking young master you said you liked care to come? How much ought I to pay him? I never know these things. I don't mean the drunk one, tho' he was sweet too.'

"I think that must be you, don't you?" said Beste-Chetwynde; "it can hardly be Captain Grimes."

"Well, I must think that over," said Paul. "It sounds rather a good idea."

"Well, yes," said Beste-Chetwynde doubtfully, "it might be all right, only there mustn't be too much of the school master about it. That man Prendergast beat me the other evening."

"And there'll be no organ lessons, either," said Paul.

Grimes did not receive the news as enthusiastically as Paul had hoped; he was sitting over the Common Room fire despondently biting his nails.

"Good, old boy! That's splendid," he said abstractedly. "I'm glad; I am really."

"Well, you don't sound exactly gay."

"No, I'm not. Fact is, I'm in the soup again."

"Badly?"

"Up to the neck."

"My dear chap, I *am* sorry. What are you going to do about it?"

"I've done the only thing: I've announced my engagement."

"That'll please Flossie."

"Oh, yes, she's as pleased as hell about it all, damn her nasty little eyes."

"What did the old man say?"

"Baffled him a bit, old boy. He's just thinking things out at the moment. Well, I expect everything'll be all right."

"I don't see why it shouldn't be."

"Well, there *is* a reason. I don't think I told you before, but fact is, I'm married already."

That evening Paul received a summons from the Doctor. He wore a double-breasted dinner jacket, which he smoothed uneasily over his hips at Paul's approach. He looked worried and old.

"Pennyfeather," he said, "I have this morning received a severe shock, two shocks in fact. The first was disagreeable, but not wholly unexpected. Your colleague, Captain

Grimes, has been convicted before me, on evidence that leaves no possibility of his innocence, of a crime—I might almost call it a course of action—which I can neither understand nor excuse. I daresay I need not particularize. However, that is all a minor question. I have quite frequently met with similar cases during a long experience in our profession. But what has disturbed and grieved me more than I can moderately express is the information that he is engaged to be married to my elder daughter. That, Pennyfeather, I had not expected. In the circumstances it seemed a humiliation I might reasonably have been spared. I tell you all this, Pennyfeather, because in our brief acquaintance I have learned to trust and respect you."

The Doctor sighed, drew from his pocket a handkerchief of *crêpe de chine*, blew his nose with every accent of emotion, and resumed:

"He is *not* the son-in-law I should readily have chosen. I could have forgiven him his wooden leg, his slavish poverty, his moral turpitude, and his abominable features; I could even have forgiven him his incredible vocabulary, if only he had been a *gentleman*. I hope you do not think me a snob. You may have discerned in me a certain prejudice against the lower orders. It is quite true. I *do* feel deeply on the subject. You see, I married one of them. But that, fortunately, is neither here nor there. What I really wished to say to you was this: I have spoken to the unhappy young woman my daughter, and find that she has no particular inclination towards Grimes. Indeed, I do not think that any daughter of mine could fall as low as that. But she is, for some reason, uncontrollably eager to be married to somebody fairly soon. Now, I should be quite prepared to offer a partnership in Llanabba to a son-in-law of whom I approved. The income of the school is normally not less than three thousand a year—that is with the help of dear Diana's housekeeping—and my junior partner would start at an income of a thousand and of course succeed to a larger share upon my death. It is a prospect that many young men would find inviting.

And I was wondering, Pennyfeather, whether by any chance, looking at the matter from a businesslike point of view, without prejudice, you understand, fair and square, taking things as they are for what they are worth, facing facts, whether possibly *you* . . . I wonder if I make myself plain?"

"No," said Paul. "No, sir, I'm afraid it would be impossible. I hope I don't appear rude, but—no, really, I'm afraid . . ."

"That's all right, my dear boy. Not another word! I quite understand. I was afraid that would be your answer. Well, it must be Grimes, then. I don't think it would be any use approaching Mr. Prendergast."

"It was very kind of you to suggest it, sir."

"Not at all, not at all. The wedding shall take place a week to-day. You might tell Grimes that if you see him. I don't want to have more to do with him than I can help. I wonder whether it would be a good thing to give a small party?" For a moment a light sprang up in Dr. Fagan's eyes and then died out. "No, no, there will be no party. The sports were not encouraging. Poor little Lord Tangent is still laid up, I hear."

Paul returned to the Common Room with the Doctor's message.

"Hell!" said Grimes. "I still hoped it might fall through."

"What d'you want for a wedding present?" Paul asked.

Grimes brightened. "What about that binge you promised me and Prendy?"

"All right!" said Paul. "We'll have it to-morrow."

The Hotel Metropole, Cwmpryddyg, is by far the grandest hotel in the north of Wales. It is situated on a high and healthy eminence overlooking the strip of water that railway companies have gallantly compared to the Bay of Naples. It was built in the ample days preceding the war, with a lavish expenditure on looking glass and marble. To-day it shows signs of wear, for it has never been quite as popular as its pioneers hoped. There are cracks in the cement on the main terrace, the winter garden is draughty, and one comes disconcertingly upon derelict bath chairs in the Moorish Court. Besides this, none of the fountains ever plays, the string band that used to perform nightly in the ballroom has given place to a very expensive wireless set which one of the waiters knows how to operate, there is never any note paper in the writing room, and the sheets are not long enough for the beds. Philbrick pointed out these defects to Paul as he sat with Grimes and Mr. Prendergast drinking cocktails in the Palm Court before dinner.

"And it isn't as though it was really cheap," he said. Philbrick had become quite genial during the last few days. "Still, one can't expect much in Wales, and it is something. I can't live without some kind of luxury for long. I'm not staying this evening, or I'd ask you fellows to dine with me."

"Philbrick, old boy," said Grimes, "me and my pals here have been wanting a word with you for some time. How about those yarns you spun about your being a shipowner and a novelist and a burglar?"

"Since you mention it," said Philbrick with dignity, "they were untrue. One day you shall know my full story. It is stranger than any fiction. Meanwhile I have to be back at the Castle. Good-night."

"He certainly seems quite a swell here," said Grimes as they watched him disappear into the night escorted with every obsequy by the manager and the head waiter. "I daresay he *could* tell a story if he wanted to."

"I believe it's their keys," said Mr. Prendergast suddenly. It was the first time that he had spoken. For twenty minutes he had been sitting very upright in his gilt chair and very alert, his eyes unusually bright, darting this way and that in his eagerness to miss nothing of the gay scene about him.

"What's their keys, Prendy?"

"Why, the things they get given at the counter. I thought for a long time it was money."

"Is that what's been worrying you? Bless your heart, I

thought it was the young lady in the office you were after."

"Oh, Grimes!" said Mr. Prendergast, and he blushed warmly and gave a little giggle.

Paul led his guests into the dining room.

"I haven't taught French for nothing all these years," said Grimes, studying the menu. "I'll start with some jolly old *huitres*."

Mr. Prendergast ate a grapefruit with some difficulty. "What a big orange!" he said when he had finished it. "They do things on a large scale here."

The soup came in little aluminium bowls. "What price the ancestral silver?" said Grimes. The Manchester merchants on the spree who sat all round them began to look a little askance at Paul's table.

"Some one's doing himself well on bubbly," said Grimes as a waiter advanced staggering under the weight of an ice pail from which emerged a Jeroboam of champagne. "Good egg! It's coming to us."

"With Sir Solomon Philbrick's compliments to Captain Grimes and congratulations on his approaching marriage, sir."

Grimes took the waiter by the sleeve. "See here, old boy, this Sir Solomon Philbrick—know him well?"

"He's here quite frequently, sir."

"Spends a lot of money, eh?"

"He doesn't entertain at all, but he always has the best of everything himself, sir."

"Does he pay his bill?"

"I really couldn't say, I'm afraid, sir. Would you be requiring anything else?"

"All right, old boy! Don't get sniffy. Only he's a pal of mine, see?"

"Really, Grimes," said Mr. Prendergast, "I am afraid you made him quite annoyed with your questions, and that stout man over there is staring at us in the most marked way."

"I've got a toast to propose. Prendy, fill up your glass. Here's to Trumpington, whoever he is, who gave us the money for this binge!"

"And here's to Philbrick," said Paul, "whoever *he* is!"

"And here's to Miss Fagan," said Mr. Prendergast, "with our warmest hopes for her future happiness!"

"Amen," said Grimes.

After the soup the worst sort of sole. Mr. Prendergast made a little joke about soles and souls. Clearly the dinner party was being a great success.

"You know," said Grimes, "look at it how you will, marriage is rather a grim thought."

"The three reasons for it given in the Prayer book have always seemed to me quite inadequate," agreed Mr. Prendergast. "I have never had the smallest difficulty about the avoidance of fornication, and the other two advantages seem to me nothing short of disastrous."

"My first marriage," said Grimes, "didn't make much odds either way. It was in Ireland. I was tight at the time, and so was every one else. God knows what became of Mrs. Grimes. It seems to me, though, that with Flossie I'm in for a pretty solemn solemnization. It's not what I should have chosen for myself, not by a long chalk. Still, as things are, I suppose it's the best thing that could have happened. I think I've about run through the schoolmastering profession. I don't mind telling you I might have found it pretty hard to get another job. There are limits. Now I'm set up for life, and no more worry about testimonials. That's something. In fact, that's all there is to be said. But there have been moments in the last twenty-four hours, I don't mind telling you, when I've gone cold all over at the thought of what I was in for."

"I don't want to say anything discouraging," said Mr. Prendergast, "but I've known Flossie for nearly ten years now, and—"

"There isn't anything you can tell me about Flossie that I don't know already. I almost wish it was Dingy. I suppose it's too late now to change. Oh, dear!" said Grimes despondently, gazing into his glass. "Oh, Lord! oh, Lord! That I should come to this!"

"Cheer up, Grimes. It isn't like you to be as depressed as this," said Paul.

"Old friends," said Grimes—and his voice was charged with emotion—"you see a man standing face to face with retribution. Respect him even if you cannot understand. Those that live by the flesh shall perish by the flesh. I am a very sinful man, and I am past my first youth. Who shall pity me in that dark declivity to which my steps inevitably seem to tend? I have boasted in my youth and held my head high and gone on my way careless of consequence, but ever behind me, unseen, stood stark Justice with his two-edged sword."

More food was brought them. Mr. Prendergast ate with a hearty appetite.

"Oh, why did nobody warn me?" cried Grimes in his agony. "I should have been told. They should have told me in so many words. They should have warned me about Flossie, not about the fires of hell. I've risked them, and I don't mind risking them again, but they should have told me about marriage. They should have told me that at the end of that gay journey and flower-strewn path were the hideous lights of home and the voices of children. I should have been warned of the great lavender-scented bed that was laid out for me, of the wisteria at the windows, of all intimacy and confidence of family life. But I daresay I shouldn't have listened. Our life is lived between two homes. We emerge for a little into the light, and then the front door closes. The chintz curtains shut out the sun, and the hearth glows with the fire of home, while upstairs, above our heads, are enacted again the awful accidents of adolescence. There's a home and family waiting for every one of us. We can't escape, try how we may. It's the seed of life we carry about with us like our skeletons, each one of us unconsciously pregnant with desirable villa residences. There's no escape. As individuals we simply do not exist. We are just potential home builders, beavers and ants. How do we come into being? What is birth?"

"I've often wondered," said Mr. Prendergast.

"What is this impulse of two people to build their beastly home? It's you and me, unborn, asserting our presence. All we are is a manifestation of the impulse of family life, and if by chance we have escaped the itch ourselves, Nature forces it upon us another way. Flossie's got that itch enough for two. I just haven't. I'm one of the blind alleys off the main road of procreation, but it doesn't matter. Nature always wins. Oh, Lord! oh, Lord! Why didn't I die in that first awful home? Why did I ever hope I could escape?"

Captain Grimes continued his lament for some time in deep bitterness of heart. Presently he became silent and stared at his glass.

"I wonder," said Mr. Prendergast, "I wonder whether I could have just a little more of this very excellent pheasant?"

"Anyway," said Grimes, "there shan't be any children; I'll see to that."

"It has always been a mystery to me why people marry," said Mr. Prendergast. "I can't see the smallest reason for it. Quite happy, normal people. Now I can understand it in Grimes's case. He has everything to gain by the arrangement, but what does Flossie expect to gain? And yet she seems more enthusiastic about it than Grimes. It has been the tragedy of my life that whenever I start thinking about any quite simple subject I invariably feel myself confronted by some flat contradiction of this sort. Have you ever thought about marriage—in the abstract, I mean, of course?"

"Not very much, I'm afraid."

"I don't believe," said Mr. Prendergast, "that people would ever fall in love or want to be married if they hadn't been told about it. It's like abroad: no one would want to go there if they hadn't been told it existed. Don't you agree?"

"I don't think you can be quite right," said Paul; "you see, animals fall in love quite a lot, don't they?"

"Do they?" said Mr. Prendergast. "I didn't know that. What an extraordinary thing! But then I had an aunt whose cat used to put its paw up to its mouth when it yawned. It's wonderful what animals can be taught. There is a sea lion at the circus, I saw in the paper, who juggles with an umbrella and two oranges."

"I know what I'll do," said Grimes. "I'll get a motor bicycle."

This seemed to cheer him up a little. He took another glass of wine and smiled wanly. "I'm afraid I've not been following all you chaps have said. I was thinking. What were we talking about?"

"Prendy was telling me about a sea lion who juggled with an umbrella and two oranges."

"Why, that's nothing. I can juggle with a whacking great bottle and a lump of ice and two knives. Look!"

"Grimes, don't! Every one is looking at you."

The head waiter came over to remonstrate. "Please remember where you are, sir," he said.

"I know where I am well enough," said Grimes. "I'm in the hotel my pal Sir Solomon Philbrick is talking of buying, and I tell you this, old boy: if he does, the first person to lose his job will be you. See?"

Nevertheless he stopped juggling, and Mr. Prendergast ate two *pêches Melba* undisturbed.

"The black cloud has passed," said Grimes. "Grimes is now going to enjoy his evening."

CHAPTER THIRTEEN

The Passing of a Public-School Man

SIX days later the school was given a half holiday, and soon after luncheon the bigamous union of Captain Edgar Grimes and Miss Florence Selina Fagan was celebrated at the Llanabba Parish Church. A slight injury to his hand prevented Paul from playing the organ. He walked down the church with Mr. Prendergast, who, greatly to his dismay, had been instructed by Dr. Fagan to give away the bride.

"I do not intend to be present," said the Doctor. "The whole business is exceedingly painful to me." Everybody else, however, was there except little Lord Tangent, whose foot was being amputated at a local nursing home. The boys for the most part welcomed the event as a pleasant variation to the rather irregular routine of their day. Clutterbuck alone seemed disposed to sulk.

"I don't suppose that their children will be terribly attractive," said Beste-Chetwynde.

There were few wedding presents. The boys had subscribed a shilling each and had bought at a shop in Llandudno a silver-plated teapot, coyly suggestive of *art nouveau*. The Doctor gave them a cheque for twenty-five pounds. Mr. Prendergast gave Grimes a walking stick— "because he was always borrowing mine"—and Dingy, rather generously, two photograph frames, a calendar, and a tray of Benares brassware. Paul was the best man.

The service passed off without a hitch, for Grimes's Irish wife did not turn up to forbid the banns. Flossie wore a frock of a rather noticeable velveteen and a hat with two pink feathers to match.

"I was so pleased when I found he didn't want me to wear white," she said, "though, of course, it might have been dyed afterwards."

Both bride and bridegroom spoke up well in the responses, and afterwards the Vicar delivered a very moving address on the subject of Home and Conjugal Love.

"How beautiful it is," he said, "to see two young people in the hope of youth setting out with the Church's blessing to face life together; how much more beautiful to see them when they have grown to full manhood and womanhood coming together and saying, 'Our experience of life has taught us that *one* is not enough.'"

The boys lined the path from the church door to the lych gate, and the head prefect said: "Three cheers for Captain and Mrs. Grimes!"

Then they returned to the Castle. The honeymoon had

been postponed until the end of term, ten days later, and the arrangements for the first days of their married life were a little meagre. "You must do the best you can," the Doctor had said. "I suppose you will wish to share the same bedroom. I think there would be no objection to your both moving into the large room in the West Tower. It is a little damp, but I daresay Diana will arrange for a fire to be lighted there. You may use the morning room in the evenings, and Captain Grimes will of course have his meals at my table in the dining room, not with the boys. I do not wish to find him sitting about in the drawing room, nor, of course, in my library. He had better keep his books and gown in the Common Room, as before. Next term I will consider some other arrangement. Perhaps I could hand over one of the lodges to you or fit up some sort of sitting room in the tower. I was not prepared for a domestic upheaval."

Diana, who was really coming out of the business rather creditably, put a bowl of flowers in their bedroom, and lit a fire of reckless proportions, in which she consumed the remains of a desk and two of the boys' play boxes.

That evening, while Mr. Prendergast was taking "Prep." at the end of the passage, Grimes visited Paul in the Common Room. He looked rather uncomfortable in his evening clothes.

"Well, dinner's over," he said. "The old man does himself pretty well."

"How are you feeling?"

"Not too well, old boy. The first days are always a strain, they say, even in the most romantic marriages. My father-in-law is *not* what you might call easy. Needs thawing gently, you know. I suppose as a married man I oughtn't to go down to Mrs. Roberts?"

"I think it might seem odd on the first evening; don't you?"

"Flossie's playing the piano; Dingy's making up the accounts; the old man's gone off to the library. Don't you think we've time for a quick one?"

Arm in arm they went down the familiar road.

"Drinks are on me to-night," said Grimes.

The silver band were still sitting with their heads together discussing the division of their earnings.

"They tell me that married this afternoon you were?" said the station master.

"That's right," said Grimes.

"And my sister-in-law never at all you would meet whatever," he continued reproachfully.

"Look here, old boy," said Grimes, "just you shut up. You're not being tactful. See? Just you keep quiet, and I'll give you all some nice beer."

When Mrs. Roberts shut her doors for the night, Paul and Grimes turned back up the hill. A light was burning in the West Tower.

"There she is, waiting for me," said Grimes. "Now it might be a very romantic sight to some chaps, a light burning in a tower window. I knew a poem about a thing like that once. Forgot it now, though. I was no end of a one for poetry when I was a kid—love and all that. Castle towers came in quite a lot. Funny how one grows out of that sort of thing."

Inside the Castle he turned off down the main corridor.

"Well, so long, old boy! This is the way I go now. See you in the morning." The baize door swung to behind him, and Paul went up to bed.

Paul saw little of Grimes during the next few days. They met at prayers and on the way to and from their class rooms, but the baize door that separated the school from the Doctor's wing was also separating them. Mr. Prendergast, now in unchallenged possession of the other easy chair, was smoking away one evening when he suddenly said:

"You know, I miss Grimes. I didn't think I should, but I do. With all his faults, he was a very cheery person. I think I was beginning to get on better with him."

"He doesn't look as cheery as he did," said Paul. "I don't believe that life 'above stairs' is suiting him very well."

As it happened, Grimes chose that evening to visit them.

"D'you chaps mind if I come in for a bit?" he asked with unwonted diffidence. They rose to welcome him. "Sure you don't mind? I won't stay long."

"My dear man, we were just saying how much we missed you. Come and sit down."

"Won't you have some of my tobacco?" said Prendergast.

"Thanks, Prendy! I just had to come in and have a chat. I've been feeling pretty fed up lately. Married life is *not* all beer and skittles, I don't mind telling you. It's not Flossie, mind; she's been hardly any trouble at all. In a way I've got quite to like her. She likes me, anyway, and that's the great thing. The Doctor's my trouble. He never lets me alone, that man. It gets on my nerves. Always laughing at me in a nasty kind of way and making me feel small. You know the way Lady Circumference talks to the Clutterbucks—like that. I tell you I simply dread going into meals in that dining room. He's got a sort of air as though he always knew exactly what I was going to say before I said it, and as if it was always a little worse than he'd expected. Flossie says he treats *her* that way sometimes. He does it to me the whole time, damn him."

"I don't expect he means it," said Paul, "and anyway I shouldn't bother about it."

"That's the point. I'm beginning to feel he's quite right. I suppose I am a pretty coarse sort of chap. I don't know anything about art, and I haven't met any grand people, and I don't go to a good tailor, and all that. I'm not what he calls 'out of the top drawer.' I never pretended I was, but the thing is that up till now it hasn't worried me. I don't think I was a conceited sort of chap, but I felt just as good as anyone else, and I didn't care what people thought as long as I had my fun. And I *did* have fun, too, and, what's more, I enjoyed it. But now I've lived with that man for a week, I feel quite different. I feel half ashamed of myself all the time. And I've come to recog-

nize that supercilious look he gives me in other people's
eyes as well.'

"Ah, how well I know that feeling!" sighed Mr. Prendergast.

"I used to think I was popular among the boys, but
you know I'm not, and at Mrs. Roberts's they only pretended to like me in the hope I'd stand 'em drinks. I did,
too, but they never gave me one back. I thought it was
just because they were Welsh, but I see now it was because
they despised me. I don't blame them. God knows I despise myself. You know, I used to use French phrases a
certain amount—things like *savoir faire* and *je ne sais
quoi*. I never thought about it, but I suppose I haven't got
much of an accent. How could I? I've never been in
France except for that war. Well, every time I say one of
them now the Doctor gives a sort of wince as if he's bitten
on a bad tooth. I have to think the whole time now before
I say anything, to see if there's any French in it or any of
the expressions he doesn't think refined. Then when I do
say anything my voice sounds so funny that I get in a
muddle and he winces again. Old boy, it's been hell this
last week, and it's worrying me. I'm getting an inferiority
complex. Dingy's like that. She just never speaks now.
He's always making little jokes about Flossie's clothes,
too, but I don't think the old girl sees what he's driving
at. That man'll have me crazy before the term's over."

"Well, there's only a week more," was all that Paul
could say to comfort him.

Next morning at prayers Grimes handed Paul a letter.
"Irony," he said.

Paul opened it and read:

JOHN CLUTTERBUCK & SONS
Wholesale Brewers and Wine Merchants

MY DEAR GRIMES:
    The other day at the sports you asked whether there

was by any chance a job open for you at the brewery. I don't know if you were serious in this, but if you were a post has just fallen vacant which I feel might suit you. I should be glad to offer it to any friend who has been so kind to Percy. We employ a certain number of travellers to go round to various inns and hotels to sample the beer and see that it has not been diluted or in any way adulterated. Our junior traveller, who was a friend of mine from Cambridge, has just developed D.T.'s and has had to be suspended. The salary is two hundred a year with car and travelling expenses. Would this attract you at all? If so, will you let me know during the next few days.

> Yours sincerely,
> SAM CLUTTERBUCK.

"Just look at that," said Grimes. "God's own job, and mine for the asking! If that had come ten days ago my whole life might have been different."

"You don't think of taking it now?"

"Too late, old boy, too late. The saddest words in the English language."

In "break" Grimes said to Paul: "Look here, I've decided to take Sam Clutterbuck's job, and be damned to the Fagans!" His eyes shone with excitement. "I shan't say a word to them. I shall just go off. They can do what they like about it. I don't care."

"Splendid!" said Paul. "It's much the best thing you can do."

"I'm going this very afternoon," said Grimes.

An hour later, at the end of morning school, they met again. "I've been thinking over that letter," said Grimes. "I see it all now. It's just a joke."

"Nonsense!" said Paul. "I'm sure it isn't. Go and see the Clutterbucks right away."

"No, no, they don't mean it seriously. They've heard about my marriage from Percy, and they're just pulling my leg. It was too good to be true. Why should they offer *me* a job like that, even if such a wonderful job exists?"

"My dear Grimes, I'm perfectly certain it was a genuine offer. Anyway, there's nothing to lose by going to see them."

"No, no, it's too late, old boy. Things like that don't happen." And he disappeared beyond the baize door.

Next day there was fresh trouble at Llanabba. Two men in stout boots, bowler hats, and thick gray overcoats presented themselves at the Castle with a warrant for Philbrick's arrest. Search was made for him, but it was suddenly discovered that he had already left by the morning train for Holyhead. The boys crowded round the detectives with interest and a good deal of disappointment. They were not, they thought, particularly impressive figures as they stood in the hall fingering their hats and drinking whisky and calling Dingy "miss."

"We've been after 'im for some time now," said the first detective. "Ain't we, Bill?"

"Pretty near six months. It's too bad, his getting away like this. They're getting rather restless at H. Q. about our travelling expenses."

"Is it a very serious case?" asked Mr. Prendergast. The entire school were by this time assembled in the hall. "Not shooting or anything like that?"

"No, there ain't been no bloodshed up to date, sir. I oughtn't to tell about it, really, but seeing as you've all been mixed up in it to some extent, I don't mind telling you that I think he'll get off on a plea of insanity. Loopy, you know."

"What's he been up to?"

"False pretences and impersonation, sir. There's five charges again' him in different parts of the country, mostly at hotels. He represents himself as a rich man, stays there for some time living like a lord, cashes a big cheque and then goes off. Calls 'isself Sir Solomon Philbrick. Funny thing is, I think he really believes his tale 'isself. I've come across several cases like that one time or another. There was a bloke in Somerset what thought 'e was Bishop of

Bath and Wells and confirmed a whole lot of kids—very reverent, too."

"Well, anyway," said Dingy, "he went without his wages from here."

"I always felt there was something untrustworthy about that man," said Mr. Prendergast.

"Lucky devil!" said Grimes despondently.

"I'm worried about Grimes," said Mr. Prendergast that evening. "I never saw a man more changed. He used to be so self-confident and self-assertive. He came in here quite timidly just now and asked me whether I believed that Divine retribution took place in this world or the next. I began to talk to him about it, but I could see he wasn't listening. He sighed once or twice and then went out without a word while I was still speaking."

"Beste-Chetwynde tells me he has kept in the whole of the third form because the blackboard fell down in his class room this morning. He was convinced they had arranged it on purpose."

"Yes, they often do."

"But in this case they hadn't. Beste-Chetwynde said they were quite frightened at the way he spoke to them. Just like an actor, Beste-Chetwynde said."

"Poor Grimes! I think he is seriously unnerved. It will be a relief when the holidays come."

But Captain Grimes's holiday came sooner than Mr. Prendergast expected, and in a way which few people could have foreseen. Three days later he did not appear at morning prayers, and Flossie, red eyed, admitted that he had not come in from the village the night before. Mr. Davies, the station master, confessed to seeing him earlier in the evening in a state of depression. Just before luncheon a youth presented himself at the Castle with a little pile of clothes he had found on the seashore. They were identified without difficulty as having belonged to the Captain. In the breast pocket of the jacket was an envelope addressed to the Doctor, and in it a slip of paper inscribed with the words "THOSE THAT LIVE BY THE FLESH SHALL PERISH BY THE FLESH."

As far as was possible this intelligence was kept from the boys.

Flossie, though severely shocked at the untimely curtailment of her married life, was firm in her resolution not to wear mourning. "I don't think my husband would have expected it of me," she said.

In these distressing circumstances the boys began packing their boxes to go away for the Easter holidays.

Part Two

CHAPTER ONE

King's Thursday

MARGOT BESTE-CHETWYNDE had two houses in England—one in London and the other in Hampshire. Her London house, built in the reign of William and Mary, was, by universal consent, the most beautiful building between Bond Street and Park Lane, but opinion was divided on the subject of her country house. This was very new indeed; in fact, it was scarcely finished when Paul went to stay there at the beginning of the Easter holidays. No single act in Mrs. Beste-Chetwynde's eventful and in many ways disgraceful career had excited quite so much hostile comment as the building, or rather the re-building, of this remarkable house.

It was called King's Thursday, and stood on the place which since the reign of Bloody Mary had been the seat of the Earls of Pastmaster. For three centuries the poverty and inertia of this noble family had preserved its home unmodified by any of the succeeding fashions that fell upon domestic architecture. No wing had been added, no window filled in; no portico, façade, terrace, orangery, tower or battlement marred its timbered front. In the craze for coal gas and indoor sanitation, King's Thursday had slept unscathed by plumber or engineer. The estate carpenter, an office hereditary in the family of the original joiner who had panelled the halls and carved the great staircase, did such restorations as became necessary from

time to time for the maintenance of the fabric, working
with the same tools and with the traditional methods, so
that in a few years his work became indistinguishable
from that of his grandsires. Rushlights still flickered in
the bedrooms long after all Lord Pastmaster's neighbours
were blazing away electricity, and in the last fifty years
Hampshire had gradually become proud of King's Thursday. From having been considered rather a blot on the
progressive county, King's Thursday gradually became
the Mecca of week-end parties. "I thought we might go
over to tea at the Pastmasters'," hostesses would say after
luncheon on Sundays. "You really must see their house.
Quite unspoilt, my dear. Professor Franks, who was here
last week, said it was recognized as the finest piece of domestic Tudor in England."

It was impossible to ring the Pastmasters up, but they
were always at home and unaffectedly delighted to see
their neighbours, and after tea Lord Pastmaster would
lead the newcomers on a tour round the house, along the
great galleries and into the bedrooms, and would point
out the priest hole and the closet where the third Earl
imprisoned his wife for wishing to rebuild a smoking
chimney. "That chimney still smokes when the wind's in
the east," he would say, "but we haven't rebuilt it yet."

Later they would drive away in their big motor cars to
their modernized manors, and as they sat in their hot
baths before dinner the more impressionable visitors
might reflect how they seemed to have been privileged to
step for an hour and a half out of their own century into
the leisurely, prosaic life of the English Renaissance, and
how they had talked at tea of field sports and the reform
of the Prayer book just as the very-great-grandparents of
their host might have talked in the same chairs and before
the same fire three hundred years before, when their own
ancestors, perhaps, slept on straw or among the aromatic
merchandise of some Hanse ghetto.

But the time came when King's Thursday had to be
sold. It had been built in an age when twenty servants
were not an unduly extravagant establishment, and it was

scarcely possible to live there with fewer. But servants, the Beste-Chetwyndes found, were less responsive than their masters to the charms of Tudor simplicity; the bedrooms originally ordained for them among the maze of rafters that supported the arches of uneven stone roof were unsuited to modern requirements, and only the dirtiest and most tipsy of cooks could be induced to inhabit the enormous stone-flagged kitchen or turn the spits at the open fire. Housemaids tended to melt away under the recurring strain of trotting in the bleak hour before breakfast up and down the narrow servants' staircases and along the interminable passages with jugs of warm water for the morning baths. Modern democracy called for lifts and labour-saving devices, for hot-water taps and cold-water taps and (horrible innovation!) drinking water taps, for gas rings and electric ovens.

With rather less reluctance than might have been expected, Lord Pastmaster made up his mind to sell the house; to tell the truth, he could never quite see what all the fuss was about; he supposed it was very historic, and all that, but his own taste lay towards the green shutters and semi-tropical vegetation of a villa on the French Riviera, in which, if his critics had only realized it, he was fulfilling the traditional character of his family far better than by struggling on at King's Thursday. But the county was slow to observe this, and something very like consternation was felt, not only in the Great Houses, but in the bungalows and the villas for miles about, while in the neighbouring rectories antiquarian clergymen devised folk tales of the disasters that should come to crops and herds when there was no longer a Beste-Chetwynde at King's Thursday. Mr. Jack Spire in the *London Hercules* wrote eloquently on the *Save King's Thursday Fund* urging that it should be preserved for the nation, but only a very small amount was collected of the very large sum which Lord Pastmaster was sensible enough to demand, and the theory that it was to be transplanted and re-erected in Cincinnati found wide acceptance.

Thus the news that Lord Pastmaster's rich sister-in-law

had bought the family seat was received with the utmost
delight by her new neighbours and by Mr. Jack Spire, and
all sections of the London Press which noticed the sale.
Teneat Bene Beste-Chetwynde, the motto carved over the
chimney piece in the great hall, was quoted exultantly on
all sides, for very little was known about Margot Beste-
Chetwynde in Hampshire, and the illustrated papers were
always pleased to take any occasion to embellish their
pages with her latest portrait; the reporter to whom she
remarked, "I can't think of anything more bourgeois and
awful than timbered Tudor architecture," did not take in
what she meant or include the statement in his "story."

King's Thursday had been empty for two years when
Margot Beste-Chetwynde bought it. She had been there
once before, during her engagement.

"It's worse than I thought, far worse," she said as she
drove up the main avenue which the loyal villagers had
decorated with the flags of the sometime allied nations in
honour of her arrival. "Liberty's new building cannot be
compared with it," she said, and stirred impatiently in
the car, as she remembered, how many years ago, the romantic young heiress who had walked entranced among
the cut yews, and had been wooed, how phlegmatically,
in the odour of honeysuckle.

Mr. Jack Spire was busily saving St. Sepulchre's Egg
Street (where Dr. Johnson is said once to have attended
Matins), when Margot Beste-Chetwynde's decision to rebuild King's Thursday became public. He said, very seriously: "Well, we did what we could," and thought no
more about it.

Not so the neighbours, who as the work of demolition
proceeded, with the aid of all that was most pulverizing
in modern machinery, became increasingly enraged, and,
in their eagerness to preserve for the county a little of
the great manor, even resorted to predatory expeditions,
from which they would return with lumps of carved stone
work for their rock gardens, until the contractors were
forced to maintain an extra watchman at night. The pan-

elling went to South Kensington, where it has come in for a great deal of admiration from the Indian students. Within nine months of Mrs. Beste-Chetwynde's taking possession the new architect was at work on his plans.

It was Otto Friedrich Silenus's first important commission. "Something clean and square," had been Mrs. Beste-Chetwynde's instructions, and then she had disappeared on one of her mysterious world tours, saying as she left: "Please see that it is finished by the spring."

Professor Silenus—for that was the title by which this extraordinary young man chose to be called—was a "find" of Mrs. Beste-Chetwynde's. He was not yet very famous anywhere, though all who met him carried away deep and diverse impressions of his genius. He had first attracted Mrs. Beste-Chetwynde's attention with the rejected design for a chewing-gum factory which had been reproduced in a progressive Hungarian quarterly. His only other completed work was the *décor* for a cinema film of great length and complexity of plot—a complexity rendered the more inextricable by the producer's austere elimination of all human characters, a fact which had proved fatal to its commercial success. He was starving resignedly in a bed-sitting room in Bloomsbury, despite the untiring efforts of his parents to find him—they were very rich in Hamburg—when he was offered the commission of rebuilding King's Thursday. "Something clean and square"—he pondered for three hungry days upon the æsthetic implications of these instructions and then began his designs.

"The problem of architecture as I see it," he told a journalist who had come to report on the progress of his surprising creation of ferro concrete and aluminium, "is the problem of all art—the elimination of the human element from the consideration of form. The only perfect building must be the factory, because that is built to house machines, not men. I do not think it is possible for domestic architecture to be beautiful, but I am doing my best. All ill comes from man," he said gloomily; "please tell your readers that. Man is never beautiful; he is never happy except when he becomes the channel for the distribution of mechanical forces."

The journalist looked doubtful. "Now, Professor," he said, "tell me this. Is it a fact that you have refused to take any fee for the work you are doing, if you don't mind my asking?"

"It is not," said Professor Silenus.

"Peer's Sister-in-Law's Mansion Builder on Future of Architecture," thought the journalist happily. "Will machines live in houses? Amazing forecast of Professor-Architect."

Professor Silenus watched the reporter disappear down the drive and then, taking a biscuit from his pocket, began to munch.

"I suppose there ought to be a staircase," he said gloomily. "Why can't the creatures stay in one place? Up and down, in and out, round and round! Why can't they sit still and work? Do dynamos require staircases? Do monkeys require houses? What an immature, self-destructive, antiquated mischief is man! How obscure and gross his prancing and chattering on his little stage of evolution! How loathsome and beyond words boring all the thoughts and self-approval of this biological by-product! this half-formed, ill-conditioned body! this erratic, maladjusted mechanism of his soul: on one side the harmonious instincts and balanced responses of the animal, on the other the inflexible purpose of the engine, and between them man, equally alien from the *being* of Nature and the *doing* of the machine, the vile *becoming!*"

Two hours later the foreman in charge of the concrete mixer came to consult with the Professor. He had not moved from where the journalist had left him; his fawn-like eyes were fixed and inexpressive, and the hand which had held the biscuit still rose and fell to and from his mouth with a regular motion, while his empty jaws champed rhythmically; otherwise he was wholly immobile.

CHAPTER TWO

Interlude in Belgravia

ARTHUR POTTS knew all about King's Thursday and Professor Silenus.

On the day of Paul's arrival in London he rang up his old friend and arranged to dine with him at the Queen's Restaurant in Sloane Square. It seemed quite natural that they should be again seated at the table where they had discussed so many subjects of public importance, budgets and birth control and Byzantine mosaics. For the first time since the disturbing evening of the Bollinger dinner he felt at ease. Llanabba Castle, with its sham castellations and preposterous inhabitants, had sunk into the oblivion that waits upon even the most lurid of nightmares. Here were sweet corn and pimentoes, and white Burgundy, and the grave eyes of Arthur Potts, and there on the peg over his head hung the black hat he had bought in St. James's that afternoon. For an evening at least the shadow that has flitted about this narrative under the name of Paul Pennyfeather materialized into the solid figure of an intelligent, well-educated, well-conducted young man, a man who could be trusted to use his vote at a general election with discretion and proper detachment, whose opinion on a *ballet* or a critical essay was rather better than most people's, who could order a dinner without embarrassment and in a creditable French accent, who could be trusted to see to luggage at foreign railway stations, and might be expected to acquit himself with decision and decorum in all the emergencies of civilized life. This was the Paul Pennyfeather who had been developing in the placid years which preceded this story.

In fact, the whole of this book is really an account of the mysterious disappearance of Paul Pennyfeather, so that readers must not complain if the shadow which took his name does not amply fill the important part of hero for which he was originally cast.

"I saw some of Otto Silenus's work at Munich," said Potts. "I think that he's a man worth watching. He was in Moscow at one time and in the Bauhaus at Dessau. He can't be more than twenty-five now. There were some photographs of King's Thursday in a paper the other day. It looked extraordinarily interesting. It's said to be the only really *imaginative* building since the French Revolution. He's got right away from Corbusier, anyway."

"If people only realized," said Paul, "Corbusier is a pure nineteenth century, Manchester school utilitarian, and that's why they like him."

Then Paul told Potts about the death of Grimes and the doubts of Mr. Prendergast, and Potts told Paul about rather an interesting job he had got under the League of Nations and how he had decided not to take his Schools in consequence and of the unenlightened attitude adopted in the matter of Potts's father.

For an evening Paul became a real person again, but next day he woke up leaving himself disembodied somewhere between Sloane Square and Onslow Square. He had to meet Beste-Chetwynde and catch a morning train to King's Thursday, and there his extraordinary adventures began anew. From the point of view of this story Paul's second disappearance is necessary, because, as the reader will probably have discerned already, Paul Pennyfeather would never have made a hero, and the only interest about him arises from the unusual series of events of which his shadow was witness.

CHAPTER THREE

Pervigilium Veneris

"I'M LOOKING forward to seeing our new house," said Beste-Chetwynde as they drove out from the station. "Mamma says it may be rather a surprise."

The lodges and gates had been left undisturbed, and the lodge-keeper's wife, white-aproned as Mrs. Noah, bobbed at the car as it turned into the avenue. The temperate April sunlight fell through the budding chestnuts and revealed between their trunks green glimpses of parkland and the distant radiance of a lake. "English spring," thought Paul. "In the dreaming ancestral beauty of the English country." Surely, he thought, these great chestnuts in the morning sun stood for something enduring and serene in a world that had lost its reason and would so stand when the chaos and confusion were forgotten? And surely it was the spirit of William Morris that whispered to him in Margot Beste-Chetwynde's motor car about seed time and harvest, the superb succession of the seasons, the harmonious interdependence of rich and poor, of dignity, innocence, and tradition? But at a turn in the drive the cadence of his thoughts was abruptly transected. They had come into sight of the house.

"Golly!" said Beste-Chetwynde. "Mamma has done herself proud this time."

The car stopped. Paul and Beste-Chetwynde got out, stretched themselves, and were led across a floor of bottle-green glass into the dining room, where Mrs. Beste-Chetwynde was already seated at the vulcanite table beginning her luncheon.

"My dears," she cried, extending a hand to each of them, "how divine to see you! I have been waiting for this to go straight to bed."

She was a thousand times more beautiful than all Paul's feverish recollections of her. He watched her, transported.

"Darling boy, how are you?" she said. "Do you know, you're beginning to look rather lovely in a coltish kind of way. Don't you think so, Otto?"

Paul had noticed nothing in the room except Mrs. Beste-Chetwynde; he now saw that there was a young man sitting beside her, with very fair hair and large glasses, behind which his eyes lay like slim fish in an aquarium; they woke from their slumber, flashed iridescent in the light, and darted towards little Beste-Chetwynde.

"His head is too big, and his hands are too small," said Professor Silenus. "But his skin is pretty."

"How would it be if I made Mr. Pennyfeather a cocktail?" Beste-Chetwynde asked.

"Yes, Peter, dear, do. He makes them rather well. You can't think what a week I've had, moving in and taking the neighbours round the house and the Press photographers. Otto's house doesn't seem to be a great success with the county, does it, Otto? What was it Lady Vanbrugh said?"

"Was that the woman like Napoleon the Great?"

"Yes, darling."

"She said she understood that the drains were satisfactory, but that, of course, they were underground. I asked her if she wished to make use of them, and said that I did, and went away. But, as a matter of fact, she was quite right. They are the only tolerable part of the house. How glad I shall be when the mosaics are finished, and I can go!"

"Don't you like it?" asked Peter Beste-Chetwynde over the cocktail shaker. "I think it's so good. It was rather Chokey's taste before."

"I hate and detest every bit of it," said Professor Silenus. "Nothing I have ever done has caused me so much disgust." With a deep sigh he rose from the table and walked from the room, the fork with which he had been eating still held in his hand.

"Otto has real genius," said Mrs. Beste-Chetwynde. "You must be sweet to him, Peter. There's a whole lot of people coming down to-morrow for the week-end and, my dear, that Maltravers has invited himself again. You wouldn't like him for a stepfather, would you, darling?"

"No," said Peter. "If you must marry again do choose some one young and quiet."

"Peter, you're an angel. I will. But now I'm going to bed. I had to wait to see you both. Show Mr. Pennyfeather the way about, darling."

The aluminium lift shot up, and Paul came down to earth.

"That's an odd thing to ask me in a totally strange house," said Peter Beste-Chetwynde. "Anyway, let's have some luncheon."

It was three days before Paul next saw Mrs. Beste-Chetwynde.

"Don't you think that she's the most wonderful woman in the world?" said Paul.

"Wonderful? In what way?"

He and Professor Silenus were standing on the terrace after dinner. The half-finished mosaics at their feet were covered with planks and sacking; the great colonnade of black glass pillars shone in the moonlight; beyond the polished aluminium balustrade the park stretched silent and illimitable.

"The most beautiful and the most free. She almost seems like the creature of a different species. Don't you feel that?"

"No," said the Professor after a few moments' consideration. "I can't say that I do. If you compare her with other women of her age you will see that the particulars in which she differs from them are infinitesimal compared with the points of similarity. A few millimetres here and a few millimetres there, such variations are inevitable in the human reproductive system; but in all her essential functions—her digestion, for example—she conforms to type."

"You might say that about anybody."

"Yes, I do. But it's Margot's variations that I dislike so much. They are small, but obtrusive, like the teeth of a saw. Otherwise I might marry her."

"Why do you think she would marry you?"

"Because, as I said, all her essential functions are normal. Anyway, she asked me to twice. The first time I said I would think it over, and the second time I refused. I'm sure I was right. She would interrupt me terribly. Besides, she's getting old. In ten years she will be almost worn out."

Professor Silenus looked at his watch—a platinum disc from Cartier, the gift of Mrs. Beste-Chetwynde. "Quarter to ten," he said. "I must go to bed." He threw the end of his cigar clear of the terrace in a glowing parabola. "What do you take to make you sleep?"

"I sleep quite easily," said Paul, "except on trains."

"You're lucky. Margot takes veronal. I haven't been to sleep for over a year. That's why I go to bed early. One needs more rest if one doesn't sleep."

That night as Paul marked his place in *The Golden Bough,* and, switching off his light, turned over to sleep, he thought of the young man a few bedrooms away, lying motionless in the darkness, his hands at his sides, his legs stretched out, his eyes closed and his brain turning and turning regularly all the night through, drawing in more and more power, storing it away like honey in its intricate cells and galleries, till the atmosphere about it became exhausted and vitiated and only the brain remained turning and turning in the darkness.

So Margot Beste-Chetwynde wanted to marry Otto Silenus, and in another corner of this extraordinary house she lay in a drugged trance, her lovely body cool and fragrant and scarcely stirring beneath the bedclothes; and outside in the park a thousand creatures were asleep; and beyond that, again, were Arthur Potts, and Mr. Prender-

gast, and the Llanabba station master. Quite soon Paul
fell asleep. Downstairs Peter Beste-Chetwynde mixed himself another brandy and soda and turned a page in Have-
lock Ellis, which, next to *The Wind in the Willows*, was
his favourite book.

The aluminium blinds shot up, and the sun poured in
through the vita-glass, filling the room with beneficent
rays. Another day had begun at King's Thursday.

From his bathroom window Paul looked down on to
the terrace. The coverings had been removed, revealing
the half-finished pavement of silver and scarlet. Professor Silenus was already out there directing two workmen
with the aid of a chart.

The week-end party arrived at various times in the
course of the day, but Mrs. Beste-Chetwynde kept to her
room while Peter received them in the prettiest way possible. Paul never learned all their names, nor was he ever
sure how many of them there were. He supposed about
eight or nine, but as they all wore so many different
clothes of identically the same kinds, and spoke in the
same voice, and appeared so irregularly at meals, there
may have been several more or several less.

The first to come were the Hon. Miles Malpractice and
David Lennox, the photographer. They emerged with little shrieks from an Edwardian electric brougham and
made straight for the nearest looking glass.

In a minute the panatrope was playing, David and Miles
were dancing, and Peter was making cocktails. The party
had begun. Throughout the afternoon new guests arrived,
drifting in vaguely or running in with cries of welcome
just as they thought suited them best.

Pamela Popham, square-jawed and resolute as a big-
game huntress, stared round the room through her spectacles, drank three cocktails, said: "My God!" twice, cut
two or three of her friends, and stalked off to bed.

"Tell Olivia I've arrived when she comes," she said to
Peter.

After dinner they went to a whist drive and dance in

the village hall. By half-past two the house was quiet; at half-past three Lord Parakeet arrived, slightly drunk and in evening clothes, having "just escaped less than one second ago" from Alastair Trumpington's twenty-first birthday party in London.

"Alastair was with me some of the way," he said, "but I think he must have fallen out."

The party, or some of it, reassembled in pyjamas to welcome him. Parakeet walked round birdlike and gay, pointing his thin white nose and making rude little jokes at every one in turn in a shrill, emasculate voice. At four the house was again at rest.

Only one of the guests appeared to be at all ill at ease: Sir Humphrey Maltravers, the Minister of Transportation. He arrived early in the day with a very large car and two very small suitcases, and from the first showed himself as a discordant element in the gay little party by noticing the absence of their hostess.

"Margot? No, I haven't seen her at all. I don't believe she's terribly well," said one of them, "or perhaps she's lost somewhere in the house. Peter will know."

Paul found him seated alone in the garden after luncheon, smoking a large cigar, his big red hands folded before him, a soft hat tilted over his eyes, his big red face both defiant and disconsolate. He bore a preternatural resemblance to his caricatures in the evening papers, Paul thought.

"Hullo, young man!" he said. "Where's everybody?"

"I think Peter's taking them on a tour round the house. It's much more elaborate than it looks from outside. Would you care to join them?"

"No, thank you, not for me. I came here for a rest. These young people tire me. I have enough of the House during the week." Paul laughed politely. "It's the devil of a session. You keen on politics at all?"

"Hardly at all," Paul said.

"Sensible fellow! I can't think why I keep on at it. It's

a dog's life, and there's no money in it, either. If I'd stayed at the Bar I'd have been a rich man by now."

"Rest, rest and riches," he said—"it's only after forty one begins to value things of that kind. And half one's life, perhaps, is lived after forty. Solemn thought that. Bear it in mind, young man, and it will save you from most of the worst mistakes. If every one at twenty realized that half his life was to be lived after forty . . .

"Mrs. Beste-Chetwynde's cooking and Mrs. Beste-Chetwynde's garden," said Sir Humphrey meditatively. "What could be desired more except our fair hostess herself? Have you known her long?"

"Only a few weeks," Paul said.

"There's no one like her," said Sir Humphrey. He drew a deep breath of smoke. Beyond the yew hedges the panatrope could be faintly heard. "What did she want to build this house for?" he asked. "It all comes of this set she's got into. It's not doing her any good. Damned awkward position to be in—a rich woman without a husband! Bound to get herself talked about. What Margot ought to do is to marry—some one who would stabilize her position, some one," said Sir Humphrey, "with a position in public life."

And then, without any apparent connection of thought, he began talking about himself. " 'Aim high' has been my motto," said Sir Humphrey, "all through my life. You probably won't get what you want, but you may get something; aim low, and you get nothing at all. It's like throwing a stone at a cat. When I was a kid that used to be great sport in our yard; I daresay you were throwing cricket balls when you were that age, but it's the same thing. If you throw straight at it, you fall short; aim above, and with luck you score. Every kid knows that. I'll tell you the story of my life."

Why was it, Paul wondered, that every one he met seemed to specialize in this form of autobiography? He supposed he must have a sympathetic air. Sir Humphrey told of his early life: of a family of nine living in two rooms, of a father who drank and a mother who had fits, of a sister who went on the streets, of a brother who went to prison, of another brother who was born deaf-mute. He told of scholarships and polytechnics, of rebuffs and encouragements, of a University career of brilliant success and unexampled privations.

"I used to do proof reading for the Holywell Press," he said; "then I learned shorthand and took down the University sermons for the local papers."

As he spoke the clipped yews seemed to grow gray with the soot of the slums, and the panatrope in the distance took on the gay regularity of a barrel organ heard up a tenement staircase.

"We were a pretty hot lot at Scone in my time," he said, naming several high officers of state with easy familiarity, "but none of them had so far to go as I had."

Paul listened patiently, as was his habit. Sir Humphrey's words flowed easily, because, as a matter of fact, he was rehearsing a series of articles he had dictated the evening before for publication in a Sunday newspaper. He told Paul about his first briefs and his first general election, the historic Liberal campaign of 1906, and of the strenuous days just before the formation of the Coalition.

"I've nothing to be ashamed of" said Sir Humphrey. "I've gone further than most people. I suppose that, if I keep on, I may one day lead the party. But all this winter I've been feeling that I've got as far as I shall ever get. I've got to the time I should like to go into the other House and give up work and perhaps keep a race horse or two"—and his eyes took on the far-away look of a popular actress describing the cottage of her dreams—"and a yacht and a villa at Monte. The others can do that when they like, and they know it. It's not till you get to my age that you really feel the disadvantage of having been born poor."

On Sunday evening Sir Humphrey suggested a "hand of cards." The idea was received without enthusiasm.

"Wouldn't that be rather *fast?*" said Miles. "It *is* Sunday. I think cards are divine, particularly the kings. Such *naughty* old faces! But if I start playing for money I always lose my temper and cry. Ask Pamela; she's so brave and manly."

"Let's all play billiards and make a Real House Party of it," said David, "or shall we have a Country House Rag?"

"Oh, I do feel such a *rip*," said Miles, when he was at last persuaded to play. Sir Humphrey won. Parakeet lost thirty pounds, and opening his pocketbook, paid him in ten-pound notes.

"How he did cheat!" said Oliva on the way to bed.

"Did he, darling? Well, let's *jolly well* not pay him," said Miles.

"It never occurred to me to do such a thing. Why, I couldn't afford to possibly."

Peter tossed Sir Humphrey double or quits, and won.

"After all, I am host," he explained.

"When I was your age," said Sir Humphrey to Miles, "we used to sit up all night sometimes playing poker. Heavy money, too."

"Oh, you wicked old thing!" said Miles.

Early on Monday morning the Minister of Transportation's Daimler disappeared down the drive. "I rather think he expected to see Mamma," said Peter. "I told him what was the matter with her."

"You shouldn't have done that," said Paul.

"No, it didn't go down awfully well. He said that he didn't know what things were coming to and that even in the slums such things were not spoken about by children of my age. What a lot he ate! I did my best to make him feel at home, too, by talking about trains."

"I thought he was a very sensible old man," said Professor Silenus. "He was the only person who didn't think it necessary to say something polite about the house. Besides, he told me about a new method of concrete construction they're trying at one of the Government Superannuation Homes."

Peter and Paul went back to their cylindrical study and began another spelling lesson.

As the last of the guests departed Mrs. Beste-Chetwynde reappeared from her little bout of veronal, fresh and exquisite as a seventeenth-century lyric. The meadow of green glass seemed to burst into flower under her feet, as she passed from the lift to the cocktail table.

"You poor angels!" she said. "Did you have the hell of a time with Maltravers? And all those people? I quite forget who asked to come this week-end. I gave up inviting people long ago," she said, turning to Paul, "but it didn't make a bit of difference." She gazed into the opalescent depths of her *absinthe frappé*. "More and more I feel the need of a husband, but Peter is horribly fastidious."

"Well, your men are all so awful," said Peter.

"I sometimes think of marrying old Maltravers," said Mrs. Beste-Chetwynde, "just to get my own back, only 'Margot Maltravers' does sound a little too much, don't you think? And if they give him a peerage, he's bound to choose something quite awful. . . ."

In the whole of Paul's life no one had ever been quite so sweet to him as Margot Beste-Chetwynde was during the next few days. Up and down the shining lift shafts, in and out of the rooms and along the labyrinthine corridors of the great house he moved in a golden mist. Each morning as he dressed a bird seemed to be singing in his heart, and as he lay down to sleep he would pillow his head against a hand about which still hung a delicate fragrance of Margot Beste-Chetwynde's almost unprocurable scent.

"Paul, dear," she said one day as hand in hand, after a rather fearful encounter with a swan, they reached the shelter of the lake house, "I can't bear to think of you going back to that awful school. Do, please, write and tell Dr. Fagan that you won't."

The lake house was an eighteenth-century pavilion, built on a little mound above the water. They stood there for a full minute still hand in hand on the crumbling steps.

"I don't quite see what else I could do," said Paul.

"Darling, *I* could find you a job."

"What sort of job, Margot?" Paul's eyes followed the swan gliding serenely across the lake; he did not dare to look at her.

"Well, Paul, you might stay and protect me from swans, mightn't you?" Margot paused and then, releasing her hand, took a cigarette case from her pocket. Paul struck a match. "My dear, what an unsteady hand! I'm afraid you're drinking too many of Peter's cocktails. That child has a lot to learn yet about the use of vodka. But seriously I'm sure I can find you a better job. It's absurd your going back to Wales. I still manage a great deal of my father's business, you know, or perhaps you didn't. It was mostly in South America in—in places of entertainment, cabarets and hotels and theatres, you know, and things like that. I'm sure I could find you a job helping in that, if you think you'd like it."

Paul thought of this gravely. "Oughtn't I to know Spanish?" he said. It seemed quite a sensible question, but Margot threw away her cigarette with a little laugh and said: "It's time to go and change. You are being difficult this evening, aren't you?"

Paul thought about this conversation as he lay in his bath—a sunk bath of malachite—and all the time while he dressed and as he tied his tie he trembled from head to foot like one of the wire toys which street vendors dangle from trays.

At dinner Margot talked about matters of daily interest, about some jewels she was having reset, and how they had come back all wrong, and how all the wiring of her London house was being overhauled because of the fear of fire; and how the man she had left in charge of her villa at Cannes had made a fortune at the Casino and given her notice, and she was afraid she might have to go out there to arrange about it; and how the Society for the Preservation of Ancient Buildings was demanding a guarantee that she would not demolish her castle in Ireland; and how her cook seemed to be going off his head that night, the dinner was so dull; and how Bobby Pastmaster was trying to borrow money from her again, on the grounds that she had misled him when she bought his house and that if he had known she was going to pull it down he would have made her pay more. "Which is not logical of Bobby," she said. "The less I valued his house, the less I ought to have paid, surely? Still, I'd better send him something, otherwise he'll go and marry, and I think it may be nice for Peter to have the title when he grows up."

Later, when they were alone, she said: "People talk a great deal of nonsense about being rich. Of course it is a bore in some ways, and it means endless work, but I wouldn't be poor, or even moderately well off, for all the ease in the world. Would you be happy if you were rich, do you think?"

"Well, it depends how I got the money," said Paul.

"I don't see how that comes in."

"No, I don't quite mean that. What I mean is that I think there's only one thing that could make me really happy, and if I got that I should be rich too, but it wouldn't matter being rich, you see, because, however rich I was, and I hadn't got what would make me happy, I shouldn't be happy, you see."

"My precious, that's rather obscure," said Margot, "but I think it may mean something rather sweet." He looked up at her, and her eyes met his unfalteringly. "If it does, I'm glad," she added.

"Margot, darling, beloved, please, will you marry me?" Paul was on his knees by her chair, his hands on hers.

"Well, that's rather what I've been wanting to discuss with you all day." But surely there was a tremor in her voice?

"Does that mean that possibly you might, Margot? Is there a chance that you will?"

"I don't see why not. Of course we must ask Peter about

it, and there are other things we ought to discuss first," and then, quite suddenly, "Paul dear, dear creature, come here."

They found Peter in the dining room eating a peach at the sideboard.

"Hullo, you two!" he said.

"Peter, we've something to tell you," said Margot. "Paul says he wants me to marry him."

"Splendid!" said Peter. "I *am* glad. Is that what you've been doing in the library?"

"Then you don't mind?" said Paul.

"Mind? It's what I've been trying to arrange all this week. As a matter of fact, that's why I brought you here at all. I think it's altogether admirable," he said, taking another peach.

"You're the first man he's said that about, Paul. I think it's rather a good omen."

"Oh, Margot, let's get married at once."

"My dear, I haven't said that I'm going to yet. I'll tell you in the morning."

"No, tell me now, Margot. You do like me a little, don't you? Please marry me just terribly soon."

"I'll tell you in the morning. There's several things I must think about first. Let's go back to the library."

That night Paul found it unusually difficult to sleep. Long after he had shut his book and turned out the light he lay awake, his eyes open, his thoughts racing uncontrollably. As in the first night of his visit, he felt the sleepless, involved genius of the house heavy about his head. He and Margot and Peter and Sir Humphrey Maltravers were just insignificant incidents in the life of the house: this new-born monster to whose birth ageless and forgotten cultures had been in travail. For half an hour he lay looking into the darkness until gradually his thoughts began to separate themselves from himself, and he knew he was falling asleep. Suddenly he was roused to consciousness by the sound of his door opening gently. He could see nothing, but he heard the rustle of silk as some one came into the room. Then the door shut again.

"Paul, are you asleep?"

"Margot!"

"Hush, dear! Don't turn on the light. Where are you?" The silk rustled again as though falling to the ground. "It's best to make sure, isn't it, darling, before we decide anything? It may be just an idea of yours that you're in love with me. And, you see, Paul, I like you so very much, it would be a pity to make a mistake, wouldn't it?"

But happily there was no mistake, and next day Paul and Margot announced their engagement.

CHAPTER FOUR

Resurrection

CROSSING the hall one afternoon a few days later, Paul met a short man with a long red beard stumping along behind the footman towards Margot's study.

"Good Lord!" he said.

"Not a word, old boy!" said the bearded man as he passed on.

A few minutes later Paul was joined by Peter. "I say, Paul," he said, "who do you think's talking to Mamma?"

"I know," said Paul. "It's a very curious thing."

"I somehow never felt he was dead," said Peter. "I told Clutterbuck that to try and cheer him up."

"Did it?"

"Not very much," Peter admitted. "My argument was that if he'd really gone out to sea he would have left his wooden leg behind with his clothes, but Clutterbuck said he was very sensitive about his leg. I wonder what he's come to see Mamma about?"

A little later they ambushed him in the drive, and Grimes told them. "Forgive the beaver," he said, "but it's rather important at the moment."

"In the soup again?" asked Paul.

"Well, not exactly, but things have been rather low lately. The police are after me. That suicide didn't go down well. I was afraid it wouldn't. They began to fuss a bit about no body being found and about my game leg. And then my other wife turned up, and that set them thinking. Hence the vegetation. Clever of you two to spot me."

They led him back to the house, and Peter mixed him a formidable cocktail, the principal ingredients of which were absinthe and vodka.

"It's the old story," said Grimes. "Grimes has fallen on his feet again. By the way, old boy, I have to congratulate you, haven't I? You've done pretty well for yourself, too." His eye travelled appreciatively over the glass floor, and the pneumatic rubber furniture, and the porcelain ceiling, and the leather-hung walls. "It's not every one's taste," he said, "but I think you'll be comfortable. Funny thing, I never expected to see you when I came down here."

"What we want to know," said Peter, "is what brought you down to see Mamma at all."

"Just good fortune," said Grimes. "It was like this. After I left Llanabba I was rather at a loose end. I'd borrowed a fiver from Philbrick just before he left, and that got me to London, but for a week or so things were rather thin. I was sitting in a pub one day in Shaftesbury Avenue, feeling my beard rather warm and knowing I only had about five bob left in the world, when I noticed a chap staring at me pretty hard in the other corner of the bar. He came over after a bit and said: 'Captain Grimes, I think?' That rather put the wind up me. 'No, no, old boy,' I said, 'quite wrong, rotten shot. Poor old Grimes is dead, drowned. Davy Jones' locker, old boy!' And I made to leave. Of course it wasn't a very sensible thing to say, because, if I hadn't been Grimes, it was a hundred to

one against my knowing Grimes was dead, if you see what
I mean. 'Pity,' he said, 'because I heard old Grimes was
down on his luck, and I had a job I thought might suit
him. Have a drink, anyway.' Then I realized who he was.
He was an awful stout fellow called Bill, who'd been
quartered with me in Ireland. 'Bill,' I said, 'I thought you
were a bobby.' 'That's all right, old boy,' said Bill. Well,
it appeared that this Bill had gone off to the Argentine
after the war and had got taken on as a manager of
a . . ."—Grimes stopped as though suddenly reminded of
something—"a place of entertainment. Sort of night club,
you know. Well, he'd done rather well in that job, and
had been put in charge of a whole chain of places of entertainment all along the coast. They're a syndicate owned
in England. He'd come back on leave to look for a couple
of chaps to go out with him and help. 'The Dagos are no
use at the job,' he said, 'not dispassionate enough.' Had
to be chaps who could control themselves where women
were concerned. That's what made him think of me. But
it was a pure act of God, our meeting.

"Well, apparently the syndicate was first founded by
young Beste-Chetwynde's grandpapa, and Mrs. Beste-
Chetwynde still takes an interest in it, so I was sent down
to interview her and see if she agreed to the appointment.
It never occurred to me it was the same Mrs. Beste-Chetwynde who came down to the sports the day Prendy got so
tight. Only shows how small the world is, doesn't it?"

"Did Mamma give you the job?" asked Peter.

"She did, and fifty pounds advance on my wages, and
some jolly sound advice. It's been a good day for Grimes.
Heard from the old man lately, by the way?"

"Yes," said Paul, "I got a letter this morning," and
he showed it to Grimes:

Llanabba Castle,
North Wales.

My dear Pennyfeather:
   Thank you for your letter and for the enclosed cheque!
I need hardly tell you that it is a real disappointment to

me to hear that you are not returning to us next term. I had looked forward to a long and mutually profitable connection. However, my daughters and I join in wishing you every happiness in your married life. I hope you will use your new influence to keep Peter at the school. He is a boy for whom I have great hopes. I look to him as one of my prefects in the future.

The holidays so far have afforded me little rest. My daughters and I have been much worried by the insistence of a young Irish woman of most disagreeable appearance and bearing who claims to be the widow of poor Captain Grimes. She has got hold of some papers which seem to support her claim. The police, too, are continually here asking impertinent questions about the number of suits of clothes my unfortunate son-in-law possessed.

Besides this, I have had a letter from Mr. Prendergast stating that he too wishes to resign his post. Apparently he has been reading a series of articles by a popular bishop and has discovered that there is a species of person called a "Modern Churchman" who draws the full salary of a beneficed clergyman and need not commit himself to any religious belief. This seems to be a comfort to him, but it adds greatly to my own inconvenience.

Indeed, I hardly think that I have the heart to keep on at Llanabba. I have had an offer from a cinema company, the managing director of which, oddly enough, is called Sir Solomon Philbrick, who wish to buy the Castle. They say that its combination of mediæval and Georgian architecture is a unique advantage. My daughter Diana is anxious to start a nursing home or an hotel. So you see that things are not easy.

YOURS sincerely,
AUGUSTUS FAGAN.

There was another surprise in store for Paul that day. Hardly had Grimes left the house when a tall young man with a black hat and thoughtful eyes presented himself at the front door and asked for Mr. Pennyfeather. It was Potts.

"My dear fellow," said Paul, "I am glad to see you."

"I saw your engagement in *The Times,*" said Potts, "and, as I was in the neighbourhood, I wondered if you'd let me see the house."

Paul and Peter led him all over it and explained its intricacies. He admired the luminous ceiling in Mrs. Beste-Chetwynde's study and the indiarubber fungi in the recessed conservatory and the little drawing room, of which the floor was a large kaleidoscope, set in motion by an electric button. They took him up in the lift to the top of the great pyramidical tower, from which he could look down on the roofs and domes of glass and aluminium which glittered like Chanel diamonds in the afternoon sun. But it was not this that he had come to see. As soon as he and Paul were alone he said, as though casually: "Who was that little man I met coming down the drive?"

"I think he was something to do with the Society for the Preservation of Ancient Buildings," said Paul. "Why?"

"Are you sure?" asked Potts in evident disappointment. "How maddening! I've been on a false scent again."

"Are you doing Divorce Court shadowings, Potts?"

"No, no, it's all to do with the League of Nations," said Potts vaguely, and he called attention to the tank of octopuses which was so prominent a feature of the room in which they were standing.

Margot invited Potts to stay to dinner. He tried hard to make a good impression on Professor Silenus, but in this he was not successful. In fact, it was probably Potts's visit which finally drove the Professor from the house. At any rate, he left early the next morning without troubling to pack or remove his luggage. Two days later, when they were all out, he arrived in a car and took away his mathematical instruments, and some time after that again appeared to fetch two clean handkerchiefs and a change of underclothes. That was the last time he was seen at King's Thursday. When Margot and Paul went up to London, they had his luggage packed and left downstairs for him in case he should come again, but there it stayed, none of the male servants finding anything in it that he would care to wear. Long afterwards Margot saw the head gardener's son going to church in a *batik* tie of Professor Silenus's period. It was the last relic of a great genius, for before that King's Thursday had been again rebuilt.

CHAPTER FIVE

The Latin-American Entertainment Co., Ltd.

AT THE end of April Peter returned to Llanabba, Dr. Fagan having announced that the sale of the Castle had not been effected, and Margot and Paul went up to London to make arrangements for the wedding, which, contrary to all reasonable expectation, Margot decided was to take place in church with all the barbaric concomitants of bridesmaids, Mendelssohn, and Mumm. But before the wedding she had a good deal of South American business to see to.

"My first honeymoon was rather a bore," she said, "so I'm not taking any chances with this one. I must get everything settled before we start, and then we're going to have the three best months of your life."

The work seemed to consist chiefly of interviewing young women for jobs in cabarets and as dancing partners. With some reluctance Margot allowed Paul to be present one morning as she saw a new batch. The room in which she conducted her business was the Sports Room, which had been decorated for her, in her absence, by little Davy Lennox, the society photographer. Two stuffed buffaloes stood one on each side of the door. The carpet was of grass-green marked out with white lines, and the walls were hung with netting. The lights were in glass footballs, and the furniture was ingeniously designed of bats and polo sticks and golf clubs. Athletic groups of the early 'nineties and a painting of a prize ram hung on the walls.

"It's terribly common," said Margot, "but it rather impresses the young ladies, which is a good thing. Some of them tend to be rather mannery if they aren't kept in order."

Paul sat in the corner—on a chair made in the shape of an inflated Channel swimmer—enraptured at her business ability. All her vagueness had left her; she sat upright at the table, which was covered with Balmoral tartan, her pen poised over an inkpot, which was set in a stuffed grouse, the very embodiment of the Feminist movement. One by one the girls were shown in.

"Name?" said Margot.

"Pompilia de la Conradine."

Margot wrote it down.

"Real name?"

"Bessy Brown."

"Age?"

"Twenty-two."

"Real age?"

"Twenty-two."

"Experience?"

"I was at Mrs. Rosenbaum's, in Jermyn Street, for two years, mum."

"Well, Bessy, I'll see what I can do for you. Why did you leave Mrs. Rosenbaum's?"

"She said the gentlemen liked a change."

"I'll just ask her." Margot took up the telephone, which was held by a boxing glove. "Is that Mrs. Rosenbaum? This is Latin-American Entertainments, Ltd., speaking. Can you tell me about Miss de la Conradine? . . . Oh, that was the reason she left you? Thank you so much! I rather thought that might be it." She rang off. "Sorry, Bessy; nothing for you just at present."

She pressed the bell, which was in the eye of a salmon trout, and another young lady was shown in.

"Name?"

"Jane Grimes."

"Who sent you to me?"

"The gentleman at Cardiff. He gave me this to give you." She produced a crumpled envelope and handed it across the table. Margot read the note. "Yes, I see. So you're new to the business, Jane?"

"Like a babe unborn, mum."

"But you married?"

"Yes, mum, but it was in the war, and he was very drunk."

"Where's your husband?"

"Dead, so they do say."

"That's excellent, Jane. You're just the sort we want. How soon can you sail?"

"How soon would you be wanting me to?"

"Well, there's a vacancy in Rio I'm filling at the end of the week. I'm sending out two very nice girls. Would you like to be going with them?"

"Yes, mum, very pleased, I'm sure."

"D'you want any money in advance?"

"Well, I could do with a bit to send my dad if you could spare it."

Margot took some notes from a drawer, counted them, and made out the receipt.

"Sign this, will you? I've got your address. I'll send you your tickets in a day or so. How are you off for clothes?"

"Well, I've got a fine silk dress, but it's at Cardiff with the other things. The gentleman said I'd be getting some new clothes, perhaps."

"Yes, quite right. I'll make a note of that. The arrangement we generally make is that our agent chooses the clothes and you pay for them out of your salary in instalments."

Mrs. Grimes went out, and another girl took her place.

By luncheon time Margot Beste-Chetwynde was tired. "Thank heavens, that's the last of them," she said. "Were you terribly bored, my angel?"

"Margot, you're wonderful. You ought to have been an empress."

"Don't say that you were a Christian slave, dearest."

"It never occurred to me," said Paul.

"There's a young man just like your friend Potts on the other side of the street," said Margot at the window. "And, my dear, he's picked up the last of those poor girls, the one who wanted to take her children and her brother with her."

"Then it can't be Potts," said Paul lazily. "I say, Margot, there was one thing I couldn't understand. Why was it that the less experience those chorus girls had, the more you seemed to want them? You offered much higher wages to the ones who said they'd never had a job before."

"Did I, darling? I expect it was because I feel so absurdly happy."

At the time this seemed quite a reasonable explanation, but, thinking the matter over, Paul had to admit to himself that there had been nothing noticeably light-hearted in Margot's conduct of her business.

"Let's have luncheon out to-day," said Margot. "I'm tired of this house."

They walked across Berkeley Square together in the sunshine. A footman in livery stood on the steps of one of the houses. A hatter's van, emblazoned with the royal arms, trotted past them on Hay Hill, two cockaded figures upright upon the box. A very great lady, bolstered up in an old-fashioned landaulette, bowed to Margot with an inclination she had surely learned in the court of the Prince Consort. All Mayfair seemed to throb with the heart of Mr. Arlen.

Philbrick sat at the next table at the *Maison Basque* eating the bitter little strawberries which are so cheap in Provence and so very expensive in Dover Street.

"Do come and see me some time," he said. "I'm living up the street at Batts's."

"I hear you're buying Llanabba," said Paul.

"Well, I thought of it," said Philbrick. "But I'm afraid it's too far away, really."

"The police came for you soon after you left," said Paul.

"They're bound to get me some time," said Philbrick. "But thanks for the tip all the same! By the way, you might warn your fiancée that they'll be after her soon, if she's not careful. That League of Nations Committee is getting busy at last."

"I haven't the least idea what you mean," said Paul, and returned to his table.

"Obviously the poor man's dotty," said Margot when he told her of the conversation.

CHAPTER SIX

A Hitch in the Wedding Preparations

MEANWHILE half the shops in London were engaged on the wedding preparations. Paul asked Potts to be his best man, but a letter from Geneva declined the invitation. In other circumstances this might have caused him embarrassment, but during the past fortnight Paul had received so many letters and invitations from people he barely remembered meeting that his only difficulty in filling his place was the fear of offending any of his affectionate new friends. Eventually he chose Sir Alastair Digby-Vaine-Trumpington, because he felt that, however indirectly, he owed him a great deal of his present good fortune. Sir Alastair readily accepted, at the same time borrowing the money for a new tall hat, his only one having come to grief a few nights earlier.

A letter from Onslow Square, which Paul left unanswered, plainly intimated that Paul's guardian's daughter would take it as a personal slight, and as a severe blow to her social advancement, if she were not chosen as one of the bridesmaids.

For some reason or other, Paul's marriage seemed to

inspire the public as being particularly romantic. Perhaps they admired the enterprise and gallantry with which Margot, after ten years of widowhood, voluntarily exposed herself to a repetition of the hundred and one horrors of a fashionable wedding, or perhaps Paul's sudden elevation from schoolmaster to millionaire struck a still vibrant chord of optimism in each of them, so that they said to themselves over their ledgers and typewriters: "It may be me next time." Whatever the reason, the wedding was certainly an unparalleled success among the lower orders. Inflamed by the popular Press, a large crowd assembled outside St. Margaret's on the eve of the ceremony equipped, as for a first night, with collapsible chairs, sandwiches, and spirit stoves, while by half-past two, in spite of heavy rain, it had swollen to such dimensions that the police were forced to make several baton charges, and many guests were crushed almost to death in their attempts to reach the doors, and the route down which Margot had to drive was lined as for a funeral with weeping and hysterical women.

Society was less certain in its approval, and Lady Circumference, for one, sighed for the early 'nineties, when Edward Prince of Wales, at the head of *ton,* might have given authoritative condemnation to this ostentatious second marriage.

"It's maddenin' Tangent having died just at this time," she said. "People may think that that's my reason for refusin'. I can't imagine that *any one* will go."

"I hear your nephew Alastair Trumpington is the best man," said Lady Vanbrugh.

"You seem to be as well informed as my chiropodist," said Lady Circumference with unusual felicity, and all Lowndes Square shook at her departure.

In the unconverted mewses of Mayfair and the upper rooms of Shepherd's Market and North Audley Street, where fashionable bachelors lurk disconsolately on their evenings at home, there was open lamentation at the prey that had been allowed to slip through their elegantly gloved fingers, while more than one popular dancing man

inquired anxiously at his bank to learn whether his
month's remittance had been paid in as usual. But Margot remained loyal to all her old obligations, and invitations to her wedding reception were accepted by whole
bevies of young men who made it their boast that they
never went out except to a square meal, while little Davy
Lennox, who for three years had never been known to
give any one a "complimentary sitting," took two eloquent photographs of the back of her head and one of the
reflection of her hands in a bowl of ink.

Ten days before the wedding Paul moved into rooms at
the Ritz, and Margot devoted herself seriously to shopping. Five or six times a day messengers appeared at his
suite bringing little by-products of her activity—now a
platinum cigarette case, now a dressing gown, now a tie
pin or a pair of links—while Paul, with unaccustomed
prodigality, bought two new ties, three pairs of shoes, an
umbrella and a set of Proust. Margot had fixed his personal allowance at two thousand a year.

Far away in the Adriatic feverish preparations were
being made to make Mrs. Beste-Chetwynde's villa at
Corfu ready for the first weeks of her honeymoon, and
the great bed, carved with pineapples, that had once belonged to Napoleon III, was laid out for her reception
with fragrant linen and pillows of unexampled softness.
All this the newspapers retailed with uncontrolled profusion, and many a young reporter was handsomely commended for the luxuriance of his adjectives.

However, there was a hitch.

Three days before the date fixed for the wedding Paul
was sitting in the Ritz opening his morning's post, when
Margot rang him up.

"Darling, rather a tiresome thing's happened," she said.
"You know those girls we sent off to Rio the other day?
Well, they're stuck at Marseilles, for some reason or other.
I can't quite make out why. I think it's something to do
with their passports. I've just had a very odd cable from
my agent there. He's giving up the job. It's such a bore
all this happening just now. I do so want to get every-

thing fixed before Thursday. I wonder if you could be an angel and go over and see to it for me? It's probably only a matter of giving the right man a few hundred francs. If you fly you'll be back in plenty of time. I'd go myself, only you know, don't you, darling, I simply haven't one minute to spare."

Paul did not have to travel alone. Potts was at Croydon, enveloped in an ulster and carrying in his hand a little attaché case.

"League of Nations business," he said, and was twice sick during the flight.

At Paris Paul was obliged to charter a special aëroplane. Potts saw him off.

"Why are you going to Marseilles?" he asked. "I thought you were going to be married."

"I'm only going there for an hour or two, to see some people on business," said Paul.

How like Potts, he thought, to suppose that a little journey like this was going to upset his marriage. Paul was beginning to feel cosmopolitan, the Ritz to-day, Marseilles to-morrow, Corfu next day, and afterwards the whole world stood open to him like one great hotel, his way lined for him with bows and orchids. How pathetically insular poor Potts was, he thought, for all his talk of internationalism.

It was late evening when Paul arrived at Marseilles. He dined at Basso's in the covered balcony off bouillabaisse and Meursault at a table from which he could see a thousand lights reflected in the still water. Paul felt very much a man of the world as he paid his bill, calculated the correct tip, and sat back in the open cab on his way to the old part of the town.

"They'll probably be at *Alice's,* in the Rue de Reynarde," Margot had said. "Anyway, you oughtn't to have any difficulty in finding them if you mention my name."

At the corner of the Rue Ventomargy the carriage stopped. The way was too narrow and too crowded for traffic. Paul paid the driver. *"Merci, Monsieur! Gardez*

bien votre chapeau," he said as he drove off. Wondering
what the expression could mean, Paul set off with less
certain steps down the cobbled alley. The houses over-
hung perilously on each side, gaily alight from cellar to
garret; between them swung lanterns; a shallow gutter
ran down the centre of the path. The scene could scarcely
have been more sinister had it been built at Hollywood
itself for some orgiastic incident of the Reign of Terror.
Such a street in England, Paul reflected, would have been
saved long ago by Mr. Spire and preserved under a public
trust for the sale of brass toasting forks, picture post
cards, and "Devonshire teas." Here the trade was of a
different sort. It did not require very much worldly wisdom to inform him of the character of the quarter he was
now in. Had he not, guide book in hand, traversed the for-
saken streets of Pompeii?

No wonder, Paul reflected, that Margot had been so
anxious to rescue her protégées from this place of temptation and danger.

A Negro sailor, hideously drunk, addressed Paul in no
language known to man, and invited him to have a drink.
He hurried on. How typical of Margot that, in all her
whirl of luxury, she should still have time to care for the
poor girls she had unwittingly exposed to such perils.

Deaf to the polyglot invitations that arose on all sides,
Paul pressed on his way. A young lady snatched his hat
from his head; he caught a glimpse of her bare leg in a
lighted doorway; then she appeared at a window, beck-
oning him to come in and retrieve it.

All the street seemed to be laughing at him. He hesitated; and then, forsaking, in a moment of panic, both
his black hat and his self-possession, he turned and fled
for the broad streets and the tram lines where, he knew
at heart, was his spiritual home.

By daylight the old town had lost most of its terrors.
Washing hung out between the houses, the gutters ran
with fresh water, and the streets were crowded with old

women carrying baskets of fish. *Chez Alice* showed no sign of life, and Paul was forced to ring and ring before a tousled old concierge presented himself.

"*Avez-vous les jeunes filles de Madame Beste-Chetwynde?*" Paul asked, acutely conscious of the absurdity of the question.

"Sure, step right along, Mister," said the concierge; "she wired us you was coming."

Mrs. Grimes and her two friends were not yet dressed, but they received Paul with enthusiasm in dressing gowns which might have satisfied the taste for colour of the elder Miss Fagan. They explained the difficulty of the passports, which, Paul thought, was clearly due to some misapprehension by the authorities of their jobs in Rio. They didn't know any French, and of course they had explained things wrong.

He spent an arduous morning at consulates and police bureaux. Things were more difficult than he had thought, and the officials received him either with marked coldness or with incomprehensible winks and innuendo.

Things had been easier six months ago, they said, but now, with the League of Nations— And they shrugged their shoulders despairingly. Perhaps it might be arranged once more, but Madame Beste-Chetwynde must really understand that there were forms that must be respected. Eventually the young ladies were signed on as stewardesses.

"And if they should not go further with me than Rio," said the captain, "well, I have a sufficient staff already. You say there are posts waiting for them there? No doubt their employers will be able to arrange things there with the authorities."

But it cost Paul several thousand francs to complete the arrangements. "What an absurd thing the League of Nations seems to be!" said Paul. "They seem to make it harder to get about instead of easier." And this, to his surprise, the officials took to be a capital joke.

Paul saw the young ladies to their ship, and all three

kissed him good-bye. As he walked back along the quay he met Potts.

"Just arrived by the morning train," he said. Paul felt strongly inclined to tell him his opinion of the League of Nations, but remembering Potts' prolixity in argument and the urgency of his own departure, he decided to leave his criticisms for another time. He stopped long enough in Marseilles to cable to Margot "Everything arranged satisfactorily. Returning this afternoon. All my love" and then left for Paris by air, feeling that at last he had done something to help.

At ten o'clock on his wedding morning Paul returned to the Ritz. It was raining hard, and he felt tired, unshaven, and generally woebegone. A number of newspaper reporters were waiting for him outside his suite, but he told them that he could see no one. Inside he found Peter Beste-Chetwynde, incredibly smart in his first morning coat.

"They've let me come up from Llanabba for the day," he said. "To tell you the truth, I'm rather pleased with myself in these clothes. I bought you a buttonhole in case you'd forgotten. I say, Paul, you're looking tired."

"I am, rather. Turn on the bath for me like an angel."

When he had had his bath and shaved he felt better. Peter had ordered a bottle of champagne and was a little tipsy. He walked round the room, glass in hand, talking gaily, and every now and then pausing to look at himself in the mirror. "Pretty smart," he said, "particularly the tie; don't you think so, Paul? I think I shall go back to the school like this. That would make them see what a superior person I am. I hope you notice that I gave you the grander buttonhole? I can't tell you what Llanabba is like this term, Paul. Do try and persuade Mamma to take me away. Clutterbuck has left, and Tangent is dead, and the three new masters are quite awful. One is like your friend Potts, only he stutters, and Brolly says he's

got a glass eye. He's called Mr. Makepeace. Then there's
another one with red hair who keeps beating every one
all the time, and the other's rather sweet, really, only he
has fits. I don't think the Doctor cares for any of them
much. Flossie's been looking rather discouraged all the
time. I wonder if Mamma could get her a job in South
America? I'm glad you're wearing a waistcoat like that. I
nearly did, but I thought perhaps I was a bit young.
What do you think? We had a reporter down at the
school the other day wanting to know particulars about
you. Brolly told a splendid story about how you used to
go out swimming in the evenings and swim for hours
and hours in the dark composing elegiac verses, and then
he spoiled it by saying you had webbed feet and a pre-
hensile tail, which made the chap think he was having
his leg pulled. I say, am I terribly in the way?"

As Paul dressed his feeling of well-being began to return. He could not help feeling that he too looked rather
smart. Presently Alastair Digby-Vaine-Trumpington came
in, and drank some champagne.

"This wedding of ours is about the most advertised
thing that's happened for a generation," he said. "D'you
know, the *Sunday Mail* has given me fifty pounds to put
my name to an article describing my sensations as best
man. I'm afraid every one will know it's not me, though;
it's too jolly well written. I've had a marvellous letter
from Aunt Greta about it, too. Have you seen the presents? The Argentine Chargé d'Affaires has given you the
works of Longfellow bound in padded green leather, and
the Master of Scone has sent those pewter plates he used
to have in his hall."

Paul fastened the gardenia in his buttonhole, and they
went down to luncheon. There were several people in the
restaurant obviously dressed for a wedding, and it gave
Paul some satisfaction to notice that he was the centre of
interest of the whole room. The maître d'hôtel offered his
graceful good wishes as he led them to their table. Peter,
earlier in the morning, had ordered the luncheon.

"I doubt if we shall have time to eat it all," he said,

"but fortunately the best things all come at the beginning."

As he was peeling his second gull's egg Paul was called away to the telephone.

"Darling," said Margot's voice, "how are you? I've been so anxious all the time you were away. I had an awful feeling something was going to stop you coming back. Are you all right, dearest? Yes, I'm terribly well. I'm at home having luncheon in my bedroom and feeling, my dear, I can't tell you how virginal, really and truly completely débutante. I hope you'll like my frock. It's Boulanger, darling; do you mind? Good-bye, my sweet. Don't let Peter get too drunk, will you?"

Paul went back to the dining room.

"I've eaten your eggs," said Peter. "I just couldn't help it."

By two o'clock they had finished their luncheon. Mrs. Beste-Chetwynde's second best Hispano Suiza was waiting in Arlington Street.

"You must just have one more drink with me before we go," said the best man; "there's heaps of time."

"I think perhaps it would be a mistake if I did," said Peter.

Paul and his best man refilled their glasses with brandy.

"It is a funny thing," said Alastair Digby-Vaine-Trumpington. "No one could have guessed that when I had the Boller blind in my rooms it was going to end like this."

Paul turned the liqueur round in his glass, inhaled its rich bouquet for a second, and then held it before him.

"To Fortune," he said, "a much-maligned lady!"

"Which of you gentlemen is Mr. Paul Pennyfeather?"

Paul put down his glass and turned to find an elderly man of military appearance standing beside him.

"I am," he said. "But I'm afraid that, if you're from the Press, I really haven't time . . ."

"I'm Inspector Bruce, of Scotland Yard," said the stranger. "Will you be so good as to speak to me for a minute outside?"

"Really, officer," said Paul, "I'm in a great hurry. I suppose it's about the men to guard the presents. You should have come to me earlier."

"It's not about presents, and I couldn't have come earlier. The warrant for your arrest has only this minute been issued."

"Look here," said Alastair Digby-Vaine-Trumpington, "don't be an ass. You've got the wrong man. They'll laugh at you like blazes over this at Scotland Yard. This is the Mr. Pennyfeather who's being married to-day."

"I don't know anything about that," said Inspector Bruce. "All I know is, there's a warrant out for his arrest, and that anything he says may be used as evidence against him. And as for you, young man, I shouldn't attempt to obstruct an officer of the law, not if I was you."

"It's all some ghastly mistake," said Paul. "I suppose I must go with this man. Try and get on to Margot and explain to her."

Sir Alastair's amiable pink face gaped blank astonishment. "Good God," he said, "how damned funny! At least it would be at any other time." But Peter, deadly white, had left the restaurant.

Part Three

CHAPTER ONE

Stone Walls Do Not a Prison Make

PAUL's trial, which took place some weeks later at the Old Bailey, was a bitter disappointment to the public editors and the jury and counsel concerned. The arrest at the Ritz, the announcement at St. Margaret's that the wedding was postponed, Margot's flight to Corfu, the refusal of bail, the meals sent in to Paul on covered dishes from Boulestin's, had been "front-page stories" every day. After all this, Paul's conviction and sentence were a lame conclusion. At first he pleaded guilty on all charges, despite the entreaties of his counsel, but eventually he was galvanized into some show of defence by the warning of the presiding judge that the law allowed punishment with the cat-o'-nine-tails for offences of this sort. Even then things were very flat. Potts as chief witness for the prosecution was unshakable, and was later warmly commended by the court; no evidence, except of previous good conduct, was offered by the defence; Margot Beste-Chetwynde's name was not mentioned, though the judge in passing sentence remarked that "no one could be ignorant of the callous insolence with which, on the very eve of arrest for this most infamous of crimes, the accused had been preparing to join his name with one honoured in his country's history, and to drag down to his own pitiable depths of depravity a lady of beauty, rank, and stainless reputation. The just censure of society," remarked the judge, "is accorded to those so inconstant and intemperate that they must take their pleasures in the unholy market of humanity that still sullies the fame of our civilization; but for the traders themselves, these human vampires who prey upon the degradation of their species, society has reserved the right of ruthless suppression." So Paul was sent off to prison, and the papers headed the column they reserve for home events of minor importance with "Prison for Ex-society Bridegroom. Judge on Human Vampires," and there, as far as the public were concerned, the matter ended.

Before this happened, however, a conversation took place which deserves the attention of all interested in the confused series of events of which Paul had become a part. One day, while he was waiting for trial, he was visited in his cell by Peter Beste-Chetwynde.

"Hullo!" he said.

"Hullo, Paul!" said Peter. "Mamma asked me to come in to see you. She wants to know if you are getting the food all right she's ordered for you. I hope you like it, because I chose most of it myself. I thought you wouldn't want anything very heavy."

"It's splendid," said Paul. "How's Margot?"

"Well, that's rather what I've come to tell you, Paul. Margot's gone away."

"Where to?"

"She's gone off alone to Corfu. I made her, though she wanted to stay and see your trial. You can imagine what a time we've had with reporters and people. You don't think it awful of her, do you? And listen, there's something else. Can that policeman hear? It's this. You remember that awful old man Maltravers. Well, you've probably seen, he's Home Secretary now. He's been round to Mamma in the most impossible Oppenheim kind of way, and said that if she'd marry him he could get you out. Of course he's obviously been reading books. But Mamma thinks it's probably true, and she wants to know how you feel about it. She rather feels the whole thing's her fault, really, and, short of going to prison herself, she'll do anything to help. You can't imagine Mamma in prison, can you? Well, would you rather get out now and her marry Maltravers, or wait until you do get out and marry her yourself? She was rather definite about it."

Paul thought of Professor Silenus's "In ten years she will be worn out," but he said:

"I'd rather she waited if you think she possibly can."

"I thought you'd say that, Paul. I'm so glad. Mamma said: 'I won't say I don't know how I shall ever be able to make up to him for all this, because I think he knows I can.' Those were her words. I don't suppose you'll get more than a year or so, will you?"

"Good Lord, I hope not," said Paul.

His sentence of seven years' penal servitude was rather a blow. "In ten years she will be worn out," he thought as he drove in the prison-van to Blackstone Gaol.

On his first day there Paul met quite a number of people, some of whom he knew already. The first person was a warder with a low brow and distinctly menacing manner. He wrote Paul's name in the "Body Receipt Book" with some difficulty and then conducted him to a cell. He had evidently been reading the papers.

"Rather different from the Ritz Hotel, eh?" he said. "We don't like your kind 'ere, see? And we knows 'ow to treat 'em. You won't find nothing like the Ritz 'ere, you dirty White Slaver."

But there he was wrong, because the next person Paul met was Philbrick. His prison clothes were ill-fitting, and his chin was unshaven, but he still bore an indefinable air of the grand manner.

"Thought I'd be seeing you soon," he said. "They've put me on to reception bath cleaner, me being an old hand. I've been saving the best suit I could find for you. Not a louse on it, hardly." He threw a little pile of clothes, stamped with the broad arrow, on to the bench.

The warder returned with another, apparently his superior officer. Together they made a careful inventory of all Paul's possessions.

"Shoes, brown, one pair; socks, fancy, one pair; suspenders, black silk, one pair," read out the warder in a sing-song voice. "Never saw a bloke with so much clothes."

There were several checks due to difficulties of spelling, and it was some time before the list was finished.

"Cigarette case, white metal, containing two cigarettes; watch, white metal; tie pin, fancy"—it had cost Margot considerably more than the warder earned in a year, had he only known—"studs, bone, one pair; cuff links, fancy, one pair." The officers looked doubtfully at Paul's gold cigar piercer, the gift of the best man. "What's this 'ere?"

"It's for cigars," said Paul.

"Not so much lip!" said the warder, banging him on the top of his head with the pair of shoes he happened to be holding. "Put it down as 'instrument.' That's the lot," he said, "unless you've got false teeth. You're allowed to keep them, only we must make a note of it."

"No," said Paul.

"Truss or other surgical appliance?"

"No," said Paul.

"All right! You can go to the bath."

Paul sat for the regulation ten minutes in the regulation nine inches of warm water—which smelt reassuringly of disinfectant—and then put on his prison clothes. The loss of his personal possessions gave him a curiously agreeable sense of irresponsibility.

"You look a treat," said Philbrick.

Next he saw the Medical Officer, who sat at a table covered with official forms.

"Name?" said the Doctor.

"Pennyfeather."

"Have you at any time been detained in a mental home or similar institution? If so, give particulars."

"I was at Scone College, Oxford, for two years," said Paul.

The Doctor looked up for the first time. "Don't you dare to make jokes here, my man," he said, "or I'll soon have you in the strait-jacket in less than no time."

"Sorry," said Paul.

"Don't speak to the Medical Officer unless to answer a question," said the warder at his elbow.

"Sorry," said Paul, unconsciously, and was banged on the head.

"Suffering from consumption or any contagious disease?" asked the M. D.

"Not that I know of," said Paul.

"That's all," said the Doctor. "I have certified you are capable of undergoing the usual descriptions of punishment as specified below, to wit, restraint of handcuffs, leg chains, cross irons, body belt, canvas dress, close confinement, No. 1 diet, No. 2 diet, birch rod, and cat-o'-nine-tails. Any complaints?"

"But must I have all these at once?" asked Paul, rather dismayed.

"You will if you ask impertinent questions. Look after that man, officer; he's obviously a troublesome character."

"Come 'ere, you," said the warder. They went up a passage and down two flights of iron steps. Long galleries with iron railings stretched out in each direction, giving access to innumerable doors. Wire netting was stretched between the landings. "So don't you try no monkey tricks. Suicide isn't allowed in this prison. See?" said the warder. "This is your cell. Keep it clean, or you'll know the reason why, and this is your number." He buttoned a yellow badge on to Paul's coat.

"Like a flag day," said Paul.

"Shut up, you —— ——," remarked the warder, and locked the door.

"I suppose I shall learn to respect these people in time," thought Paul. "They all seem so much less awe-inspiring than any one I ever met."

His next visit was from the Schoolmaster. The door was unlocked, and a seedy-looking young man in a tweed suit came into the cell.

"Can you read and write, D.4.12?" asked the newcomer.

"Yes," said Paul.

"Public or secondary education?"

"Public," said Paul. His school had been rather sensitive on this subject.

"What was your standard when you left school?"

"Well, I don't quite know. I don't think we had standards."

The Schoolmaster marked him down as "Memory defective" on a form and went out. Presently he returned with a book.

"You must do your best with that for the next four weeks," he said. "I'll try and get you into one of the morning classes. You won't find it difficult, if you can read fairly easily. You see, it begins there," he said helpfully, showing Paul the first page.

It was an English Grammar published in 1872.

"A syllable is a single sound made by one simple effort of the voice," Paul read.

"Thank you," he said; "I'm sure I shall find it useful."

"You can change it after four weeks if you can't get on with it," said the Schoolmaster. "But I should stick to it, if you can."

Again the door was locked.

Next came the Chaplain. "Here is your Bible and a book of devotion. The Bible stays in the cell always. You can change the book of devotion any week if you wish to. Are you Church of England? Services are voluntary—that is to say, you must either attend all or none." The Chaplain spoke in a nervous and hurried manner. He was new to his job, and he had already visited fifty prisoners that day, one of whom had delayed him for a long time with descriptions of a vision he had seen the night before.

"Hullo, Prendy!" said Paul.

Mr. Prendergast looked at him anxiously. "I didn't recognize you," he said. "People look so much alike in those clothes. This is most disturbing, Pennyfeather. As soon as I saw that you'd been convicted I was afraid they might send you here. Oh, dear! oh, dear! It makes everything still more difficult."

"What's the matter, Prendy? Doubts again?"

"No, no, discipline, my old trouble. I've only been at

the job a week. I was very lucky to get it. My bishop said
he thought there was more opening for a Modern Churchman in this kind of work than in the parishes. The Governor is very modern too. But criminals are just as bad as
boys, I find. They pretend to make confessions and tell
me the most dreadful things just to see what I'll say, and
in chapel they laugh so much that the warders spend all
their time correcting them. It makes the services seem so
irreverent. Several of them got put on No. 1 diet this
morning for singing the wrong words to one of the hymns,
and of course that only makes me more unpopular.
Please, Pennyfeather, if you don't mind, you mustn't call
me Prendy, and if any one passes the cell will you stand
up when you're talking to me. You're supposed to, you
see, and the Chief Warder has said some very severe
things to me about maintaining discipline."

At this moment the face of the warder appeared at
the peep-hole in the door.

"I trust you realize the enormity of your offence and the
justice of your punishment?" said Mr. Prendergast in a
loud voice. "Pray for penitence."

A warder came into the cell.

"Sorry to disturb you, sir, but I've got to take this one
to see the Governor. There's D.4.18 down the way been
asking for you for days. I said I'd tell you, only, if you'll
forgive my saying so, I shouldn't be too soft with 'em, sir.
We know 'im of old. 'E's a sly old devil, begging your
pardon, sir, and 'e's only religious when 'e thinks it'll
pay."

"I think that I am the person to decide that, officer,"
said Mr. Prendergast with some dignity. "You may take
D.4.12 to the Governor."

Sir Wilfred Lucas-Dockery had not been intended by
nature or education for the Governor of a prison; his appointment was the idea of a Labour Home Secretary who
had been impressed by an appendix on the theory of
penology which he had contributed to a report on the
treatment of "Conscientious Objectors." Up to that time
Sir Wilfred had held the Chair of Sociology at a Mid-

land university; only his intimate friends and a few specially favoured pupils knew that behind his mild and professional exterior he concealed an ardent ambition to serve in the public life of his generation. He stood twice for Parliament, but so diffidently that his candidature passed almost unnoticed. Colonel MacAdder, his predecessor in office, a veteran of numberless unrecorded campaigns on the Afghan frontier, had said to him on his retirement: "Good luck, Sir Wilfred! If I may give you a piece of advice, it's this. Don't bother about the lower warders or the prisoners. Give hell to the man immediately below you, and you can rely on him to pass it on with interest. If you make prison bad enough, people'll take jolly good care to keep out of it. That's been my policy all through, and I'm proud of it" (a policy which soon became quite famous in the society of Cheltenham Spa).

Sir Wilfred, however, had his own ideas. "You must understand," he said to Paul, "that it is my aim to establish personal contact with each of the men under my care. I want you to take a pride in your prison and in your work here. So far as possible, I like the prisoners to carry on with their avocations in civilized life. What was this man's profession, officer?"

"White Slave traffic, sir."

"Ah, yes. Well, I'm afraid you won't have much opportunity for that here. What else have you done?"

"I was nearly a clergyman once," said Paul.

"Indeed? Well, I hope in time, if I find enough men with the same intention, to get together a theological class. You've no doubt met the Chaplain, a very broad-minded man. Still for the present we are only at the beginning. The Government regulations are rather uncompromising. For the first four weeks you will have to observe the solitary confinement ordained by law. After that we will find you something more creative. We don't want you to feel that your personality is being stamped out. Have you any experience of art leather work?"

"No, sir."

"Well, I might put you into the Arts and Crafts Workshop. I came to the conclusion many years ago that almost all crime is due to the repressed desire for æsthetic expression. At last we have the opportunity for testing it. Are you an extravert or an introvert?"

"I'm afraid I'm not sure, sir."

"So few people are. I'm trying to induce the Home Office to instal an official psychoanalyst. Do you read the *New Nation,* I wonder? There is rather a flattering article this week about our prison called *The Lucas-Dockery Experiments.* I like the prisoners to know these things. It gives them corporate pride. I may give you one small example of the work we are doing that affects your own case. Up till now all offences connected with prostitution have been put into the sexual category. Now I hold that an offence of your kind is essentially acquisitive and shall grade it accordingly. It does not, of course, make any difference as far as your conditions of imprisonment are concerned—the routine of penal servitude is prescribed by Standing Orders—but you see what a difference it makes to the annual statistics."

"The human touch," said Sir Wilfred after Paul had been led from the room, "I'm sure it makes all the difference. You could see with that unfortunate man just now what a difference it made to him to think that, far from being a mere nameless slave, he has now become part of a great revolution in statistics."

"Yes, sir," said the Chief Warder; "and, by the way, there are two more attempted suicides being brought up to-morrow. You must really be more strict with them, sir. Those sharp tools you've issued to the Arts and Crafts School is just putting temptation in the men's way."

Paul was once more locked in, and for the first time had the opportunity of examining his cell. There was little to interest him. Besides his Bible, his book of devotion—*Prayers on Various Occasions of Illness, Uncertainty and*

Loss, by the Rev. Septimus Bead, M.A., Edinburgh, 1863
—and his English Grammar, there were a little glazed
pint pot, a knife and spoon, a slate and slate pencil, a
salt jar, a metal water can, two earthenware vessels, some
cleaning materials, a plank bed upright against the wall,
a roll of bedding, a stool and a table. A printed notice
informed him that he was not permitted to look out of
the window. Three printed cards on the wall contained
a list of other punishable offences, which seemed to include every human activity, some Church of England
prayers, and an explanation of the "system of progressive stages." There was also a typewritten "Thought for
the Day," one of Sir Wilfred Lucas-Dockery's little in-
novations. The message for the first day of Paul's imprisonment was: *"SENSE OF SIN IS SENSE OF WASTE,
the Editor of the 'Sunday Express.'"* Paul studied the
system of progressive stages with interest. After four
weeks, he read, he would be allowed to join in associated
labour, to take half an hour's exercise on Sundays, to
wear a stripe on his arm, if illiterate to have school in-
struction, to take one work of fiction from the library
weekly, and, if special application were made to the Governor, to exhibit four photographs of his relatives or of
approved friends; after eight weeks, provided that his
conduct was perfectly satisfactory, he might receive a
visit of twenty minutes' duration and write and receive a
letter. Six weeks later he might receive another visit and
another letter and another library book weekly.

Would Davy Lennox's picture of the back of Margot's
head be accepted as the photograph of an approved
friend, he wondered?

After a time his door was unlocked again and opened a
few inches. A hand thrust in a tin, and a voice said,
"Pint pot quick!" Paul's mug was filled with cocoa, and
the door was again locked. The tin contained bread,
bacon, and beans. That was the last interruption for
fourteen hours. Paul fell into a reverie. It was the first
time he had been really alone for months. How very re-
freshing it was, he reflected.

The next four weeks of solitary confinement were among the happiest of Paul's life. The physical comforts were certainly meagre, but at the Ritz Paul had learned to appreciate the inadequacy of purely physical comfort. It was so exhilarating, he found, never to have to make any decision on any subject, to be wholly relieved from the smallest consideration of time, meals, or clothes, to have no anxiety ever about what kind of impression he was making; in fact, to be free. At some rather chilly time in the early morning a bell would ring, and the warder would say, "Slops outside!"; he would rise, roll up his bedding, and dress; there was no need to shave, no hesitation about what tie he should wear, none of the fidgeting with studs and collars and links that so distracts the waking moments of civilized man. He felt like the happy people in the advertisements for shaving soap who seem to have achieved very simply that peace of mind so distant and so desirable in the early morning. For about an hour he stitched away at a mail bag, until his door was again unlocked to admit a hand with a lump of bread and a large ladle of porridge. After breakfast he gave a cursory polish to the furniture and crockery of his cell and did some more sewing until the bell rang for chapel. For a quarter of an hour or twenty minutes he heard Mr. Prendergast blaspheming against the beauties of six-teenth-century diction. This was certainly a bore, and so was the next hour, during which he had to march round the prison square, where between concentric paths of worn asphalt a few melancholy cabbages showed their heads. Some of the men during this period used to fall out under the pretence of tying a shoe lace and take furtive bites at the leaves of the vegetables. If observed they were severely punished. Paul never felt any temptation to do this. After that the day was unbroken save for luncheon, supper, and the Governor's inspection. The heap of sacking which every day he was to turn into mail bags was supposed by law to keep him busy for nine hours. The prisoners in the cells on either side of him, who were not quite in their right minds, the warder told Paul,

found some difficulty in finishing their task before lights
out. Paul found that with the least exertion he had finished long before supper, and spent the evenings in
meditation and in writing up on his slate the thoughts
which had occurred to him during the day.

CHAPTER TWO

The Lucas-Dockery Experiments

SIR WILFRED LUCAS-DOCKERY, as has already been suggested, combined ambition, scholarship, and genuine optimism in a degree rarely found in his office. He looked
forward to a time when the Lucas-Dockery experiments
should be recognized as the beginning of a new epoch in
penology, and he rehearsed in his mind sentences from
the social histories of the future which would contain
such verdicts as *"One of the few important events of this
Labour Government's brief tenure of power was the appointment as Governor of Blackstone Gaol of Sir Wilfred Lucas-Dockery. The administration of this intrepid
and far-seeing official is justly regarded as the foundation
of the present system of criminal treatment. In fact, it
may safely be said that no single man occupies so high a
place in the history of the social reform of his century,
etc."* His eminent qualities, however, did not keep him
from many severe differences of opinion with the Chief
Warder. He was sitting in his study one day working at a
memorandum for the Prison Commissioners—one of the
neglected series of memoranda whose publication after
his retirement indicated Sir Wilfred's claim to be the
pioneer of artificial sunlight in prisons—when the Chief
Warder interrupted him.

"A bad report from the Bookbinding Shop, sir. The
instructor says that a practice is growing among the men

of eating the paste issued to them for their work. They say it is preferable to their porridge. We shall either have to put on another warder to supervise the bookbinding or introduce something into the paste which will make it unpalatable."

"Has the paste any nutritive value?" asked Sir Wilfred.

"I couldn't say, sir."

"Weigh the men in the Bookbinding Shop, and then report to me any increase in weight. How many times must I ask you to ascertain *all* the facts before reporting on any case?"

"Very good, sir! And there's a petition from D.4.12. He's finished his four months' solitary, and he wants to know if he can keep at it for another four."

"I disapprove of cellular labour. It makes a man introvert. Who is D.4.12?"

"Long sentence, sir, waiting transference to Egdon."

"I'll see D.4.12 myself."

"Very good, sir!"

Paul was led in.

"I understand you wish to continue cellular labour instead of availing yourself of the privilege of working in association. Why is that?"

"I find it so much more interesting, sir," said Paul.

"It's a most irregular suggestion," said the Chief Warder. "Privileges can only be forfeited by a breach of the regulations witnessed and attested by two officers. Standing Orders are most emphatic on the subject."

"I wonder whether you have narcissistic tendencies?" said the Governor. "The Home Office has not as yet come to any decision about my application for a staff psychoanalyst."

"Put him in the observation cell," said the Chief Warder. "That brings out any insanity. I've known several cases of men you could hardly have told were mad—just eccentric, you know—who've been put on observation, and after a few days they've been raving lunatics. Colonel MacAdder was a great believer in the observation cells."

"Did you lead a very lonely life before conviction? Perhaps you were a shepherd or a lighthouse keeper, or something of the kind?"

"No, sir."

"Most curious. Well, I will consider your case and give you my answer later."

Paul was led back to his cell, and next day was again summoned before the Governor.

"I have considered your application," said Sir Wilfred, "with the most minute care. In fact, I have decided to include it in my forthcoming work on the criminal mind. Perhaps you would like to hear what I have written about you?"

CASE R. [he read]:

A young man of respectable family and some education. No previous criminal record. Committed to seven years' penal servitude for traffic in prostitution. Upon completing his first four months R. petitioned for extension of cellular labour. Treatment as prescribed by Standing Orders: either (a) detention in observation cell for the Medical Officer to satisfy himself about the state of prisoner's mind or (b) compulsory work in association with other prisoners unless privilege forfeited by misdemeanour.

Treatment by Sir Wilfred Lucas-Dockery.—I decided that R. was suffering from misanthropic tendencies induced by a sense of his own inferiority in the presence of others. R.'s crime was the result of an attempt to assert individuality at the expense of community. (Cp. Cases D, G, and I.) Accordingly I attempted to break down his social inhibitions by a series of progressive steps. In the first stage he exercised daily for half an hour in the company of one other prisoner. Conversation was allowed during this period upon approved topics, history, philosophy, public events, etc., the prisoners being chosen among those whose crimes would tend as little as possible to aggravate and encourage R.'s.

"I have not yet thought of the other stages of your treatment," said Sir Wilfred, "but you can see that individual attention is being paid to your reclamation. It may cause you some gratification to realize that, thanks to my report, you may in time become a case of scientific interest throughout the world. Sir Wilfred Lucas-Dockery's treatment of Case R. may haply become a precedent for generations yet unborn. That is something to lift you above the soul-destroying monotony of routine, is it not?"

Paul was led away.

"The men in the kitchen have lodged a complaint that they cannot work with C.2.9," said the Chief Warder. "They say he has an infectious skin disease all over his hands."

"I can't be worried with things like that," said the Governor irritably. "I am trying to decide upon Case R.'s—I mean D.4.12's—third stage of reclamation."

Case R. of the Lucas-Dockery experiments began on the new *régime* that afternoon.

"Come out," said the warder, unlocking his cell, "and bring your 'at."

The parade ground, empty of its revolving squads, looked particularly desolate.

"Stand there and don't move till I come back," said the warder.

Presently he returned with a little bony figure in prison dress.

"This 'ere's your pal," he said; "this 'ere's the path you've got to walk on. Neither of you is to touch the other or any part of 'is clothing. Nothing is to be passed from one to the other. You are to keep at a distance of one yard and talk of 'istory, philosophy, or kindred subjects. When I rings the bell you stops talking, see? Your pace is to be neither quicker nor slower than average walking pace. Them's the Governor's instructions, and Gawd 'elp yer if yer does anything wrong. Now walk."

"This is a silly dodge," said the little man. "I've been

in six prisons, and I never seen nothing to touch it. Most irregular. You doesn't know where you are these days. This blinking prison is going to the dogs. Look at the Chaplain. Wears a wig!"

"Are you here for long?" asked Paul politely.

"Not this time. They couldn't get a proper charge against me. 'Six months for loitering with intent.' They'd been watching me for weeks, but I wasn't going to let them have a chance this time. Now six months is a very decent little sentence, if you take my meaning. One picks up with old friends, and you like it all the more when you comes out. I never minds six months. What's more, I'm known here, so I always gets made 'landing cleaner.' I expect you've seen my hand often enough coming round with the grub. The warders know me, see, so they always keeps the job open for me if they hears I'm coming back. If you're nice to 'em the first two or three times you're 'ere, they'll probably do the same for you."

"Is it a very good job?"

"Well, not as jobs go, but it's a nice start. The best job of all is Reception cleaner. One doesn't get that for years, unless you've special recommendations. You see, you has all the people coming in fresh from outside, and you hears all the news and gets tobacco sometimes and racing tips. Did you see the cleaner when you come in? Know who he is?"

"Yes," said Paul, "as a matter of fact, I do. He's called Philbrick."

"No, no, old man, you've got the wrong chap. I mean a big stout man. Talks a lot about hotels and restaurants."

"Yes, that's the man I mean."

"Why, don't you know who that is? That's the Governor's brother: Sir Solomon Lucas-Dockery. Told me so hisself. 'Ere for arson. Burnt a castle in Wales. You can see he's a toff."

CHAPTER THREE

The Death of a Modern Churchman

SOME days later Paul entered on another phase of his reclamation. When he came into the prison square for his afternoon exercise he found that his companion's place had been taken by a burly man of formidable aspect. He had red hair and beard, and red-rimmed eyes, and vast red hands which twirled convulsively at his sides. He turned his ox-like eyes on Paul and gave a slight snarl of welcome.

"Your new pal," said the warder. "Get on with it."

"How do you do?" said Paul politely. "Are you here for long?"

"Life," said the other. "But it doesn't matter much. I look daily for the Second Coming."

They marched on in silence.

"Do you think that this is a good plan of the Governor's?" asked Paul.

"Yes," said his companion. They walked on in silence, once round, twice round, three times round.

"Talk, you two," shouted the warder. "That's your instructions. Talk."

"It makes a change," said the big man.

"What are you here for?" asked Paul. "You don't mind my asking, do you?"

"It's all the Bible," said the big man. "You should read about it there. Figuratively, you know," he added. "It wouldn't be plain to you, I don't suppose, not like it is to me."

"It's not an easy book to understand, is it?"

"It's not understanding that's needed. It's vision. Do you ever have visions?"

"No, I'm afraid I don't."

"Nor does the Chaplain. He's no Christian. It was a vision brought me here, an angel clothed in flame, with a crown of flame on his head, crying 'Kill and spare not. The kingdom is at hand.' Would you like to hear about it? I'll tell you. I'm a carpenter by profession, or at least I was, you understand." He spoke a curious blend of cockney and Biblical English. "Not a joiner—a cabinet-maker. Well, one day I was just sweeping out the shop before shutting up when the angel of the Lord came in. I didn't know who it was at first. 'Just in time,' I said. 'What can I do for you?' Then I noticed that all about him there was a red flame and a circle of flame over his head, same as I've been telling you. Then he told me how the Lord had numbered His elect and the day of tribulation was at hand. 'Kill and spare not,' he says. I'd not been sleeping well for some time before this. I'd been worrying about my soul and whether I was saved. Well, all that night I thought of what the angel had told me. I didn't see his meaning, not at first, same as you wouldn't. Then it all came to me in a flash. Unworthy that I am, I am the Lord's appointed," said the carpenter. "I am the sword of Israel; I am the lion of the Lord's elect."

"And did you kill anybody?" asked Paul.

"Unworthy that I am, I smote the Philistine; in the name of the Lord of hosts, I struck off his head. It was for a sign in Israel. And now I am gone into captivity, and the mirth is turned into weeping, but the Lord shall deliver me in His appointed time. Woe unto the Philistine in that day! woe unto the uncircumcised. It were better that a stone were hanged about his neck and he were cast into the depths of the sea."

The warder rang his bell. "Inside, you two!" he shouted.

"Any complaints?" asked the Governor on his rounds.

"Yes, sir," said Paul.

The Governor looked at him intently. "Are you the man I put under special treatment?"

"Yes, sir."

"Then it's ridiculous to complain. What is it?"

"I have reason to believe that the man I have to take exercise with is a dangerous lunatic."

"Complaints by one prisoner about another can only be considered when substantiated by the evidence of a warder or of two other prisoners," said the Chief Warder.

"Quite right," said the Governor. "I never heard a more ridiculous complaint. All crime is a form of insanity. I myself chose the prisoner with whom you exercise. I chose him for his peculiar suitability. Let me hear no more on this subject, please."

That afternoon Paul spent another disquieting half hour on the square.

"I've had another vision," said the mystical homicide. "But I don't yet know quite what it portends. No doubt I shall be told."

"Was it a very beautiful vision?" asked Paul.

"No words can describe the splendour of it. It was all crimson and wet like blood. I saw the whole prison as if it were carved of ruby, hard and glittering, and the warders and the prisoners creeping in and out like little red ladybirds. And then as I watched all the ruby became soft and wet, like a great sponge soaked in wine, and it was dripping and melting into a great lake of scarlet. Then I woke up. I don't know the meaning of it yet, but I feel that the hand of the Lord is hanging over this prison. D'you ever feel like that, as though it were built in the jaws of a beast? I sometimes dream of a great red tunnel like the throat of a beast and men running down it, sometimes one by one and sometimes in great crowds, running down the throat of the beast, and the breath of the beast is like the blast of a furnace. D'you ever feel like that?"

"I'm afraid not," said Paul. "Have they given you an interesting library book?"

"*Lady Almina's Secret*," said the lion of the Lord's elect. "Pretty soft stuff, old-fashioned too. But I keep reading the Bible. There's a lot of killing in that."

"Dear me, you seem to think about killing a great deal."

"I do. It's my mission, you see," said the big man simply.

Sir Wilfred Lucas-Dockery felt very much like Solomon at ten o'clock every morning of the week except Sunday. It was then that he sat in judgment upon the cases of misconduct among the prisoners that were brought to his notice. From this chair Colonel MacAdder had delivered sentence in undeviating accordance with the spirit and the letter of the Standing Orders Concerning the Government of His Majesty's Prisons, dispensing automatic justice like a slot machine: in went the offence; out came the punishment. Not so Sir Wilfred Lucas-Dockery. Never, he felt, was his mind more alert or resourceful or his vast accumulation of knowledge more available than at his little court of summary justice. "No one knows what to expect," complained warders and prisoners alike.

"Justice," said Sir Wilfred, "is the capacity for regarding each case as an entirely new problem." After a few months of his administration, Sir Wilfred was able to point with some pride to a marked diminution in the number of cases brought before him.

One morning, soon after Paul began on his special *régime* of reclamation, his companion was called up before the Governor.

"God bless my soul!" said Sir Wilfred; "that's the man I put on special treatment. What is he here for?"

"I was on night duty last night between the hours of 8 P.M. and 4 A.M.," testified the warder in a sing-song voice, "when my attention was attracted by sounds of agitation coming from the prisoner's cell. Upon going to the observation hole I observed the prisoner pacing up and down his cell in a state of high excitement. In one hand he held his Bible, and in the other a piece of wood which he had broken from his stool. His eyes were staring; he was breathing heavily, and at times muttering verses of the Bible. I remonstrated with the prisoner when he addressed me in terms prejudicial to good discipline."

"What are the words complained of?" asked the Chief Warder.

"He called me a Moabite, an abomination of Moab, a wash pot, an unclean thing, an uncircumcised Moabite, an idolater, and a whore of Babylon, sir."

"I see. What do you advise, officer?"

"A clear case of insubordination, sir," said the Chief Warder. "Try him on No. 1 diet for a bit."

But when he asked the Chief Warder's opinion Sir Wilfred was not really seeking advice. He liked to emphasize in his own mind, and perhaps that of the prisoners', the difference between the official view and his own.

"What would you say was the most significant part of the evidence?" he asked.

The Chief Warder considered. "I think whore of Babylon, on the whole, sir."

Sir Wilfred smiled as a conjuror may who has forced the right card.

"Now I," he said, "am of a different opinion. It may surprise you, but I should say that the *significant* thing about this case was the fact that the prisoner held a piece of the stool."

"Destruction of prison property," said the Chief Warder. "Yes, that's pretty bad."

"Now what was your profession before conviction?" asked the Governor, turning to the prisoner.

"Carpenter, sir."

"*I knew it*," said the Governor triumphantly. "We have another case of the frustrated creative urge. Now listen, my man. It is very wrong of you to insult the officer, who is clearly none of the things you mentioned. He symbolizes the just disapproval of society and is, like all the prison staff, a member of the Church of England. But I understand your difficulty. You have been used to creative craftsmanship, have you not, and you find prison life deprives you of the means of self-expression, and your energies find vent in these foolish outbursts? I will see to it

that a bench and a set of carpenter's tools are provided
for you. The first thing you shall do is to mend the piece
of furniture you so wantonly destroyed. After that we will
find other work for you in your old trade. You may go.
Get to the cause of the trouble," Sir Wilfred added when
the prisoner was led away; "your Standing Orders may
repress the symptoms; they do not probe to the underlying
cause."

Two days later the prison was in a state of intense excitement. Something had happened. Paul woke as the
bell rang at the usual time, but it was nearly half an hour
before the doors were unlocked. He heard the warder's
"Slops outside!" getting nearer and nearer, interjected
with an occasional "Don't ask questions," "Mind your
own business," or a sinister "You'll know soon enough,"
in reply to the prisoners' questions. They, too, had sensed
something unusual. Perhaps it was an outbreak of some
disease—spotted fever, Paul thought, or a national disaster
in the world outside—a war or revolution. In their en-
forced silence the nerves of all the men were tightened to
an acuteness of perception. Paul read wholesale massacres
in the warder's face.

"Anything wrong?" he asked.

"I should bleeding well say there was," said the warder,
"and the next man as asks me a question is going to cop it
hot."

Paul began scrubbing out his cell. Dissatisfied curiosity
contended in his thoughts with irritation at this interruption of routine. Two warders passed his door talking.

"I don't say I'm not sorry for the poor bird. All I says
is, it was time the Governor had a lesson."

"It might have been one of us," said the other warder
in a hushed voice.

Breakfast arrived. As the hand appeared at his door
Paul whispered: "What's happened?"

"Why, ain't you 'eard? There's been a murder, shocking
bloodthirsty."

"Get on there," roared the warder in charge of the landing.

So the Governor had been murdered, thought Paul; he had been a mischievous old bore. Still, it was very disturbing, for the news of a murder which was barely noticed in the gay world of trams and tubes and boxing matches caused an electric terror in this community of silent men. The interval between breakfast and chapel seemed interminable. At last the bell went. The doors were opened again. They marched in silence to the chapel. As it happened, Philbrick was in the next seat to Paul. The warders sat on raised seats, watchful for any attempt at conversation. The hymn was the recognized time for the exchange of gossip. Paul waited for it impatiently. Clearly it was not the Governor who had been murdered. He stood on the chancel steps, Prayer book in hand. Mr. Prendergast was nowhere to be seen. The Governor conducted the service. The Medical Officer read the lessons, stumbling heavily over the longer words. Where was Mr. Prendergast?

At last the hymn was announced. The organ struck up, played with great feeling by a prisoner who until his conviction had been assistant organist at a Welsh cathedral. All over the chapel the men filled their chests for a burst of conversation.

" 'O God, our help in ages past,' [sang Paul].
    'Where's Prendergast to-day?'
 'What, ain't you 'eard? 'e's been done in.'
    'And our eternal home.'

" 'Old Prendy went to see a chap
    What said he'd seen a ghost;
 Well, he was dippy, and he'd got
    A mallet and a saw.'

" 'Who let the madman have the things?'
    'The Governor; who d'you think?

> He asked to be a carpenter,
>   He sawed off Prendy's head.
>
> " 'A pal of mine what lives next door,
>   'E 'eard it 'appening;
> The warder must 'ave 'eard it too,
>   'E didn't interfere.'
>
> " 'Time, like an ever-rolling stream,
>   Bears all its sons away.'
> " 'Poor Prendy 'ollored fit to kill
>   For nearly 'alf an hour.
>
> " 'Damned lucky it was Prendergast,
>   Might 'ave been you or me!
> The warder says—and I agree—
>   It serves the Governor right.' "

                                             "Amen."

From all points of view it was lucky that the madman had chosen Mr. Prendergast for attack. Some people even suggested that the choice had been made in a more responsible quarter. The death of a prisoner or warder would have called for a Home Office inquiry which might seriously have discouraged the Lucas-Dockery reforms, and also reflected some discredit upon the administration of the Chief Warder. Mr. Prendergast's death passed almost unnoticed. His assassin was removed to Broadmoor, and the life of the prison went on smoothly. It was observed, however, that the Chief Warder seemed to have more influence with his superior than he had had before. Sir Wilfred concentrated his attention upon the statistics, and the life of the prison was equitably conducted under the Standing Orders. It was quite like it had been in old MacAdder's day, the warders observed. But Paul did not reap the benefits of this happy reversion to tradition, because some few days later he was removed with a band of others to the Convict Settlement at Egdon Heath.

CHAPTER FOUR

Nor Iron Bars a Cage

THE granite walls of Egdon Heath Penal Settlement are visible, when there is no mist, from the main road, and it is not uncommon for cars to stop there a few moments while the occupants stand up and stare happily about them. They are looking for convicts, and as often as not they are rewarded by seeing move across the heath before them a black group of men chained together and uniformly dressed, with a mounted and armed warder riding at their side. They give an appearance of industry which on investigation is quite illusionary, for so much of the day at Egdon is taken up with marching to and from the quarries, in issuing and counting tools, in guarding and chaining and releasing the workmen, that there is very little work done. But there is usually something to be seen from the road, enough, anyway, to be imagined from the very aspect of the building to send the trippers off to their teas with their consciences agreeably unquiet at the memory of small dishonesties in railway trains, inaccurate income tax returns, and the hundred and one minor infractions of law that are inevitable in civilized life.

Paul arrived from Blackstone late one afternoon in early autumn with two warders and six other long-sentence prisoners. The journey had been spent in an ordinary third-class railway carriage, where the two warders smoked black tobacco in cheap little wooden pipes and were inclined towards conversation.

"You'll find a lot of improvements since you were here last," said one of them. "There's two coloured-glass windows in the chapel, presented by the last Governor's

widow. Lovely they are, St. Peter and St. Paul in prison
being released by an angel. Some of the Low Church prisoners don't like them, though.

"We had a lecture last week, too, but it wasn't very
popular—'The Work of the League of Nations,' given by
a young chap of the name of Potts. Still, it makes a
change. I hear you've been having a lot of changes at
Blackstone."

"I should just about think we have," said one of the
convicts, and proceeded to give a somewhat exaggerated
account of the death of Mr. Prendergast.

Presently one of the warders, observing that Paul
seemed shy of joining in the conversation, handed him a
daily paper. "Like to look at this, sonny?" he said. "It's
the last you'll see for some time."

There was very little in it to interest Paul, whose only
information from the outside world during the last six
weeks had come from Sir Wilfred Lucas-Dockery's weekly
bulletins (for one of the first discoveries of his captivity
was that interest in "news" does not spring from genuine
curiosity, but from the desire for completeness. During his
long years of freedom he had scarcely allowed a day to
pass without reading fairly fully from at least two newspapers, always pressing on with a series of events which
never came to an end. Once the series was broken, he
had little desire to resume it), but he was deeply moved
to discover on one of the middle pages an obscure but recognizable photograph of Margot and Peter. "The Honourable Mrs. Beste-Chetwynde," it said below, "and her
son Peter, who succeeds his uncle as Earl of Pastmaster."
In the next column was an announcement of the death of
Lord Pastmaster and a brief survey of his uneventful life.
At the end it said, "It is understood that Mrs. Beste-Chetwynde and the young Earl, who have been spending the
last few months at their villa in Corfu, will return to
England in a few days. Mrs. Beste-Chetwynde has for
many years been a prominent hostess in the fashionable
world and is regarded as one of the most beautiful women
in Society. Her son's succession to the earldom recalls the

sensation caused in May of this year by the announcement
of her engagement to Mr. Paul Pennyfeather and the dra-
matic arrest of the bridegroom at a leading West End
hotel a few hours before the wedding ceremony. The new
Lord Pastmaster is sixteen years old, and has up till now
been educated privately."

Paul sat back in the carriage for a long time looking at
the photograph, while his companions played several
hands of poker in reckless disregard of Standing Orders.
In his six weeks of solitude and grave consideration he
had failed to make up his mind about Margot Beste-Chetwynde; it was torn and distracted by two conflicting
methods of thought. On one side was the dead weight of
precept, inherited from generations of schoolmasters and
divines. According to these, the problem was difficult but
not insoluble. He had "done the right thing" in shielding
the woman: so much was clear, but Margot had not quite
filled the place assigned to her, for in this case she was
grossly culpable, and he was shielding her, not from misfortune nor injustice, but from the consequence of her
crimes; he felt a flush about his knees as Boy Scout honour
whispered that Margot had got him into a row and ought
jolly well to own up and face the music. As he sat over his
post bags he had wrestled with this argument without
achieving any satisfactory result except a growing conviction that there was something radically inapplicable
about this whole code of ready-made honour that is the
still small voice, trained to command, of the Englishman
all the world over. On the other hand was the undeniable
cogency of Peter Beste-Chetwynde's "You can't see Mamma
in prison, can you?" The more Paul considered this, the
more he perceived it to be the statement of a natural law.
He appreciated the assumption of comprehension with
which Peter had delivered it. As he studied Margot's photograph, dubiously transmitted as it was, he was strength-
ened in his belief that there was, in fact, and should be,
one law for her and another for himself, and that the raw
little exertions of nineteenth-century Radicals were essentially base and trivial and misdirected. It was not simply

that Margot had been very rich or that he had been in love with her. It was just that he *saw* the *impossibility* of Margot in prison; the bare connection of vocables associating the ideas was obscene. Margot dressed in prison uniform, hustled down corridors by wardresses—all like the younger Miss Fagan—visited by philanthropic old ladies with devotional pamphlets, set to work in the laundry washing the other prisoners' clothes—these things were *impossible,* and if the preposterous processes of law had condemned her, then the woman that they actually caught and pinned down would not have been Margot, but some quite other person of the same name and somewhat similar appearance. It was impossible to imprison the Margot who had committed the crime. If some one had to suffer that the public might be discouraged from providing poor Mrs. Grimes with the only employment for which civilization had prepared her, then it had better be Paul than that other woman with Margot's name, for anyone who has been to an English public school will always feel comparatively at home in prison. It is the people brought up in the gay intimacy of the slums, Paul learned, who find prison so soul destroying.

How lovely Margot was, Paul reflected, even in this absurd photograph, this gray-and-black smudge of ink! Even the most hardened criminal there—he was serving his third sentence for blackmail—laid down his cards for a moment and remarked upon how the whole carriage seemed to be flooded with the delectable savour of the Champs Élysées in early June. "Funny," he said. "I thought I smelt scent."

And that set them off talking about women.

Paul found another old friend at Egdon Heath Prison: a short, thick-set, cheerful figure who stumped along in front of him on the way to chapel, making a good deal of noise with an artificial leg. "Here we are again, old boy!" he remarked during one of the responses. "I'm in the soup as per usual."

"Didn't you like the job?" Paul asked.

"Top hole," said Grimes, "but the hell of a thing happened. Tell you later."

That morning, complete with pickaxes, field telephone and two armed and mounted warders, Paul and a little squad of fellow criminals were led to the quarries. Grimes was in the party.

"I've been here a fortnight," said Grimes as soon as they got an opportunity of talking, "and it seems too long already. I've always been a sociable chap, and I don't like it. Three years is too long, old boy. Still, we'll have God's own beano when I get out. I've been thinking about that day and night."

"I suppose it was bigamy?" said Paul.

"The same. I ought to have stayed abroad. I was arrested as soon as I landed. You see, Mrs. Grimes turned up at the shop, so off Grimes went. There are various sorts of hell, but that young woman can beat up a pretty lively one of her own."

A warder passed them by, and they moved apart, banging industriously at the sandstone cliff before them.

"I'm not sure it wasn't worth it, though," said Grimes, "to see poor old Flossie in the box and my sometime father-in-law. I hear the old man's shut down the school. Grimes gave the place a bad name. See anything of old Prendy ever?"

"He was murdered the other day."

"Poor old Prendy! He wasn't cut out for the happy life, was he? D'you know, I think I shall give up schoolmastering for good when I get out. It doesn't lead anywhere."

"It seems to have led us both to the same place."

"Yes. Rather a coincidence, isn't it? Damn, here's that policeman again."

Soon they were marched back to the prison. Except for the work in the quarries, life at Egdon was almost the same as at Blackstone.

"Slops outside," chapel, privacy.

After a week, however, Paul became conscious of an alien influence at work. His first intimation of this came from the Chaplain.

"Your library books," he said one day, popping cheerfully into Paul's cell and handing him two new novels, still in their wrappers, and bearing inside them the label of a Piccadilly bookseller. "If you don't like them I have several for you to choose from." He showed him rather coyly the pile of gaily bound volumes he carried under his arm. "I thought you'd like the new Virginia Wolf. It's only been out two days."

"Thank you, sir," said Paul politely. Clearly the library of his new prison was run on a much more enterprising and extravagant plan than at Blackstone.

"Oh there's this book on Theatrical Design," said the Chaplain, showing him a large illustrated volume that could hardly have cost less than three guineas. "Perhaps we might stretch a point and give you that as well as your 'educational work.'"

"Thank you, sir," said Paul.

"Let me know if you want a change," said the Chaplain. "And, by the way, you're allowed to write a letter now, you know. If, by any chance, you're writing to Mrs. Beste-Chetwynde, do mention that you think the library good. She's presenting a new pulpit to the chapel in carved alabaster," he added irrelevantly, and popped out again to give Grimes a copy of Smile's *Self-Help,* out of which some unreceptive reader in the remote past had torn the last hundred and eight pages.

"People may think as they like about well-thumbed favourites," thought Paul, "but there is something incomparably thrilling in first opening a brand-new book. Why should the Chaplain want me to mention the library to Margot?" he wondered.

That evening at supper Paul noticed without surprise that there were several small pieces of coal in his dripping: that kind of thing did happen now and then; but he was somewhat disconcerted, when he attempted to scrape them out, to find that they were quite soft. Prison food was often rather odd; it was a mistake to complain; but still. . . . He examined his dripping more closely. It had a pinkish tinge that should not have been there and was unusually firm and sticky under his knife. He tasted it dubiously. It was *pâté de foie gras*.

From then onward there was seldom a day on which some small meteorite of this kind did not mysteriously fall from the outside world. One day he returned from the heath to find his cell heavy with scent in the half dark, for the lights were rarely lit until some time after sundown, and the window was very small. His table was filled with a large bunch of winter roses, which had cost three shillings each that morning in Bond Street. (Prisoners at Egdon are allowed to keep flowers in their cells, and often risk severe reprimand by stooping to pick pimpernels and periwinkles on their way from work.)

On another occasion the prison doctor, trotting on his daily round of inspection, paused at Paul's cell, examined his name on the card hanging inside his door, looked hard at him and said: "You need a tonic." He trotted on without more ado, but next day a huge medicine bottle was placed in Paul's cell. "You're to take two glasses with each meal," said the warder, "and I hopes you like it." Paul could not quite decide whether the warder's tone was friendly or not, but he liked the medicine, for it was brown sherry.

On another occasion great indignation was aroused in the cell next door to him, whose occupant—an aged burglar—was inadvertently given Paul's ration of caviare. He was speedily appeased by the substitution for it of an unusually large lump of cold bacon, but not before the warder in charge had suffered considerable alarm at the possibility of a complaint to the Governor.

"I'm not one to make a fuss usually," said the old burglar, "but I will be treated fair. Why, you only had to look at the stuff they give me to see it was bad, let alone taste it. And on bacon night, too! You take my tip," he said to Paul as they found themselves alone in the quarries one day, "and keep your eyes open. You're a new one, and they might easily try and put a thing like that over on you. Don't eat it; that's putting you in the wrong. Keep it and show it to the Governor. They ain't got no right to try on a thing like that, and they know it."

Presently a letter came from Margot. It was not a long one.

DARLING PAUL [it said]:

It is so difficult writing to you because, you know, I never can write letters, and it's so particularly hard with you because the policemen read it and cross it all out if they don't like it, and I can't really think of anything they will like. Peter and I are back at King's Thursday. It was divine at Corfu, except for an English doctor who was a bore and would call so often. Do you know, I don't really like this house terribly, and I'm having it redone. Do you mind? Peter has become an earl—did you know?—and is rather sweet about it, and very self-conscious, which you wouldn't expect, really, would you, knowing Peter? I'm going to come and see you some time—may I?—when I can get away, but Bobby P.'s death has made such a lot of things to see to. I do hope you're getting enough food and books and things, or will they cross that out? Love, Margot. I was cut by Lady Circumference, my dear, at Newmarket, a real point-blank Tranby Croft cut. Poor Maltravers says if I'm not careful I shall find myself socially ostracized. Don't you think that will be marvellous? I may be wrong, but d'you know, I rather believe poor little Alastair Trumpington's going to fall in love with me. What shall I do?

Eventually Margot came herself.

It was the first time they had met since the morning in June when she had sent him off to rescue her distressed protégées in Marseilles. The meeting took place in a small room set aside for visitors. Margot sat at one end of the table, Paul at the other, with a warder between them.

"I must ask you both to put your hands on the table in front of you," said the warder.

"Like Up Jenkins," said Margot faintly, laying her exquisitely manicured hands with the gloves beside her bag.

Paul for the first time noticed how coarse and ill-kept his hands had become. For a moment neither spoke.

"Do I look awful?" Paul said at last. "I haven't seen a looking glass for some time."

"Well, perhaps just a little *mal soigné,* darling. Don't they let you shave at all?"

"No discussion of the prison régime is permitted. Prisoners are allowed to make a plain statement of their state of health, but must on no account make complaints or comments upon their general condition."

"Oh, dear!" said Margot; "this is going to be very difficult. What are we to say to each other? I'm almost sorry I came. You are glad I came, aren't you?"

"Don't mind me, mum, if you wants to talk personal," said the warder kindly. "I only has to stop conspiracy. Nothing I hears ever goes any further, and I hears a good deal, I can tell you. They carry on awful, some of the women, what with crying and fainting and hysterics generally. Why, one of them," he said with relish, "had an epileptic fit not long ago."

"I think it's more than likely I shall have a fit," said Margot. "I've never felt so shy in my life. Paul, *do* say something, please."

"How's Alastair?" said Paul.

"Rather sweet, really. He's always at King's Thursday now. I like him."

Another pause.

"Do you know," said Margot, "it's an odd thing, but I do believe that after all these years I'm beginning to be regarded as no longer a respectable woman. I told you when I wrote, didn't I, that Lady Circumference cut me the other day? Of course she's just a thoroughly bad-mannered old woman, but there have been a whole lot of things rather like that lately. Don't you think it's rather awful?"

"You won't mind much, will you?" said Paul. "They're awful old bores, anyway."

"Yes, but I don't like *them* dropping *me*. Of course, I don't mind, really, but I think it's a pity, particularly for

Peter. It's not just Lady Circumference, but Lady Vanbrugh and Fanny Simpleforth and the Stayles and all those people. It's a pity it should happen just when Peter's beginning to be a little class-conscious, anyway. It'll give him all the wrong ideas, don't you think?"

"How's business?" asked Paul abruptly.

"Paul, you mustn't be nasty to me," said Margot in a low voice. "I don't think you'd say that if you knew quite how I was feeling."

"I'm sorry, Margot. As a matter of fact, I just wanted to know."

"I'm selling out. A Swiss firm was making things difficult. But I don't think that business has anything to do with the—the ostracism, as Maltravers would say. I believe it's all because I'm beginning to grow old."

"I never heard anything so ridiculous. Why, all those people are about eighty, and anyway you aren't at all."

"I was afraid you wouldn't understand," said Margot, and there was another pause.

"Ten minutes more," said the warder.

"Things haven't turned out quite as we expected them to, have they?" said Margot.

They talked about some parties Margot had been to and the books Paul was reading. At last Margot said: "Paul, I'm going. I simply can't stand another moment of this."

"I've just decided something rather important," said Margot, "just this minute. I am going to be married quite soon to Maltravers. I'm sorry, but I am."

"I suppose it's because I look so awful?" said Paul.

"No, it's just everything. It's that, too, in a way, but not the way you mean, Paul. It's simply something that's going to happen. Do you understand at all, dear? It may help you, too, in a way, but I don't want you to think that that's the reason, either. It's just how things are going to happen. Oh, dear! How difficult it is to say anything."

"If you should want to kiss good-bye," said the gaoler, "not being husband and wife, it's not unusual. Still, I don't mind stretching a point for once . . ."

"Oh, God!" said Margot, and left the room without looking back.

Paul returned to his cell. His supper had already been served out to him, a small pie from which protruded the feet of two pigeons; there was even a table napkin wrapped round it. But Paul had very little appetite, for he was greatly pained at how little he was pained by the events of the afternoon.

CHAPTER FIVE

The Passing of a Public-School Man

A DAY or two later Paul again found himself next to Grimes in the quarry. When the warder was out of ear-shot Grimes said: "Old boy, I can't stand this much longer. It just ain't good enough."

"I don't see any way out," said Paul. "Anyway, it's quite bearable. I'd as soon be here as at Llanabba."

"Not so Grimes," said Grimes. "He just languishes in captivity, like the lark. It's all right for you—you like reading and thinking, and all that. Well, I'm different, you know. I like drink and a bit of fun, and chatting now and then to my pals. I'm a sociable chap. It's turning me into a giddy machine, this life, and there's an awful chaplain, who gives me the pip, who keeps butting in in a breezy kind of way and asking if I feel I'm 'right with God.' Of course I'm not, and I tell him so. I can stand most sorts of misfortune, old boy, but I can't stand repression. That was what broke me up at Llanabba, and it's what's going to break me up here, if I don't look out for myself. It seems to me it's time Grimes flitted off to another clime."

"No one has ever succeeded in escaping from this prison," said Paul.

"Well, just you watch Grimes next time there's a fog!"

As luck would have it, there was a fog next day, a heavy, impenetrable white mist which came up quite suddenly while they were at work, enveloping men and quarry in the way that mists do on Egdon Heath.

"Close up there," said the warder in charge. "Stop work and close up. Look out there, you idiot!" for Grimes had stumbled over the field telephone. "If you've broken it you'll come up before the Governor to-morrow."

"Hold this horse," said the other warder, handing the reins to Grimes.

He stooped and began to collect the chains on which the men were strung for their march home. Grimes seemed to be having some difficulty with the horse, which was plunging and rearing farther away from the squad. "Can't you even hold a horse?" said the warder. Suddenly Grimes, with remarkable agility considering his leg, was seen to be in the saddle riding away into the heath.

"Come back," roared the warder, "come back, or I'll fire." He put his rifle to his shoulder and fired into the fog. "He'll come back all right," he said. "No one ever gets away for long. He'll get solitary confinement and No. 1 diet for this, poor fish."

No one seemed to be much disturbed by the incident, even when it was found that the field telephone was disconnected.

"He hasn't a hope," said the warder. "They often do that, just put down their tools sudden and cut and run. But they can't get away in those clothes and with no money. We shall warn all the farms to-night. Sometimes they stays out hiding for several days, but back they comes when they're hungry, or else they get arrested the moment they shows up in a village. I reckon it's just nerves makes them try it."

That evening the horse came back, but there was no sign of Grimes. Special patrols were sent out with blood-hounds straining at their leashes; the farms and villages on the heath were warned, and the anxious inhabitants barred their doors closely and more pertinently forbade their children to leave the house on any pretext whatever; the roads were watched for miles, and all cars were stopped and searched, to the intense annoyance of many law-abiding citizens. But Grimes did not turn up. Bets were slily made among the prisoners as to the day of his recovery; but days passed, and rations of bread changed hands, but still there was no Grimes.

A week later at morning service the Chaplain prayed for his soul: the Governor crossed his name off the Body Receipt Book and notified the Home Secretary, the Right Honourable Sir Humphrey Maltravers, that Grimes was dead.

"I'm afraid it was a terrible end," said the Chaplain to Paul.

"Did they find the body?"

"No, that is the worst thing about it. The hounds followed his scent as far as Egdon Mire; there it ended. A shepherd who knows the paths through the bog found his hat floating on the surface at the most treacherous part. I'm afraid there is no doubt that he died a very horrible death."

"Poor old Grimes!" said Paul. "And he was an old Harrovian, too."

But later, thinking things over as he ate peacefully, one by one, the oysters that had been provided as a "relish" for his supper, Paul knew that Grimes was not dead. Lord Tangent was dead; Mr. Prendergast was dead; the time would even come for Paul Pennyfeather; but Grimes, Paul at last realized, was of the immortals. He was a life force. Sentenced to death in Flanders, he popped up in Wales; drowned in Wales, he emerged in South America; engulfed in the dark mystery of Egdon Mire, he would rise again somewhere at sometime, shaking from his limbs the musty integuments of the tomb. Surely he had followed in the Bacchic train of distant Arcady, and played on the reeds of myth by forgotten streams, and taught the childish satyrs the art of love? Had he not suffered unscathed the fearful dooms of all the offended gods of all the histories, fire, brimstone, and yawning earthquakes, plague and pestilence? Had he not stood, like the Pompeian sentry, while the Citadels of the Plain fell to ruin about his ears? Had he not, like some grease-caked Channel swimmer, breasted the waves of the Deluge? Had he not moved unseen when darkness covered the waters?

"I often wonder whether I am blameless in the matter," said the Chaplain. "It is awful to think of some one under my care having come to so terrible an end. I tried to console him and reconcile him with his life, but things are so difficult; there are so many men to see. Poor fellow! To think of him alone out there in the bog, with no one to help him!"

CHAPTER SIX

The Passing of Paul Pennyfeather

A FEW days later Paul was summoned to the Governor's room.

"I have an order here from the Home Secretary granting leave for you to go into a private nursing home for the removal of your appendix. You will start under escort, in plain clothes, this morning."

"But, sir," said Paul, "I don't want to have my appendix removed. In fact, it was done years ago when I was still at school."

"Nonsense!" said the Governor. "I've got an order here from the Home Secretary especially requiring that it shall be done. Officer, take this man away and give him his clothes for the journey."

Paul was led away. The clothes in which he had been tried had been sent with him from Blackstone. The warder took them out of a locker, unfolded them and handed them to Paul. "Shoes, socks, trousers, waistcoats, coat,

shirt, collar, tie and hat," he said. "Will you sign for
them? The jewellery stays here." He collected the watch,
links, tie pin, note case, and the other odds and ends that
had been in Paul's pockets and put them back in the
locker. "We can't do anything about your hair," said the
warder, "but you're allowed a shave."

Half an hour later Paul emerged from his cell, looking
for all the world like a normal civilized man, such as you
might see daily in any tube railway.

"Feels funny, don't it?" said the warder who let him
out. "Here's your escort."

Another normal civilized man, such as you might see
daily in any tube railway, confronted Paul.

"Time we started, if you're quite ready," he said.
Robbed of their uniforms, it seemed natural that they
should treat each other with normal consideration. Indeed, Paul thought he detected a certain deference in the
man's tone.

"It's very odd," said Paul in the van that took them to
the station; "it's no good arguing with the Governor, but
he's made some ridiculous mistake. I've had my appendix
out already."

"Not half," said the warder with a wink, "but don't go
talking about it so loud. The driver's not in on this."

A first-class carriage had been reserved for them in the
train. As they drew out of Egdon Station the warder said:
"Well, that's the last you'll see of the old place for some
time. Solemn thought, death, ain't it?" And he gave another shattering wink.

They had luncheon in their carriage, Paul feeling a
little too shy of his closely cropped head to venture hat-
less into the restaurant car. After luncheon they smoked
cigars. The warder paid from a fat note case. "Oh, I nearly
forgot," he said. "Here's your will for you to sign, in case
anything should happen." He produced a long blue paper
and handed it to Paul. *The Last Will and Testament of
Paul Pennyfeather* was handsomely engrossed at the top.
Below, it was stated, with the usual legal periphrases, that
he left all he possessed to Margot Beste-Chetwynde. Two

witnesses had already signed below the vacant space. "I'm sure this is all very irregular," said Paul, signing; "I wish you'd tell me what all this means."

"I don't know nothing," said the warder. "The young gentleman give me the will."

"What young gentleman?"

"How should I know?" said the warder. "The young gentleman what's arranged everything. Very sensible to make a will. You never know with an operation what may happen, do you? I had an aunt died having gall stones taken out, and she hadn't made a will. Very awkward it was, her not being married properly, you see. Fine, healthy woman, too, to look at her. Don't you get worried, Mr. Pennyfeather; everything will be done strictly according to regulations."

"Where are we going? At least you must know that."

For answer the warder took a printed card from his pocket.

Cliff Place, Worthing [he read]. *High-class Nursing and Private Sanatorium. Electric thermal treatment under medical supervision. Augustus Fagan, M.D., Proprietor.* "Approved by the Home Secretary," said the warder. "Nothing to complain of."

Late in the afternoon they arrived. A car was waiting to take them to Cliff Place.

"This ends my responsibility," said the warder. "From now on the doctor's in charge."

Like all Dr. Fagan's enterprises, Cliff Place was conceived on a large scale. The house stood alone on the seashore some miles from the town, and was approached by a long drive. In detail, however, it showed some signs of neglect. The verandah was deep in driven leaves; two of the windows were broken. Paul's escort rang the bell at the front door, and Dingy, dressed as a nurse, opened it to them.

"The servants have all gone," she said. "I suppose this is the appendicitis case. Come in." She showed no signs of recognizing Paul as she led him upstairs. "This is your room. The Home Office regulations insisted that it should be on an upper story with barred windows. We have had to put the bars in specially. They will be charged for in the bill. The surgeon will be here in a few minutes."

As she went out she locked the door. Paul sat down on the bed and waited. Below his window the sea beat on the shingle. A small steam yacht lay at anchor some distance out to sea. The gray horizon faded indistinctly into the gray sky.

Presently steps approached, and his door opened. In came Dr. Fagan, Sir Alastair Digby-Vaine-Trumpington, and an elderly little man with a drooping red moustache, evidently much the worse for drink.

"Sorry we're late," said Sir Alastair, "but I've had an awful day with this man trying to keep him sober. He gave me the slip just as we were starting. I was afraid at first that he was too tight to be moved, but I think he can just carry on. Have you got the papers made out?"

No one paid much attention to Paul.

"Here they are," said Dr. Fagan. "This is the statement you are to forward to the Home Secretary, and a duplicate for the Governor of the prison. Shall I read them to you?"

" 'Sh'all right!" said the surgeon.

"They merely state that you operated on the patient for appendicitis, but that he died under the anæsthetic without regaining consciousness."

"Poor old chap!" said the surgeon. "Poor, poor l'il girl!" And two tears of sympathy welled up in his eyes. "I daresay the world had been very hard on her. It's a hard world for women."

"That's all right," said Sir Alastair. "Don't worry. You did all that was humanly possible."

"That's the truth," said the surgeon, "and I don't care who knows it."

"This is the ordinary certificate of death," said Dr. Fagan. "Will you be so good as to sign it there?"

"Oh, death, where is thy sting-a-ling-a-ling?" said the surgeon, and with these words and a laboured effort of the pen he terminated the legal life of Paul Pennyfeather.

"Splendid!" said Sir Alastair. "Now here's your money. If I were you I should run off and have a drink while the pubs are still open."

"D'you know, I think I will," said the surgeon, and left the sanatorium.

There was a hush for nearly a minute after he had left the room. The presence of death, even in its coldest and most legal form, seemed to cause an air of solemnity. It was broken at length by the arrival of Flossie, splendidly attired in magenta and green.

"Why, here you all are!" she said with genuine delight. "And Mr. Pennyfeather too, to be sure! Quite a little party!"

She had said the right thing. The word "party" seemed to strike a responsive note in Dr. Fagan.

"Let us go down to supper," he said. "I'm sure we all have a great deal to be thankful for."

After supper Dr. Fagan made a little speech. "I think this an important evening for most of us," he said, "most of all for my dear friend and sometime colleague Paul Pennyfeather, in whose death to-night we are all to some extent participants. For myself as well as for him it is the beginning of a new phase of life. Frankly, this nursing home has not been a success. A time must come to every man when he begins to doubt his vocation. You may think me almost an old man, but I do not feel too old to start light-heartedly on a new manner of life. This evening's events have made this possible for me. I think," he said, glancing at his daughters, "that it is time I was alone. But this is not the hour to review the plans of my future. When you get to my age, if you have been at all observant of the people you have met and the accidents which have happened to you, you cannot help being struck with an amazing cohesiveness of events. How promiscuously we who are here this evening have been thrown together!

How enduring and endearing the memories that from now onwards will unite us! I think we should drink a toast—to Fortune, a much-maligned lady."

Once before Paul had drunk the same toast. This time there was no calamity. They drank silently, and Alastair rose from the table.

"It's time Paul and I were going," he said.

They walked down to the beach together. A boat was waiting for them.

"That's Margot's yacht," said Alastair. "It's to take you to her house at Corfu until you've decided about things. Good-bye. Good luck!"

"Aren't you coming any farther?" asked Paul.

"No, I've got to drive back to King's Thursday. Margot will be anxious to know how things have gone off."

Paul got into the boat and was rowed away. Sir Alastair, like Sir Bedivere, watched him out of sight.

CHAPTER SEVEN

Resurrection

THREE weeks later Paul sat on the verandah of Margot's villa, with his evening *apéritif* before him, watching the sunset on the Albanian hills across the water change, with the crude brilliance of a German picture postcard, from green to violet. He looked at his watch, which had that morning arrived from England. It was half-past six.

Below him in the harbour a ship had come in from Greece and was unloading her cargo. The little boats hung round her like flies, plying their trade of olive wood souvenirs and forged francs. There were two hours before dinner. Paul rose and descended the arcaded street into the square, drawing his scarf tight about his throat; the evenings began to get cold about this time. It was odd

being dead. That morning Margot had sent him a bunch
of Press cuttings about himself, most of them headed
"Wedding Sensation Echo" or "Death of Society Bridegroom Convict." With them were his tie pin and the rest
of his possessions which had been sent to her from Egdon.
He felt the need of the bustle of the Cafés and the quay
side to convince him fully of his existence. He stopped at
a stall and bought some Turkish delight. It was odd being
dead.

Suddenly he was aware of a familiar figure approaching
him across the square.

"Hullo!" said Paul.

"Hullo!" said Otto Silenus. He was carrying on his
shoulders a shapeless knapsack of canvas.

"Why don't you give that to one of the boys? They'll
take it for a few drachmas."

"I have no money. Will you pay him?"

"Yes."

"All right! Then that will be best. I suppose you are
staying with Margot?"

"I'm staying at her house. She's in England."

"That's a pity. I hoped I should find her here. Still I
will stay for a little, I think. Will there be room for me?"

"I suppose so. I'm all alone here."

"I have changed my mind. I think, after all, I will
marry Margot."

"I'm afraid it's too late."

"Too late?"

"Yes, she's married some one else."

"I never thought of that. Oh, well, it doesn't matter
really. Whom did she marry? That sensible Maltravers?"

"Yes, he's changed his name now. He's called Viscount
Metroland."

"What a funny name!"

They walked up the hill together. "I've just been to
Greece to see the buildings there," said Professor Silenus.

"Did you like them?"

"They are unspeakably ugly. But there were some nice
goats. I thought they sent you to prison."

"Yes, they did, but I got out."

"Yes, you must have, I suppose. Wasn't it nice?"

"Not terribly."

"Funny! I thought it would suit you so well. You never can tell with people, can you, what's going to suit them?"

Margot's servants did not seem surprised at the arrival of another guest.

"I think I shall stay here a long time," said Professor Silenus after dinner. "I have no money left. Are you going soon?"

"Yes, I'm going back to Oxford again to learn theology."

"That will be a good thing. You used not to have a moustache, used you?" he asked after a time.

"No," said Paul. "I'm just growing one now. I don't want people to recognize me when I go back to England."

"I think it's uglier," said Professor Silenus. "Well, I must go to bed."

"Have you slept any better lately?"

"Twice since I saw you. It's about my average. Good-night."

Ten minutes later he came back on to the terrace, wearing silk pyjamas and a tattered old canvas dressing gown.

"Can you lend me a nail file?" he asked.

"There's one on my dressing table."

"Thank you." But he did not go. Instead he walked to the parapet and leant out, looking across the sea. "It's a good thing for you to be a clergyman," he said at last. "People get ideas about a thing they call life. It sets them all wrong. I think it's poets that are responsible chiefly. Shall I tell you about life?"

"Yes, do," said Paul politely.

"Well, it's like the big wheel at Luna Park. Have you seen the big wheel?"

"No, I'm afraid not."

"You pay five francs and go into a room with tiers of seats all round, and in the centre the floor is made of a great disc of polished wood that revolves quickly. At first you sit down and watch the others. They are all trying to sit in the wheel, and they keep getting flung off, and that makes them laugh, and you laugh too. It's great fun."

"I don't think that sounds very much like life," said Paul rather sadly.

"Oh, but it is, though. You see, the nearer you can get to the hub of the wheel the slower it is moving and the easier it is to stay on. There's generally some one in the centre who stands up and sometimes does a sort of dance. Often he's paid by the management, though, or, at any rate, he's allowed in free. Of course at the very centre there's a point completely at rest, if one could only find it. I'm not sure I am not very near that point myself. Of course the professional men get in the way. Lots of people just enjoy scrambling on and being whisked off and scrambling on again. How they all shriek and giggle! Then there are others, like Margot, who sit as far out as they can and hold on for dear life and enjoy that. But the whole point about the wheel is that you needn't get on it at all, if you don't want to. People get hold of ideas about life, and that makes them think they've got to join in the game, even if they don't enjoy it. It doesn't suit every one.

"People don't see that when they say 'life' they mean two different things. They can mean simply existence, with its physiological implications of growth and organic change. They can't escape that—even by death, but because that's inevitable they think the other idea of life is too—the scrambling and excitement and bumps and the effort to get to the middle. And when we do get to the middle, it's just as if we never started. It's so odd.

"Now you're a person who was clearly meant to stay in the seats and sit still and if you get bored watch the others. Somehow you got onto the wheel, and you got thrown off again at once with a hard bump. It's all right for Margot, who can cling on, and for me, at the centre, but you're static. Instead of this absurd division into sexes they ought to class people as static and dynamic. There's a real distinction there, though I can't tell you how it comes. I think we're probably two quite different species spiritually."

"I used that idea of the wheel in a cinema film once. I think it rather sounds like it, don't you? What was it I came back for?"

"A nail file."

"Oh, yes, of course. I know of no more utterly boring and futile occupation than generalizing about life. Did you take in what I was saying?"

"Yes, I think so."

"I think I shall have my meals alone in future. Will you tell the servants? It makes me feel quite ill to talk so much. Good-night."

"Good-night," said Paul.

Some months later Paul returned to Scone College after the absence of little more than a year. His death, though depriving him of his certificates, left him his knowledge. He sat successfully for Smalls and Matriculation and entered his old college once more, wearing a commoner's gown and a heavy cavalry moustache. This and his natural diffidence formed a complete disguise. Nobody recognized him. After much doubt and deliberation he retained the name of Pennyfeather, explaining to the Chaplain that he had, he believed, had a distant cousin at Scone a short time ago.

"He came to a very sad end," said the Chaplain, "a wild young man."

"He was a *very* distant cousin," said Paul hastily.

"Yes, yes, I am sure he was. There is no resemblance between you. He was a thoroughly degenerate type, I am afraid."

Paul's scout also remembered the name.

"There used to be another Mr. Pennyfeather on this staircase once," he said, "a very queer gentleman indeed. Would you believe it, sir, he used to take off all his clothes and go out and dance in the quad at night. Nice quiet gentleman, too, he was, except for his dancing. He must have been a little queer in his head, I suppose. I don't know what became of him. They say he died in prison." Then he proceeded to tell Paul about an Annamese student who had attempted to buy one of the Senior Tutor's daughters.

On the second Sunday of term the Chaplain asked Paul to breakfast. "It's a sad thing," he said, "the way that the 'Varsity breakfast—'brekker' we used to call it in my day— is dying out. People haven't time for it. Always off to lectures at nine o'clock, except on Sundays. Have another kidney, won't you?"

There was another don present, called Mr. Sniggs, who addressed the Chaplain rather superciliously, Paul thought, as "Padre."

There was also an undergraduate from another college, a theological student called Stubbs, a grave young man with a quiet voice and with carefully formed opinions. He had a little argument with Mr. Sniggs about the plans for rebuilding the Bodleian. Paul supported him.

Next day Paul found Stubbs' card on his table, the corner turned up. Paul went to Hertford to call on Stubbs, but found him out. He left his card, the corner turned up. Two days later a little note came from Hertford:

Dear Pennyfeather:

I wonder if you would care to come to tea next Tuesday, to meet the College Secretary of the League of Nations Union and the Chaplain of the Oxford prison. It would be so nice if you could.

Paul went and ate honey buns and anchovy toast. He liked the ugly, subdued little College, and he liked Stubbs.

As term went on Paul and Stubbs took to going for walks together, over Mesopotamia to Old Marston and Beckley. One afternoon, quite light-hearted at the fresh weather, and their long walk, and their tea, Stubbs signed *Randal Cantuar* in the visitors' book.

Paul rejoined the League of Nations Union and the O. S. C. U. On one occasion he and Stubbs and some other friends went to the prison to visit the criminals there and sing part songs to them.

"It opens the mind," said Stubbs, "to see all sides of

life. How those unfortunate men appreciated our singing!"

One day in Blackwell's bookshop Paul found a stout volume, which, the assistant told him, was rapidly becoming a best seller. It was called *Mother Wales, by Augustus Fagan*. Paul bought it and took it back with him. Stubbs had already read it.

"Most illuminating," he said. "The hospital statistics are terrible. Do you think it would be a good idea to organize a joint debate with Jesus on the subject?" The book was dedicated *"To my wife, a wedding present."* It was eloquently written. When he had read it Paul put it on his shelves next to Dean Stanley's *Eastern Church*.

One other incident recalled momentarily Paul's past life.

One day, at the beginning of his second year, as Paul and Stubbs were bicycling down the High from one lecture to another, they nearly ran into an open Rolls-Royce that swung out of Oriel Street at a dangerous speed. In the back, a heavy fur rug over his knees, sat Philbrick. He turned round as he passed and waved a gloved hand to Paul over the hood.

"Hullo!" he said; "hullo! How are you? Come and look me up one day. I'm living on the river—Skindle's."

Then the car disappeared down the High Street, and Paul went on to his lecture.

"Who was your opulent friend?" asked Stubbs, rather impressed.

"Arnold Bennett," said Paul.

"I thought I knew his face," said Stubbs.

Then the lecturer came in, arranged his papers, and began a lucid exposition of the heresies of the second century. There was a bishop in Bithynia, Paul learned, who had denied the Divinity of Christ, the immortality of the soul, the existence of good, the legality of marriage, and the validity of the Sacrament of Extreme Unction. How right they had been to condemn him!

Epilogue

IT WAS Paul's third year of uneventful residence at Scone.

Stubbs finished his cocoa, knocked out his pipe, and rose to go. "I must be off to my digs," he said. "You're lucky staying in college. It's a long ride back to Walton Street on a night like this."

"D'you want to take Von Hugel?" asked Paul.

"No, not to-night. May I leave it till to-morrow?"

Stubbs picked up his scholar's gown and wrapped it round his shoulders. "That was an interesting paper to-night about the Polish plebiscites."

"Yes, wasn't it?" said Paul.

Outside there was a confused roaring and breaking of glass.

"The Bollinger seem to be enjoying themselves," said Paul. "Whose rooms are they in this time?"

"Pastmaster's, I think. That young man seems to be going a bit fast for his age."

"Well, I hope he enjoys it," said Paul. "Good-night."

"Good-night, Paul," said Stubbs.

Paul put the chocolate biscuits back in the cupboard, refilled his pipe, and settled down in his chair. Presently he heard footsteps and a knock at his door.

"Come in," he said, looking round.

Peter Pastmaster came into the room. He was dressed in the bottle-green and white evening coat of the Bollinger Club. His face was flushed and his dark hair slightly disordered.

"May I come in?"

"Yes, do."

"Have you got a drink?"

"You seem to have had a good many already."

"I've had the Boller in my rooms. Noisy lot. Oh, hell! I must have a drink."

"There's some whisky in the cupboard. You're drinking rather a lot these days, aren't you, Peter?"

Peter said nothing, but helped himself to some whisky and soda.

"Feeling a bit ill," he said. Then, after a pause, "Paul, why have you been cutting me all this time?"

"I don't know. I didn't think there was much to be gained by our knowing each other."

"Not angry about anything?"

"No, why should I be?"

"Oh, I don't know." Peter turned his glass in his hand, staring at it intently. "I've been rather angry with you, you know."

"Why?"

"Oh, I don't know—about Margot and the man Maltravers and everything."

"I don't think I was much to blame."

"No, I suppose not, only you were part of it all."

"How's Margot?"

"She's all right—*Margot Metroland*. D'you mind if I take another drink?"

"I suppose not."

"Viscountess Metroland," said Peter. "What a name! What a man! Still, she's got Alastair all the time. Metroland doesn't mind. He's got what he wanted. I don't see much of them really. What do you do all the time, Paul?"

"I'm going to be ordained soon."

"Wish I didn't feel so damned ill. What were we saying? Oh, yes, about Metroland. You know, Paul, I think it was a mistake you ever got mixed up with us; don't you? We're different somehow. Don't quite know how. Don't think that's rude, do you, Paul?"

"No, I know exactly what you mean. You're dynamic, and I'm static."

"Is that it? Expect you're right. Funny thing you used to teach me once; d'you remember? Llanabba—Latin sentences, *Quominus* and *Quin,* and the organ; d'you remember?"

"Yes, I remember," said Paul.

"Funny how things happen. You used to teach me the organ; d'you remember?"

"Yes, I remember," said Paul.

"And then Margot Metroland wanted to marry you; d'you remember?"

"Yes," said Paul.

"And then you went to prison, and Alastair—that's Margot Metroland's young man—and Metroland—that's her husband—got you out; d'you remember?"

"Yes," said Paul, "I remember."

"And here we are talking to one another like this, up here, after all that! Funny, isn't it?"

"Yes, it is rather."

"Paul, do you remember a thing you said once at the Ritz—Alastair was there—that's Margot Metroland's young man, you know—d'you remember? I was rather tight then too. You said, 'Fortune, a much-maligned lady.' D'you remember that?"

"Yes," said Paul, "I remember."

"Good old Paul! I knew you would. Let's drink to that now; shall we? How did it go? Damn, I've forgotten it. Never mind. I wish I didn't feel so ill."

"You drink too much, Peter."

"Oh, damn, what else is there to do? You going to be a clergyman, Paul?"

"Yes."

"Damned funny that. You know you ought never to have got mixed up with me and Metroland. May I have another drink?"

"Time you went to bed, Peter, don't you think?"

"Yes, I suppose it is. Didn't mind my coming in, did you? After all, you used to teach me the organ; d'you remember? Thanks for the whisky!"

So Peter went out, and Paul settled down again in his chair. So the ascetic Ebionites used to turn towards Jerusalem when they prayed. Paul made a note of it. Quite right to suppress them. Then he turned out the light and went into his bedroom to sleep.